MW01487546

Settling
The
Wind

Kari August

Mountain Track Publishing

Colorado

Published by Mountain Track Publishing
Estes Park Colorado

ISBN: 9781973319672

Cover design: Caroline Christner

Cover art: Kamil Vojnar @ Trevillion Images

Inquiries should be sent to:
Mountain Track Publishing
2181 Highway 66
Estes Park, Colorado 80517

For Caroline,

who also had an adventure in independence this last year,

and succeeded

Settling

The

Wind

Prologue

1875
Colorado Territory

My Dearest Sister,

I trust the town of Fort Collins is still treating you well. Clarissa, I have the most wonderful news. I will be settling in Estes Park, having purchased a picturesque cabin, already built, with a cookstove. I have new friends and neighbors who can help me if trouble arises. I hope you will visit me in the future, but for now I request that you send my wagonload of belongings by way of the freight service. I know I have made the correct decision concerning my future.

Love,

Henrietta

P.S. Give the kids a hug from me.

Clarissa was a woman of action and didn't dally long after receiving the letter from her younger sister. She wrote a note to their brother immediately.

Dear Herman,

Greetings from Fort Collins. Hope you and your cattle ranch are prospering in the rough country of Wyoming Territory. Eddie is doing well with his butcher shop and the kids remain lively. I don't know where the hours go by each day, I'm so busy.

Unfortunately, I am writing to you with some serious news. I am now convinced that our younger sister has lost her senses. Perhaps it is a reaction to her

i

grief from losing her husband, or just plain foolishness. Whatever the cause, she has gone and bought a cabin in the mountainous backwoods of Estes Park, Colorado!

Now before you get it into your head that I, in any way, contributed to this decision, I want to assure you that when Henrietta told me she required some time to herself, I encouraged her to visit the much more refined Manitou Springs. But you remember even as a child how stubborn Henrietta could be—insisting that ragtag stray mutt she once found was the prettiest thing ever, comes to mind. Well, she just up and vowed to tour Estes Park, not listening to any kind of reasoning. Now look where this has gotten her. I would appreciate your help in any way you can. For now, I am placating her and sending her belongings on to Estes Park. Surely, one cold winter will be enough to convince her to come back and stay with me and mine.

Your loving sister,
Clarissa

Chapter One

Spring
1875
Fort Collins, Colorado Territory

One month before . . .

Henrietta felt as if a jumble of emotions were coming at her from every possible direction, assailing her all at the same time. Just a few short weeks ago, her vigorous husband had decided to go for a hike and never returned, tragically killed by a hunter's stray bullet. And just like that, her whole world had turned upside down.

Not that erratic gunfire was all that surprising in the West where many people with little experience were equipped with pistols and rifles. And of course, the wrongdoer of the misdeed had never been found. But overwhelmed with sudden grief, Henrietta had made some quick decisions, sold their home in the small mountain town of Grand Lake, Colorado, packed up her possessions, and with her older sister's encouragement, had moved in with her family at Fort Collins. But now she was feeling unsettled, almost trapped. She was living in a situation that did not suit her.

Henrietta looked out the parlor window, her attention drawn by the noise her active nephews were making in the yard, excitably playing ball. Her husband and she had not been able to conceive children of their own, despite being married for several years. It was a personal sorrow that felt even rawer now. Henrietta couldn't imagine ever loving another man as much as she had loved her Charles, knew she would never remarry and therefore never have any kids of her own.

Henrietta couldn't help feeling envious of her sister. Clarissa had made a good match with a prosperous butcher, lived in a sprawling home, had two sons and an infant daughter and could not be more content. Clarissa had never made Henrietta feel like an intruder in her idyllic setting, and she wasn't, she knew that, yet this wasn't her home, and she wasn't sure it would ever deem so.

Between the crushing sorrow, and the regrets for what would never be, Henrietta felt almost smothered by life. She stopped watching the boys romping, released a long breath and sat down on the settee. Perhaps all these feelings were a usual part of mourning and would pass as she settled down to a life of spinsterhood as the children's favorite aunt. But she suspected—no knew— there was more to her complicated feelings.

Because mixed in with the sadness and disappointment and yes, anger, at the turn of events, was a strong lament that she had found herself falling into the same familiar pattern of behavior that she had always found somewhat frustrating.

Put plainly, she had never known true independence—ever—and she had always craved the experience.

Henrietta had gone from living with her family back East, to venturing out West with her brother and sister when their parents had passed, to married life with Charles, to moving in with her sister's family now. Henrietta could not even recall a single night her entire life that she had spent alone. Even after Charles had died, neighbors hurried over to keep her company. Henrietta knew that her appearance never helped matters. She had always been petite and thin, almost delicate appearing—though she knew she was not fragile—prompting even strangers to take on an attitude of overprotectiveness. No, Henrietta had never known a moment of true self-reliance.

Certainly, she was grateful for every good fortune life had brought her way. She knew not everyone could boast a pair of kind, if meddling, siblings or once having such a loving husband. But if she had had her druthers, would she have even gone out West in the first place or married so quickly despite having fallen in love?

Henrietta had always just done what was expected of her at the time, as in moving in with her sister now. Of course, there were a few women, especially in the West, who were an independent sort, but they were few and far between, and looked on as oddities for the most part. Women were supposed to follow the rules, obey what custom dictated, and raise families while the menfolk looked out for them.

She reached over to the side table and unfolded the local newspaper. She perused the headlines, not really registering anything that she was reading. She absently turned the page, stopping abruptly short at what

3

she saw in the bottom corner, "Travel for the Adventurer and Rest for the Weary Soul."

Henrietta had just finished avidly taking in the ad, when Clarissa entered the room, cradling a sleeping Ellie on her shoulder. Henrietta looked over as Clarissa gingerly sat her plump matronly figure down on the other end of the settee. "Lord, if I make the wrong move, this little hellion might awaken and start up again."

Henrietta put down the paper. "Want me to hold her a while?"

Clarissa shook her head. "Too dangerous a maneuver to attempt." Clarissa then took on her authoritative, "older sister" tone of voice that she specialized in, as she eyed Henrietta. "So, what response will I get today when I inquire about your plans on unpacking your wagonload of belongings?"

Henrietta hesitated, not sure how she wanted to reply this time. Clarissa had been pestering her with the same question the last couple of weeks, but Henrietta had hedged giving a precise answer. She chose now to be more honest about her thoughts. "I'll know what to do with the wagonload when I decide where I should live permanently."

Clarissa huffed out a breath, frustratingly. "How can you even consider living any place else? There's plenty of room, your company is welcome, the boys adore their aunt—"

"And I love them, but I want . . ."

"What?" Her sister frowned.

"I'm just not really sure in the long term—"

"Oh, good Lord." Clarissa rolled her eyes. "Spare me."

Henrietta handed over the newspaper. "Look at this advertisement I found. I think I'd like to visit Estes Park."

Her sister quickly read the print, then looked up incredulously. "Are you out of your mind? Estes Park is scarcely settled. This MacGregor establishment can't be much—probably just some squat cabin."

"They allow camping in tents on their property."

"Camping? You want to go *camping*? As a *single woman*?"

Henrietta tried to explain. "I want some time to think—some time alone."

Clarissa nodded slowly, sagely. "Okay, fine. Now I can see that. Truly I can. But why don't you visit Manitou Springs instead? It's only about a hundred miles south of here, an easy ride by rail. Eddie and I went there before we started this brood and it was glorious." Her face lit up excitedly. "You know all the fashionable set goes there nowadays."

"I'd scarcely call myself part of that crowd."

"So what if you're not one of those snobbish Easterners or European nobility that visit there—your Charles was respected in these parts. But besides the grand hotels, the place has soda springs and bath houses, and . . . and even a bowling alley! You could see nearby Pikes Peak and the Garden of the Gods. Why it's called the Saratoga of the West. Do you know what celebrities visited there last year?"

"Clarissa, I don't know and the topic doesn't interest me. The place is not for me—at least not in my present frame of mind."

Henrietta wasn't exactly sure why she so preferred a trip to Estes Park over Manitou Springs. She knew both places were picturesque mountain settings, stunning beyond belief, at least that's what her friend Rocky Mountain Jim had always told her. But also, she realized that Estes Park would lack the pretentiousness of a resort such as Manitou Springs. Staying there would be a simple and inexpensive affair. And that's what she wanted now, just an easy time with . . . life.

Her sister pursed her lips briefly, before stating, "You know you could meet a wealthy new husband in Manitou Springs."

"Clarissa! That's the last thing I want."

"Well, at least Charles managed to leave you a good inheritance to live by on your own."

"That's not the only reason I'm not interested in a husband. Nobody and I mean *nobody* could ever replace . . ." Henrietta could feel the tears that were always just beneath the surface, threatening to spill over again.

Clarissa held up her hand. "You say that now, but just wait and see how you feel in a year."

"No." Henrietta shook her head. "You couldn't be more wrong."

"We'll see." Her sister arched her brow and smiled smugly.

Henrietta ran her hand over her head and adjusted her bun in back. She couldn't see how living here was possibly going to work. Henrietta loved her sister, her zest for life, but Clarissa's opinions could exasperate her like nobody else's in the world. Just then Eddie, Junior and Wally charged into the parlor, waking

Ellie, who immediately began wailing. Clarissa got up off the settee and paced, while admonishing her sons.

And Henrietta started yearning all over again, with her entire being, that she was in her sister's shoes, with a robust husband, a couple of overly frisky sons and a fitful daughter.

Without saying a word, Henrietta walked to the front entrance, grabbed her hat and shawl and departed to make the necessary arrangements for her excursion to Estes Park.

Chapter Two

Henrietta boarded the stagecoach at Namaqua and began her journey a few days later. She was one of nine passengers in the coach that day—three narrow benches with three people crammed next to each other on each. She sat in the front row, the area usually reserved for women. Next to her sat a middle-aged woman with a friendly but weathered face and an attractive young lady Henrietta guessed was in her teens and the woman's daughter. In the rows behind Henrietta were men of all ages interested in fishing, hiking and hunting—at least that was what she had gathered so far by their loud conversation.

Henrietta tried to adjust her draped overskirt with the pleated frilled underskirt in back—she couldn't do anything about the bustle—and then tugged on the ruffled cuffs of the long tight sleeves of her maroon jacket-bodice with the high buttoned neckline. She tipped her small straw hat with the flat crown and long trailing ribbons fashionably forward. She should have been wearing all black from head to toe for the next year as custom dictated, but she was purposely not in mourning clothes—instead she was dressed in the traveling outfit her husband liked to see her in the most. She knew that was what Charles would have wanted.

She could hear him now. *Henrietta, if I ever end up in heaven, don't let me look down and see you in black. Life's too precious and short to waste any time grieving over me.*

Then he would playfully grab her bun in back and give it a teasing tug. Since the day she had met Charles, she didn't think she had ever worn a perfectly arranged bun. Henrietta blinked back tears. Her bun was straight as an arrow now, and the loose blond strands around her face were neatly arranged.

Henrietta glimpsed out the small adjacent window and saw the three-other horse-drawn wagonloads that were making the journey with the stagecoach today. The stagecoach driver appeared and lowered the leather flaps over the windows to help keep out the dust. The air in the coach immediately began to feel a bit stifling, and they hadn't even started the trip yet. By the pungent smells, some of the men were definitely drinkers and smokers and did not believe in bathing. Henrietta next heard the driver adjusting the luggage on top and then settling into his seat in front. With a lurch, the coach took off.

Since booking the trip, Henrietta had purposely put on an assured and calm face in front of her sister despite some occasional uneasiness, but now that she was actually on her way, she felt a sudden formidable shudder of apprehension course through her. This *was* crazy for her to attempt on her own, wasn't it? So much could go wrong—from something as basic as having trouble setting up her tent to as serious as an assault.

But stagecoach travel being as it was, her worries were soon displaced by concerns about staying in her seat. The ride was bouncy and bumpy and after a particularly rough jolt, Henrietta glanced at the woman next to her and was met with a welcoming smile. The woman chortled, "Could the driver find a hole just a little bit bigger to drive this contraption through? He hasn't succeeded yet in eliminating all feeling in my rump."

Henrietta burst out in a chuckle which almost felt like a novel sensation after the last month. She took an immediate liking to the down-to-earth woman who held out her hand to Henrietta. "Hi! I'm Mrs. Horace Ferguson but you can call me Sallee or Sal for short." She nudged the young woman next to her who looked over with a pleasing grin. "And this here is my daughter Anna."

Henrietta shook their hands. "I'm Mrs. Charles Schodde." She hesitated, then continued. "Actually, I'm recently widowed." And Henrietta found she was blinking back tears yet again. This was the problem with losing a loved one as an adult. People scarcely talked about it but the unfortunate truth was that tears could come when you least expected or wanted them to. Here she sat with a complete stranger and she was revealing her anguished feelings even though she hadn't intended to. She found it embarrassing. Perhaps it was the woman's kind face which had allowed her to open up, but if Henrietta's friend could be believed, she should expect this uncomfortable behavior out of herself for at least a couple years. Good Lord.

Henrietta briefly glanced down at her clothes and wondered if she should explain why she wasn't wearing a mourning outfit but decided to let it pass as Sal reached over and patted her hand in her lap. "Are you travelling alone?"

Henrietta sniffled and nodded.

Sal smiled warmly. "Now don't you worry about a thing, dearie. Horace and I will look after you on this trip. We're headed to Estes Park to set up our homestead."

"Oh, thank you for your concern." She managed a watery smile. "Please call me Henrietta." And just as quickly as the tears had come, Henrietta could now feel a lightening in her mood again.

"So, you're a tourist, Henrietta?"

"Yes, I plan to stay at the MacGregor ranch."

"They're good people, I hear tell. Wouldn't know myself since this is my first trip there."

"Truly? You're moving to Estes Park, and you've never seen the place?"

"Nope, but Horace sure has—says it's gorgeous. We hope to set up a cattle ranch. Horace is driving one of the wagons you see out the window. One of my sons is leading the wagon loaded with chickens. The cattle will trail up separately."

"What made you decide to move there?"

"What didn't?" Sal harrumphed.

The coach slammed in and out of another rut in the trail and they bounced rigorously on their bench. Sal clapped her hands briefly. "Oh, bravo, driver. Thataway." And Henrietta found herself laughing again. "Horace and I hail originally from Tennessee. We were actually farmers and then merchants before Horace got it into his head in '71 to move his wife and five kids out to the new agricultural community south of Greeley, Colorado."

Henrietta perked up. "Oh, that's the place where Horace Greeley—that famous *New York Tribune* editor—decided to form a utopian society. Didn't he coin the phrase, 'Go West, young man'?"

"Yep, he did. But Greeley didn't actually start the colony, it was merely named after him by one of his newspaper reporters, Nathan Meeker, and no matter how much the place was supposed to be a land of agriculture, education, religion, and temperance, it was surely a far cry from being utopian." Sal shook her head ruefully. "We were going to be cattle ranchers, but see, that's a little difficult when the conditions your first winter are so harsh that ninety-five of your heifers and steers just drift away not to be found again."

Henrietta's eyes widened. "Oh, that's bad."

"You bet. So the next year we planted fifteen acres of vegetables. They were doing just fine until a scourge of grasshoppers descended."

Henrietta shook her head as Sal continued. "But I guess you could say we're a stubborn group of people because in '73 and '74 we tried a crop of oats and wheat. But, as in much of Colorado and the West, the grasshoppers continued devastating everything in sight. My God, they even devoured the leather reins to Horace's horse." She looked over at Henrietta then. "What did your husband do? Did he have to deal with those insufferable grasshoppers too?"

"He was a general practitioner. I mean some of the people he treated had grasshopper problems but not him." Henrietta was relieved she could say something about her husband without tears.

"Lucky him. Anyways, as you can imagine, we were in desperate straits by the fall of '74."

Henrietta nodded thoughtfully. "And did you say with five kids to feed?"

"Yep."

"So how did you manage?"

"Let's just say scarcely. But then we read in the *Denver Press* that an English lord named Dunraven might be involved in filing false land claims in Estes Park. You know what I'm talking about?"

Henrietta nodded. "Oh, yes. I heard all about it. My friend Mountain Jim tried to stop it. Dunraven was hiring lowlifes from Denver to file homesteading claims in Estes Park and then buying them cheaply from them. He apparently desired or still wants to establish a cattle ranch and his own personal game preserve so that only he and his wealthy friends can enjoy the area."

"Yeah, that's what we read also." Sal smirked. "So Horace headed over to Estes Park last fall to see what was what. Do you know that in just three days Horace nabbed eleven deer with just his old muzzle loading rifle and caught so many trout he had to quit counting? But our real luck came when Horace met the Farrar brothers, Clint, Hank, and Ike. Have you heard about them?"

Henrietta shook her head.

"Those boys are only in their twenties but have already made a real name for themselves as hunters. Well, anyhow, the Farrar brothers were having trouble getting their game to the Denver market. A round trip of their loaded wagons could take six full days, and that's if there were no mishaps. So Horace struck a deal with

13

them. Our son Hunter is going to haul their fish and meat and get two-thirds the purchase price while we set up our homestead about a half-mile from Mary's Lake. Horace figures that's an area overlooked by Dunraven or if not, where Dunraven has filed one of his false claims. Hope he knows what he's doing because Hank Farrar and Horace have already built us a log cabin. It's only a couple rooms, mud chinked, and sod roofed, but it has a fine fireplace . . . or so I've been told."

"So now you'll be cattle ranchers again? Aren't you worried?"

"Honey, I'm always worried. But I've heard that the sheltered valleys there are easier on the livestock. We'll have to see, of course."

Sal kept up a conversation until the driver finally stopped to rest the horses. Sal stiffly climbed out after all the bouncing while spry Anna and Henrietta alighted with greater ease. They noticed a nearby group of pines and quickly headed over out of necessity. That was another problem with coach travel. One had to watch how much one drank before leaving or potentially suffer the consequences.

Afterwards Henrietta helped Sal spread blankets on the ground for a quick repast for everyone. Her tall and thin husband Horace was obviously accustomed to his sociable wife adding tagalongs to their family gatherings. In fact, Sal hailed over a merchant from Longmont, a Mr. Richard Hubbell, after she noticed him standing by himself. Like mother, like daughter, Anna immediately started up a conversation with the gentleman.

After adjusting the traces on his wagon, their son Hunter sat down next to Henrietta. "I lost the coin toss."

Henrietta looked over. "Beg pardon?"

Hunter was tall like his father but more built with a handsome face and twinkling eyes. "Don't think I willingly agreed to drive a wagon full of clucking and screeching hens. They just love the excitement of being jostled on the road."

Henrietta smiled. "Oh, I see."

"Actually, we're becoming friends. I've started to name them. Yeah, over there you see Shrieky and Squawky and that big one in front—that's Chubs."

Henrietta chuckled. "Would you like some of my bread and cheese?"

He held up his hand. "Hold on a sec." He looked over at Sal. "Hey, Ma. Time for chicken dinner."

"Oh, go on with you now. No, it's not." Sal answered affectionately.

He looked back at Henrietta. "Bread and cheese it is."

As they ate Henrietta gazed around at the rolling foothills of the Rockies with a sense of excitement. They had been following the Little Thompson River for much of the way. She asked Horace if it would be too much longer before they were actually in the mountains. Horace half-smiled. "Well, see, if we were birds, we'd be there shortly. As is, some of the worst stretch is yet to come."

Henrietta looked at Sal, their eyes widened, and they broke out in chuckles. An hour later, the dire prediction that Horace made proved more than true. The stage coach driver nearly broke his arm trying to get the

15

coach over the worst of the rocks. But steadily the group climbed and within a few more hours they were at heights following a trail that could be called a road in only the most generous of terms. Henrietta looked uneasily out the window, the flaps having been raised as conditions became less dusty. Their coach was now approaching a cliff with a steep slope. Suddenly a shout pierced the air.

Sal gasped. "That's Hunter yelling!" She leaned over toward the window. "What's going on?"

With horror, the women saw the wagon holding the chickens fall over the fifty-foot precipice, careening rapidly down the sharp drop until crashing at the bottom.

Sal wailed, "Oh, my Lord. My son. My son." She hastily started towards the door but was blocked by the men in the coach who were already trying to scramble to the scene. Sal sat back down.

The women could do nothing but look out the window at the horrific scene until the crowd at the door climbed out. Horses were pulling ineffectually at their traces and whinnying, while chickens flapped and flailed on the ground. They couldn't see Hunter, but the wagon was leaning forebodingly against a group of jagged rocks.

Sal hung her head in her hands. "I can't look any more." Anna started weeping softly on her shoulder.

After an agonizing moment, Henrietta thought she saw some staggering movement in the shrubbery part way down the slope. She looked more closely and realized it was Hunter getting to his feet, standing a bit shakily, but still alive. She grabbed Sal's arm. "Look! Hunter made it. He must have jumped before the crash."

Sal leaned on top of Henrietta, stared out the window, and whispered, "I think I just got my own life back."

Tears of gladness came to Henrietta's eyes. "I know exactly what you mean."

The women made their way to the door and climbed out of the coach. The scene below was still chaos. The chickens, who had managed to escape out of their broken cages, were squawking everywhere while the horses continued their attempts at bolting. Yelling men were having difficulty making it down the steep drop, but eventually the younger ones of the bunch reached the crash site.

Miraculously, it was only a short while later before the horses were calmed and the wagon pulled out of the crag. A dozen chickens had been killed, but otherwise the brush along the slope had apparently slowed and softened the blow.

Giving her son a big hug, Sal said, "Now, Hunter, that appetite of yours is something else. There are easier ways than that to get me to cook you chicken dinner."

Hunter grinned. "Sure, thing, Ma. I'll try to remember that next time."

Henrietta helped Anna and Sal hastily field dress a few of the birds before departing. Within a few hours, the group had reached the half-way house where they would spend the night. The women agreed, with its cramped rooms, the log structure wasn't much to speak of, but at least it appeared clean. The chickens were cooked and the women retired to one of the rooms— Anna, Henrietta and Sal all sharing one bed. The only other guest room and bed was shared by three of the men—the burly owner requesting that they remove their boots first—the remaining men sleeping on the floor of the main room or underneath the wagons out-of-doors. Henrietta woke up the next morning wondering suspiciously if the bed had had bugs—most establishments serving tourists did. They were on their way after a breakfast of coffee and eggs.

Within a couple hours the foothills became so steep that on one occasion horses from three wagons were teamed together to get just one cart to the top. By the second night they were in Muggins Gulch, a park-like setting five miles from the main settlement of Estes Park. Henrietta knew of the area, though she had never been there herself before. Rocky Mountain Jim had once lived in Muggins Gulch and had talked of his home in detail to her. She had become friends with the famous trapper when Charles and she had helped him mend from a grizzly bear attack that had occurred near their home at Grand Lake. And though Mountain Jim had lived a vastly different lifestyle than herself—was older, rougher, and struggled with his own personal demons— they had developed a special bond. Funny, how in life the most unlikely companions could become close friends—but it had happened with them. She had known that forever more, if he possibly could, he would always come to her assistance if she ever required help, and she would do the same for him as she showed when she had then travelled all the way to Fort Collins—staying with her sister again—to help him mend after another unfortunate incident. But Mountain Jim was gone now and knew nothing of her current woes.

A hawk suddenly circled close by, pulling her from her thoughts, and she gazed at the view before her. Though the valley with the surrounding hills was beautiful, she realized few of the travelers appreciated the splendor as much as Henrietta. Most were consumed with excitement over the new wooden toll road that was being built extending from Saint Vrain Creek in Boulder County, heading northwesterly, passing Muggins Gulch, to the easterly side of the Big Thompson in Estes Park, terminating eventually at the Macgregor ranch. The idea had apparently been hatched by Alex Macgregor and with financial backing, including money from his mother-in-law, construction had begun in the last year.

Henrietta learned all this and more because the construction foreman's temporary residence was where they spent the second night. Usually Israel Rowe was a hunter, transporting his game to Denver or Longmont to be sold or exchanged for flour and sugar or other essentials. But Alex Macgregor had hired him as the crew foreman and his wife Harriet as the cook for the workers.

At dinner Sal leaned over to Henrietta and said in a low voice, "Wanna bet only Israel is getting paid? And who do you think is working more, Israel or Harriet? She is not only keeping the house and cooking for the men, but Harriet has her little ones to look after also. Small kids are demanding at that age."

Henrietta looked over at the red-headed woman bustling about to keep everybody happy, with her daughter Dora clinging to her skirt. Even having never met the woman before, Henrietta could see the fatigue on her face.

19

Sal smirked. "I've told Horace that one of these days I'm going to join those suffragettes. He doesn't believe me, but just you wait and see." Sal nodded smugly and Henrietta smiled. The group of women, mainly easterners, who had banded together for women being allowed to vote were a vocal crowd who were often the butt of jokes for newspaper editors across the nation. But the notion was not so foreign to westerners. Wyoming women had had the right to vote in their territory since 1869.

Sal looked over intently at Henrietta. "What's to stop you from joining?"

At the reminder that she no longer had a husband, her face dropped.

Sal immediately was contrite. "Ah, honey, I wished I hadn't said that."

Henrietta shook her head. "No, it's okay. I think I just have to toughen up."

"No, you do not. Just give it time, darlin'. The grieving won't be as raw as time passes. I promise you that."

By the next day Henrietta already valued her new friendship with Sal and was sorry to see the Fergusons depart the group to move to their homestead while the majority of the travelers headed to the MacGregors'. But Sal assured her that if she could find no room with the MacGregors, she was welcome to stay at their cabin, cramped as it would be. Henrietta promised to visit Sal in the next couple of weeks.

Henrietta wasn't quite sure what she had been expecting at the MacGregors', but she found herself taken aback several times. First, the setting was more

20

magnificent than she could have imagined. The gently sloping hillside of the area known as Black Canyon faced impressive Longs Peak, the highest mountain in this part of the Rockies. A few cattle grazed nearby, making for a pretty, romantic scene. Secondly, there was a virtual tent city near the main lodge. Numerous light-colored canvases with wide awnings stood in stark relief against the backdrop of dark pines. The field of campers mingling about included men, women and children. Additionally, it appeared as if a group of small cabins were being built close by. But perhaps the most surprising find was the MacGregors themselves.

Henrietta climbed out of the stagecoach, gathered her belongings and approached the main house. She knocked determinedly on the log cabin door. An attractive, diminutive woman answered. Despite the rugged setting, she was stylishly dressed and had her auburn hair pulled up neatly in a bun.

"Mrs. MacGregor?"

"Yes, come in, please." She held open the door.

Henrietta entered the small cabin and looked briefly around at the fine furnishings and oil paintings on the walls. There was even a piano in the corner. "I'm Henrietta Schodde. I read your advertisement in the Fort Collins paper and was hoping to stay at least a couple of weeks. I brought a tent and some camping supplies."

"Wonderful. We'd love to have you. How many are in your party?"

"Just myself."

Mrs. MacGregor frowned slightly. "Have you camped before?"

Henrietta hesitated. "With my family in the past."

"Have a seat and let's chat a bit."

Henrietta was wary now whether she would be allowed to stay or strongly encouraged to take the returning stage back. And just then she realized how much this trip meant to her. She somehow sensed that although her grief would always be with her, this excursion in such a pleasant setting would somehow start the process of recovery.

After being served tea in a delicate porcelain cup, Henrietta related the events in the last month that had brought her to their door. Clara, as she insisted being called, then explained how the MacGregors had come to Estes Park. Three years ago, Clara had been studying at the art academy in Chicago—thus the surrounding landscapes and refined atmosphere—but had decided to visit the West on a sketching trip and had met her future husband Alex that summer in Colorado. Her husband was ambitious and apparently a real worker. Being raised by an impoverished widow, he had started working at a newspaper when he was only eight and become a printer by age fourteen. Five years ago, he had travelled to Denver and begun studying law. Though he still practiced as an attorney in Denver and Fort Collins, the MacGregors had placed a squatter's claim above Black Canyon a couple years ago. Realizing the area would attract tourists, Alex had then started the toll road last year.

Henrietta was surprised. "So you've just recently come to Estes Park yourselves?"

Clara grinned. "Yes! Alex and Hank Farrar only built this pole and bough-roofed cabin a few months ago." She looked around the room. "It took them scarcely nine days to finish it. I was staying in Denver at the time because I had just had our baby. Little Georgie and I only moved in here a couple months ago."

"But there are already so many tourists camping here!"

Clara chuckled. "I know! Between the advertisements and word-of-mouth, the news has travelled quickly."

Just then the front door opened and banged shut. An average height man with dark hair, a mustache and goatee entered as an infant began to wail in an adjoining room. He spoke sheepishly, "Oops, sorry about that."

Clara shook her head and smiled. "Alex, you have a real knack for waking Georgie out of his naps. Let me go get him while you introduce yourself to my new friend, Henrietta Schodde."

Alex had a pleasant voice but sharp eyes, and Henrietta suspected he made a formidable attorney. "How do you manage to handle all your responsibilities if you are still practicing law?"

Clara walked back into the room with her infant son, "I'll tell you how. While he's off to Fort Collins or Loveland or Longmont or Heavens-knows-where, I'm running the show here."

Alex smiled while reaching for Georgie. "And a fine job you do, Clara."

"Why thank you, Alex." She looked at Henrietta. "At least my mother has filed an adjoining claim this year to be near us. She'll be a big help."

Alex arched his brows, smiling. "And the toll road will be forever indebted to Georgiana Heeney and her cash flow." He began tickling little Georgie, who squealed with delight.

Clara asked Alex, "Was there anything important in the mail the stage brought?"

Alex stopped teasing his son and looked at Clara. "There was, and I have to get to Denver on business. If it's okay with you, I'll take the returning coach."

Clara blew out a breath. "How long do you expect to be gone?"

Alex grimaced slightly. "I'm not sure. You know how it is . . ." He trailed off.

Clara turned to Henrietta. "You weren't really interested in camping, were you? 'Cause I suddenly have room for you in the cabin if you'd like to stay with me."

"I'd love to, Clara," burst out of Henrietta before she realized that her grand plan for true independence and spending a night alone had just been thwarted. But at least it had been her decision. She turned to Alex. "Thank you for the accommodations, Mr. MacGregor."

Clara smiled. "Oh, you can call him Alex. Believe me, Henrietta, people get to know each other, for good or bad, real quick out on the frontier. If you don't already know that, you soon will."

24

Chapter Three

Henrietta was at peace. She had been in Estes Park for a week and for the first time since the death of Charles actually felt as if she wasn't struggling to hold her emotions together. She realized she had spent most of the last month fleeing—trying, in her way, to escape from the reality of what had happened. Well, she had stopped running.

Every morning after helping Clara with her chores, Henrietta would go on a long hike—sometimes with other guests, but mostly alone. And during those treks, she found she could reminisce without bursting into tears. She could work through her irrational anger at Charles for leaving her—which came as a revelation to her on one hike that she was even holding in any ire. She started to feel more herself. She began to act more herself.

And with that came a tentative enjoyment for living. Yes, Charles had died, but she was yet alive and still had a yearning to sample some of what life had to offer. She had been dealt a devastating blow, but she could pull herself up and out of the mire. Oh, she was still bursting into tears at times. Last night all it had taken was the sight of another guest wearing the same hat style that Charles had favored. But her sobs weren't prolonged affairs of a month ago. In fact, they were often accompanied by sweet remembrances.

Henrietta was feeling so much better that she was going to try her hand at camping. Alex had returned last night and although the MacGregors had offered space in their cabin for her still, she welcomed a new adventure. So this morning she had picked out a site and begun unpacking her tent. Before she had even struck the first stake, however, she had attracted a small interested crowd who pitched in to help.

George Bode stopped by after the tent was assembled. Henrietta had met George a couple days before when he had visited with Clara, hoping to ask Alex some legal advice. George was a rancher who had immigrated from Germany and owned a small herd of cattle. He was a stout, shy man who had scarcely been able to look Henrietta in the eye, blushing repeatedly, until he found out that her parents had moved from Germany also. Then George had opened up, sprinkling his conversation with a few German phrases.

Today he was taking Henrietta horseback riding. Henrietta had never been much of an equestrian, to say the least, but could see that if she learned how to ride better, a whole lot more of Estes Park would open up to her. George was an excellent rider and once he had learned that Henrietta had never received proper instruction as a youth and had mainly gotten by riding carriages most of her life, he had offered to give her lessons. Considering she was nearing thirty years of age, she figured it was about time she learned.

"*Guten Tag,* George. *Wie geht es Dir?*"

George smiled sweetly. "*Gut, Henrietta.*"

Even if Henrietta had been interested in other men—which she most assuredly was not—George was not the type of man who would have attracted her attention. She had sensed that George also had no romantic interest in her either when they had initially met. Their shared German heritage was what appealed to him.

Henrietta looked at the horse George had brought with him for her to ride and started laughing. "How old is that poor beast? She looks ancient."

"Ach now, Henrietta, we don't want you to feel any fear of being thrown."

"Well, there's certainly no possibility of that."

"Liebchen will be good to you."

"You named that nag *Liebchen?*" She bit back a smile. *Liebchen* was a German term of endearment meaning "loved one" and Henrietta realized that George either had a wry sense of humor or was impossibly dear.

George tightened the cinch on the mare. "I borrowed a side saddle from Clara."

"Thank you, George. Most considerate of you." George helped Henrietta mount and led the way toward the trail along the Fall River.

An hour later, despite George's and Henrietta's best efforts, she still bounced along awkwardly and clumsily. And Liebchen had absolutely no regard for her, the horse quickly determining that *she,* and *not* Henrietta, would be the boss. Currently Liebchen was grazing on grass, though George had told Henrietta multiple times not to allow it since the mare should learn that she was the one who should decide when the horse could eat or ride.

Henrietta pulled back on the reins to get her to stop, but Liebchen wagged her head vigorously until she could munch again.

George blew out an exasperated breath. "Here, watch me ride her."

Henrietta dismounted, then held the reins to George's horse as George straddled and then expertly commanded Liebchen to do whatever he wanted. And the obstinate horse obeyed! Henrietta knew a choice word she thought the mare should be renamed but kept her opinion to herself. Besides the fact that Henrietta never used foul language, George was obviously attached to the wicked horse.

She shook her head after George alighted. "I'm a horrible rider. Do you think I'll ever learn?"

"Well, you are not a natural . . . er, perhaps more practice . . ." George frowned slightly. "Uh . . ."

Henrietta raised a corner of her mouth. "What is it, George?"

He prevaricated some more. "It's . . . er . . ."

"George, just say it. You think I'm hopeless. I don't have it in me, do I?"

George blushed again for no obvious reason that Henrietta could see but then said, "Ach, no. It's not that. It's just I don't know how anybody can learn how to ride properly on a side saddle. I think you should try riding astride . . . like a man."

Henrietta opened her mouth to say something, then clicked it shut. George was correct. She couldn't get over the feeling that she was going to drop off the edge of her mount at any moment. Sitting squarely on the horse seemed so much more sensible. Of course, some of her ankles and legs might be revealed which would be embarrassing . . . but perhaps if she wore her most voluminous skirt, it would hide some of her lower limbs. Now if she had one of those new bloomer bottoms or riding outfits with a split skirt she had seen in a magazine, she would be all set, but riding astride was the last thing that had been on her mind while packing for this trip. "I'll give it a try."

George grinned, obviously relieved she hadn't been offended by the suggestion. "Excellent, Henrietta. Shall we say tomorrow then? I'll bring Liebchen by for another lesson."

Henrietta inwardly groaned about him bringing the horse from hell but then acknowledged beggars shouldn't be choosers. George was being nice enough taking time out from his busy life as a rancher to teach her so she agreed.

That evening Henrietta was invited to join in a group meal with the other campers. Henrietta agreed to supply the corn bread and managed not to burn the bottom of it over her campfire—quite the accomplishment she found. When dinner was finished, Henrietta helped clean the dishes with the other women, then headed to her shelter. She was actually excited about spending her first night alone.

She entered her tent, secured the ties at the entrance, and then proceeded to bundle up as best she could—putting an additional sweater and coat on. Nights were often chilly even in the summer in the mountains. She spread out a couple of blankets and snuggled down into them, amazed at the fact that she was completely by herself for the first time in her life. All alone.

This should have been a highly momentous occasion, but she quickly realized total solitude was not exactly the way to describe the situation and she was only fooling herself. She was in the midst of a large, noisy campground. Some of the campers, the men especially, had talked during the meal about building a bonfire for entertainment. After an hour of listening to drinking, happy laughter, and an occasional raucous shout, Henrietta decided to take a peek at what was still going on.

She untied a portion of her tent and peered at the sight. An enormous fire had been built. Huge soaring flames reached into the evening sky, lighting the surrounding campers enjoying the spectacle. She had never seen a blaze so big and hesitated a moment about whether to join the crowd.

But though she was slowly recovering from her recent tragic past, she realized she still was not up to spending an evening in merriment—and might never be for that matter—so she returned to her bed. It was several hours later before the crowd quieted and dispersed. But then, just as Henrietta was drifting off to sleep, she heard a soft rustling noise outside her tent.

She sat up, instantly alert and holding her breath, and strained to hear what it was. She couldn't quite make it out. Oh, Lord. Now what?

But after a few more moments she chided herself that surely no bear or mountain lion would venture so close to so many campers—would it? She shook her head, trying to calm herself. No, of course not—or at least, *probably* not. She lay back down slowly and the indistinct sound at last disappeared. An hour later, she finally fell asleep.

George appeared with Liebchen late the following morning. He looked at Henrietta with a slightly puzzled expression on his face.

"What's wrong, George?"

"You look *dicker* today."

Henrietta chuckled. "Oh, I suppose I do look fat. I bought some trousers from one of the youngsters who had outgrown them." She raised her skirt and showed off her pant leg.

George blushed.

Henrietta decided to ignore his shyness. She went up to Liebchen and stroked her mane, determined to make friends and take control of the evil horse.

Liebchen snorted loudly and then proceeded to poop.

Henrietta turned to George. "Well, should we begin?"

George made a move to help Henrietta mount again, but she held up her hand. "No, I want to try myself." But the problem was that even though Henrietta knew she had the strength to hoist herself up, every time she placed her foot in the stirrup, Liebchen would take a couple small steps. Just a couple, but it was enough to throw her off balance and she would have to try again.

After several attempts, George exclaimed, "Liebchen knows better."

Oh, Henrietta was sure of that. "George, give us a moment here, would you?" Henrietta took Liebchen by the bridle and guided the horse a few feet away.

She then proceeded to have a talk with Liebchen, woman to woman. George pretended not to hear but obviously could. "Now, look here, Liebchen. I lost my husband recently. Did you know that? And I'm trying to make a life of my own. You would think that as another woman, you would try to be as supportive as possible."

George raised his brows, looked away, and muttered, "*Ach, du leibe Zeit.* She's gone *verruckt.*"

Henrietta continued despite the accusation of craziness. "All I am asking is for a little cooperation here." Liebchen stamped one of her hooves. "I'll take that as a yes. And I want you to know that I think with this other saddle I might improve, making it easier for you also. Now are you with me?"

Liebchen surprised her by nuzzling her shoulder. Of course, she did it a bit too vigorously, nearly pushing her over, but Henrietta decided to take that as progress, even if George was now frowning.

"Liebchen, I am going to attempt mounting again and you are going to hold still."

Henrietta straddled successfully. She looked at George. "We're ready now."

Henrietta experienced a near instant transformation by riding astride. She felt more confident and rode with less fear. Liebchen took a little longer to be convinced of a change, but gradually after a few more lessons, the two were a united pair. So much so, that George allowed Henrietta to stable Liebchen at the MacGregors' and ride her while she remained in Estes Park. He refused to take any money for the use of the

32

mare, but Henrietta thought she knew of a way to repay him for his generosity.

She took over the kitchen at the main house one day. Henrietta had always loved to bake and had even once dreamed of owning a bakery. She made German bread and pastries with recipes she had grown up on as a child. She gave some to the MacGregors and other campers, but the next day when George came by to talk to Alex, she surprised him with the baked goods.

George blushed and said nothing at first, perhaps embarrassed by receiving the present—which was nonsensical to Henrietta—but when he took a bite of the strudel, he finally exclaimed, *"Mein Gott."*

Henrietta chuckled. "So, you like it?"

"Can you make me some more? I will pay you."

"How about as long as I can use your horse, I will supply you with baked goods?"

George practically shouted, "Deal!"

Later that afternoon Henrietta headed over to the Fergusons'. Alex offered to watch Georgie so Clara could accompany her.

Along the way, Clara observed, "So Liebchen and you are getting along now."

"Haven't you noticed how sprightlier she is?"

Clara looked at the horse and lowered the corners of her mouth, dubiously.

"She absolutely is. I think it's because she finds herself useful again."

"Well, nobody likes being put out to pasture I would guess."

They passed by a newly constructed cabin and Henrietta asked who owned it.

"The McClintocks. Alex is providing long term leases on our Black Canyon property for families wanting to build their own cabin."

"Alex has so many plans, doesn't he?"

"Besides the cattle and our vegetable garden, now he's working on growing some oats and wheat, but the oats are best since they can be threshed here on the ranch whereas wheat has to be milled in Longmont."

"Yesterday I heard him talking about harvesting ice this winter."

"Oh, that's nothing. He also wants to run a general store and a milk house and a meat house and let's not forget the water-powered sawmill."

Henrietta gawked, speechless a moment.

"Just watch. He'll do it all also."

"Good Lord." She shook her head.

Three miles later, the women were drinking coffee and eating some of the pie Henrietta had brought, around a rough-hewn table when Sal commented, "I can see this mountain air suits you, Henrietta. You have a new glow."

She smiled. "I love it here. I'm actually looking forward to the Fourth of July celebrations, and a month ago I couldn't imagine taking pleasure in anything again."

Clara elaborated. "The campers are holding a contest for who can build the biggest bonfire. Some even have a few fireworks. Your family should join us, Sal."

Henrietta enthused, "Do come, Sal. You should see the pictures Clara has painted herself."

"Oh, you never have to ask a Ferguson twice to attend a celebration. We'll all be there if we can."

Henrietta frowned slightly. "But tell me, Sal, how have you been making out?"

"Considering I'm living with a sod roof again, I'd say pretty well. Can't say I like the dirt crumbling down on me occasionally, and it'd be nice to have more light in the cabin. Oh, and the rain leaked in with that heavy downpour a few days ago, but all and all I'm doing fine. Horace plans on adding more rooms shortly and that ought to help. Just have to get him from fishing all the time. He's like a man possessed." Sal chuckled and shook her head.

A week later Henrietta sat on the bank of the Fall River with Clara and Sal, waiting for the fireworks to start. Henrietta looked between the two women who had become fast friends, visiting another time in the last week. She gazed up at the full moon rising over the mountains in the twilight sky and tried to commit the scene to memory. A stagecoach was due to arrive the day after tomorrow and her excursion to Estes Park would be at an end. She blew out a long breath.

Sal put her arm around Henrietta's shoulders. "You missing Charles, honey?"

She nodded. "Always. But it's more than that. I've really come to cherish this place. I can't imagine leaving in a day's time."

Clara nodded. "That's what everybody says. The family who told us today that they had to give up their cabin were in tears and not only because of their financial straits. This place affects most people's core in a special way. They're looking now for someone to buy their home, but I'm sure it will go fast."

Henrietta turned to Clara intently. "Which cabin is it?"

"Remember the one we passed on the way to Sal's?"

"On your land?"

"No, the cabin by the Thompson River."

Henrietta breathed in excitedly. "Oh. Oh. It's so picturesque. Perhaps *I* could purchase it from them."

Clara and Sal stared at her wide-eyed a moment. Sal was the first to break the stunned silence. "You want to buy a house? And live here permanently? *By yourself?*"

Henrietta paused a moment and then nodded slowly as she realized that was exactly what she wanted to do.

Sal grinned. "Well, I'll be."

Clara started warming to the idea. "But you really wouldn't be here by yourself. You have Sal and me and of course, George. And the Rowes plan on building a place a little east of here once the toll road's finished."

Sal added, "And don't forget about the Farrar brothers. Have you met the boys yet?"

Henrietta shook her head. "I guess they've been away hunting."

Clara explained, "They'd be your closest neighbors since their cabin is where the Thompson meets the Fall River."

Henrietta bit her lip and no one said anything more for a few moments. Moving to Estes Park would be one of the most fulfilling experiences she could imagine. The thought was a bit scary, and yet, she wanted to do it. "I suppose I should see the cabin on the inside before I make a definite decision."

Sal snorted. "I'd say so." And the three women started giggling.

Henrietta looked at her new friends. "This is a bit crazy, isn't it?"

Sal smiled. "Nah, just adventurous, honey. But I got a good feeling about this. Clara, I think we got ourselves a new neighbor."

Henrietta visited the three-room log cabin the next day and was smitten with the place. Besides the main living area, there were two small bedrooms off the back. A step-top cook stove stood in the kitchen that she could buy from the owners. The yard held an empty chicken coop and a small stable that was half-built but large enough for a couple horses. Water could be obtained easily from the river. The structures including the house showed some wear already but were doable as far as Henrietta was concerned. The land was flat, making for an easy garden plot, and held magnificent views of the surrounding mountains. She couldn't imagine a more perfect place for herself.

Henrietta felt a moment of guilt taking the family's home, but caught up in her enthusiasm, made an offer that evening that was accepted. She was now the proud owner of a home in Estes Park.

Henrietta wrote a letter to her sister explaining her purchase and requesting that her belongings be sent to her. She had no doubt what her sister's reaction was going to be. She imagined Clarissa would write complaining to their brother Herman but realize that the deed was done.

Her first night in her new home, Henrietta wondered if she had made a dreadful mistake.

Chapter Four

Collan Wallace knew he had made a mistake as soon as he took a bite of the stale bun and dry sliced cheese he had purchased and realized it would not satisfy his hunger. But he could do nothing more about the situation at present as he sat on a train, steaming its way from Cheyenne, Wyoming to Denver, Colorado. The food had been the best fare he could buy off the platform during the quick stop when the locomotive had taken on more water for its boilers.

He looked over at the passenger across from him. The plump woman was happily eating some tasty meal she had been smart enough to *bring with her*. That had been his error—he should have done the same. At least he hadn't purchased a third-class ticket. That train car had only wooden benches and an outhouse style washroom at one end shared by all. Collan was in second class where the individual leather seats were padded and there were separate washrooms at either end of the car. Of course, it would have been nice if he could have ridden in one of the new sleeper cars where seats folded or else dropped down from the ceiling into beds, but that car had already been full. The best car, though, was the one made to look luxuriously comfortable, like a fancy hotel room, in which only the very wealthy enjoyed the car completely to themselves. But that type of car was entirely out of Collan's price range.

Collan gnawed on another bite. But the food wasn't the only thing that Collan was discontented about. The parting comment made by his friend was sticking in Collan's craw also. Most recently Collan had been earning a wage helping his childhood friend Herm with his cattle ranch north of Laramie, Wyoming. But he had felt restless—which was increasingly becoming a usual state of affairs during his adult life—and had decided to wander over to Cheyenne and now down to Denver for a bit. It wasn't that Collan was some vagabond just scraping by from one line of work to another, he just couldn't seem to presently settle.

Before he had departed, his friend had accused him of becoming a bit rootless, bouncing from one thing to the next. Herm had warned him that if he was trying to escape from his own inner thoughts—whatever they could be—that those notions would just find him in the next place. Collan had just shrugged the comment off at the time, not really even sure if he had got the gist of what Herm had been trying to tell him anyway. But now Herm's aside observation kept returning to his thoughts.

What had Herm seen Collan do or heard Collan say to give him the impression that he had *any* inner thoughts to escape from? Good God. Sounded a bit deep and Collan didn't like to think too much on these types of matters, and yet . . .

To say Collan was discontented or troubled would not be exactly correct either. He was happy . . . well, sort of . . . but feeling all the same as if his life lacked . . . he wasn't sure—or perhaps actually didn't want to admit to himself what.

40

If it was consistent and steady work, though, that he was lacking, he knew for certainty that he was not interested in becoming a merchant out West. No, sir. He had had enough of that back East.

Collan stared out the window at the plains and distant mountains going by, frowning. He intuitively knew, however, that Herm had meant his comment to apply to something much more meaningful. In other words . . . what was missing in Collan's life that would give it more depth and satisfaction so he wasn't so restless? What something *or someone*?

There, he had recognized—as much as he desired at present—the true issue for what it was. So . . . now what? Did that mean he should keep wandering around until he found this something or someone to fill this void in his life or was he supposed to go back to Herm's and just sit on his ass, thinking more on what specifically was this hollow in his life—God, that sounded particularly unpleasant.

Collan shook his head. This was too much. As far as he was concerned, he was better off in his ignorance. "Escaping from inner thoughts." He muttered to himself. "What unnecessary bullshit."

The woman across from him, briefly stopped eating and glared at his language. He apologized and then ignored her. He was going to travel to Denver and . . . and . . . have some fun, then find some work . . . or not.

He shrugged—if he felt like it, he could always travel further southwest . . . or perhaps northwest—he had never been on either route before.

When the much-anticipated toll road opened to excited fanfare towards noon on a pleasant July day, Henrietta's wagon was one of the first to travel the route. She had paid one dollar for the mules the MacGregors owned, Dutch and Honey, to haul her belongings to her new cabin. George helped unload her small collection of furniture and got Liebchen settled in the stable. George refused to sell the mare to Henrietta, preferring her steady supply of baked goods over cash.

Sal sent over her smiling, thirteen-year-old son, Willy, newly arrived with some cattle to Estes Park. He was as sociable as the rest of the family and helped hustle to and from the wagon the numerous other items.

Henrietta had made arrangements for eggs, flour, sugar, and other necessities to be supplied to her from the store the MacGregors had begun but found that her sister Clarissa had assumed she would have to supplement her wagon with provisions. Her husband had added an axe, a hammer, a hoe, some nails, a shovel and some tool she had no idea what its use was for. Henrietta, therefore, had not only a surplus amount of goods, but also luxury spices that Clarissa knew Henrietta liked to bake with. Before George and Willy departed, Henrietta gave them some cookies she had baked.

The remaining part of the day, Henrietta kept busy unpacking and settling in. She slipped between her sheets that night, tired but with a feeling of contentment. She was finally going to spend a night all by herself. Not only that, she was in her new home. She closed her eyes and snuggled into her bed, proud of herself and what she had accomplished.

Bang . . . bang bang . . .bang . . . bang bang bang. What was that? She sat up and listened to the repetitive noise. She knew the wind had kicked up the last hour. Possibly a shingle was loose on the roof, but it would have to wait until the morning for fixing. She settled back in her bed to sleep.

An eerie noise then came from her window with a sudden gust. A moment later, the unsettling moaning emanated again from the glass frame.

Convinced now she wouldn't be able to rest unless she went outside to investigate, Henrietta had just slipped on her robe over her nightdress and placed one foot in her boots, when she next heard a loud thump. Henrietta stopped frozen in her tracks and listened.

Oh, no. Something had landed on her roof. Something *big*. She couldn't fathom how any beast could have jumped up there until she remembered the large pine in the back of her house. So what could have launched from the tree to her gable? Stomp, stomp, stomp. The creature was walking around now. Perhaps it was just a raccoon. But what if it was something more menacing?

Henrietta quickly ran to the front door to make sure the bolt was set, then seized a kitchen knife and hurried back to her bed. She grabbed at the covers and tried to hide beneath them, only allowing a small slit to view the dark bedroom. Bang . . . bang bang . . . oooooeeeeeooooo . . . thump thump thump . . . bang . . . bang bang bang . . . repeated itself for a few minutes until Henrietta realized with relief that at least the clomping on her roof had finally stopped. Oh, thank God. The animal must have jumped down.

Henrietta took a couple deep breaths, trying to calm herself. Fine, she could deal with the noise coming from the wind. So what if it sounded like a ghost was entering her kitchen window? So what if something was banging? She could fix it in the morning. She could do this. She could fall asleep all alone. Yes, she could.

Then she heard what sounded like pawing at her front door. She gasped and then shouted, "You go away!" and the noise stopped. But the image of what could be out there, trying to get in, kept her awake for several hours and when she did finally manage to fall asleep, she tossed and turned.

The next morning when she awoke, Henrietta remained in bed, trying to convince herself she hadn't made a huge mistake. But she couldn't get around the gnawing feeling that she would not be able to manage by herself. She was too much of a fraidy-cat and why she hadn't realized that before, she didn't know. No, actually, she knew. Because she had always lived with someone else, noises at night hadn't bothered her so much.

And just how exactly did one go about fixing a loose shingle? Huh? Somebody tell her that. She knew how to cook, sew, garden, darn, knit, crotchet, embroider and now ride a horse—well, ride a little. Oh, and she had gone fishing a few times but did not especially like placing the worm on the hook. She did not know how to chop, hammer, saw, or properly handle a gun.

What had she been thinking buying this property?

She felt like a failure already. All her proud plans of experiencing independence, making her own decisions, doing exactly what she wanted to do, living a life of self-rule were obviously only an illusion for someone like her.

She got up disconsolately and slipped her feet into a pair of her husband's old boots. She went out onto the porch still only in her nightgown. What difference did it make? There wasn't anybody to see her. She was all alone—that was for sure. She gazed around her yard and surroundings. The sight was so beautiful with the river winding around her property before the distant mountains that she found herself inwardly smiling.

She just had to give this living arrangement a longer try. She didn't want to give this place up.

She went back to her bedroom, slipped on her oldest dress and this time her own scuffed up boots and walked again to the porch. She closed the door behind her. She didn't want any animals getting in while she did some chores. Liebchen stirred in the stables, seeing her.

She walked over and stroked her mane. "And how are you this morning?"

The mare stomped a foot. Henrietta poured some grain in a bucket and placed it in front of the horse who eagerly started chomping. George had advised Henrietta that his mare should not require extra feeding as long as she could be allowed to graze, but Henrietta didn't want to worry that the horse wasn't getting enough to eat. She would prefer a fat mount to a starving one. While she waited for Liebchen to finish, Henrietta surveyed her roof. She didn't see any obvious loose shingle, but there was a branch hanging over from the adjacent tree that might have been pounding her roof with the wind. That animal last night had also probably used that limb to jump over to the top of her house.

She decided cutting down that branch would be her first chore for the day, but she required a way to get up the tree where the bough met the trunk. She remembered there was a crude ladder in the back of the stables that the prior owners had not taken with them. She hauled the heavy item out into the yard and studied it a moment.

Oh. No wonder they hadn't wanted it. One of the rungs was broken. Henrietta went back into the house and got her hammer. She loosened the broken board from the ladder, trying not to bend the nails. She looked around for something she could use as a replacement rung but did not find one readily. She would have to improvise and make her own board. Perhaps she could chop or saw a log in half and nail that onto the front of the ladder as the missing rung.

Yes, *that* would actually be her first chore—chopping and sawing logs. Henrietta had always heard that one of the most important chores for any homesteader was to make sure there was enough fuel for cooking and as extra to keep warm in the coming winter.

She had never chopped a log in her life, but she was going to today. She knew there were some fallen timber in the back of her house. She looked over at Liebchen and decided to saddle her and then have the mount drag one of the logs over to her yard.

Liebchen eyed her warily as she hoisted the saddle onto her back, as if she knew something unusual was up. Henrietta patted her neck. "Don't worry. We'll figure this out."

But when Henrietta straddled her and tried to rein her towards the back of the house, Liebchen instead walked over to some nearby grass to graze. Henrietta rolled her eyes. "Oh, no you don't. Just because George isn't around doesn't mean you have to return to your old ways."

Liebchen ignored her and continued grazing. Henrietta had enough to do besides arguing with her horse so she dismounted and grabbed the mare by the bridle. She walked her over to the area where several pines had fallen. One in particular appeared lighter and smaller and had fallen atop of another tree. Henrietta took the rope she had brought with her and now tied one end as tightly as she could around the tree. She then tied the other end of the rope to the saddle.

She grabbed Liebchen's bridle and coaxed her to walk toward the house. As soon as the rope was fully uncoiled and taut, the mare stopped. Henrietta commanded, "Pull, Liebchen, pull."

Liebchen dropped her head and started grazing again. Henrietta blew out a long breath. "Oh, for heaven's sake. Can't you even try?"

Liebchen ignored her. Henrietta stomped back to her home, muttering, "Fine, fine. I'll haul the logs myself." She went into her cabin and grabbed the axe and saw, leaning by the front door. She would first saw the tree into smaller pieces and then lug everything back to her home. Then she would chop a board off of one of the pieces and nail it onto the ladder which she would then climb to saw down the branch that was banging against her roof.

An hour later Henrietta had managed to saw only a couple sections off the fallen tree. She couldn't believe how difficult it was to get the saw to actually cut the tree and not get repeatedly stuck in the gliding motion. Her arm already felt fatigued from the unfamiliar motion. She decided to accept for today what she had accomplished and tried lifting one of the sections to carry back to her yard. She wobbled underneath the weight and dropped it back to the ground. She thought briefly about trying to get Liebchen, who was still contentedly grazing, to haul the small section back for her but quickly dismissed the idea. She was wasting too much time on this chore as is without involving her stubborn horse.

Henrietta tried rolling the log into her yard and found she could do that without too much effort. She went back for the next section of log and after she tied the axe and saw to her saddle, Liebchen followed her back to the yard. She went into her cabin for a drink of water but quickly returned to her yard. She upended the log and took the axe by the handle. She lifted it above her shoulder and slammed down on the log. She scarcely made an impression. Huh.

Henrietta patted the raised section of the log. Was this some unusually firm tree? No, it couldn't be. It was just one of the fallen pines. She tried again with the axe and made only a slightly larger gap. Good Lord. This was going to take forever.

An hour later, Henrietta had finally chopped into jagged pieces one section of the tree. After several failed attempts, she had figured out that she had to raise the axe well above her head and then with a sliding motion of her hand on the handle, let the axe drop into the wood with her momentum. The only problem was that now she felt so tired from the activity that she didn't think she could do more of it for today.

She went back into her cabin for another drink and also snagged a piece of bread. She sat on her porch steps gobbling the morsel down. Now what? She had planned to get started on her garden today. Should she forget about the ladder and the banging tree branch? Because just how long was it going to take her to finish that chore? The rest of the day? My God, how did anyone get everything done that had to get completed around a homestead? No wonder farmers had huge families. They required all the helping hands.

At least she had the money to hire help if it came to that. But wouldn't that be defeating the purpose of her living her independent life? She frowned a moment in thought. She didn't know and was honestly too tired to figure out the answer to that question just now.

She decided to go back to her ladder project. She picked up the broken rung with the nails still sticking in it off the ground. She grabbed her hammer and sat back on the porch steps. She pulled the nails from the board. Unfortunately, one of the nails turned out bent. She hammered it on her porch step, trying to straighten it. She was only partially successful. She shrugged, thinking the nail would probably do and walked back over to the ladder. She grabbed the straightest piece of chopped log that she could find and managed to nail it onto the front of the ladder. She hauled the ladder over to the tree with the hanging branch and positioned it against the trunk. She tested her new rung for strength with her arms. It seemed to hold.

Tentatively, she started to climb the ladder, holding her saw with one hand. She made it up to the point where she could cut the branch. She leaned forward and began sawing. She was pleased to see she was getting better at this.

She started moving more vigorously as the branch began to drop off. Just when she was finishing and the branch hung by a thin strip of bark, the ladder gave way, sliding off to the side of the trunk. She dropped her saw abruptly and grabbed hold of the trunk with her arms. The ladder stopped moving.

Now what? How was she supposed to get down without falling? She stepped slowly to the rung below and scraped along the tree trunk with her arms. The ladder held. She took another step, then another and another. She finally placed her foot on her improvised rung and heard a cracking immediately before she half-banged, half-plummeted, her way to the ground.

She lay still on the dirt, trying to catch her breath. The wind was knocked out of her and she suddenly felt defenseless. She struggled to breathe evenly and finally after a few moments, she felt better.

She shook her head. No more chores involving ladders for her—at least not for a while. She felt sore all over as she struggled to sit up and when she tried to put weight on both arms, she felt a piercing in the wrist she had stretched out to dampen her fall.

Oh, no. Not on her very first full day at her homestead. This couldn't be. She wriggled the wrist back and forth a few times. Yes, it was definitely affected but probably not broken. At least she didn't think so and at least it was not her dominant arm. She rested the arm against her side as she finally managed to stand.

She looked over at the ladder still leaning crookedly against the tree. She was determined to finish this chore. She kicked the ladder fully on the ground and pulled with a load grunt, one-handed, the hanging branch until *finally* it broke from the tree, peeling some of the bark with it. She felt immediate satisfaction. There. The morning had not been a complete failure.

She decided it was time to take a break and make herself a meal. She gathered some of the pieces of timber off the ground that she had chopped, resting them gently on her arm—and wasn't that really something that she had also sawed the logs herself—and went towards her cabin to place them in her cook stove. Despite the wrist, she was actually proud of herself.

She stepped lively up the steps, opened her cabin door excitedly and was suddenly struck upon entering this time that she was all alone.

Somehow in her brief euphoria she had forgotten that she was a widow, that Charles was not inside her cabin, just waiting to hear about her homesteading accomplishments. That not only wasn't Charles not there cheering her on, but that there was *no one* to hear about her morning.

She stopped in her tracks and listened. She could hear the river, the slight rustling of the wind in the trees and one short bird call. But her home was completely silent. She wasn't used to a home that didn't have any noise in it. Someone had always been bustling about with her. She didn't know if she liked it. She didn't know if she would ever get used to it. She did know, however, that she missed her husband at that moment with a longing so deep that she had to sit down.

She wiped at her tears, remembering him. Her husband's passing was a problem that she could not make better. He was gone for good and there was nothing she could do about it. She knew this. Of course, she knew this, but it didn't stop her from feeling at that instant every little anguish there was to feel about her sorrow.

She no longer felt hungry and let the logs simply fall to the cabin floor. She had kept busy since he had passed, one way or another, and had done her best to handle her sadness—and she recognized it wasn't so awfully raw as it had been a month ago, she had been doing better lately—but still . . . she suffered.

She allowed herself the indulgence of solitude to take it all in. Really take it all in. Time passed as she sat, staring into space.

Eventually, she heard an animal screech outside and remembered her surroundings. She got up from the table, absently broke away a piece of bread and then walked over to look out her window. Her wrist was puffy, but she tried to ignore it. She nibbled discontentedly—meals alone would be another aspect of her new life she would have to become accustomed to.

She swallowed her last bite, then blew out a long breath. She should try to pull herself together. Charles would want her to. She decided to spend the afternoon gardening, wrist and all. The ground should be prepared for planting. Perhaps the activity out-of-doors would help her forget, at least temporarily again, all that troubled her.

Three hours later, she collapsed on her bed. She was famished, but she had to take a nap. She just felt so tired. Her garden plot was also going to take longer than she had thought. The ground was workable but loaded with rocks—so many that she already had a pile of them forming around the bed.

She snuggled into her pillow, resting her wrist off to the side. Yes, she would just lie down for a few minutes and then get up to make some stew. . . .

She awoke briefly later to find her cabin now fully dark. She adjusted her covers and fell back to sleep, no longer interested in feeding herself.

The next morning Henrietta turned over in bed and awoke suddenly to a bad feeling in her wrist. Light was streaming into the room, and she realized she had slept in longer than usual. She looked at her arm. She could scarcely bend her wrist and it had become as large as a turnip. Her first thought was to ask Charles to have a look at it. But, ahhh . . . that was impossible now, wasn't it? She had briefly forgotten again in her sleep that he had passed.

She got up and awkwardly tied a large scarf from around her neck to her wrist to support it. That wasn't the only thing that proved difficult. An hour later she gave up trying to make any decent kind of meal for herself or doing any substantial work outside. She knew from experience that she was better off letting her wrist rest than pushing it. So after giving Liebchen some grain and fetching water from the river, she decided just to head back to her cabin. She looked at the ground as she walked, too dispirited to enjoy the surrounding scenery. She stopped suddenly, sloshing water over the side of the bucket, as she noticed a curious print in the dirt.

What had caught her attention was how big it was—as if the ball of the animal's foot was extremely large. She looked more closely. Could it actually be a boot print instead? She didn't see any indentations from claws. She pressed her own shoe into the dirt next to it to compare. This print was either from a man's foot or a formidable animal. She looked around for some similar prints but saw none in the surrounding rocks embedded in the ground. She shook her head. This really was nothing for her to get frightened about. So what if some large creature had passed through recently? He wasn't here now. That was all that mattered.

She entered her cabin and dragged a chair out onto the porch. She sat down and opened the first of several newspapers she had found in a trunk that her sister had sent along with her belongings. After reading the top article Henrietta wondered if Clarissa had hand-picked which editions to send her—as a warning so to speak.

Apparently, a gang of outlaws had recently robbed several stagecoaches. A posse was being formed to track the bandits. It was believed that the gang hung out in Owl Canyon which was an area of foothills about fifteen miles north of Fort Collins, but the worry was whether the gang had escaped south into the mountains. That put them potentially in Henrietta's direction. Oh, that wasn't good.

The next newspaper began with an article about recent Indian attacks. Okay. At least she didn't have to worry about that . . . much. All the local settlers had assured her that the last Indians had basically disappeared from the Estes Park area over the last decade. But this article discussed the special society of Cheyenne Dog Soldiers. This powerful group of Cheyenne warriors rejected the notion of living on reservations or Americans expanding westward and had been raiding along the Platte River. Henrietta blew a breath of relief. Okay, that was pretty far from here. But, oh no. They also roamed the foothills and mountains of Montana and Wyoming. So what would stop them from coming to Colorado and Estes Park, Henrietta wondered. She read further. These men were named after a Cheyenne legend in which dogs transformed into fierce fighters. They were known for wearing large headdresses and sashes made from buffalo. And, oh good God. During battle, the dog soldier would stake his sash to the ground and fight from that location no matter what. He could not leave until the battle was over or he was unpinned by a fellow warrior. Henrietta shook her head. She moved on to the next newspaper.

The lead articled concerned the problem with wolves. Now that the buffalo and other large game were disappearing, being hunted for food or sport, the wolves were turning to cattle as prey. Henrietta shuddered in horror. One rancher described a particularly gruesome attack in which the wolf had devoured only the cow's udder and hindquarters so he had had to kill the cow himself to put her out of her misery.

Henrietta set the newspaper down. She had read enough. But the problem was that Henrietta could not get the scary images out of her head for the rest of the day. By evening she still felt down despite her wrist already improving slightly from the morning.

She managed to fall asleep as darkness fell, but awoke to Liebchen nickering once loudly from the stables. She sat up in bed. That was kind of unusual. What had disturbed her? Henrietta got out of bed and walked over to her kitchen window. She could not see a thing the night was so cloudy.

Just then she heard a howling. A WOLF howling. Her eyes widened. Surely wolves wouldn't attack a much bigger horse, would they? But then Liebchen was old and slow. She listened intently to the night noises a moment longer. There was another yowl or was that a hoot? Her imagination flooded. Could word have spread already that she was alone and an easy victim? Perhaps that wasn't a wolf at all, but Indians or *outlaws* signally to each other in the dark. What if someone was trying to steal poor Liebchen?

She quickly lit the lantern on her table. Before she lost her courage, Henrietta wrapped a shawl around her shoulders and then grabbed her husband's old rifle. Her plan was to fire a warning. She walked to the door, and ignoring the discomfort in her wrist, opened it a crack and peered out. She saw nothing moving. She opened the door wider and took a step onto her porch. Then another and another as she descended her steps into the yard.

She peered over by the stables. "Liebchen? Are you still there?"

She heard no sounds and could see nothing in the distance. The darkness was absolute this shrouded night except for the small area of faint light filtering out through the door from her lantern on the table. She took another step, then gasped as she caught a set of eyes flashing at her.

She turned and tore back into her cabin, slamming and bolting the door behind her. She had no idea whose set of eyes those belonged to, animal or crouching person.

She sank down, leaning her back against the door, panting. She looked at the rifle she had thrown on the floor upon hurriedly entering—she hadn't even gotten off a warning with the darn thing. Then she chuckled mirthlessly as she grabbed it. The gun wasn't even loaded, she now remembered. She was hopelessly pathetic at defending herself or her horse. And now she was too afraid to even walk across the room to get some ammunition because she had lit the lantern and any person could see her through the kitchen window so doing.

Minutes went by and then an hour. And though she heard no more unusual noises, she stayed by the door. She awoke the next morning, slumped sideways on the floor, still clutching the useless rifle. So this was going to be the way of things. She was ready to begin packing up to leave, but then she heard Liebchen, neighing by the stables. She blew out a breath. At least she was still alive and not stolen. Perhaps Henrietta would give the place one more day try.

She was eating breakfast when Clara stopped by a week later. She looked Henrietta over a moment and raised her brows. "Well, how is it going?"

"Do I look that bad?"

"Perhaps a little tired."

Henrietta snorted. "I'm exhausted." She hesitated, then divulged, "I'm thinking about selling my home."

Chapter Five

"What?" Clara looked startled by her revelation.

"Some evenings if I sleep even an hour straight, it's a miracle. Every noise has me convinced there's a creature outside just waiting to burst into my home. Though surprisingly, that hasn't been a problem the last couple of nights because I'm so tired, I sleep so soundly a whole gang of bandits could break in on me and I don't think I'd stir."

"Oh, I see."

Henrietta shook her head, disgustedly. "And I realize I didn't know the first thing about running a homestead myself."

"Most people don't, but they learn." Clara smiled slightly. "You seemed so happy about purchasing this place."

Henrietta rested her head on the table and said unenthusiastically, "I was deluded by the excitement of being independent for once in my life."

"Oh."

"Chores that always looked so easy and obvious to accomplish when my brother or father or husband had done them are a lot more difficult than I thought. I'm sure you saw on your way in that pathetic excuse for a log pile. That's three days of working every morning for at least an hour." She showed Clara her wrist. "Of course, I had to give this a few days rest after it puffed up like a watermelon the day after I fell on it when the ladder gave way."

Clara bugged her eyes.

Henrietta continued, not waiting for any further response. "I mean I know I'm not a total failure—"

"Of course not. You're brave and heroic for even attempting to carve your own path out here."

Henrietta shrugged, uncertainly. "Anyways, I've learned to get into a routine of sorts. First thing in the morning, I haul water from the river and then handle everything that Liebchen requires—you know grain, mucking out her stall—then I grab a quick bite and tackle some chore." She frowned slightly. "But it is becoming increasingly obvious that it's going to be a choice between growing plants this summer and raising chickens. That coop requires some repair before I can do that. Oh, and you can forget about baking anything fun like pastry and pies. I mean I can handle extra bread for George, but just to get a decent meal on the table is plenty enough to do." She stopped briefly and asked, "Did you know that recently chopped logs make terrible fires? They mainly just smoke a lot. I had to find old, dry timber and twigs to make any kind of cooking fire. Somehow that fact had always slipped my attention until I was the one who was actually hauling in the cooking fuel."

She resumed her original topic. "Anyways, at night, I try getting the mending or washing done, but I can scarcely stay awake!" Her frown deepened. "Really, I should do the washing before I start the chopping or hoeing so that it can dry outside, but that log pile is so measly it has me worried." She blew out a long breath.

60

"Liebchen could also use an enclosed area to graze. I wonder how difficult it is to build a fence—"

"Henrietta, stop!"

She looked over. "What?"

"Why do you feel *you* have to do all this? I thought you had some inheritance to hire help."

She nodded. "I do, it's just . . ."

"What?"

"I've been meaning to find the time to figure this all out, but I'm not sure if I hire help if I'll still be living independently."

"And that's important to you."

"Yes."

Clara shook her head. "Well, you better take a break from this whirlwind and start enjoying life more, if you want my opinion."

Henrietta was quiet a moment, then said, "I have some dried cherries."

"And?"

"I want to make a pie with them. You know I love baking."

"Then do it."

Henrietta nodded, noncommittedly. "Perhaps . . . but all these chores aren't the only problem."

"What else?"

"I always used to have so much more energy, but if I don't get at least a quick nap in the afternoon, I'm finished."

"And?"

Clara already knew her well enough that she could tell Henrietta was holding something further back. Henrietta shrugged and glanced away briefly. "I don't know if I can get used to how quiet this house is with only me roaming about." She looked back earnestly. "I mean it's really kind of lonely eating all your meals by yourself." *And without Charles,* she would have added but stopped herself, not wanting to burst into tears.

She swallowed, then continued softly. "I thought I would enjoy the privacy, but I'm not so sure." She waved her hand in the air listlessly. "Anyways, I don't really know *what* I think about anything anymore, and I'm just too tired to ponder it further."

Clara was silent a moment, then said, "I think you should get a dog."

Henrietta raised her head, perking up. "A dog? Oh, I adore dogs, but there was always one reason or another why I couldn't get one the last few years." She suddenly liked the idea, finally feeling enthused again about something. Even if she sold her cabin, she could still keep the pooch. She asked, "But where would I find one?"

"Hmmm. Let's go over to the Evans'. They always seem to have a pack running around. Perhaps they'd sell you one."

A couple hours later, Clara and Henrietta rode their horses up to the Evans' front porch. Liebchen had decided to obey on the way over to Henrietta's great relief. Henrietta would have found it embarrassing to admit to Clara how obstinate her horse had become again.

Griff Evans and his family were some of the original settlers to Estes Park, having purchased their property from Joel Estes, the town's namesake, which they then sold to the Englishman, Lord Dunraven. The

Evans helped manage the estate now. But because of their association with the unpopular Lord Dunraven, who was accused of land swindling for his own gain, the Evans were almost considered as outsiders themselves now.

But it was not an Evans, but a Mr. Theodore Whyte, who greeted them when they knocked on the door. Henrietta had heard about but not yet met, the snooty Englishman who Lord Dunraven had also hired to help run the domain. Besides his offensive attitude, he was also known for riding around Estes Park in an expensive riding outfit on a fine English mount, jumping barriers and fences with ease—an unusual sight for the area.

Clara made the introductions and stated they were hoping to acquire a dog.

Mr. Whyte sniffed, then said, "The Evans have all departed for a trip to Denver. Perhaps you should return another time."

Henrietta could take a hint, especially one so rude. They were obviously bothering him. She was just turning to leave when she spied an older appearing dog, limping badly across the yard. There was something familiar about the mutt. Was that actually . . .?

She hurried down the front steps. "Ring? Is that you?"

Ring looked over and started wagging his tail. Henrietta rushed over to meet him halfway and gave the dog a loving hug and pet. "What are you doing here?"

She looked back at Mr. Whyte. "I thought that family in Fort Collins took him in after Mountain Jim departed."

He shook his head. "No, Griff wasn't going to give up such a great hunting dog. He's useless now, of course."

"Oh, Ring. Are you not feeling well?" Ring licked her face. Henrietta knew the dog well because he had stayed with her when she had helped Mountain Jim mend. Besides the limp, he looked thin and neglected, his fur dirty and matted. She turned back to Mr. Whyte. "I'd like him."

Whyte waved his hand dismissively. "Take him. He's yours. But you better also get Sally out of the barn. They're usually inseparable."

"Griff took Mountain Jim's puppy also?"

"Yes, before she proved unserviceable, also. She's gun-shy since her ear got blown off in a hunting accident."

Clara muttered, "I've heard enough." She shook her head, disgustedly, as she stomped over to the barn.

Henrietta thought Whyte was a vile man, but at least he helped hoist Ring before her on her saddle. Ring did not protest. Whyte then lifted Sally before Clara. Sally was missing an ear, but more important, was not the active, friendly puppy Henrietta remembered. She cowered and shook with fear.

Once out of hearing range, Clara exploded. "How deplorable that was. Whyte is a rude man. And the Evans have surely taken a slide since their dealings began with that Dunraven. We're not on the best of terms, as you probably gathered. Alex has made his opinion known what he thinks of this whole Dunraven business."

Henrietta nodded. "At least I've got the dogs."

64

"Yes, at least that."

Once at the cabin, over the next few days Henrietta lavished attention and home cooking on the dogs, sharing large portions of beef stew with them. She set up soft beds made with extra blankets in the corner of her bedroom. She gave them both baths. She hugged them, babbling assuring words, whenever they were near. And the dogs responded. Sally no longer cowered and Ring seemed to be smiling, or so she thought.

And Henrietta benefited also. They were company for her. Perhaps not the talking kind but still noise makers in the house. They were someone to love. But even with their added comradery to her household, Henrietta realized no one and no living thing would ever come close to filling the void from her husband's passing.

As difficult as it was, she forced herself resignedly to the fact that she would just have to settle to this feeling of hollowness for the rest of her life. She could do it. She had to do it.

One day George came by for some bread, but he did not stay long. He had too many chores to do on his own spread, but before he departed he promised to find some time to show her how to fix things around her cabin. He then asked about Liebchen.

Henrietta smiled. "Oh, she's just fine." She did not want to admit to George that the horse was a stubborn mess.

But not so long after, Henrietta realized—if she excluded Liebchen from her musings—things were actually looking a bit up and she no longer had the urge to sell her cabin. Yes, she had had her initial sorrowful troubles, but that was okay. She was doing better now and proving she was a capable woman. Yes, she was. Just look at her growing pile of logs.

A few days later, Henrietta was even humming as she turned soil over in her new garden. She glanced warmly at Ring and Sally who were now sprawled contentedly on her front porch. But when the dogs started barking excitedly and she turned around to see what was causing the commotion, she suddenly dropped her shovel in horror.

Three of the most ragged appearing men approached on horses. Their clothes were dirty, stained and torn. They were all thin to the point of gauntness and frowned as they rode closer. They appeared to be a group of highly desperate characters. This was one of her worse nightmares coming to life.

Henrietta fought the urge to run into her cabin for the gun that Charles had owned. She had fired the weapon once in the last week but didn't feel she had much control over her aim. She blew out a long breath and decided she had better try standing her ground as the men drew nearer. The dogs continued barking vigorously, but strangely stayed on the porch. If she survived this encounter, Henrietta vowed to teach her dear pooches how to be better watch dogs.

She managed a tentative smile as the men came up to her. The tallest fellow in front took off his scruffy fur hat and gave a curt nod. "Mrs. Schodde? I'm Hank Farrar and these here are my brothers Clint and Ike. Miss Clara sent us over to see if you be wantin' any help around here."

Henrietta clasped her chest and staggered backwards a few feet with relief. "Oh, good Lord." Ring and Sally stopped barking and started wagging their tails.

He tilted his head puzzled. "Are you doing okay, Ma'am?"

Henrietta brushed her dirty hands over her skirt and reached up to shake his hand. "Oh, Mr. Farrar. I've heard a lot about you. Won't you all get down and have some coffee with me?"

"We'd be much obliged." The three brothers dismounted and looked hesitantly around the yard. Hank spoke up again as he removed his hat. "You living here by yourself, Mrs. Schodde?"

"Why, yes I am."

They all exchanged glances with each other, brows raised.

She ignored the looks. "Please call me Henrietta."

"Yes, ma'am. And you can call me Hank, Miss Henrietta." He slugged his nearest brother and motioned with his head and a frown for Clint to remove his hat. Ike followed suit.

"Well, come on in. The coffee will just take a minute to heat."

The brothers followed Henrietta into the cabin and stood around the table awkwardly, shuffling their feet, until Henrietta remembered to tell them to have a seat. They watched her intently as she put the pot on the stove and added more kindling to the fire. She then sat down at the table and smiled pleasantly. "It's nice to meet you all at last."

Hank nodded once, Clint blushed, and Ike looked around the cabin, mouth open.

"So I guess we're neighbors."

Hank nodded again. "We're where the Thompson meets the Fall River."

"And you hunt for a living?"

Clint spoke up. "And fish."

Henrietta searched for a topic of conversation and drew a blank. She wondered how hunters with such a successful reputation could look so haggard. Surely, they must have plenty to eat with their line of work. But some motherly instinct kicked in, and she offered, "I have beef stew. Would you like some?"

Ike finally spoke and smiled widely. "You bet, Miss Henrietta. My brothers can't cook for shit."

Hank huffed. "Now what the heck did I tell you, Ike, about watching your language?"

"Sorry, Hank. I'm just so hungry and look at that pie over there."

Henrietta jumped up. "Oh, my. You can certainly have a piece of that, also. I was just waiting for the coffee to heat." She put the pot of stew on the stove and turned back around.

Clint groaned. "We burn dab near everything."

Ike shook his head. "And the corn bread comes out so dry you can't near swallow it."

Hank explained, "We got the fixin's but can't manage to do the makin'."

Henrietta took pity on the sorry lot. "Well, I could probably help you with that. Why don't you bring me over some of your meat, and I'll make it into a meal for you?"

All three brothers gazed silently at her a moment. Finally Hank spoke again. "You'd do that for us, Miss Henrietta?"

She smiled. "Certainly. I love to cook. And *bake.* I really like to bake when I force the time. But it's not as much fun when it's only for the dogs and me."

Hank said hesitantly, "Would, uh, . . . would next Saturday be fine with you?"

"Absolutely."

Henrietta awoke a few days later to the sound of chopping logs and pounding on her roof. She looked out her window and recognized Ike in her still unfinished garden plot, plowing up a lane. She quickly drew her coat over her nightie and walked out of the cabin, Ring and Sally in her wake, both yawning loudly. She looked up at Hank on her roof. "What's going on?"

Hank glanced over while working. "We noticed your roof required some repairs, Miss Henrietta."

She frowned slightly. "It did?" She hadn't noticed but of course, she didn't really know what to look for.

Clint asked, "Is this a good place for your timber?"

She glanced over at the growing pile of chopped logs. "That'd be fine, Clint."

Ike shouted from the garden. "You want me to mix in some of that horse shit for your garden, Miss Henrietta?"

Hank threw down his hammer and yelled. "Dab blame it, watch the language, Ike!"

Ike looked sheepish. "I mean horse poop, Miss Henrietta."

Clint guffawed. "It's horse *manure,* you oaf. That's what reeefined people call it."

Hank commanded, "Get back to work. Add the manure, Ike." Hank jumped down from the roof and walked over to his horse. "We brought you some elk meat, trout, and venison. We weren't sure which you wanted to make."

Henrietta took the proffered game and fish. "Why don't I try to cook it all? Is cherry pie and spice cookies fine for dessert?"

Their mouths dropped.

When the meal was ready, Henrietta had the men wash their faces and hands in the basin she placed by her front door. They entered her cabin shyly again and took their seats. Henrietta realized that the other day, Hank must have instructed his brothers to be on their best behavior. They had been restrained and eaten quietly what she had offered but had not requested seconds. This meal began with their rapt silent attention again as she placed the roasted elk, potatoes, gravy, and bread and butter on the table. She served each a generous portion.

Ike took the first bite. He pounded with his fist on the table causing his plate to jump, then said, "Lord, have mercy, we've died and gone to heaven."

Clint looked over. "Just so, Miss Henrietta."

She smiled, "Why, thank you. Eat up." And eat up they did. No longer holding back—probably since they had provided the meat—they dug in with relish, devouring, groaning, and slurping with pleasure. The elk, grilled trout and venison were wolfed down rapidly and totally. A second and then third loaf of bread were demolished. The potatoes and gravy gobbled down. The pie disposed of in minutes. By the time the meal was finished only a few crumbs from the spice cookies remained on their plates.

Henrietta wasn't sure what to say. "Well, that was, uh . . . something. I guess you boys were hungry."

Hank glanced at her sheepishly. "Sorry about not leaving you any for the next week, Miss Henrietta. We'll bring more next time."

And they certainly did. As the succeeding weeks progressed, if the Farrars weren't out hunting, they visited every three or four days for meals in exchange for chores.

They started to fill out and she could see with their curly blond hair and strong tall physiques that if they bothered to put in a little effort at grooming they might be considered handsome. She took pity on them again. One day she broached the subject of their attire.

They had just finished consuming baked trout, elk steaks, five loaves of bread and cake. They were relaxing on the front porch with the dogs. Ring and Sally had turned into their devoted followers. Her dogs obviously knew where the grub and scraps came from that was passed freely to them during meals.

She smiled pleasantly. "Hank and Ike, I noticed you had tears in your shirts." They surveyed their clothes as if they had never noticed before and both shrugged.

She turned to Clint. "And your pants could use some fixing."

Clint looked over suddenly abashed. "Sorry, Miss Henrietta."

71

"Now that's okay." She said cheerfully. "Your clothes are all just a bit filthy and torn. Nothing we can't make better."

Ike spoke up surprised. "We can?"

"Why sure. Just a little mending and scrubbing."

Ike was still confused. "But why would we do that? They're just going to get all dirty again."

"Well, don't you want to look nice?"

Ike frowned. "For who?"

Clint slugged him in the arm. "So's Miss Henrietta ain't embarrassed to be seen with us, you stupid oaf."

"And you might want to court some women someday."

Hank was now interested. "What do you have in mind, Miss Henrietta?"

"Well, first, we could pull out my washtub and you could all take a bath."

That was met with loud protest at once. "In front of you?" "Today?" "Whatever for?"

But Henrietta felt she was now on a mission and disregarded their objections. Over the remainder of the day and into the evening she had them all bathe and then change into some old clothes belonging to Charles while she washed, dried, and mended theirs.

On the next visit, she trimmed their mops and beards. The following week she worked on teaching them some table manners and even instructed them on a simple dance step.

But this was not all a one-sided affair. Henrietta's home site was turning into one of the best kept places in Estes Park. Besides repairing her cabin and preparing a garden, the Farrars finished building the stable and constructed a fenced area for Liebchen to graze in. She bought some chicks, hens and a rooster from Sal Ferguson and the Farrar brothers caged in her coop. Henrietta started peddling her eggs to campers who were staying with Clara. Word also spread about her baking, and she began getting requests and selling bread, cookies, pies and strudel from her cabin.

Eventually, the well-fed Farrars started splitting their current wardrobe at the seams. Now showing some pride in their appearance, they decided to buy some new clothes and departed on a trip to Denver. Shortly thereafter, George swung by for some loaves of bread.

Over a cup of coffee, Henrietta said, "I don't know how you do it all. I don't have a cattle herd like you and the Farrars are helping me out. How can you possibly find the time to cook, clean, wash, feed the livestock, garden, and then ranch?"

He shrugged. "Now you see why this bread is more valuable to me than money."

Henrietta nodded slowly. "I could use a milk cow. That would save me the effort of running over to buy some milk, though I do like chatting with my women friends."

George blushed. Now what had she said? Henrietta was running over their conversation in her mind, trying to figure it out when George suddenly blurted out, "Ach, you want a husband, Henrietta? That would be easier for you."

Was he volunteering for the position?! Oh, Lord. She hoped not. She tried to make a joke out of it. "No, I am definitely not getting married again. I don't want a husband, but I could sure use *a wife* to help around here."

George smiled, looking vastly relieved, as if he had been saved from an execution. Henrietta quirked a corner of her mouth over at George but decided not to take that as the insult it appeared. Little did she realize that by the next afternoon, she would have her wife.

Chapter Six

Henrietta had just finished tossing scraps to the one-legged hawk she had named Harry, who now regularly perched, half-leaning, on her fence post and then gone inside to refresh the water bowl of Snuggles—the baby rabbit she kept in the corner of her kitchen after finding the poor thing in the field next to his lifeless mother—when she glanced out the window, hearing shouting. Ring and Sally, who had been snoozing by the cook stove, sprang to their feet and started barking.

Henrietta wasn't at first sure what to make out of the scene before her. Across the Thompson River, a rough appearing fellow was dismounting from his horse, yelling loudly, clad in a fur cap and hide shirt, like the image of an old trapper—though there were scarcely any nowadays what with the decimated beaver population. He staggered as he placed his foot on the ground and then swayed as he took a swig from a flask.

Henrietta then noticed a woman with her tresses in long braids, angrily hollering at the drunkard. As she stomped towards the man, Henrietta caught glimpses of a tall pair of moccasins underneath her cotton skirt.

She watched for a few moments but when their argument turned violent, and the man took a swing at the woman, landing his punch in her gut, causing her to collapse on the ground, Henrietta had seen enough. She strode determinedly out of her cabin, slamming the door on her snarling and yapping pooches, who she did not want to see possibly come to harm.

She shouted as she walked towards the horrid man, "Hey, you there, what do you think you're doing?"

The reprobate turned around to face her as Henrietta agilely crossed the stream, jumping from rock to rock. He slurred his words. "What's it your business, you old whore."

Henrietta gasped. "Why, I never." She walked unwaveringly up to within a few feet of the scalawag. He was more built and taller than she had first realized, but she didn't back down. "This is my property, sir, and I want you to leave at once. Your wife can stay if she wants." Henrietta knew this strip of land across from the river was not actually hers, but now was not the time for petty details.

Henrietta's eyes widened as his countenance turned even uglier, and he raged towards her. "I don't take commands from the likes of you, woman."

He backhanded her on the side of her head before she realized his intent. She sailed, sprawling face down into the dirt. A moment later she looked back up at him stunned, and to her horror he had picked up a large rock.

She tried to scramble away across the ground, but he proved quicker. He stumbled towards her, menacingly raising the rock above himself. Just as she was sure he was going to slam it down on top of her head, a BOOM pierced the air. He dropped the rock abruptly and howled in agony. He staggered a few feet as he tried to grab at his leg, before collapsing on the ground.

Henrietta looked over aghast at his wife, holding the gun, and then at the drunkard's lifeless appearing form. Henrietta hurried to her feet and noticed a spreading red stain along his filthy pants leg. She pulled the man over onto his back, and the wife tore his pants at the seam with a knife. Henrietta ripped a portion of her petticoat and tied it around the man's leg to staunch the flow, though the hurt did not appear that deep. She then leaned over his face. "Oh, thank goodness. He's still breathing. Must be just passed out drunk."

The wife was already shoving the rifle back into its scabbard, along the side of the saddle as the horse stood motionless. "Too bad I didn't hit him higher. The old bastard had it coming."

Henrietta gazed stunned, as she studied the woman more closely. She appeared to be an Indian, with dark coloring and a broad face. She looked in her forties or perhaps thirties, but weathered, as if she hadn't spent much time indoors.

The woman shrugged. "Next time I'll do better."

Henrietta finally stirred. "Well, what should we do now?"

"Let the coyotes have him."

Henrietta frowned. "I guess we should bring him to my cabin to clean him up and then try to get help if he doesn't get better soon." The thought of this man staying with her any longer than necessary was distinctly unpleasant.

The woman did not respond but just stared straight ahead, as Henrietta then stood still a moment also, briefly pondering. Should they tell a sheriff about the incident? But what sheriff? Was there even one here?

Henrietta didn't think so. And even if there was some authority, what was she supposed to say. That an Indian woman had struck her husband defending her . . . if he even was her husband?

No, she couldn't do that to this woman. The woman had undoubtedly saved her life, but Henrietta didn't think there was a court in Colorado that would not try to convict her for at least attempted manslaughter. And why was that? Henrietta smirked. Because the men in Colorado, in all their supposed infinite wisdom, had established a policy of Indian extermination. No Indian was a good Indian as far as a lot of them were concerned. All Indians should leave, one way or another. And if one harmed a member of the so-called fairer and nobler race, then that Indian most assuredly should suffer also. Even if it had been all in her defense!

Henrietta turned back to the drunk, lying still on the ground. She motioned to the woman. "Come on. Let's try lifting him onto his horse and leading him back to my cabin."

The woman shook her head, disgustedly, but quietly helped. Unfortunately, the man proved too large and unyielding to raise more than a couple feet off the ground—as if he was some gargantuan limp ragdoll. He did mumble a few soft incoherent words of protest, however, during their attempt, reassuring Henrietta that he was coming around at least. Just as Henrietta contemplated their next move, she glanced up to one of the surrounding ridges.

Oh, no! A gentleman in a fine riding outfit sat motionless atop an English steed, observing the sight far below him. Just what had the lord's horrible minion,

78

Theodore Whyte, seen? The whole unfortunate event, part of it, or just the last few minutes? Had he heard the gun go off? Did he think the drunkard was actually dead?

His horse made a motion toward them, and Henrietta made a quick decision. If she could, she would try to convince him that *she* had hit the man in self-defense. She would keep the Indian woman completely out of it. Henrietta knew she was a horrible liar but hoped she could act her way through the skewed account.

His mount took a few more steps in her direction, and Henrietta wanly waved, but as she watched, Theodore Whyte seemed to change his mind, did not acknowledge her greeting and reined his horse around in the opposite direction. A minute later, he was gone from sight.

Henrietta blew out a long breath and briefly contemplated what it meant. It was too puzzling to fathom. What gentleman would just leave her to deal with a man lying still on the ground? Did he just not want to get involved in any way or was he going for help? Or worse, was he heading to the authorities with what he had seen?

But she didn't ponder for long, because the Indian woman was now walking in the direction of her cabin. She hurried to catch up. "Where are you going? We can't just leave your husband lying on the ground!"

The woman shrugged. "I'm staying with you."

"Oh, sure. Uh, that would be fine." Henrietta tried to smile pleasantly. "We should talk I think. But *after* we deal with your husband."

They both turned around, hearing a grumbling commotion behind them. The husband had now amazingly managed to get up and mount his horse. He slurred threateningly, "I'm going to get you bitches." Then he reined and rode off, leaning over the horse's neck.

The woman turned back to Henrietta. "You want to talk?" She shook her head. "I don't talk." She continued on her way towards the cabin, Henrietta following closely in step.

After a moment, though, Henrietta glanced back around, to take one more glimpse of her husband. He was off at a distance now, but yet discernable. As if he had sensed her hesitation, he also briefly reined his horse around to look. Was that expression on his face actually regret and sorrow? It was difficult for Henrietta to accept that a man could be so despicable.

But his expression changed further to one of such obvious malevolence that Henrietta suddenly felt scared to her soul. Before she could say anything in warning, he abruptly reined back around and rode off.

Henrietta set her sights again on the woman, but found that she herself was the one being surveyed, up and down.

"I now help you." She raised both brows at Henrietta. "You one stupid woman."

Henrietta paused in her tracks again.

The woman wasn't lying about not wanting to talk. It took several more days before Henrietta finally got her story out of her. Magpie had grown up with the Southern Cheyenne, but considering how taciturn she could be,

Henrietta could only imagine that Magpie had changed dramatically over the years or the tribe had a rich ironic sense of humor when naming people.

She was actually raised part of Black Kettle's tribe and became quite vocal as she described the famous Washita Valley massacre by troops led by Custer, in which he had attacked before light in the winter of '68, despite a flag of peace flying over the chief's tepee. Black Kettle had tried to stop the battle before it started, but Custer and his men had killed Black Kettle without negotiation, and then murdered more, including innocent children and women, many of whom had just risen from their bed to start their day, not fully dressed yet. The survivors managed to flee to surrounding cover but had then watched in horror while Custer and his men gathered their belongings—including tepees and winter supplies—into a pile and set the items aflame. The Indian mule and pony herd was slaughtered next—more than eight hundred animals. The remaining tribe was taken captive and forced to follow through the snow to the nearest fort without adequate clothing or shelter. Magpie claimed Custer had compelled her beautiful best friend to be his mistress and had allowed his men to take advantage of other women in the tribe. Henrietta was disgusted hearing the story which was so different from the version the newspapers had described of the victory of the supposedly happily married hero.

Shortly thereafter, Magpie's father had then agreed to a marriage between her and a trapper visiting the fort, thinking her future might be better if she learned English and his ways. At first, their union apparently progressed well, but as the supply of beaver and game

81

dwindled and her husband took to drinking, she suffered through his abuse and neglect. The day Henrietta had met them, her husband was accusing her of walking too slowly. He had recently sold her horse for liquor, and she had been on foot. Magpie had come to despise his brutality but had not thought he would live much longer anyway, because he had of late been throwing up blackish content. She showed little regret over his leaving her and did not seem concerned about whether he would return.

Henrietta, however, fretted the first few days about someone finding out what had happened to her husband and whether he would come back for revenge. But when Whyte failed to appear accusing them of wrongdoings and there was no further sign of her husband returning, Henrietta began to relax. Not fully, because she didn't trust Whyte or the scary husband, but at least enough to continue on with her life. She decided that unless she was confronted, she would divulge to no one what had happened and made Magpie promise the same. Magpie rolled her eyes, not seeing the seriousness of the situation.

Magpie settled into the bedroom next to Henrietta's, but after several days Henrietta asked if she planned to move to a reservation. She shook her head. "Reservation bad."

Henrietta frowned. "But the government wants all Indians on reservations. I don't think you will be allowed to roam free."

Magpie shrugged.

So Henrietta ventured, "Do you want to live on my land now?"

"This land cannot be owned." She smirked, not recognizing any manmade boundaries in nature. "Do you think you own the air I breathe also?"

Henrietta shook her head. What could she say to that?

But as further time progressed, Henrietta could see that Magpie was a big help with chores and became reconciled to the fact that she now had a roommate and "the wife" she had asked for. She chose not to view the situation as her losing part of her independence since she could still make her own decisions. And if Magpie could be a little grumpy—to put it mildly? Well, at least she didn't talk too much. But she wondered what her friends were going to think about the arrangement. And more important, whether their shared secret could possibly come to light.

Chapter Seven

Denver Colorado

Collan was of proud Scottish descent and like his forebears, did not suffer fools lightly. He had just stepped up to the bar at the Moose Saloon, when he was approached by a stranger asking if he was new to town.

Collan frowned slightly. "And what business is it of yours, sir?"

"I'm looking for gentlemen who know a superb opportunity when they see one." A smarmy smile followed that statement. Collan looked the fellow once over and noticed he wore a business suit that had seen better days.

Collan *was* actually newly arrived in town and still trying to decide where in the West he would stake his future since departing his friend's ranch in Wyoming.

He took a sip of his beer. "And just what are you offering?"

"Ah, I can see you are interested."

Collan smirked. "Or perhaps I'm just bored and looking to pass the time."

Overhearing Collan, another fellow at a nearby table chuckled. Collan turned and the gent smiled wryly, nodding his head once in greeting. He sat assured in his seat, one leg stretched out underneath the table.

"Have you heard of a quaint village by the name of Breckenridge?"

Collan turned back to the businessman with a glowering expression. Oh, Collan had definitely heard of Breckenridge. He had once tried panning for nuggets there with his best friend and his friend's sisters a dozen years ago, but whereas Herman had departed the town richer thus allowing him to start his cattle ranch in Wyoming, Collan had gone broke. Not only that, his parents had begged him to return to Pennsylvania. They were getting too old to run the family's general store by themselves. And with the passing of his older brother during the war the responsibility had fallen squarely on him. So Collan had returned East, though he hadn't been pleased, knowing he yearned for a life more adventurous. But once his parents had passed and the store had begun to falter in the recession of '73, Collan had sold out, pocketing a modest sum, but enough to start a new life out West. Of course, that meant leaving the girl he was courting, but Collan had heard rumors that she had been seen stepping out with other gents anyways.

The businessman didn't seem to notice Collan's scowl and continued. "Would you like to purchase a claim for prospecting that is sure to make you wealthy?"

And with that Collan had heard enough. There was nothing remaining in Breckenridge to mine and only poor pushovers didn't know that. Collan grabbed the fellow by the back of his jacket and forcefully escorted the swindler out the door with a loud, "Not in this lifetime."

He returned into the saloon to see the gent at the table laughing. As he neared him on his way to the bar, the man said, "That scoundrel tried the same con with me a few days ago."

"Hope you showed him the boot also."

"No, but I should have." He smiled. "Have a seat. Abner Sprague is the name. And you are?"

Collan shook hands, then grabbed his unfinished beer off the bar. "Collan Wallace. Newly arrived to Denver but not stupid as shit."

Abner chuckled again, making his mouth once more temporarily disappear underneath his voluminous mustache. Abner looked to be in his twenties and was on the short side, but had a strong wiry build. Collan took an immediate liking to this man and over the next hour ended up telling him his life story. When he had finished, he shook his head. "You would think that a man in his thirties, who has worked all his life, would be established by now, but . . ." He shook his head. "And now that I got my freedom to go anywhere and do anything, I can't seem to settle." He paused, pondering. "I might just be afflicted with eternal wanderlust."

Abner leaned forward. "Nothing wrong with that."

Collan chuckled. "Oh, you got a similar suffering?"

"At one time I did. Now I'm preparing to set my claim in Estes Park."

"How'd that come about?"

86

"My parents moved the family by wagon train a decade ago to northeast Colorado. But just viewing the mountains from that one room cabin wasn't good enough. I wanted to explore them. So in '68, I went on a hiking trip with my friends and stumbled upon a fellow named Griff Evans just where Estes Park begins. He was putting in a fence for his home with this talkative trapper named Mountain Jim. I was told by them where to wander to see 'the most beautiful sights ever.' So of course, I had to venture back a couple more times and by '74 I had climbed Longs Peak."

Collan whistled low. "That's a tall one."

"Sure is, but the view's spectacular."

"I bet."

"Now I can't imagine living anywhere else. Only problem is that some greedy Englishman has his sights set on the same place. I hear tell he's got most of Estes Park except for parts along the Wind River, Beaver Meadows, and this place I'm heading to, Willow Park. But even if he thinks he has a claim to where I'm going, I'm prepared to defy him because there's a good chance it's fraudulent. I'm betting he'll let me stay than cause himself trouble."

"You mean he's filing false homesteading titles?"

"By hiring every troublemaker he can find off the streets of Denver to do so and then buying their fraudulent claims for cheap in return. I hear a lot of these claims don't have the required shelter built to maintain the claim as valid. And that's where I think I can get him for any difficulty he might try to cause me."

87

"Just like an Englishman, huh? Not surprised considering his country's history of devouring Scotland." He paused a moment in thought then raised his beer. "A toast to you. I'd sure like thwarting that kind of greed."

"Well, you can. The claim adjacent to mine is open. I was going to team up with a fellow who recently got himself killed, accusing another man of cattle thieving."

Collan shook his head, then hesitated again, pondering the possibilities. "The most beautiful place I'll ever see, you say?"

"Without a doubt."

"And what do you plan to do with your land."

"Farming, ranching, perhaps a little prospecting. We wouldn't have to partner, but we could help build each other's cabin, share cooking and supplies, at least in the beginning."

Collan smiled. "I think I might like owning my own ranch. A lot of work, though."

"That it is."

"So when do you leave?"

A week later, Collan mailed a letter before departing Denver.

Dear Herman,

Greetings from Colorado. I want to tell you that all your advice about cattle ranching in Wyoming has not gone to waste. You might be a bit surprised to learn that I am starting my own spread in the small mountain community of Estes Park. You probably recall that it is in the vicinity of Longs Peak and supposedly beautiful. I wouldn't know since I've never been there before, but life's an adventure, is it not? Wish me luck for I fear I will require some!

Regards,
Collan

Three weeks later, Collan was startled to receive a response from Herman so quickly.

Dear Collan,

Glad to hear you have settled, and I bid you well. Let me know when you are ready to purchase some livestock as I desire to sell off part of the herd and can give you a good price. Your letter was fortuitous in timing for me. I hope I can impose on you for a simple favor. I have learned since you departed Wyoming that my sister Henrietta has settled in Estes Park herself. Her husband has recently passed away and Clarissa is fit to be tied, worried that she will perish in the hinterlands. Could you look in on her for me? I would really appreciate it.

All the best,
Herm

Collan pored over the letter once more to make sure he hadn't read it wrong. Etta was in Estes Park? He groaned aloud. Oh, hell. As if he had time for this kind of nonsense.

Chapter Eight

The Farrar brothers were either absolutely intimidated by Magpie or else too worried about losing Henrietta's cooking skills. Those were the only explanations Henrietta could come up with to explain what occurred when they returned.

Henrietta had just gathered some eggs into her apron and was walking back towards her cabin when they rode up with wide grins on their faces. The dogs swarmed around their horses cheerfully barking.

"Oh, welcome back." She smiled. "Did you have a good trip to Denver?"

"Hank did." Ike chuckled.

Clint gave a knowing wink. "He can't wait to get back."

"Tomorrow if he could, wouldn't you say?" Ike raised his brows.

Hank dismounted. "Oh, hush now. Miss Henrietta, we got you a present."

Clint protested. "Hey, it was my idea. I was going to give her that."

Ike stepped down. "Well I helped picked it out."

"But Hank made sure he paid for it." Clint chuckled. "Even though one of them is *pink*!"

"She said it was roseblush, you oaf." Ike playfully kicked Clint.

"Oh, is that what the salesgirl told old Hank, along with a whole lot of other stuff?" Clint grinned.

Henrietta smiled. "Hank, how wonderful. And were you wearing your new clothes and all spiffed up?"

Hank briefly closed his eyes in agony. "Can we talk about something else?"

Ike motioned dramatically. "Well, give her the present."

Henrietta started towards the cabin. "Come on inside for some coffee. I can unwrap it there."

That was when they first noticed Magpie standing in the doorway, arms crossed, her usual smirk across her face.

They stopped walking.

Ike frowned. "Is that an Injun woman? What's she doing here?"

Henrietta smiled pleasantly. "Oh, let me introduce Magpie. She swung by one day and decided to stay. She's a big help." Henrietta was glad she could tell the truth even if some important details had to be omitted.

"Magpie? Meet Clint, Hank, and Ike. The Farrar brothers. They're famous hunters from around here."

Magpie snorted.

"Well, well, shall we all go in?"

Once inside, they each took a seat around the table and after Henrietta poured coffee she began undoing the string tied around the paper packaging of the present. Once unwrapped, she saw that inside were a couple long lengths of cotton fabric, one cerise with flowers and the other blue with birds. "Oh, my. I can make the kitchen curtains I wanted. Thank you so much."

Clint smiled shyly. "You're welcome, Miss Henrietta."

Henrietta wasn't surprised the gift had been Clint's idea, Ike had helped pick out the playful patterns, and then to learn that Hank had taken command of the situation. Hank was always the leader, Clint the sweetest and Ike the funniest.

She picked up the flowery fabric and smiled. "I was thinking about putting this table outside on the porch for campers who come by for my baked goods. They could relax, have a cup of coffee or tea, and view the beautiful scenery. Now I can make a tablecloth for it also." She looked at Hank who was the best carpenter between the brothers. "Do you think you could make me a bigger dining table for inside, perhaps with some benches?"

Hank nodded. "You bet."

"Oh, and guess what?" Henrietta said excitedly. "George told me last time he was here that Clara has got one of those new sewing machines and she said I can use it."

"Yeah, we saw that newfangled invention last time we were by. Clara pushes a foot treadle and it makes the thread go in and out, and in and out, in tiny little steps." Clint shook his head. "Ike neart jumped out of his pants he was so surprised."

"I did no such fool thing, Clint."

"Did, too, Ike."

"Did, not!"

Henrietta rested her head on her hand. "Now if only someone could figure out a machine for washing dishes. Wouldn't that be something?"

Hank shook his head. "Won't happen, Miss Henrietta. Too complicated, I'd expect."

Ike looked over at Henrietta. "I'm hungry. How long 'til supper?"

Clint kicked him underneath the table. "She wants to chat with us now, you oaf."

Henrietta stood quickly. "No, no. I can start cooking."

Ike smiled and stood. "That's great, Miss Henrietta. I'll get the fixings." He ran outside and returned shortly with wrapped bundles of the usual elk, trout and venison which he placed on the table.

Magpie spoke up for the first time and asked simply, "Where are the hides?"

Hank answered amiably. "Oh, we cut out the best meat and usually leave the carcasses for the animals."

Magpie shook her head with obvious disdain. "Oh, and I suppose the *great* hunters take only the *tongue* of the buffalo also."

Ike looked around perplexed. "What's she getting at? What buffalo? They're all neart killed."

Hank tried explaining. "It'd be too much work to handle everything just so on every animal we catch."

Magpie crossed her arms again. "Next time, I go with you."

"What?!" Ike looked over at Hank, eyes widened, obviously horrified at the thought. "She can't do that, can she, Hank?"

Clint was shaking his head, vigorously.

Henrietta knew that the brothers were known for never divulging their best fishing and hunting areas to anyone who asked, and she doubted Hank would agree to Magpie coming along. But Magpie was looking particularly mulish so Henrietta tried to make peace. "Oh, I'm sure she'd be an awful good help. Wouldn't you, Magpie?"

Magpie grunted. "Help? I teach them how to hunt."

Ike gaped. "She can't say *that*, can she, Hank?"

Hank raised his hand and finally spoke. "Miss Magpie, we Farrar brothers hunt alone. No exceptions."

Magpie looked straight ahead, not meeting his eye. "I come."

Hank puckered his brow.

Henrietta tried to intervene again. "Magpie? How about if they bring you back a hide next time? Wouldn't that be nice?"

Now Magpie was frowning also. "I come."

Henrietta turned to Hank. "Well, what if Magpie goes along with you just this once? Say, as a favor to me? Perhaps you could fetch another horse for her to ride from your homestead."

Hank squirmed in his seat. But a few hours later, when the brothers were departing, none said another word of protest as Magpie mounted the horse that Ike had led back for her to ride. She trailed close behind them.

Collan's trip over to the MacGregors' was supposed to have been just a quick affair—pick up some more

94

coffee, flour, and sugar and then get back to helping Abner build his cabin. They had agreed to start on his home first and once that was complete, both work on building Collan some shelter. They were toiling as fast as they could, not wanting to be caught without cover in the autumn weather expected to arrive in a couple months.

But as soon as Collan had reached the MacGregors', he had received that letter from Herman, and he knew he couldn't just return to assisting Abner. He had to swing by Henrietta's place immediately, so he obtained directions and began his journey without even stopping to buy the supplies first. Collan shook his head while riding. Considering their history, it just figured Etta was causing him trouble now.

They had known each other for years, having grown up together back East. Her brother Herman, a year older than Collan, had become his best friend. Etta was a full three years younger than Collan and just why they had always found a reason to go at it with each other, he wasn't quite sure. Considering her sister Clarissa was only a year younger than Collan, one might think that the two of them would have had more interaction with each other, but no, Clarissa had never been of particular interest to him. It had always been petite and sassy Etta who had drawn him in. Of course, most people who met Etta did not know about this feisty side of her character, but Collan sure did, because he had always had a special talent in bringing it out.

Even as a little girl, Etta had liked to play the lady, pretending that she was the cultivated, gentile, and restrained sort—dressing daintily and prettily, enjoying acting as if she lived her life in a calm and refined manner. But Collan had always known otherwise. That little spitfire could show a will of iron.

Perhaps if she hadn't been so much fun to tease, Collan would have stopped. But Etta gave as good as she got. If he dunked her braid in an inkwell, she would throw his homework assignment into the outhouse. If he dropped a frog down her dress, she would stick her foot out and trip him. If he sneaked a rotten piece of trout into her satchel, she would hide his fishing pole.

Of course, the teacher had known none of these going-ons. No, Etta had liked to play the perfect pet, and Miss Marble had adored her. Etta gave her flower posies while Collan let loose lizards underneath her desk. Etta wrote in a neat script while Collan scrawled sloppily. Etta eagerly picked apples so Miss Marble could show how she made her special applesauce while Collan looked for the ones with worms. No, Miss Marble had never liked Collan, and Collan had never eaten her stupid applesauce. In fact, he still hated applesauce to this day, but he was sure Etta still loved the stuff.

But even after Etta's parents had passed and Herm had decided to prospect out West and his sisters had followed him, the scrapping between them hadn't stopped. Once Collan joined them in Breckenridge, he had found more ways to annoy her. Hell, just slipping too much salt into her baked goods could get a significant rile out of her.

But everything between them had come to a crashing end the day her precious Charles had arrived in Breckenridge also. He wasn't sure why, but it had actually bothered him to see his fellow tormentor and her future husband courting and dancing and talking together. So Collan had kept his distance and the last he had known Charles and she had happily settled down.

But that had been until he had received her brother Herman's letter. So here he was now, on a rise above her property, surveying her homestead. The view was spectacular, he'd give her that. And there was a trim cabin with a large front porch overlooking the meandering river. His eyes wandered around the yard, and he finally saw Etta. He couldn't hold back a smile at the sight of her once more.

She looked about the same with her petite frame and hair in a bun. Or actually, he realized as a gust of wind flattened her dress against her and nearly blew her over, she was perhaps just a bit fuller in figure. She was stroking the mane of some absolutely ancient horse while some frisky roan horse nuzzled her. He shook his head. Is that what she considered adequate mounts? Collan shrugged. Probably didn't make any difference since she most likely still rode like a bump on a log.

He then saw her versions of watchdogs. One was a gimpy old pooch, hobbling off the porch while the other was a mangy mutt with one ear gone that was chasing a butterfly. Neither had noticed him.

He heard some pounding and turned his head to see that a tall blond fellow was hammering some boards together on the far side of the stable. Near him a woman, who looked an awful lot like a squaw, was stretching some hide on a frame. Were they her hired help?

Etta was now walking back to her cabin and the laughable watchdogs, still oblivious to his presence, were cheerfully following her. Etta staggered a little as

97

another sudden gust of wind swooshed over her. Collan shook his head. Fool woman hadn't placed her cabin near a windbreak. Everybody out West knew to do that, except obviously, Etta.

More movement then caught his eye as he observed the blond gent head over to the cabin also. Collan frowned as he entered without knocking as if he owned the damn place. Collan had seen enough. He was going to find out just what was what.

Henrietta tilted her head to one side. "I think your corner, Ike, should be juuust a bit higher." Ike raised his end an inch. He and Clint were standing on a bench helping Henrietta put up a rod for her new kitchen curtains. "Hmmm. Now Clint down juuust a tiny smidgeon."

Clint asked, "Izthizgood?" He and Ike were trying to speak around the pins in their mouths.

Henrietta smiled. "Yes, I think that will be perfect." She turned around to Hank. "If you can now nail in the brackets, Clint and Ike can then pin the fabric over the rod so I can see how it will look and then I can pin a hem and then we can take down the rod and then I'll get to sewing." She smiled again happily.

Hank had just positioned the first support when she thought she heard a soft knock and the door swung open, banging against the wall.

"Well, hello, Etta. I see you're up to more mischief—or so I've heard."

The dogs started barking loudly, but Henrietta did not even have to turn around. She knew exactly who had barged into her cabin. Because in a world of millions of people, there was only one individual who insisted on calling her by the nickname she despised. And why did he do it? Oh, to annoy her, to provoke her, to make her yearn to punch him. But she pivoted nonetheless to find Collan Wallace standing in the doorway, mouth agape, as if he had never seen anyone put up curtains before. She pursed her lips briefly, then answered in kind. "What are *you* doing here, Collie?"

Collan frowned because she knew that he hated the name she had come up with ages ago to call him. In fact, there was a time when she would sometimes add a "ruff, ruff" as in barking to emphasize the similarity of his name to the dog of the same title. But she was more dignified now. And besides, there was no use aggravating the situation anymore since the Farrar brothers had dropped all the curtain trappings to surround her defensively. Collan, in true childish form, merely smirked, "You tell me first what's going on."

Henrietta rolled her eyes. "What does it look like? I'm homesteading."

Collan grunted. "No, more like worrying your family to pieces, Etta."

"Oh, is that so."

"Yes!" Collan practically roared.

With that outburst, her baby rabbit tried jumping out of her box. Henrietta hurried over to pick the poor thing up. She admonished Collan. "Now look what you've done. Poor Snuggles is scared." She caressed the rabbit soothingly and then placed her back in her box. "There, there Snuggles. Don't worry. I'll protect you from the big rude loudmouth."

Collan scoffed. "Poor Snuggles. It's a damn rabbit for Christ's sake, Etta. And you should be thanking me, Etta, instead of scolding me."

She placed her hand on her hip. "And why is that?"

"Before I came in here, I shooed some one-legged hawk out of your yard."

"Harry? You attacked poor Harry, too?"

"He was going to get at your chickens."

"No, he was not. He was just waiting for his daily scraps."

"You feed a damn hawk now too?"

She found herself raising her own voice now. "He has only one leg!"

Collan then looked at the ceiling. "My God. It's a loony bin here. Wait 'til Herm hears about this."

Clint then stepped forward. "Miss Henrietta? You want some help with this here fella?"

Henrietta turned and attempted to smile pleasantly. "No thanks, Clint. It won't be necessary. He's actually a friend of the family."

But Collan wasn't done complaining. "Yes! And this sure is some greeting I've gotten."

She pivoted again to face Collan, frowning. "Well, you're the one who charged in here without a howdy do."

He raised his hands. "Hey, I've got more important things to do than chase down some fool woman who thinks she can homestead."

"Like what?"

He puffed up. "Like build my own cabin."

She gasped. "You're moving here?"

He nodded. "Uh, huh. In Willow Park next to Abner Sprague." Which, to Henrietta's amazement, caused the brothers to suddenly relax and turn all friendly. The traitors.

Hank held out his hand. "I'm Hank Farrar and these here are my brothers Clint and Ike. Glad to meet you. Abner was telling us about you."

Collan shook their hands. "Collan Wallace. Former merchant and prospector and now hopeful rancher."

Ike then turned to Henrietta. "Is supper soon? I'm getting hungry."

Henrietta bustled over to the cook stove. "Oh, my Lord. I hope my biscuits haven't burned." She turned back around. "Please, everyone. Have a seat. It'll just be a moment while I finish up. Ike, can you tell Magpie supper's soon?"

As Henrietta finished getting the meal onto the table and took her seat, she was glad to see that at least Magpie wasn't a pushover to Collan's temporary charm. But while Magpie glared in her usual surly fashion, the Farrars continued chatting amiably with Collan. So much so that by the end of the meal, they offered to help build Abner and his cabins when they returned from their next hunting trip. The double turncoats! Apparently, Abner and Collan planned on building rough-hewn cabins, approximately fifteen by fifteen feet made with pole roofs covered with seven inches of peat from a nearby swamp. Collan surmised the rainfall would not run off but be absorbed by the peat, and these roofs would hold fine unless they got more than an inch of water at once.

Henrietta supposed the Farrars couldn't be faulted for warming up to Collan. He had always been a man's man and had attracted friends easily over the years—her own older brother for one. She briefly wondered if he had a woman in his life now, then dismissed the thought. It surely was not her concern. But she couldn't help noticing that Collan had aged well—his once boyish features had matured in a most handsome fashion. With his tall frame, dark wavy locks and striking blue eyes, she could imagine how many women were attracted to him.

An hour later the Farrars stood up, preparing to depart. Clint frowned, concerned. "You're not angry we didn't finish the curtains, are you, Miss Henrietta?"

She waved her hand dismissively. "No, you go on along. We can raise them sometime later."

Hank hesitated. "I know you want that new table so this one can be for the tourists who come by. Perhaps Clint and Ike can help Collan and Abner while I swing by on my own to help you."

"Oh, that would be wonderful." She smiled. "I could then pack up a meal for you to bring to your brothers."

The Farrars seemed satisfied with the plan, but Collan started frowning over the new arrangement. "I don't know if that's such a good idea."

She shook her head. "Why ever not?"

Collan seemed to be searching for an answer. "Well, uh . . . because . . . uh . . ." He then smiled, seemingly pleased he could conjure a response. "Oh, because your sister Clarissa won't like you unchaperoned with a man alone at your cabin. And I already got enough to explain when I write Herm next."

Henrietta blew out a breath. "Well, why don't you just keep quiet about what doesn't concern you."

"I owe it to your brother to look out for you."

Henrietta stood. "No, you do not. I am an independent woman who makes her own decisions about what concerns her. And you being here in Estes Park is not going to change that, Collan."

"Yes, it will, Etta. What are you? Some sort of suffragette now, too?"

"And why shouldn't I be? Sal Ferguson is."

"Who?"

Hank motioned with his hand. "The Fergusons live over that a way. Miss Henrietta bought her chickens from their homestead."

She pointed at Collan. "You just watch. I'm going to form an Estes Park suffragette group with Sal."

He rolled his eyes. "Oh, good Lord."

"And besides, I'm not all alone. Magpie stays with me."

Ike was now concerned. "Wait a minute. Aren't you hunting with us again, Miss Magpie?" Henrietta wasn't sure what had gone on the last trip, but since then the Farrars were now big Magpie converts.

Magpie scowled. "I go hunting."

"Well, we're talking about when you return from hunting anyways."

"Look, enough of this. After the Farrars hunt, if it's okay with them, they will first proceed over to my place to help and then we will *all* come over here to see what you want done." Collan raised his brows at Henrietta for approval.

"Fine. The more the merrier. Just bring me enough meat to feed everyone."

Clint said, "Oh, you never have to worry about that, Miss Henrietta."

"Thank you, Clint. You Farrars are all so nice." She then turned with an innocent face. "Aren't they, *Collie?*"

"Oh, ruff, ruff, Etta. Ruff, ruff. Collie my ass," he muttered which then caused Henrietta to snort back a chuckle.

Chapter Nine

After Collan departed Etta's he decided to head back to the MacGregors' to compose a quick letter to mail with the next stage and also to pick up the supplies he had originally set out to buy. He rode over distractedly and slowly, recalling what had just happened.

When he had seen Hank walk into her cabin as if he felt at home, Collan had been seized by a completely irrational feeling of jealousy. He had scarcely refrained himself from slamming the cabin door open and bellowing, "What *the hell* is going on around here?" Instead he had uttered the still impolite and sarcastic "more mischief" phrase which, of course, had gotten Etta's back immediately up which—Collan couldn't help chuckling now—he had enjoyed thoroughly provoking even more. What was it about that woman and his scrambled feelings?

And then—though he had used swear words when they were younger just to rile her and he knew better now how to treat a lady—he had sprinkled his conversation with bravado and inappropriate phrases. And just when he had gotten his emotions steady he had been gripped by another bout of jealousy at the thought of Hank possibly spending any time alone with her.

He shook his head. He vowed that the next time he saw her he would act more dignified. Yes, simply as a concerned old acquaintance. Nothing more, because they weren't anything more. He blew out a long breath and concentrated on hurrying over to the MacGregors. The day was wasting.

Collan found it amazing how refined an atmosphere it was over at the MacGregors'. As he was hitching his horse, he heard a violin and then strumming on a guitar before he knocked on the door to inquire about sending a letter. Clara had then welcomed him into her home and supplied him with paper and pen, especially after she found out that he was a friend of Etta's. He looked around the cabin with wonder at the soft armchairs, landscape paintings and other luxuries of civilization.

She also showed him the small store they had set up. Settlers and visitors could buy fresh vegetables, sugar, salt, cornmeal, flour, baking powder, bacon, fat pork, tea, coffee, candles and kerosene—all brought over the toll road from Longmont except the butter, cream, and potatoes which were produced locally. After perusing the tempting viands, Collan made his purchases and finally sat down to write his letter.

Dear Herm,

Henrietta is well and even appears to have put on some weight. She has collected a whole mix of devoted followers and misfits, persons and critters alike. I will endeavor to watch over her though she is showing some of her usual obstinacy. She fashions herself now as an independent woman. Heaven save us. I would appreciate a price on thirty head of cattle. You know what I require in regards to the number of heifers, steers and calves. Look forward to hearing from you soon.

Your friend,
Collan

P.S. Tell Clarissa that I don't think even dynamite could blast her sister out of here for now.

Collan was busy the next week working with Abner on the cabins, but during the scarce quiet times and especially at night before he fell asleep he found himself thinking about Etta. He felt an odd sort of excitement and stirring over having reestablished their acquaintance. She still was the amusing distraction he had always found her to be.

But after she had hitched up with Charles, he had purposely blocked—or at least attempted to—all thoughts of her. He had been surprised after all those years apart to feel a twinge of . . . *hurt?* . . . when Herm had mentioned her in passing in the last year when he had stayed with him in Wyoming.

Even more baffling was this feeling that he couldn't wait to see her again. Aw, perhaps it was just that she reminded him of home, and of course, it was always fun to rile her up, but still . . . how odd. Nevertheless, by the time the Farrars had returned from hunting and stopped by to help Abner and him build cabins, Collan had hustled everybody along so they could all get over to Etta's—everybody except Abner, who promised to come over later to meet her after he completed a chore he wanted to attend to.

Once at Etta's, the Farrars immediately swarmed around Magpie who was working on another hide by the stables. Magpie bothered to only nod once in greeting towards Collan as he passed her by on his way to the

107

cabin. He inwardly shook his head, wondering if the crabby woman would ever truly warm up to him.

But then Sally, the one-eared waif, approached him, wagging her tail cautiously, until he squatted down to her level and called her forward. She ran over to slurp his face effusively. He had never been a big fan of dog slobber but sensed that somehow it would be damaging to push this mutt away. Ring barked a couple times, then made the effort to climb down the porch steps himself. Collan noticed that he was limping less than even just a week ago. Etta was no doubt waiting on him hand and foot so his leg could get better.

He finally broke from the poochfest and knocked on the cabin door. Etta greeted him with a smile and the dogs followed him inside. He closed the door behind him.

He turned to face her. "Etta?"

"Yeah?" She had gone back to cooking and was standing by her stove, holding a mixing bowl in her arms, stirring.

"I meant to tell you something the last time I was here but got distracted and forgot."

Her brows puckered slightly. "What?"

He looked at her intently. "I'm sorry about your loss. Charles was a good man."

"Oh." Etta's face dropped. "Oh." She took a few ragged breaths. "Oh, fiddlesticks." And then she dropped the bowl on the table and turned away from him.

She started sniffling and then wiping her eyes quickly with the hem of her apron. Her back still facing him, she mumbled, "I'm sorry . . . I don't know what's come over me." But then she wept more loudly.

Collan walked over to her and turned her around slowly, then wrapped her in an embrace. "Etta, honey, give it time." He patted her back softly.

"I just miss him so." She muttered into his shirt.

He nodded. "I know."

She looked up at him. "But I've been doing better, Collan. Really. I haven't cried for . . . well, at least a week."

He cocked a brow and half-smiled. "*That long*, huh?"

Etta sniffed once more, then bit back a watery smile.

"You do realize, Etta, that this is the first time our entire lives that we've ever hugged."

She stepped out his arms at that. "Good Lord. How strange."

He chuckled. "Yes, well. Miracles can happen."

She picked up her bowl and began stirring again. "So tell me, have you found a girl for yourself?"

He shrugged and looked away briefly before saying, "Oh, I've courted a few, but nothing stuck. Nobody ever measured up to you, Etta."

She laughed. "Oh, I bet. Very funny, Collan."

"You ever goin' to marry again, Etta?"

She shook her head. "Oh, no. Charles was it for me." She hesitated a moment before continuing. "Besides, I can't imagine taking the risk of becoming so romantically attached to someone that I would wed again. I don't think I could survive if I possibly lost another loved one."

She then blinked and noticeably tried pulling herself together again after revealing such raw feelings and Collan attempted to help lighten the mood. "Yeah, and I suppose an *independent* woman like yourself wouldn't want to take on a husband."

"Might get in the way of my suffragette meetings." She smiled cockily now. "But how about you? You ever plan on tying the knot?"

"Absolutely. Who wouldn't want someone cleaning and cooking for ya? And don't forget about the washing and drying—"

"—and the sewing and darning—"

"—and the baby making." He raised both brows and smiled.

She gasped. "I can't believe you just said that to me. How scandalous."

"Well, we are older now, Etta. You'd have to expect our funnin' to get more sophisticated."

"Oh, is that what you call it?"

"Yeah, that there was mature humor."

She snorted just as Ike walked in. "Got the meat, Miss Henrietta."

"Thank you, Ike. Just put it on the table."

"What you makin'?" Ike walked over and picked up Snuggles. "She's gettin' big."

"This here is batter for cake."

"With frosting?"

"Yep."

"Oooeee. This sure is some special day. Miss Magpie said she's making me moccasins." He raised one of his cracked and worn leather boots. "I think I can still get a few more years out of these, though."

Etta looked skeptical. "I'm not so sure about that."

Clint and Hank walked in. Hank took Snuggles from Ike. "She's getting fat. I'm going to try to finish that table you want."

"Thanks Hank. You wouldn't believe how many campers are coming over here now for some baked goods. I've started making pies in the evenings to keep up."

Collan nodded. "Oh, I believe it. Some tourist types actually came up to Abner and me and asked if we had any fish they could buy. What do they think we do all day—laze by the river so we can feed them?"

"Well, once I get my little teashop set up on the porch, I'm going to be making even more pennies. Sure is a sight easier than trying to cattle ranch."

"Yes, Etta. You are correct. I should be serving coffee and tea with my pinky raised instead of roping old steers." Collan shook his head.

Clint asked, "So if Hank is building your table, does that mean the rest of us are hanging kitchen curtains?"

Ike groaned loudly as Collan muttered, "Oh, God."

"Well, actually, I was wondering . . ." Etta hesitated.

"Yes?" Collan asked with fake eagerness. "Just what does her Highness desire now? Oh, *please* command us—your ever so humble and obedient slaves to your cooking."

"Oh, hush, Collan. Actually, I would really like a milkcow and could use another shed."

"You mean a milkcow that is sturdy and a good producer or your usual on-its-last-legs antiquarian?"

Ike frowned. "What's an antiquery?"

"An old fart."

"Collan, that is so mean."

"Oh, very choice coming from the woman who sneaked a bottle of ink into my pants pocket so that when it spilled over my bottom, it looked like I had done it in them."

Clint was astonished. "Miss Henrietta, you really did that?"

Etta shook her head. "Nooo. Well, actually, yes. But I can assure you he had it coming."

Collan snorted as he walked towards the door. "Guess we're building a cowshed next."

A few hours later, the brothers carried in the newly made rough-hewn table and benches as Collan hauled Etta's smaller table and chairs out onto the porch. Collan inwardly smiled as Etta exclaimed enthusiastically over the whole affair as if she had just received fine furnishings.

Abner arrived shortly thereafter and the gang sat down for their meal. Collan noticed that Etta was fussing over Abner, making sure he had enough to eat. Etta had loved to play the cordial hostess even as a little girl and since she had a new visitor she was in top form. He also became aware that Magpie was scowling more than usual so he asked, "Something wrong, Miss Magpie?"

"Too many men. Talks with Hawk working too much."

"Talks with Hawk?"

Etta smiled happily. "That's what she calls *me*. Magpie's so clever with her names."

Collan chuckled. "Really? You think so? I would have thought she'd call you Talks to Devil."

"Collan! We have a new visitor."

"Aw, heck. It's just Abner."

Abner smiled. "Don't worry about me, Henrietta. I'm used to Collan's joking. Can't say I think much of some of the other new neighbors—that Whyte fella, in particular."

Collan caught Etta briefly looking over worriedly at Magpie and wondered what that was about, but Abner wasn't done talking.

"That lackey of Dunraven shows up here equipped with race horses, dogs, guns and all the usual trappings of an English gentleman and then thinks he can annoy and harass us until we leave."

Etta frowned. "What do you mean?"

"Let's just say I'm not the only one put off by his attitude. George Bode let him have it today. I witnessed it myself on my way over here."

Etta clasped her chest. *"My George?"*

Collan frowned. "What do you mean *your* George?"

Abner shook his head. "I know I shouldn't be talking about this in front of the ladies, but George and Whyte got into a brawl on that bridge a bit yonder from here."

"I don't believe this," Etta exclaimed. "George Bode is one of the sweetest men alive!"

Collan rolled his eyes. "Oh, Good God."

Abner added, "George near threw him into the creek."

Etta stood abruptly. "This is *horrible*." But then Collan watched her sway slightly and say, "Oh, I feel a bit wobbly."

He quickly grabbed her arm. "Sit down, Etta, before you keel."

Etta sat, then said, "That was odd. I guess it must be the altitude."

Clint nodded. "Yep, can get us all sometimes, Miss Henrietta."

But Magpie was shaking her head. "It's the baby."

Etta laughed lightly. "What baby? I'm not carrying a baby."

With a bored look, Magpie smirked and crossed her arms. "Talks with Hawk one stupid woman."

Confusion reigned shortly thereafter.

Chapter Ten

At first the group sat in their seats, stunned, until finally Ike broke the silence. "*A baby?!* What you gonna do with a youngun, Miss Henrietta?"

Henrietta shook her head firmly. "I couldn't be having a child. It's just impossible after so many years."

"Well, Etta." Collan raised one brow skeptically. "I did notice that you've never looked fuller in the face and . . ." He briefly glanced down at her breasts, before quickly looking away.

Henrietta pulled her dress down tighter in front and glimpsed at herself. "I've just been eating a lot. Snacking on too many of my sweets."

"Since when has that ever caused you to put on pounds, Etta?"

"I'm older now, Collan."

"And working a lot more so the reverse should be true." He frowned slightly. "Aren't women supposed to know about these things?"

"Well, yes, it's just that I've never been . . . and then with losing Charles . . ." Henrietta trailed off as she noticed all the men, including Collan, had turned beet red and were looking any place else but at her.

Magpie blew out a loud breath. "You having a baby."

Henrietta looked over at Magpie, with her insistent expression, and then couldn't hold back any longer the sudden excitement and yearning that filled her. There *had* been a few mornings in the last month when she had thought she might throw up. And all her clothes were fitting her more tightly. Oh, if only it was real. To be finally having a child would be one of her most cherished dreams coming true. If Charles were alive, he would be so proud. She started blinking back tears. "I guess I could be in a delicate way . . ." She breathed raggedly. "Oh . . .oh . . . how *wonderful.*" She burst out sobbing.

Collan reached over and began patting her back softly. "And here we go again."

"I'm . . . I'm sorry, everyone." Henrietta snuffled.

"It's fine, Etta. But if you don't stop soon, I might just have to give you a hug again."

She looked up at that and began laughing softly which caused the men to look over with an expression of vast relief. All except sweet Clint who smiled warmly and wiped at tears in his own eyes with his sleeve.

Collan then asked, "So when did you and Charles . . . uh . . . I mean how far along do you think you could be, Etta?"

The men were back to behaving awkwardly. Ike got up, muttered a "whoa," and walked towards Snuggles. Hank suddenly found Sally interesting. Clint vigorously stirred milk and sugar into his coffee. Abner commenced retying his boots. Only Collan and Magpie stared at her in earnest.

"Well, I suppose I could be a couple months . . . three? . . . no, actually, perhaps even five."

Collan mocked. "Ah, now that makes things nice and precise."

Henrietta chuckled again.

Ike sat back down with Snuggles. "So are you going to be leaving us, Miss Henrietta?"

She quickly answered, "Oh, no." But she found herself then hesitating. There was so much now to consider. But surely, she shouldn't do anything until she was certain she was with child. "At least not for now."

Ike grinned. "That's great, Miss Henrietta."

Clint kicked Ike underneath the table. "She can't be workin' for us no more, you oaf."

"I didn't say she should, you old crybaby."

Henrietta stood. "Oh, I feel fine. I can still cook for you all."

"Thanks, Miss Henrietta." Ike smiled broadly again.

But when she looked over at Collan, he frowned slightly and said nothing, obviously deep in thought.

The next week Clara stopped by. "I thought I'd bring over this letter that arrived for you."

"Thanks, Clara. Have you heard the news?" She placed a cup of coffee in front of her as she sat down at the table.

"Just this morning. There's not much privacy on the frontier. How are you feeling?"

Henrietta shrugged. "Fine. Just more tired in the afternoons."

Clara nodded. "I bet. Well, go ahead. Read your letter. Don't mind me."

Henrietta opened the envelope and pulled out the short note.

Dear Henrietta,

Enough is enough. Fall is coming on, and it is time for you to come home. Your room is waiting for you, and we all miss you. Now, you had your little adventure and time spent alone, but surely even you can see that a woman such as yourself has no business spending a winter by herself even if I heartell from Herm that Collan has moved to your area. Sell your cabin there and even if you don't settle in with us, then at least use some of the money to buy a cozy home here in Fort Collins for I have some exciting news about our growing little town.

Five, and I repeat FIVE, very eligible bachelors have moved to Fort Collins since you were here last. Now before you start shaking your head, I want to say that obviously, I am not trying to meddle in your affairs. I am just giving some sound sisterly advice as usual.

Clarissa

P.S. Ellie is growing like a weed and the boys are so active they are near driving me to distraction.

She looked up after she finished reading.

"Anything important?" Clara took a sip.

Henrietta shook her head. "My sister wants me to leave here before winter, and she doesn't even know that I could be with child."

Clara nodded. "Oh, I see."

"Let's go visit Sal and find out what she thinks."

"Didn't I tell you there was a new glow to you? I don't want to hear about you not being with child. It's probably obvious even to Horace." Sal chuckled and looked down the length of the table. "Hey, Horace. Stop tying that fishing lure. Do you think Henrietta is in a delicate way?"

Horace leaned over sideways a bit and gave Henrietta a quick look. "Yep," then concentrated again on his intricate creation.

Sal pursed her lips. "Told you."

"But do you think I should have the baby here?" Henrietta took a bite of the cornbread Sal had placed in front of her.

Sal shrugged. "Don't know and I'm the last woman you should be asking. You've already heard how many foolish things I've found myself mixed up in. What do you think, Clara?"

"I had Georgie before I arrived, but . . . well, everything's a risk. Some just more than others."

Sal nodded. "Spoken like a sage."

Horace got up without a word, snatching his fishing pole by the door before departing.

Sal half-smiled. "I guess we've all had our surprises. Little did we know what we were getting ourselves involved in when we came here."

The women looked over, waiting for her to continue.

"Horace has turned into a fishing guide for the tourists. Not that he's complaining. We thought our living would be from the cattle, but some visitors have been asking for accommodations also. We're thinking about expanding our quarters." Sal looked over at Clara and puckered her brows slightly.

Clara held up her hand. "Oh, don't worry about taking any of our business. We have more than we can handle."

Sal looked relieved. "Well, that's at least one concern out of the way. Now if we can just figure out what to do with that Whyte character."

"You're having problems with Mr. Whyte, too?" Henrietta suddenly felt uneasy again at the mention of his name. Weeks had passed since Magpie had had her unfortunate encounter with her trapper husband, and they had heard nothing further from the despicable scalawag or from Whyte about the incident. Perhaps she was fretting for nothing, but she couldn't quite drop the affair from her list of worries.

"He's claiming we're building on land owned by Dunraven and he's told us to simply leave." Sal frowned as Henrietta gasped. "Oh, no."

Sal crossed her arms. "Well, we sure aren't going without a fight. We can make a living here in Estes Park. That's becoming increasingly obvious. Hunter departed yesterday to find a surveyor and investigate our title so we can be certain what's what."

"Sounds like a good idea. You stick to your guns, Sal." Clara added.

"Oh, you bet. He's not going to bluff us out. Hunter will make sure of that."

Henrietta asked, "Did you hear what happened with George? He got into an actual scrap with Whyte though I don't know any of the details. But George is such a dear man I can't imagine it was any of his fault."

"Oh, he is." Clara nodded thoughtfully. "Such a sweet man." Clara then chuckled softly. "Good Lord. If I didn't know better, I'd think this whole place was feuding. I haven't told you about my mother yet."

Sal widened her eyes. "She got in a quarrel with Whyte, too?"

"Not Whyte, but this new settler named WilliamJames who bought land by my mother's homestead. He's claiming some of hers is his and is building a cabin on it."

"So, what's this rascal like?" Sal asked disgustedly.

Clara blew out a breath. "Oh, if all this hadn't happened, I think you might find him quite likable. He's in his thirties and came out here after his grocery business in New York failed in the depression of '73."

Henrietta spoke up. "Just like Collan. Did you know he once owned a general store?"

Clara shook her head. "Was he your beau a time ago back East?"

Henrietta snorted. "I can assure you, Collan Wallace and I *have never* and *will never* be romantically involved." But she didn't fail to catch a knowing look exchanged then between Clara and Sal.

Chapter Eleven

Collan sat on a rocky ledge overlooking his land and gazed briefly at the daisy-like flowers scattered in the grassy plains that spread out from the gurgling, meandering stream. He couldn't quite believe he owned such a beautiful place. His brother would have loved it here.

He briefly closed his eyes on the sight, willing the thought to go away. No use thinking about what could not be. His brother was gone forever along with all their shared hopes and laughter. But if Collan had learned anything from his passing, it was that life was short and should be experienced every day to the fullest. Even with that said, Collan realized that his decision to move here had been a bit crazily abrupt and certainly not completely thought out. He had grabbed at his next adventure with an eagerness that was almost like desperation. He knew that much, but he hadn't quite figured out exactly why.

A breeze suddenly blew the unopened letter that he had placed next to him off the rock and he forgot about these deep thoughts as he went to retrieve the envelope before returning to his perch. The letter was from Herm, and he could predict already what was written. Collan had penned a quick note to Herm out of a sense of duty after last seeing Etta but not really with enthusiasm. He had just known that Etta would be reticent about revealing her condition to her concerned siblings so he himself had divulged the fact to Herm. He had felt like a snitch, but more than that, he knew the pressure for her to return to Clarissa would be immense and that had bothered him. He shook his head disgustedly. And why was that?

Good Lord. He would be without one more burden to look after and a bothersome, squabbling one at that. He had plenty enough to concern himself with here in Estes Park.

Collan took out his knife and made a slit in the envelope. And why, in heavens, would he want the added chore of looking after some other man's kid—a constant reminder that Etta had chosen another man for her mate other than him. He suddenly paused in his action. Had he really just thought that?

No, he had not. His mind was obviously just wandering so he returned to pulling the note out of the envelope.

Dear Collan,

I have gathered the livestock you requested. Three of my men have started trailing them down to you already. You should be able to grow your own herd nicely. I will send an invoice once you receive the cattle.

Thank you for informing me of Henrietta's condition which she has neglected to write about herself thus far. No wonder, as I am sure she knows her siblings would want her to move. I would appreciate you encouraging her to return to her family. I know she can be stubborn, but do the best you can my friend.

Herm

Collan folded the letter and put it in his pocket. He knew he should head over to Etta's immediately and pack her up, but . . . but what?

He blew out a long breath. He just didn't feel like it.

He looked around at the scenery again. Why, anyone could see that the day was just too pretty to get in an argument, and he was sure it would involve that to get her to budge. Besides, he had plenty of chores to do on his own spread in anticipation of receiving the cattle. And of course, the Farrar brothers and he were supposed to visit her in a few days anyways to complete the cow shed. Why, certainly, her leaving could be put off until then.

Satisfied with his decision, Collan jumped off the rocky ridge and whistled for his horse.

Henrietta couldn't believe what she was hearing. "You're leaving? You're just packing up and leaving Estes Park?"

George nodded. "*Ja*, I made my decision. I don't want to fight." George had blushed after admitting to the encounter but now was digging in on the piece of strudel she had placed before him. They were both sitting on her porch at the cloth-covered tea table she had set up for tourists.

"But I don't even know what the argument was about to begin with." Henrietta didn't want George to depart. Though they didn't see as much of each other as before, he had still been one of her first friends in Estes Park—and a generous, kind, and sweet one at that.

"I put up fences to contain my cattle, and Herr Whyte thought that he could send his *schreckliche* cowboys to my land and tear them down

"Why that's just terrible. He can't do that."

"*Jawohl,* I told him so."

"I heard you nearly pushed him in the creek." Henrietta bit back a smile.

He looked up sheepishly but then smiled at her expression. "I should have." He took another bite of strudel.

"But where will you go?"

"I'll stay in Colorado but not in Estes Park."

"Well, I'm going to miss you."

George reached into his pocket and placed a small figurine of a horse in front of her. "I made this present for you."

She picked it up and wondered at the details. "You carved this? Out of pine?"

George nodded. "I wish I had time to make one nicer for you. I used to carve in *Deutschland.*"

Henrietta looked over. "Oh, no, George. This one is just lovely. *Dankeschoen.*"

"*Bitteschoen.*"

Liebchen neighed loudly and they both looked over at the stable. "Does this mean that you're taking Liebchen with you?"

George smiled wanly. "I must. We have been together many years."

Henrietta nodded. "I know." So now she required a mount. Magpie was currently out hunting with the Farrars on the roan horse that had practically turned into hers, but Henrietta did not want to buy such a frisky horse for herself.

"What will you do for a mount?"

She forced a smile. "I'm sure I can find another. Perhaps not as opinionated as Liebchen, but at least one that is tame."

"Could you do me a favor?"

"Absolutely, George. What is it?"

"I have a milk cow I was hoping you could take. She is still a producer, but a bit hobbly to be trailing to another home so far away. She's friendly. I think you will like her."

"Oh, George. Thank you. Does she have a name?"

"I just call her Beauty." He half-smiled. "You will see. She was once attacked by a mountain lion."

Henrietta shook her head. "The poor thing. Why, yes. I will be happy to take her. How much should I pay you?"

"Nothing. You are doing me a favor."

"But George—"

"Ah, okay. She costs five loaves of bread, a pie, *and* a strudel. Deal?"

She smiled. "Oh, George. Did I ever tell you how much I love you?"

He turned a deep shade of red and Henrietta chuckled. A few days later Henrietta whacked Collan on the arm.

Chapter Twelve

"Ow. *What?* I'm just stating a fact. That is the ugliest cow that ever existed in the history of mankind."

Etta gasped and rushed over to cover the cow's ears—or what remained of them—with her hands. "Don't you listen to him, Beauty. And you take that back, Collie, or I'll . . . I'll . . ."

Collan crossed his arms. "Or you'll what?"

"Yeah, what are you going to do now, Miss Henrietta?" Ike seemed genuinely interested.

Clint then spoke up. "Don't feel bad, Miss Henrietta. I'm pretty sure I once saw a cow nastier looking than Beauty. That one was attacked by a griz."

Collan chuckled.

Etta first looked over at Clint with a warm expression, stating pleasantly, "Why, thank you, Clint. That's awfully kind of you to say so."

But she turned back to Collan with a glare and it was in that precise moment that Collan knew he was going to put off having "The Talk" with Etta about her leaving Estes Park. Simply put, he realized that he was enjoying her company too much and besides, she didn't look all that much fatter. She couldn't be due all that soon.

Hank then walked up with the package of meat. "The usual, Miss Henrietta, some elk and trout."

Etta smiled. "Thank you, Hank. I have the fixin's for stew already started so it shouldn't be too long—"

Ike wailed. "Thank the Lord. I'm starved."

Magpie finally spoke up and now she was the one glowering, at Ike. "What wrong with you? I feed you. I feed you."

Ike started backing away in the new moccasins that Magpie had made for him, holding up his hands. "I know, Miss Magpie. I know. No offense. No offense. And some of your meals are real tasty. I'm just not that fond of that latest dish you made." He shuddered. "Meat mixed in with grizzle."

Magpie crossed her arms. "Hmmmph."

Etta spoke cheerily. "Well, to tie you over until supper, everybody can have some bread with the butter from Beauty I made."

Collan smiled. "Now that's a thought. Perhaps you could sell it to tourists, Etta. But instead of calling it Butter from Beauty, you could name it, say, Butter from Beastly."

The Farrars brothers all snorted back a guffaw.

Later at the dining table, Hank beat Collan in broaching the topic of finding a replacement for Liebchen. "I really don't think you should be here by yourself without a horse, Miss Henrietta, and no insult meant, but, uh . . . well, I mean, Lightning and Miss Magpie get along real well, but, uh . . . I've seen you riding and, uh . . ."

Collan interrupted. "You ride like a bag of flour with no obvious command."

Etta became indignant. "That's simply not true, Collan. George taught me how to ride and I'm a lot better. I mean, yes, Liebchen would still occasionally insist on eating the whole time we were riding, but that was only when she was in a mood and usually all I had to do was have a talk with her—"

"Save it, Etta. You're getting a horse just shy of approaching heaven."

Etta gaped. "I'm an independent woman now and I make my own decisions and you can't tell me what kind of horse to buy, Collie, and—"

Collan broke in. "Are you saying you want to buy that roan horse of the Farrars?" If she said yes, Collan knew he was going to have to put his foot down. The horse would kill her. But why couldn't he stop himself from saying what he knew was one baiting comment after another to her. Sure, it was fun to rile her—always had been—but he could see that if he pushed her too far, she might make a wrong decision for herself out of stubbornness. The thought hit him then that perhaps he persisted in his teasing because he could get attention from her—better an unpleasant response from her than none at all. God, had that always been one of the reasons for his antics? Even when they were younger? But Etta interrupted his musings.

She sat straighter and turned to Hank. "Well, yes, I would like to buy Lightning—for Magpie to own. But Hank, I was wondering if you planned to go to Denver any time soon and could look for another horse for me. Something dear with a sweet personality."

Collan felt an immediate, and he knew, irrational stab of jealousy that she wasn't asking him to find her a horse. He found himself nodding sagely and saying sarcastically, "Oh, yeah. That's always the first thing to look for when buying a horse, never mind how it's built, how old it is—"

Magpie interrupted him and was obviously also on the Hank going to Denver wagon train. "I want beads from Denver. I make baby clothes and shoes."

Collan turned back to Etta, "How about if I—"

But Ike started chuckling before Collan could suggest himself, buying the horse for Etta. "Oh, don't worry, Miss Magpie. Hank will surely get you some beads. They sell those in the store where we got the cloth for the kitchen curtains." Ike turned to Clint. "Do you think that young filly's still there behind the counter?"

Clint grinned. "You mean the one that talked all the time with Hank?"

"Yep, the very one." Ike winked.

Collan decided to persevere despite realizing that him buying the horse for Etta should not suddenly be so important. "Etta, I could—"

But Collan was interrupted again as Etta smiled. "Oh, then Hank, let me trim your beard before you leave and I want to wash and iron one of your outfits."

"What about a bath, Miss Henrietta?" Ike teased. "Aren't you goin' to make Hank take one of those?"

Now Collan had a whole new set of issues. Why was Hank going to get all this undivided attention from Etta? But Hank just rolled his eyes at Ike, and Collan quickly noticed he did not refuse her suggestions.

Then Etta sealed the deal as she said, "We'll pull out the tub after dessert and get Hank ready to leave in the morning." She turned to Hank. "I mean if that's okay with you."

Hank nodded. "Sure thing, Miss Henrietta. I'll get you a horse."

Well, it wasn't okay with Collan, though he didn't want to admit to himself the full reason exactly why.

Chapter Thirteen

A couple weeks went by and Henrietta had to admit that perhaps her newfound independence wasn't all it was cracked out to be. She knew part of her mixed feelings about being all alone was that with everyone gone, she had all her chores to do herself and she was tired *all the time*. Every afternoon she gave in to her fatigue and took naps. She couldn't make it through the day if not.

Hank was in Denver still. Magpie was usually off hunting with Clint and Ike. And Collan? Well, she knew he was busy on his own homestead, but she had thought he would occasionally stop in to see how she was doing. But apparently not. Only Abner Sprague swung by regularly now and since he was universally liked—being an amiable, industrious and sensible man—he was welcomed not only at her cabin but by the Fergusons and MacGregors as well. Friendly messages were passed through Abner back and forth between Clara and Sal and herself and she assumed he was giving progress reports to Collan about herself, but she never heard a word in return. She couldn't help thinking that perhaps Collan was avoiding her and that possibility bothered her more than she thought it would.

She decided the next time she saw Abner she would specifically ask about Collan. A few days went by before he stopped by again. Abner took his usual seat on her porch as she brought out a piece of pie.

Ring and Sally immediately took their positions at his feet. He was a sucker for giving them part of his food which, of course, endeared him all the more to her.

He spoke around a mouthful. "So, have you heard about the new family in the area?"

"No, who's that?"

"Elkanah Lamb, his wife Janie, and son Carlyle."

"Hmmm, that name almost sounds familiar. Where's he from?" Abner always knew the details. People felt comfortable opening up to him apparently.

Abner swallowed. "Originally a farmer's son in Indiana, but he prospected in Breckenridge in the '60's."

"Oh, perhaps that's where I heard the name."

Abner shrugged. "Perhaps. Lately he's been an itinerant minister organizing congregations along the South Platte, Poudre, and Thompson Rivers."

Henrietta smiled. "So civilization has finally come to Estes Park."

Abner chuckled. "Well, for those who actually want to be tamed. Most cowboys in the West, for example, are not big on organized religion."

"Really?"

"Nah. Religion is something that comes when the women and families start moving into an area. Anyways, he's fixin' on making a wagon road from the lower end of Estes Park to Longs Peak valley where he plans on building a cabin."

"What's he going to do all the way up there?"

"Well, besides still ministering, the usual— raising cattle. But the way things are going, I bet he'll also find himself putting up tourists and perhaps even acting as a guide up Longs Peak."

Henrietta nodded. She saw an opening to broach the topic she was most interested in. "Are Collan and you still being asked by tourists about accommodations and meals?"

Abner snorted. "All the time. Who knows— perhaps I'll get in the tourist business myself. I'm sure I will if my parents move out here, also."

"Do they plan to?"

"In a year or so."

She couldn't hold back any longer. "And just how is Collan? I haven't seen him for a while."

Abner tilted his head back surprised at that before composing himself again. "Honestly, he seems, well, a little sullen lately, but he's been busy building his cabin."

She frowned slightly. "What's he upset about?"

Abner shook his head. "I'm not sure he is. He might be just plum tired."

"Aren't we all?"

"Yeah, but it's a good kind of tired, don't you think?" Abner smiled. He reached down to pet Ring and Sally. "Well, I should be going. Great pie again, Henrietta."

"Thanks, Abner." But as she waved goodbye, she realized she still did not know what was going on with Collan and that perturbed her more than she thought it should.

Collan's cattle arrived and with them, a hired hand named Tinker. Tinker had shown up at Herm's hoping to be one of his cowboys, but Herm had enough men already. So, with the cowboys that had trailed the cattle, Tinker had come along and offered his help to Collan. Since Abner and his cabins were both complete, he only saw Abner occasionally—luckily just enough so that Abner could pass on a word that Etta was doing fine— and sometimes Collan felt overwhelmed with all that had to get done at his ranch. He knew he could use some help.

Collan looked over at Tinker before answering his request about work. He was a weathered, worn man, perhaps in his forties. Tall, but slight of build as if he had never been fed well. He walked with a bad limp. Collan asked the obvious question by his appearance. "I don't cotton with outlaws. You ever been in trouble before?"

Tinker puckered his brow. "They're not to my liking either. I look like I've lived a rough life because I have. I came West during the war and became a scout until an arrow messed with my leg. Since then I've wandered, trying to find something steady. Not so easy when you can't get around so well every day. But I'm a quick learner and have experience at many odd things. That's how I got my name. I've always liked to tinker with things." He stopped talking and then frowned at Collan, waiting for a response.

"I'm not sure I can pay you. I'm just starting out."

"Herm explained that. I want regular meals and a dry, warm bed at night."

Collan held out his hand for a shake. "We can give it a try."

Within a few days, Collan was comfortable around Tinker and more than appreciative of added hands for all the chores required. Tinker would have to sit frequently to get off his leg, but he finished whatever he started.

Abner swung by and seemed to take an immediate liking to Tinker. "I think you got yourself a good man there, Collan." Tinker was currently building a front porch for the cabin and could not hear what they were saying.

Collan half-smiled. "I thought he was a bandit when I first met him."

Abner chuckled. "Nah, just one down on his luck."

"So what's the news? Etta still doing well?"

"Seems to be. She says she hasn't seen you for a while and was asking about you." Abner looked at him inquiringly.

Collan blew out a long breath. "I've been busy." He knew it was an inadequate response. He was not going to reveal that he had missed her terribly the last couple of weeks and realized how much he yearned for her but had purposely refrained from visiting so he could get over his attraction. He did not want to get hopelessly hurt—actually, *again,* if he honestly considered his feelings after she had married her husband. Etta had her life and he had his to live and it would be good if he just kept remembering that. He went over his list of reasons why this was true that he had drummed into himself over the past several days. She wanted her independence. She said she was never going to marry again. She sought other people's assistance, not his, for her problems—like her lack of a horse. And, of course, the big one. She was carrying the love of her life's baby—even if he was no longer on this Earth—and probably had no room for anyone else in her emotional being.

"Did you know Hank got back? Henrietta wanted to know if you would like to see her new horse." Abner smiled, as if in on some joke.

Collan frowned. Well, that was a little different. He could at least be neighborly. "Sure, I should probably introduce Tinker to some of the folks around here anyways."

"Yeah, that would be a reason to go over there." Abner chuckled.

"What's so funny?"

Abner kept laughing. "Oh, nothing at all. Just being friendly."

Collan ignored him and started walking towards his new porch. "Hey, Tinker. We're taking a little break."

Chapter Fourteen

Etta's home was in an uproar when Collan arrived. Clint, Ike, Hank, and Magpie were all on their horses rapidly crisscrossing the field beyond the river. Etta was standing by her stables, next to an ugly nag of a horse, already saddled, talking earnestly to it.

She looked over as Collan and Tinker clopped into her yard and dismounted. "Oh, Collan. Thank God you're here."

Running up to him, she gave Collan a quick hug.

After a moment of relishing her warm greeting—though he knew that was the last thing he should be doing—he reluctantly placed her away from him so he could look into her face. "Etta, what's wrong?" He could see no harm had come to her and relaxed a little.

But she started flapping both hands in the air excitedly. "Oh, Lord. It's bad! It's real bad. And it's all my fault."

"Tell me what happened."

She huffed out a breath. "It's Snuggles! She's gone! I was trying to teach her how to live outside and I turned *for just a second* to wave to Harry who had come for a visit and when I turned back she had run off."

Collan lowered his head so she couldn't see his face and tried not to laugh. But he failed. He was just so relieved it wasn't anything serious.

Etta stamped her foot. "Collie, it's not funny. She should not be on her own yet."

Collan raised his head. "So, is that the search party across the river?"

"Yes! And I want to join in, but Buzzie will not cooperate. I mean not that I blame him because he doesn't know the gravity of the situation since he's never met Snuggles."

"Let me guess. Buzzie is your new horse."

"Yes! Doesn't he look just like a cute little bumblebee?" She smiled warmly.

Collan followed her gaze over to the decrepit hag of a horse. He couldn't see it. Not at all.

"And usually he's just a big old loverboy. I don't know what's got into him today."

Collan did. He knew the horse had figured out that he could push her around and do what he wanted—which was stand and do nothing.

Etta finally realized she had added company. She started talking to Tinker. "Oh, I do beg your pardon. How do you do?" She held out her hand. "I'm Henrietta Schodde. I'm afraid things are a little disorganized currently, but you are most welcome."

Tinker shook her hand. "Thank you, ma'am. You can call me Tinker." He then looked over at Collan for an explanation. "I'm not sure if I got what's going on. Can I be of help?"

"Mount up again and head across the river. You're looking for a rabbit."

"A rabbit?"

"Yes, still kinda on the small size."

Tinker motioned with his head for Collan to follow and started walking a few feet away as Etta headed back to Buzzie. Tinker lowered his voice. "On the way over here, I did notice a hawk, carrying what could possibly be a smallish rabbit."

Collan briefly closed his eyes. "Oh, hell. Did you happen to see if the hawk had only one leg?"

"That I couldn't quite tell."

"Well, don't say anything to Etta, but we'll make this search real short."

Collan walked over to the stables. Etta was trying to mount Buzzie. He grabbed hold of Buzzie's bridle with one hand and with the other gave Etta a boost. He handed her the reins. "Thanks, Collie. You'll help look, won't you?"

"Sure, Etta. Got nothing better to do." Collan shook his head. He had tried, but the woman had ensnared him once again.

A couple hours later, Henrietta resigned herself to Snuggles being gone. She looked down the dining table and consoled herself—at least Collan had bothered to make an appearance here. She had surprised herself at how happy she had been to see him. She had actually hurried over to embrace him. Collan and she never *hugged*. Well, near never. It was so strange, yet had felt like an honest reaction to her feelings at the time. Go figure. Henrietta decided to concentrate on her rabbit again, and asked, "Clint, do you really think Snuggles is old enough to be on her own?"

Clint nodded. "She's probably making a nice little nest for herself as we speak. Please don't cry

140

anymore, Miss Henrietta. I just can't take it." He wiped at his eyes with his sleeve.

She swallowed. Now she felt embarrassed. She hadn't realized that anyone had noticed her sniffles while she was preparing the meal. The rest had all been talking, getting to know Tinker. Well, all except Magpie, who had alternatingly watched him with wary eyes or else smirked at him.

Henrietta looked now at Tinker. The poor thing, hobbling the way he was. She was determined to fatten him up and take that sad expression off his face. "Tinker, could I get you some more stew?"

"No, thank you, ma'am. But I want to say it's been a real long time since I've had such a delicious meal."

"Well, I hope you have room for dessert. I made pie."

Tinker actually smiled, a bit tentatively, but still an attempt. "You bet."

Magpie now mumbled some incomprehensible words softly to herself.

Tinker narrowed his eyes at her and spoke what sounded like jibberish back. *That* got everyone's attention, including Collan and Hank who stopped their own conversation—something about how Buzzie was the best Hank could find for the money that didn't require breaking in.

Magpie now glared at Tinker and signed something to him.

He rapidly signed something back.

Henrietta could tell they were not having a nice conversation. "Magpie? What's happening?"

141

Ike spoke up. "Yeah, what's going on, Miss Magpie?"

Magpie just stared straight ahead, refusing to answer, so Tinker finally explained. "She said she's watching me. She doesn't trust me."

Magpie then said, "And he told me that I am a mean Cheyenne woman so I told him he looks dirty and wears old clothes."

"And I then told her that she should make me some."

Henrietta asked the obvious. "So, Tinker, you speak Cheyenne and know sign?"

He nodded once. "I learned a little as a scout."

Henrietta smiled. "Well, I'm sure I could make you a new shirt and mend and wash your clothes." She looked across the table. "And perhaps Magpie could make you a pair of moccasins. Wouldn't that be nice, Magpie, since we're welcoming him as our new neighbor?"

Magpie smirked.

"After supper, why don't I give your locks a trim and we can pull out the tub for a bath?"

Collan rolled his eyes at that as Ike slapped the table, laughing. "Miss Henrietta has got herself a new victim. Welcome to Estes Park, Tinker."

Clint frowned. "Shut up, you oaf. She's just being nice."

Ike quieted but continued to snort back a chuckle. Henrietta glanced over at Collan, smiling, but was taken aback that he appeared a bit sour in expression. Now what was wrong with him?

The following week, Collan and Tinker were again calling on Etta. She had invited them to come back, and there was no way Collan could deny Tinker the pleasure—he had talked about nothing else for days. He obviously had not been fussed over by a couple women in a long, *long* time. Collan knew, too, he would not go on his own.

So on the way over with him Collan repeated to himself—she would live her life and he would live his. He also recognized he just had to get over this petty jealousy he was feeling every time Etta gave other men her attention.

When they arrived Etta did not embrace him and Collan told himself not to be disappointed. He got to work immediately, having agreed with the Farrars to chop logs all day for a substantial pile come winter. Of course, Collan knew that there was a good chance she would not be in her cabin come winter, but he was still putting off the discussion since she seemed to be thriving where she was at. The shadows he had seen on her face just a month ago from losing her husband were fading. He suspected, having her baby was giving her a new outlook on the future.

After a few hours of toiling, they walked into the cabin for a noon meal. The smell of the elk roast, potatoes, gravy and biscuits was near overwhelming. It was beyond time he found a wife who could cook for him every day like this. She just wasn't going to be Etta.

Etta took off her apron. "I also grilled some trout if there's not enough to eat."

Ike was the first to sit down. "What's in the bowl, Miss Henrietta?"

"I made huckleberry jam for the bread if you like." Etta smiled pleasantly, but Collan knew her every expression and could tell something was up.

He ventured a guess. "Did you make any butter this week?"

"A little." She shook her head and raised her hands. "But it was all eaten up by the tourists."

"Uh, huh. I'm sure it's not because Beastly's production is already dropping off."

Etta frowned. "Stop calling Beauty that horrible name, Collie. It's really disrespectful."

Collan rolled his eyes. "Etta, you're either going to have to mate Beastly which is not going to be easy, considering her looks—I mean I'm sure bulls have their preferences—or pasture her or eat her."

Etta gasped which made Collan laugh. "You are so mean! I'm sure Beauty is just a little off because she's at a new place with strange people she doesn't know—"

"—and because she's a has-been, old broad." He just couldn't stop himself from teasing her every time he was around her. He had always reveled in her reaction—that was never going to change no matter what the reasoning behind it.

Etta put her hands on her hips. "That's it, Collie! I'm not talking to you the rest of the day. Just sit down and eat!" Collan chuckled louder but complied.

Tinker stood standing still, mouth actually agape, at their interaction. Etta turned to him. "Oh, Tinker, wait. I want you to try something on before you eat." She hurried into her bedroom and came out with a package wrapped in simple paper, tied with a string. "For you."

Tinker swallowed, obviously moved by her kindness. Etta misinterpreted and turned to the table. "Don't worry. We'll make sure there's food for you. Clint, please put a generous helping of everything on a plate for Tinker."

Clint nodded. "Sure thing, Miss Henrietta."

She turned back to Tinker. "Well, go on and open it."

Tinker unwrapped the package and pulled out a shirt, simple in design, but still much better than what he was wearing. He shook his head. "I don't know what to say—"

But Etta was shooing him. "Now go on. You can change in my bedroom."

Tinker obeyed as Ike asked, around a mouthful, "How'd you make that so quick, Miss Henrietta?"

She smiled. "Magpie and I went over to see Clara and used her new sewing machine. I really like it. What a wonderful invention."

Collan couldn't help asking about her horse. "How'd you get Buzzie off his ass?"

Etta frowned and huffed, but Magpie answered. "Buzzie follows Lightning."

He nodded. "Ah, of course."

Tinker emerged from the bedroom, now looking embarrassed to be the aim of everyone's attention but not able to hide a small smile.

"You look so nice, Tinker." Etta clasped her hands, then adjusted one of the sleeves. She turned to Magpie, still excited. "Should *I* tell him? No, no. *You* should."

Magpie stared straight ahead and not at Tinker as she said, unenthusiastically, "I make moccasins for you."

Etta grinned happily. "She has to finish fitting them to you. But she can do that this afternoon. What do you think?"

Tinker finally found his voice. "I think that's great. Really great. I'll just move my plate in front of Magpie so I can properly thank her during the meal." Clint scooted down the bench to make room.

"Oh, how nice." Etta said, as Collan started chuckling again. He had a feeling that the conversation the rest of them would not be able to follow was not necessarily going to be sweet. He also got the impression that Tinker was, nevertheless, enjoying himself.

Etta finally sat down at the table and placed her napkin on her lap. "I have some other news. Clara said she's going to hold a dance next week."

"What do you mean a dance?" Ike asked.

"Like a social, Ike." Hank said.

Ike frowned. "A social. What's a social?" Ike winked at Clint then, who grinned. "Oh, I see. You know all about these things now, Hank, don't you, now that you have your Denver gal. And just when are you goin' back to Denver? I'm sure Miss Henrietta could use some more fabric."

Etta smiled and continued. "Women can come for free, but it will cost men twenty-five cents to attend."

Ike protested immediately. "That's not fair."

Collan looked over. "Do you honestly think you could get a gal to partake with this rough group of men unless she was offered some advantage?"

"Hey, I take offense to that." Ike sat up straighter, pulling down his wrinkled shirt. "I'm quite the catch now, aren't I, Miss Henrietta? You said I was handsome last time you gave me a trim."

"Yes, I did. But I'll want you to wear your best clothes, remember the manners I taught you, and we'll have to practice dancing later today."

Clint groaned. "Oooh, do we have to?"

Etta nodded. "If you want to please a girl. And I only taught you one simple step before."

Ike put his head on the table. "I'd prefer to chop logs."

Henrietta could see that the dancing lessons were not progressing as she had hoped and Collan, the devil, would not stop laughing. At least the Farrar brothers all had their blond curls and manly, strong frames going for them.

The table had been moved to the edge of the room and Magpie and Tinker were sitting in a corner, debating the height his moccasins should take—or at least that's what she surmised they were arguing about now.

"Okay, time to change partners." She tried to stay cheerful. "Ready? One and a two and a three . . ." But Clint, who was paired with Hank, crashed into Ike as Hank stepped on Henrietta's foot, as she tried to now partner with Hank instead of Ike. Oh, dear.

There was a loud thud as Collan fell off his bench in a guffaw. She turned to him. "Will you *please* stop laughing?"

Collan raised to a sitting position on the floor and attempted to speak. "Perhaps it would help if you . . ." He broke out chuckling again.

"*Stop* it, Collie." She stomped her foot. "I mean it."

He wiped his eyes with his sleeve and looked at her. "Or you'll what? Throw my boots down your outhouse?"

She narrowed her eyes. "I just might."

"You wouldn't really do *that*, Miss Henrietta?" Clint asked alarmed. "Would you?"

She didn't answer.

But Collan got to his feet. "I think you should try something simpler. I always found the waltz easier than these country steps."

He took her in his arms and started to move before she could protest. "Shall we?"

Henrietta knew Collan was a good dancer, but *they* had never danced together before. She tried to keep a little distance between their bodies, but as he started to hum an especially sweet tune, she began to give in to the pleasing melody and their movements flowed together. She didn't know how she felt about all this and then noticed everyone watching them. Even Magpie and Tinker had paused in their squabbling to observe.

She stopped to ask. "What is that song you're humming?"

"Leo Delibes' Coppelia Waltz—just popular back East before I came out here. Do you like it?"

She looked into his face. "Yes."

He took hold of her again and turned to the Farrar brothers. "See how all you have to remember is

148

the one, two, three, one, two, three rhythm." They demonstrated to the brothers, counting out the steps, and then she stopped again.

"Hank, why don't you try leading Clint." She turned around to the corner. "And Ike will partner with Magpie." Magpie surprised everyone by getting up without protest.

She thought Tinker looked a bit longingly, so she asked him, "Would you like to dance with me?" But he shook his head, and she didn't try to convince him, considering his leg.

Collan then said, "We should go outside for more room." So they all stepped into the yard.

Collan took hold of Henrietta again. "Now men, women seem to like it if you hold them firmly." He pulled her closer.

"Wait. What are you doing?" She tried to take a step back.

But Collan ignored her and began humming the pretty melody again. So, they started to dance.

She found herself enjoying the movements with Collan again which then made her feel uncomfortable. What was she doing? Was she betraying the memory of her husband? But she couldn't seem to stop herself from also humming the appealing tune and when he twirled her rapidly around her dogs, she laughed with pleasure. Out of the corner of her eye, she saw that Clint and Hank were stomping sluggishly, but Magpie had taken ahold of Ike and was showing him the dance capably.

"Hey, Miss Magpie, this is kind of fun," he exclaimed. "Where'd you learn how to dance like this?"

"The fort."

"Which one?"

She didn't answer Ike but also joined in the humming and seemed to be taken back to a time when she was younger. Tinker started watching her avidly from the porch, as Clint and then Hank cut in with Magpie to give the dance a better try.

Meanwhile Collan and Henrietta became more fluid in their dancing, and Henrietta lost track of their companions in the yard. It only seemed natural when their bodies joined yet closer together. She caught Collan looking into her eyes earnestly and she gazed back, and . . . for what seemed like the first time in her life, she became aware of Collan as a mature man, who knew how to romance a woman, who could be charming, who, oh, God, this can't be.

"Hi, everyone. Looks like you're having fun." Abner greeted them astride his horse.

Collan and Henrietta stopped abruptly, the spell broken, and she pulled away from him. Henrietta felt flustered and she brushed down her skirt, feeling as if she had been caught in an act she should not have been doing. "Hi, Abner. Would you like something to eat?"

Abner dismounted. "Don't mind if I do."

"Come on in, then."

"I was actually hoping I'd run into you, Collan. I've got some news I don't think you'll like hearing."

Chapter Fifteen

"He did *what*?" Collan looked flabbergasted.

"You heard me correctly. Like some lord of the realm, Whyte commanded me off my land. He said I didn't own the property and neither did you, and I told him that you and I both filed proper claims at near the same time. Then he informed me that he was heading over to see you next. I guess Whyte didn't catch up with you."

"No, he did not. So what else did you say?"

Abner sat straighter at the table. "I took great pleasure in telling him to get his own surveyor." Abner had taught himself surveying, thinking he might like doing the work sometime in the future. So it was Abner who had surveyed their land for them.

Collan shook his head. "The gall of the man. I can't get over it."

"Obviously, his policy in dealing with us settlers is to ignore our claims and annoy and harass us."

Henrietta asked, "Do you know if the Fergusons have found a surveyor yet for their property?"

Abner nodded. "I just talked with them before I came here. Turns out their cabin is on their claim, but what they're using adjacent for their cattle is not."

Her eyes widened. "Oh, no. So what are they going to do?"

"They're still trying to figure that out, though all these tourists are definitely giving them a reason to stay."

Ike spoke up. "What we goin' to do if Whyte comes talkin' with us, Hank? You know our land was probably claimed by those lackeys of Dunraven."

Henrietta clasped her chest. "It was? Oh, Lord. Everyone's not going to leave me, are they?"

Hank shook his head. "The land was never bettered by building a dwelling on it—the way the homestead act requires. And until Dunraven can prove how he came by the property in the first place, I intend to stay."

"Oh, you just know the land was obtained by trickery." Abner added, disgustedly.

"You bet it was." Hank nodded.

Henrietta looked around the table at all the angry men. "Well, please promise me that none of you are going to do anything foolish. You mean a lot to me." Her eyes seemed to stray of their own volition over to Collan until she quickly glanced away.

Collan surveyed the scene before him. Ike was *dancing* with a pretty gal and Clint was conversing with another. A small band was playing that included a couple fiddlers and a guitar player. He did not see Etta or Magpie.

Last week when he had offered to pick Etta up before the dance, she had declined, and he had assumed she was coming with a friend such as Sal Ferguson—but apparently not. He felt disappointed yet he knew it was an opportunity to give another woman a chance—because Etta would live her life and he would live his, he repeated to himself. He just had to keep that in mind. So what if they had managed to dance like a couple for the first time in their lives. It didn't mean a thing because .. . tarnation, did he have to repeat the list to himself again about her not wanting to marry again and so on? No.

He was tired of the list. He quickly looked around the crowd again and noted there were plenty of attractive women here who were either settlers or tourists. He glimpsed over at the punch bowl table and saw a woman glance back at him so he approached her. Why not? She had a shapely figure.

She turned to him as he got nearer and asked, "Have we met before? You look familiar."

He shook his head. "I don't think so and I believe I would have remembered meeting you before." He smiled. She didn't, and he knew in that instant that he really didn't want to spend any more time with her. He muttered, "If you'll excuse me . . ."

He saw Anna Ferguson who he had met before and though he had no romantic interest in her, she was watching the dancing avidly. The current song was ending so he asked, "Would you like to take a spin with the next song."

Anna briefly looked around, then said, "Thank you, Mr. Wallace. I would."

And somehow her calling him his formal name instead of Collan made him feel ancient. But he also noticed that as they performed the steps to a country ditty—Buffalo gals, won't you come out tonight? And dance by the light of the moon—her head seemed to be on a swivel. She was definitely searching for someone. Sure enough, within a minute, another man asked to cut

153

in. Collan had a vague recollection that he had once met the gent who was a merchant from one of the outlying towns.

He walked back to the edge of the dance floor, determined to find a suitable partner to dance with because that was what he should be doing. But as he scrutinized the crowd, he just couldn't seem to find the drive to pursue anyone else.

He looked over to the group of men conversing on the other side of the dance floor. Tinker, standing next to Abner and Hank, appeared bored and almost grim. He wondered if the man had ever enjoyed gatherings such as this one. And yet, there was something about Tinker—the way he would occasionally talk about a variety of topics—that made Collan think that, yes, at one time Tinker had had a full life. Was it simply his awkward gait or something else that caused him to withdraw?

Collan thought about how he also had been withdrawing slowly, but surely, for years. He just didn't think his frame of mind was as obvious to the world as that which Tinker showed. But as Collan had gone from one situation to the next, he had never fully engaged with other people before he was on his way again. He wasn't even sure what he was looking for or what kind of entanglement he was *avoiding* so greatly. But something wasn't at peace with him and had not been for a while, and he finally could admit to himself that his jumbled feelings about Etta were somehow involved in the mix of emotions. Hell.

He already felt like going home.

"Collan Wallace."

He turned around at the call of his name. Clara and Sal were standing behind him, looking at him in almost a scolding fashion. "Yes?"

"What are *you* doing here?" Sal asked.

"Funny, I was asking myself the same question."

"Henrietta and Magpie are not here." Clara pointed out.

Uh, he knew that. It was the first thing he had noticed. "I know."

"And why not?" Sal asked.

He shook his head. "I'm not sure."

Clara elaborated. "I mean *I thought* Henrietta was going to attend for certain since Magpie brought over some baked goods today to share at the dance. I just didn't even bother to ask Magpie if they both were coming."

Sal snorted. "And I didn't expect to see you here, Collan, if she wasn't." She looked at Clara for confirmation as if that would be obvious. Clara nodded back to her.

Then they both put their hands on their hips and Sal asked, "*Sooo* . . . what are you going to do about it?"

"Uh, I'm going to ride over there and get them both." The thought made him feel happy for the first time this evening.

Sal smiled. "Now you're thinking, Collan. Good idea."

Clara added. "And hurry back. No excuses." She looked at Sal and they both giggled, before walking off.

Collan found Tinker again. "Mount up. We're supposed to bring Etta and Magpie to the dance."

Tinkers brows raised, but he suddenly didn't appear so grim anymore.

Henrietta watched as Magpie climbed astride her horse and followed Tinker out of the yard without complaint. There was definitely more to Magpie than what at first had been obvious. But Henrietta didn't have time to ponder that now because she was going to give it to Collie, but good. She had only been putting on a serene act in front of Tinker to be polite.

Chapter Sixteen

Collan was lounging on one of her porch chairs, petting Ring and Sally. He looked up as she turned to him. "Are you going to change or wear that to the dance?"

"I'm not going to the dance. I'm going to mash you into a million pieces, Collan, instead."

He actually started chuckling. "You've never seriously hit a thing in your life, Etta. I doubt you're going to begin now."

"Oh, yeah." She was livid. "Well, you've driven me to it. And I'm going to take great satisfaction in it. Just you watch—"

He laughed louder.

She kicked at his chair, shoving it a couple inches over. "Take that!"

Ring and Sally tilted their heads, trying to figure out what was going on.

Collan snorted. "Now look what you've done, Etta. You've scared your dogs."

"I have not! They know I would never do anything bad to them."

"Oh, but you would me." He chuckled again.

"Yes! And why are you taking such pleasure in it?"

He shrugged, grinning. "I'm not sure. Perhaps because it's a hell of a lot more entertaining than that dance."

"Really?" She couldn't help being curious. "Oh, is the turnout bad or the music poor?"

"No. The dance is fine. You're just better to watch."

"This is not some show for your amusement. I'm honestly furious with you."

"Tell me why."

"I'll show you instead." She stomped into her cabin and returned with the letter. She shoved it in front of his face. "Read this, you big gossip."

"What?" He held it up to the light, streaming out of her cabin window and started reciting aloud: *"Dear Henrietta, Congratulations. Herm informed me you will be a mother soon. I know you have wanted a child for a long time and I am happy for you."*

Collan looked up at her sheepishly. "Oh."

She put her hands on her hips. "Yeah. *Oh.* Keep reading."

"Of course, I would have expected to hear such news from you instead of our brother, but I guess now that you are such an independent woman living in the frontier of Estes Park you don't think about your sister so much. I, however, have shown nothing but concern for you."

He glanced up again. "Clarissa has always had a knack for laying it on thick, hasn't she?"

"That's not the point, Collie. You should have never told Herm."

He continued without comment. *"The reason I am writing this letter is to state unequivocally that you should PACK AT ONCE and come stay with me. You cannot have that child like some savage in the rough."*

158

He shook his head. "She sure can be dramatic."

Henrietta smirked. "Just keep reading."

"Once the baby has come into the world, he or she will find a happy, loving home here with me and mine. I am, of course, not telling you what to do—"

He nodded. "Of course."

"—but only expressing what I know you already must realize. I am very surprised you are not here already. I will be looking for your arrival in the very near future. Your loving sister, Clarissa."

Henrietta kicked his chair again. "This is all your fault."

He got up from the chair, holding both hands up. "Now listen, Etta, you know I couldn't just stay quiet about such important news."

"Do I?" She crossed her arms.

"Yeah, and we really have to talk about when you're going to leave Estes Park."

"Oh, do we? I thought it was my choice if I even leave at all."

"It is your decision. I'm just going to help you make it. But you don't have to decide tonight. Why don't I take you to the dance now?"

"You said it was boring."

He shook his head. "No, I didn't say that. It'll just be more interesting with you there."

"Because I'll beat you up?"

"Now, Etta. That's not your way."

"Yeah, well, it is now so you better watch out."

"Duly noted." He looked her up and down. "Is that really what you want to wear to the dance? It looks kind of old."

"Thanks a lot, Collie. You're a real charmer."
She looked down at her faded dress. "I wear this for
chores around the house. I have no intention of going to
that dance. I never did."

"Why not?"

"Because I'm a recent widow, who is also
having a child. It would appear unseemly."

He chuckled a little. "Well, see, everyone knows
that I came over here to escort you to the dance so if I
don't return there real quick they're probably going to
think that you and I are doing . . . you know . . . over
here."

She gaped. "Oh, my God. Then get back there!"

"I don't want to. It's boring."

She stamped her foot. "Are you saying that the
only way you will go again to the dance is with me?"

"Pretty much." He couldn't hold back a smile.

She hurried into her cabin but kept talking to
him as she frantically shuffled about. "Oh, my God.
Now what am I going to wear? My nice dress is
probably all wrinkled. I have it stored in the trunk. And,
of course, I can't do anything about its condition because
every minute I'm not at that dance, people are imagining
that you and I are going at it."

He spoke through the door. "Probably like
rabbits."

"That's not funny, Collie."

"Yeah, forget the rabbits. Probably like
monkeys."

"Will you please be quiet." She held up her best
dress in the doorway. "What do you think? Will they
notice the wrinkles?"

"Nah. And tick tock. I can feel your reputation slipping every second."

She hurried into her bedroom and slammed the door. She emerged a few minutes later and stood in the doorway again, panting. "Well, how do I look?"

He didn't say anything for a moment but just stared at her. "Real nice, Etta. Honestly."

"Really?"

"Uh, huh. You got that just tousled in the bedroom look."

"If you are still alive, Collie, at the end of the night, consider it a miracle."

Chapter Seventeen

Collan and Etta agreed it would take too much time to saddle her horse. Collan also knew that it would take too long to actually teach Etta how to ride her horse over to the dance—not that she would ever admit that was a problem.

So Etta now sat sideways in front of him on his horse, trying her best not to touch Collan more than necessary. It was impossible, of course, considering the swaying motion with riding, but she was doing her darndest which Collan found amusing. He was so used to giving his horse his head on easy rides and distracted by Etta that he inadvertently let his horse charge up a slope.

She slammed against him and he heard her gasp. He drew rein abruptly. He hoped he hadn't hurt her or, God forbid, the baby. "What's wrong?" he asked worriedly.

She didn't answer him at first but kept her hands on her belly as she stared straight ahead.

"Etta, come on—"

She waved one hand impatiently. "Shush. Wait." She placed her hands back on the skirt of her dress but then turned to him with a wide grin. "The baby's moving. I can feel it for the first time."

Collan's eyes lit up. "Really?"

"Yes! Just now again."

"Let me feel, Etta."

She nodded eagerly and placed his hand underneath hers. He didn't sense anything at first but then thought his hand moved very slightly.

She asked, "Did you feel it? Did you feel it that time?"

He wasn't sure, but he didn't want to disappoint her. "Yeah. He's going to be a real fighter, Etta."

She smiled sweetly. "Isn't it wonderful?"

He nodded, smiling back at her. He started riding again slowly and she relaxed into him now, unaware of her position in her happiness. She was honestly, truly delighted, and he cherished seeing her expression just now. He realized this was the first time since her husband passed that she had expressed her happiness without a slight shadow in her eyes. Oh, probably everyone would have disagreed, but he knew her well and recognized for at least a moment she had completely forgotten her sorrow. He didn't want the moment to pass, so he asked, "How far along does that make you, Etta?"

She puckered her brows. "I think most women feel their babies at five months."

"So you'll have a new year baby?"

She nodded. "Yeah, I guess so. But Collie, I really am going to have a child." She looked up at him excitedly and again without shadows.

He chuckled. "You had any doubt? Look how fat you are now." She scarcely had a bulge on her belly. She was that type of woman, carrying.

She punched his arm, playfully. "You're so mean, Collie. But I was just too afraid to fully hope before. But now I know for sure."

"Yep, you're going to be a mother for certain." And Collan was pleased for her, truly he was, but he couldn't help wondering again how much the child would put a barrier between her and another person. Would she become so attached to the baby that she had no more room in her life for anyone else? Would the baby be a constant reminder of the man she had married? He shook his head, not wanting to think about it anymore. They had a dance to get to.

Etta hurriedly dismounted as they reached the dance and walked eagerly over to Clara and Sal. He saw Clara touch her skirt and smile. He looked around with interest at the remaining crowd. He suddenly felt content being at the dance.

With Etta here.

Though not really with Etta since he knew she was going to spend the night with her women friends. But somehow, it was just the fact that she was present that made a difference.

Ike was dancing with one of the woman tourists and Hunter, eldest son of Sal, had corralled Magpie. Good Lord. Magpie was actually laughing at something he was saying as she effortlessly swirled around the dance floor. He could suddenly picture Magpie as she must have been as a beguiling maiden before all her troubles started. He looked to the edge of the dance floor. It appeared Tinker could also as he kept glancing her way while he talked to Clint. The song ended.

Tinker smiled as Magpie walked back over to where he was standing. A new song began—Beautiful dreamer, wake unto me, Stalight and dewdrops are waiting for thee, Sounds of the rude world, heard in the day, Lull'd by the moonlight have all pass'd away—and Clint and Ike found new partners. So did Hank he saw. Figures, the melody was the slow type they only had to sway to.

But as the dance progressed, Collan found himself satisfied with just drinking the loaded punch and talking to the other men. He had no desire to seek out a dance partner until he heard the beginning strains of a familiar waltz. Tinker had borrowed one of the fiddles and was playing the beautiful song that he had heard at Etta's. The other musicians were catching on to the melody and joining in. The crowd was mesmerized by the sweet performance and starting to waltz. And perhaps it was the liquor or just his scrambled feelings for Etta, but he found himself approaching her as she talked excitedly with the other women about how she hadn't known Tinker could play.

He looped his arm through hers and started pulling her towards the dance floor.

"What are you doing, Collie?" she asked with an exasperated tone.

He stopped. "Oh, I forgot. Dancing in front of everyone would be . . . what was that ridiculous word you used? Oh, yeah. Unseemly."

She frowned. "Unseemly is not a ridiculous word—"

He placed his finger over her mouth. "Etta, hush. Follow me."

He started walking towards one of the nearby sheds. He turned back and looked at her. She was frowning more deeply and asking, "Where are you going?"

"Etta, would you just be quiet for once in your life and come on?"

She huffed out a breath. "Oh, for heaven's sake." But she started following him. He rounded the nearby building until he came to the private rear of it.

He looked at her determinedly. "There. Now nobody can see you dancing."

"But that's not the only point—"

He placed his finger over her mouth again and quieted her. "I require more expert dancing lessons that only you can provide."

She rolled her eyes. "You do not."

"Yes, I do. I want to show off in front of that fetching maiden that came to the dance tonight."

She was suddenly interested and peered around the corner. "Which one?"

"The one with cake dribbling out of her mouth she can't devour it fast enough. I like 'em chubby—you know, like you."

She turned back to him and said, "You're despicable, Collan Wallace." But she bit back a smile.

She didn't resist when he took her in his arms. "I'm trying to figure out just how one moves when there's all this blubber to get around."

She started chuckling.

"Perhaps like this," he said and they both swayed slightly to the melody. Henrietta was tentative at first but gave in to the music as she had the day they

166

spun around in her yard—Collan knew she loved to dance.

They were perfect for each other—both relaxing into the tune. She smiled up at him and he smiled back. They swung and twirled.

They looked into each other's eyes. He couldn't hide his desire.

She recognized it and came to a halt, eyes wide.

He lowered his head for a kiss.

She fled.

Henrietta didn't think the ride back to her house could get any more awkward. They both knew what had almost happened behind that barn. Collan was now sober and subdued but urging his horse to get to her cabin as swiftly as safely possible.

She was embarrassed. And felt guilty. For betraying her husband, though she had not. For possibly leading Collan on, though she hadn't meant to. She wanted to blame it all on his drinking tonight but intuitively knew deep down that there was more to it.

She suddenly remembered something she had long forgotten. Here she was feeling guilty now the same way she had felt guilty about Collan when her husband had first started courting her. But she hadn't comprehended why then and she wasn't sure still. They had only been childish adversaries to each other who had grown a little older. There had been no romantic feelings between them then, had there? But nevertheless, she had had this sense of betrayal towards Collan as soon as she had agreed to a first date with Charles. But then she had been swept away by the charm of Charles and fallen deeply in love with him. She had forgotten about her initial unexplainable feelings of guilt towards Collan until now.

But she inwardly shook her head. She really had nothing to feel guilty about then or now. She hadn't led Collan on tonight in any way. This was all in his head. Not hers.

Her baby moved. She wanted to tell Collan again but refrained. He dropped her off at her cabin and said a soft goodbye.

Chapter Eighteen

Like her mood, the wind would not settle. Autumn had arrived. The aspen had turned yellow and the nights were colder. Unlike the summertime, the breezes seemed to blow nearly constantly now, gentle at times but with powerful gusts occurring more often. Henrietta's cabin had been placed in what seemed like a wind tunnel with no breaks to stop the draughts. The wind had never bothered her before, but she found its persistence now grating.

The Farrar brothers still stopped by regularly, Abner and Tinker each once, but Henrietta had not seen Collan since the night of the dance. That was a few weeks ago. Henrietta told herself this was for the best. She did not require him to hover over her as her protector. She had lived her life for years just fine without him. And yet, she . . . missed him. Missed his company. She wanted things between them to get back to how they always had been before. She wanted to smooth over this awkwardness. She was not sure how to go about doing that though. Despite their years of pranks and squabbling, somehow this breach seemed more serious than all the rest.

To keep her mind off Collan, she stayed busier than ever. She had come upon the idea to make and sell meat pies to the tourists. She had started by giving the Farrars some to take while they were hunting—she was so grateful to them for working so diligently on her log pile. They had said she required a huge supply to get through the winter. So now even the Farrar brothers were indirectly involved in the tourist trade as she gave them some of the cash she received selling the pies since they provided the meat.

She had not told the Farrars yet though, that she was still undecided about whether to stay here when her baby was due. She could admit to herself that the prospect was a bit frightening to have the baby with only Magpie possibly present.

Unlike Henrietta's turbulent feelings, Magpie was smiling more. She was genuinely excited about the baby and was making a beautiful beaded carrier that she showed Henrietta would strap over her back to carry her infant. One day Henrietta even caught her singing an Indian song while she was sewing.

Magpie had started storing food for them for the winter—smoked fish and a meat jerky. She also sold some of the same to the tourists. A couple tourists had even asked her to make moccasins for them that they would get from her the following summer.

But the tourist business in Estes Park was daily gradually dwindling with the chillier weather due. Conversations during mealtimes were less about local affairs. Newspapers were coming regularly with the mail, and the talk was more about what was happening in the outside world. There was much discussion of Colorado becoming a state instead of remaining a territory. Henrietta was surprised to hear that anyone was opposed to the idea. But it turned out Colorado had advantages staying as a territory—benefits supplied by the United States without putting up with the same obligations. Money for administering the government came from federal funds as a territory. There would probably be a vote on the issue in the following year.

President Grant was now reported as being despondent and grim despite winning reelection overwhelmingly in '72. Though there had been rumors of his heavy drinking in the past, she was fond of the President and did not think he had been imbibing for years. As far as she was concerned he had done some good, trying to reunite the country after the war. The president had bravely supported the Fifteenth Amendment which prohibited federal and state governments from denying a citizen voting privileges due to history of servitude or race. She had once read that he could not abide by any cruelty to animals and was especially kind to women and the downtrodden. But she knew his popularity with the public really suffered because of the economic depression of '73 and also because of the behavior of those who worked for him—several former military men who had served with him during the war—who were involved in numerous scandals, including allegations of bribery, cronyism, and fraud.

Some of these characters had become involved in the Whiskey Ring in which millions in taxes had been stolen from the federal government with the help of high officials, including Orville Babcock, the private secretary to the President. The distillers had bribed the government officials who had then helped them evade federal taxes on the whiskey they sold.

Furthermore, his Secretary of War, William Belknap, and his secretary's *wives* were found to have taken bribes in a trading post monopoly scandal, forcing soldiers on the western frontier and Indians to buy supplies at higher than market prices, leaving many destitute. Henrietta thought the President was being blamed unfairly for others' unscrupulous behavior, but Hank quickly pointed out that the President was the one who had chosen them.

Magpie cursed the President for the awful way the Indians were currently being treated, despite the President trying to pursue a peace policy with them—made futilely difficult by the ever-increasing westward expansion. The President had even initially appointed a Seneca Indian, Ely Parker, as Commissioner of Indian Affairs, but the gentleman was driven out of office unfairly due to prejudicial maneuvering, despite the fact that the man was a highly educated engineer who had served with Grant during the Civil War, had become a General and transcribed the articles of surrender at the end of the war.

Tinker agreed with her that the agents assigned to reservations were corrupt—there were food shortages with Indians starving on the reservations, yet they were not allowed to hunt for their own food. Getting to know Magpie had made all present at Henrietta's table more sensitive to the plight of the Indian, but there were few Americans who had any sympathy. Mainly the atrocities and drunkenness of the Indians made the papers, scarcely ever the horrible acts by the civilians and military. Henrietta suspected that Tinker had either taken part in or witnessed some of these tragedies as a scout for he became brooding and silent as Magpie complained about what she had experienced or heard.

But all talk of the world outside Estes Park came to a sudden end when Abner appeared again one day with the Farrar brothers. All were angry and heated and wanted to know if anything untoward had happened to Henrietta. From what she could quickly gather, Theodore Whyte, that stooge of Lord Dunraven, had become quite active again.

She sat at the end of her dining table and shook her head, trying not to look worried. "No, Whyte hasn't been by to see me." She glanced briefly at Magpie who was smirking. Magpie could not see why Henrietta made such a fuss about the man to her. Henrietta had told her several times that the man might have seen what had happened when Magpie gunned down her husband and cause some kind of trouble for them, but Magpie always just shrugged. She could also not fully comprehend the drama concerning land ownership since she didn't even think Henrietta or anyone could possess their own property to begin with.

Abner now frowned. "Well, his surveyor confirmed that Collan's and my land were properly filed and settled. So you know what he did?"

Henrietta was afraid to ask. "What?"

"He sent his low life cowboys—or should I say henchmen—over to our land and drove their cattle on to it. Can you imagine the gall?"

Henrietta was intensely aware that Collan was not with them all, sitting around the table. She was now more than ever afraid to ask what happened next. She did not want to hear that he had gotten into a fight and was now so badly off he could not ride over here. She puckered her brows. "So what happened then? Was there an argument?"

"No, the cowardly curs departed as soon as the cattle were on our land. We only found the extra herd, not them, but quickly realized whose they were."

She couldn't help asking, worriedly, "But where is Collan?"

"Oh, Tinker and he are driving the livestock back over the property line."

Henrietta blew out a long breath of relief. Collan was fine, and more than that, had a perfectly reasonable excuse for why he was not here now.

Hank spoke up. "So you know what happened next?"

Henrietta tried to concentrate on the topic at hand and not on Collan's whereabouts and asked, "What?"

"The man showed up personally at our place."

"Who?" she asked Hank. "Dunraven?"

Ike shook his head with an exasperated look. "No, Miss Henrietta. Aren't you listening? We're talking about Whyte now."

Henrietta swallowed. "Yes, yes, of course. So what did he say?"

"He told us *we're* on land belonging to Dunraven." Clint said resignedly.

Ike snorted. "Well, we already recognized *that* as a possibility."

"I just knew this was going to happen." Clint shook his head sadly.

Ike said excitedly, "But wait 'til you hear what ol' Hank told him."

Hank sat straighter. "Exactly what I said I would. Until he can prove how that wily Dunraven came by this land and made it all legal and such, we weren't going anywhere."

"And Dunraven can go to hell! That's what Hank told him." Ike added, grinning.

Clint kicked Ike underneath the table. "Don't tell her that, you oaf."

"Ow!" He glanced at Clint, clutching his leg. "Well, he *did*." He turned back to Henrietta. "And Whyte just turned his horse and deeeparted without another word. That's when Abner showed up at our place to tell us what had happened to Collan and him."

Clint then looked at Henrietta, worriedly. "He better not show up here next."

"Oh." She shook her head. "Oh, no. I don't think he will." She hoped she was correct.

Chapter Nineteen

A week later, Abner informed her that Whyte had his cowboys run their cattle onto Collan's and his land again, this time sprinkling the property with salt so the cattle would want to stay. Abner was hopping mad and was on his way to talking with Whyte himself. Henrietta felt dejected by the news.

Not only was Whyte causing unnecessary trouble for Abner and Collan, but this was huge news. And yes, okay, Collan was probably driving the cattle back over the property with Tinker and had a perfectly good excuse for not being here and telling her the news himself, but she couldn't help taking it as more.

Henrietta had apparently turned into nothing in Collan's eyes. They weren't even friends who shared their concerns with each other anymore. She felt like crying but managed to hold back the tears until Abner was out of sight over the ridgeline.

She sat down on her porch steps to brood, glad that she was all alone, with Magpie now hunting with the Farrars. Ring and Sally came over and both put their heads in her lap, and she slowly stroked their furs.

She couldn't believe she felt so sad about their state of affairs. Collan had been a nuisance and a pest to her since they were little kids. She should be relishing this break in their relations. But she wasn't. This time it felt so permanent. She wondered now if she had actually hurt Collan when she had become involved with her husband because she sure as rain felt hurt now herself by his rejection.

Her baby kicked and she tried pulling herself together, wiping her eyes with her sleeve.

She had so much to look forward to. She frowned determinedly. She was *not* going to let Collan ruin this special time in her life. No, she was not. Why he could just . . . he could just *go to hell* if he thought so.

Henrietta burst into tears again.

The next morning what she had been dreading might happen, occurred. She was in her yard, returning from fetching more water when Ring and Sally started barking ferociously from the porch. She saw the distinctive outline of Whyte on the ridge above her. No one else rode such a fine English mount with an attire to correspond.

She watched a moment more. Oh, Lord. No wonder everyone spoke of his cowboys as such a despicable lot. Even from a distance they looked like toughened criminals with their flashing guns and long spurs—she felt sorry for their horses—and one even had a whip in his hand. She could easily imagine these had been some of the same men who had filed all those false claims on the land.

They approached her slowly. Uncharacteristically, the dogs hurried off the porch and were now snarling. My God, these were the type of men who might kill her pooches to quiet them. She turned and urged the dogs back into her cabin, shutting the door tightly behind her. They continued to bark as she descended her porch steps into her yard again.

177

The men continued their unhurried way towards her property. Whyte turned around to make some comment and the cowboys snickered. For one crazy moment, she felt like fleeing. But she stood her ground as she watched them cross the river and enter her yard.

They surrounded her with their horses. Whyte dismounted with assurance and looked around at her outbuildings, her cabin, and finally studied her. She could just imagine some of the nasty thoughts that were entering his kind of mind—he was probably even trying to guess if she was with baby by her husband or after his passing.

Henrietta was suddenly angered. How dare he behave so rudely. The first thing he should have done was greet her civilly. Did he think he was some English lord and she a peasant? Well, this was part of America, Mister, and there were no nobility and those that showed up on these shores weren't even regarded highly by most working Americans either.

She decided she would have to be the better person, but she did suddenly regret that she was in her oldest dress—the one that was *sooo* comfortable in her present condition—but also in which the fabric was unfortunately faded and thin, therefore her now protruding belly button could be seen. Yet she hadn't been expecting anyone to stop by today. The tourists seemed to be gone. And if anyone had come by, she would have hurriedly changed in her bedroom to something more presentable if she had had her wits about her.

But she still didn't have her head about her because she realized she was letting his cowboys now leer at her breasts which had grown too big for the bodice of the dress—were the nipples showing, too? Oh, the horror.

She crossed her arms over her chest. Oh, *why* hadn't she changed her dress when she had put the dogs in the house? The dogs, who were now barking at a high pitch. The situation suddenly angered her even more.

She briefly looked Whyte up and down, scarcely holding in her disdain. "Good Morning, Mr. Whyte. What brings you to my home?" She blew out a breath. Now that wasn't proper. Her mother had taught her to be a lady. Manners, Henrietta. Remember your manners. So she persevered. "Would you and your men enjoy a refreshment? Perhaps some tea on my porch?"

Every single one of the men's mouths dropped. Even Whyte. But he quickly composed himself. "Good morning, Mrs. Schodde. I was hoping to discuss some business with you. A bit of tea would be welcome."

He motioned with his hand for her to proceed towards the porch steps, ignoring his men. Oh, but she was going to have some fun with this. Even if he tried to take her precious cabin or, God forbid, threaten dear Magpie and her with what he might have seen that day, she was determined now to have some merry devilment. She took a few steps, then turned back around to the dirty bunch of cowboys and asked, "Coming?"

They looked at one another puzzled and she added, "I would take it as an insult if you didn't want to join us."

They looked perplexed and stayed mounted. She continued. "Of course, if you don't like pie with your tea, you might not want to partake."

179

That did it. They all dismounted and hobbled their mounts while Whyte frowned at his men. She wanted to laugh out loud. The silly wannabe Lord was going to have to eat with his subjects.

As they all approached the cabin, Ring and Sally could now be heard growling and pouncing at the door they were so disturbed by the men's presence. She turned to Whyte. "I want to thank you for my beloved dogs. They're both so sweet." As if on cue, the dogs barked even more ferociously.

She walked up the steps and then slipped inside the cabin while the men took seats either at the table or on the porch steps. She quietly bolted the door. Once in the house her bravado started to fade as she glanced out the window while putting the tea kettle on the stove. Whyte was obviously angered and the men were looking amused . . . but still dangerous. Lord, that gun was big in that short one's holster.

She swallowed and then blew out a breath. She could do this. She really could. She hadn't been in training all these years with Collan and his and hers antics for nothing. She walked to her bedroom and put on her most conservative dress. The one with the buttoned sleeves, high, high collar and thick fabric that revealed nothing. Unfortunately, the dress hiked higher in the front to cover her belly, but there was nothing for it. She looked towards the front door. The dogs continued a low growl. She was so proud of them, trying to protect her. She would give them extra stew tonight.

She went back into the kitchen and cut slices of pie. She placed some everyday ceramicware cups on a tray. She then went into her trunk in her bedroom and pulled out her most delicate porcelain tea set that she only used for extra special occasions. It was a service for four. She would give one cup to Whyte and save the other three for his most appalling looking cowboys.

She went back into the kitchen and prepared the tea. She had to make multiple trips in and out of the cabin to bring everything over to the outside table, slamming the door each time to keep her faithful, snarling pooches inside, but eventually all was ready to be portioned.

She briefly considered serving Whyte last but thought that was going too far. She handed a dainty cup and saucer filled with tea to him. "Milk? Sugar?"

He shook his head. "No, thank you." He raised his cup but then returned it to the saucer, knowing he should wait until the hostess was seated and had taken a sip first of her own.

She looked around. Oh, yes. The one with the big gun, the one with the whip and the one with a large blade hanging off his belt. She served them tea in the special set. They scarcely could figure out how to hold the cups. They all requested generous amounts of sugar.

Finally she served the remaining couple men and herself in the everyday cups.

Once the pie was served, she sat down across from Whyte at the table. The men with the tiny, fine cups were now drinking, gripping the items as if they were beer mugs. Oh, no. That wouldn't do.

She turned to Big Gun and frowned like a prudish marm. She said in a pleasant voice, "Hasn't anyone taught you how to hold a tea cup?" She gripped her cup with her forefinger and thumb and raised her pinky to put on an especially effeminate show. "Like this." She looked around at all the men who were watching her with amused curiosity—all except Whyte, who could not hold back a glare. "I would appreciate if you men all showed your proper manners and drank the same way." One of the men snorted, but they all obeyed.

Whyte glanced around at his ridiculous looking men and turned back to her. "Mrs. Schodde, this isn't a tea party with a set of dolls. We have business to discuss."

She raised her hand imperiously. "Please, Mr. Whyte. Your manners. Not until we have all finished our refreshments." Another cowboy snorted back a chuckle. The frown Whyte wore deepened, but he complied and took a bite of the pie. She could tell he liked it. He asked her, "Do you often bake?"

She fanned her hand once like a lady. "Oh, yes. Breads, cakes, pies, and German strudel."

That got Big Blades attention. "You make strudel?" She looked at him more closely. He did look of German descent, but what a *dummkopf* to have gotten involved with Whyte.

She smiled. *"Jawohl."*

Whyte then suggested, "Perhaps some arrangement could be made where we buy—"

"Mr. Whyte! Your manners again. Everyone is not finished eating. Please no business until then." Several men chuckled as Whyte now huffed loudly.

She could tell she had pushed her luck too far. It wouldn't do to humiliate Lord Wannabe anymore in front of his men, and further, she could see that the men had all already gobbled down their pies. She said, "Ah, I see we have finished."

Whyte glanced around. "Yes, we have." He then said sarcastically to his men. "If you'd please excuse us."

The men slowly stood and walked over to their horses. They obviously were sorry to see the show come to an end.

She looked at Whyte inquiringly and waited for him to start talking. She suddenly felt frightened again but tried not to show it.

He puckered his brow. "Mrs. Schodde, it has come to my attention that this property you have claimed is part of the Dunraven estate."

She almost sagged with relief. Was that all? As long as he didn't try to put Magpie in jail she could deal with any of this other nonsense. She smiled. "Whatever do you mean, Mr. Whyte? I purchased this cabin and land properly from the original owners."

"That is a matter of opinion, Mrs. Schodde."

"I highly doubt that, Mr. Whyte." She replied curtly.

"Lord Dunraven is a powerful personage who can apply all his resources to—"

"Well, he hasn't met me!"

Whyte stood. "I can see it will do no good to simply command you to vacate the premises."

"Certainly not." She stood also.

"I'll be sending my surveyor over and you can be sure your title will be investigated. Expect to hear back from me in the next few weeks."

"With pleasure, Mr. Whyte!" She swirled around him to her cabin entrance. The dogs had resumed barking again with her raised voice. She inwardly thought, title? What *title*? Just where was that thing?

Before she could open the door and slip inside she heard a familiar voice. "What the hell is going on here, Whyte?"

She turned to see Hank and his brothers, with Magpie following, riding into the yard. Oh, thank God. Some cavalry for support.

Whyte answered, "None of your business, Farrar."

Henrietta then looked around at the scene. Oh, no. The cowboys all had a hand on their holsters and were frowning. Clint and Ike were dismounting hurriedly and reaching for their rifles. And Whyte? He was staring at Magpie with an intent expression, probably trying to recall when he had seen her last. Henrietta had to put a stop to all of this. And now. But what was she going to do?

She looked again at the precious Farrar brothers, trying to defend her and dear, dear Magpie and knew she just had to do the one thing that went completely against her grain. She had not bought a house and finally become an independent woman who made her own decisions to lower herself to this. But she couldn't think of any other solution at the moment so she forced herself to do it.

She started sniffling and sobbing—loudly. "Oh, me. Poor me." Sob, sob. "A helpless woman, attacked by robber barons." Hacking sobs. She could hear the dogs now howling and wailing. They wanted to get to her and console her.

She collapsed on the porch step for effect—bent over, her head in her arms. She could hear Clint say as he walked towards her, "Now look what you've done, Whyte." He patted her back, softly. "Please, don't cry, Miss Henrietta. You know I can't take it."

She ventured a quick peek at the remaining others. Magpie was smirking. She wasn't fooled, but those cowboys Whyte had brought were looking at her sympathetically—she guessed they really had liked the pie and didn't want to ruin any chances for more, let alone Herr Big Blade and the prospect of strudel—he apparently knew how much more difficult and time-consuming strudel was to make. He sure didn't want to be on her bad side. But Lord Wannabe? Well, he just looked disgusted.

She lowered her head again and shook her shoulders, for more of a show, as if now silently crying.

Finally it worked. Whyte commanded, "Ride out."

Henrietta looked up and saw them gallop away.

Clint helped her stand. Hank was shaking his head and asking, "What happened?"

Henrietta brushed her dress. Darn, one of her good dresses was now all dusty, but she looked over at Hank and said, "Oh, he's trying to take my property, also, but he isn't going to get it."

Hank frowned. "I'm riding over to see Abner and Collan and let them know."

Ike, who had been surprisingly quiet, finally spoke up. "You mean before we *eat*?"

Hank nodded once. "This shouldn't wait."

"Awww." He stamped his foot but started to remount.

Henrietta raised her hand. "Wait. Just a minute." She hurried into her cabin as the dogs burst out. She grabbed a big basket and placed a cherry pie in it. She tossed several meat pies in a napkin and placed them on top. She looked around. There was no way to give them any of the stew. No, there was. She spooned some of it in one of her baking dishes and wrapped another napkin over it. She grabbed the handle of the basket and flew out the door.

She walked over to Ike. "Take this, but try not to toss it or the stew will spill over before you get there."

Ike smiled. "Thanks, Miss Henrietta. Do I have to share it?"

Clint and Hank both said, "Yes."

Henrietta and Magpie watched them ride toward Collan's. She probably should have stopped them from going. She had handled the situation just fine on her own. But perhaps, just perhaps, when Collan heard about her recent going-ons, he would finally come over for a visit. She wanted to talk to him.

Chapter Twenty

Theodore Whyte sat on the front porch of his cabin, adjusted his cravat and the lapels of his coat, and opened the newspaper. He crossed his legs and tried perusing the headlines. But he couldn't seem to pay attention to what was written on the page. Things were not going how he had planned.

He looked up and watched Griff Evans, who acted as a type of steward to Dunraven and his holdings, cross the yard and open the door to his family's home. Before he entered he gave a jovial wave over to Theodore. He waved back but inwardly shook his head. Any merriment coming out of Griff Evans was all false cheer. Anybody with eyes could see that. The man was not the type to kill a person and take it lightly. But that was what Griff had done last year in some drunken affair before Theodore had arrived to stay in Estes Park. Theodore did not know the full details, however, the final results were that even though Griff did not end up going to jail, he was a broken, damaged man nonetheless, who was shunned by much of the Estes Park community. That had not always been the situation. Apparently, he had been a much-loved person in the settlement before he had become involved with Dunraven and the gunning down tragedy had occurred.

Theodore had overheard Griff talking to his wife a few weeks ago. Once they saved enough money, they were going to leave Estes Park and try starting anew as lodgekeepers. Theodore would then try to buy their home because unlike them, he wanted to remain in Estes Park. He liked the climate, the bountiful fishing and hunting, the views and more important, he truly believed eventually he could become a person of power and prominence in the area.

Growing up in Devonshire, as the younger son of a British colonel, what he had lacked in riches, he did not now lack in ambition and cleverness. Just look at what he had accomplished thus far. He had travelled to America a decade ago, had tried his hand in mining and trapping, and then struck fast when the real opportunity had presented itself.

Three years ago, he had walked into a Denver watering hole and recognized Lord Dunraven at the bar. He had walked up to him and presumed a connection with the man since Dunraven and his father were both Irish landholders. He had talked as if he were an expert on Estes Park though he had only visited the area once or twice himself. The following year he had acted as a guide for Dunraven when the Lord had wanted to hunt in Estes Park. And then, *and then*, Theodore's true genius had come to the fore.

Theodore had suggested forming the Estes Park Company, better known in these parts now as the English Company. Since Dunraven was a foreigner and could not take part in the homesteading act, Theodore had suggested that they find men who were able to do so and then purchase the properties for cheap back from them. Theodore had had no trouble finding unscrupulous individuals off the streets of Denver. Everything had been going exactly to plan—uh, that was until the last year.

The English Company had accumulated vast tracts of land throughout Estes Park. Of course, most claims had not been improved with a shelter of some kind as required by law, but he scarcely thought anyone would take notice. After all, what the English Company was accomplishing in Estes Park was occurring all over different parts of the West as the English acquired land the Americans still impoverished from the Civil War could not purchase themselves.

But he hadn't counted on how much resistance the English Company would find from the local settlers. Theodore had naively supposed that as long as he played the part of an aristocratic arrogant Englishman that the American rustics would fall in line. He had equipped himself with fine mounts and hunting dogs, shown off his riding skills by jumping gates with ease and had dressed impeccably no matter the occasion. But instead of showing respect, these local settlers had looked at him as an oddity.

He recounted his efforts the last several months. First, he had tried bluster and merely commanded certain settlers to leave their property as Dunraven now owned it. That certainly hadn't worked with settlers such as the Fergusons. He curled his lip. That Ferguson woman had had a particularly smart mouth with him and their situation was still up in the air. Unfortunately, the surveyor found that their house, if not their remaining land, was on their own property, and he just knew that that stubborn woman would run a lodge for tourists if nothing else. So he had moved on for now.

Then he had thought if he harassed certain other settlers, they would fold. He had almost ended up in the creek in an altercation—how undignified—after he had instructed his men to tear down the fence of that German. Oh, the German had finally departed, but now Theodore realized that he could probably have used that man and so his one true success was essentially a failure.

And why could he use that cloddish German? Because Theodore had written Dunraven that the tourist industry could perhaps prove more profitable in the end than the cattle business. And what had he received in reply? Oh, a letter from Dunraven that had sent him into a complete tumult.

Dunraven now thought he wanted to build a hotel, someplace absolutely splendid, for his guests and him to stay at, and *not only that*, he would be visiting in the next year to pick out a site—oh, and of course, Theodore knew, to assess his progress with land acquisitions.

First off, just where was Theodore supposed to find all the skilled craftsmen to build that hotel? That German had carved amazingly intricate designs into just the pine porch columns of his cabin, and Theodore had essentially forced him away. He shook his head, exasperated.

But Theodore had prudently decided that he would have to get quite aggressive in his land dealings if he was going to have any real successes to show Dunraven. So he had driven cattle over several settlers' properties. Multiple times. And even sprinkled salt so the cattle would want to stay. But that was when he had discovered the grit of Abner Sprague and Collan Wallace.

Theodore had always supposed his greatest threat in the community would be that cunning lawyer Alex MacGregor. Hell, he seemed to be as ambitious as Theodore with not only a law practice, but a booming homestead and a toll road serving tourists.

MacGregor had made it plain up front that he was opposed to any land swindling and planned to take Dunraven to court. Theodore had at least had the satisfaction of knowing that anything Alex the Nuisance did would take years in all probability to accomplish with the judicial system.

He blew out a breath. Such a pity to be at odds with one of the most refined families in the area. Theodore pictured a day when he would bring a wife here who would want to make friends.

Anyways, his mind was wandering. What he really should be doing now is concentrating on that Abner Sprague. That shorty was a force to reckon with and could prove to be the biggest threat to his enterprise. Yesterday afternoon he had stormed over here, making threats if Dunraven and his men caused any more trouble for his friend Collan's and his homesteads. Not only that, he had made it obvious that he had kept track of every single going-ons with Theodore, listing every settler that he knew Theodore and his team had harassed one way or another. Apparently, the man got around the community regularly and knew how to establish allies. The stupid busybody.

So this morning Theodore had tried going after what he assumed would be the easy targets, and he had brought his men for additional intimidation. Theodore pursed his lips. He actually might have found it amusing what that Schodde woman had done if he hadn't felt so humiliated at the time. Serving tea to his rough cowboys. He shook his head and rolled his eyes.

But there was something peculiar about today's visit besides the tea party and he was now trying to remember what. Hmmm. What was it?

Oh, yes. When he had said that she was on Dunraven property she had almost looked relieved. What could that possibly mean? What a strange reaction. Had that Schodde woman expected him to say something more damaging? What could that be? He scarcely knew the woman, having only met her when she had taken away those useless mutts.

No, wait. There had been that time when he had heard a gun go off and looked over her ridge. Let's see. What had he seen? Oh, yes. The Schodde woman had been talking with another woman, who had been dressed *like that squaw he saw today in her yard,* both seemingly oblivious at the time to the fact that some drunk was stumbling and swaying behind them until he finally mounted his horse. Theodore had turned away in disgust at that point and rode off. It had been none of his concern and he hadn't wanted to get involved in any possible sordid mess.

But was there more to it? Was the lowlife actually drunk or *hit* by the gunfire he had heard and by that Schodde woman? Theodore highly doubted it had been the squaw at fault. Why would the Schodde woman possibly want to cover for an Indian savage? Americans hated them—Americans were not as enlightened as the

English. The whole situation was a puzzle for now, but he had the feeling that this salacious tidbit he had seen might come in handy if that woman required more convincing to leave that property.

He frowned. But for now, he required a plan that would get a whole group of these settlers to leave. He wasn't sure what that was and would have to think about it later. He was being motioned over to come in for dinner. Probably the usual dull fare. No pie. Nor strudel. Not that he really knew what the hell strudel was anyways.

Chapter Twenty-one

Collan could not believe what he was hearing. He felt terrible. "So she was actually sobbing?"

Clint nodded glumly. "Just awful to take." He reined his mount away from the men so they could not see his face.

Collan was now really concerned. "What did they do to her?" He looked around at the remaining brothers, waiting for one to answer.

Hank shrugged sheepishly as his horse side-stepped, sensing the strain of the men. "We didn't ask such a personal question. We came over here before we got all the details."

Collan strode rapidly across his yard towards his horse. "Well, I'm finding out just what the hell happened and so help me God, they're going to pay."

Hank nodded. "We'll find Abner and join you at her house."

Tinker grimly headed towards his own mount without saying a word.

Ike then spoke up. "But what about all this grub she packed in this basket I've been hauling around. Ain't we gonna at least eat some first?"

Collan stopped and turned around, frowning. "She gave you food to take before you came here?" Something was not quite adding up here, but he didn't have time now to ponder it.

Clint reined back around and nodded. "Miss Henrietta knew we were hungry."

"We'll eat it back at her house, Ike." Hank commanded.

"Awww, hell. I'm starved." Ike complained, but he followed his brothers to find Abner.

Tinker remained silent as they hurried over to Etta's, so Collan had his thoughts to himself. He hadn't seen Etta since the dance a few weeks ago—by his own choice and for his own self-protection. He had behaved like an ass that night, trying to plant a kiss on her. What had he been thinking? He hadn't been, that's for sure. He had been embarrassed beyond dreams when she had fled and could scarcely manage a word on the ride home. The situation had been humiliating and . . . hurtful. Once again.

Just when was he going to learn? She couldn't have made it any plainer over the years that she harbored absolutely no romantic feelings toward him. Hell, she married another man. And okay, he hadn't exactly given the impression at the time—when Collan, Etta and her siblings, had all been mining in Breckenridge—that his feelings towards her had developed and matured into something more than his viewing her as just his partner in pranks. But he hadn't felt then that their relationship required spelling out and if it had, he was sure he would have gotten around to telling her so eventually. As far as he had been concerned, she was *his* Etta and always had been, and everyone had seemed to realize it except her future husband when he arrived on the scene.

Collan had been flabbergasted, catching them courting. And then hurt. So he had backed off, waiting for Etta to come to her senses. But she had only fallen deeply in love and everyone had realized that also.

So Collan had departed Breckenridge—broke financially and with his parents begging him to help with their general store back East—and done his best over the years to forget her.

And he had done well at that. In fact, he had convinced himself that his feelings for her had been nothing more than youthful folly and infatuation. He had actually initially felt annoyed when he had received the letter from Herm, requesting that he look out for her in Estes Park. Annoyed because she would take time away from building his new homestead and perhaps . . . annoyed because he hadn't wanted to take the chance of her slipping underneath his well-formed defenses.

But she had slowly, but surely, insinuated herself again into his passions so that he couldn't do a thing in Estes Park now without thinking about her constantly. And wanting to see her *all the time*. The last few weeks had been torture, staying away from her. And he had almost given in a few times, but then he would hear some report about her from Abner or Tinker that she was doing fine and he would control himself and stay at his spread. After all, he knew it was in his best interest to conquer these romantic feelings. He was more than tired of her hurting him.

But this whole situation now with that Englishman and his rough cowboys was different. Even if Etta and he were fated to be nothing more than pals— and he would do his best to remind himself of that

196

often—he still had an obligation to look out for her. He had promised her family he would.

So onward he rode, eagerly—*damnation!*—and dreadfully, waiting to find out exactly what had happened today and also, sadly, to see whether his interference was welcome or not since their awkward last encounter.

Collan stopped and looked over the ridge at Etta's homestead. All looked quiet. Nothing moved in the yard except the tail of that horse of hers, flicking at the few flies. Ring and Sally were sleeping on the porch. He wasn't sure whether to feel relieved or not. She could still be inside, distressed. He kicked his horse into a trot and descended towards her yard.

Once there, Ring and Sally came off the porch to greet Tinker and him, but Etta did not appear at the door. He dismounted and handed his reins to Tinker. "Mind tending the horses?"

Tinker shook his head and took the reins, guiding Collan's and his mount over to the river for a drink.

Collan stepped onto her porch with trepidation and knocked softly as he pushed the door open. He quickly glanced around the room. Magpie was at the dining table sewing.

Then he saw Etta at the cookstove. She turned around, hearing the door and smiled. "Oh, you came!"

She dropped her spatula onto the side of the griddle and hurried over to where he was standing. "You haven't been to visit for so long!" She wrapped her arms around him in a warm embrace and his mouth dropped open. This was *not* the reception he had been expecting.

He wanted to hug her back but refrained—they were pals, remember—and instead patted her back. His first thought was that she had grown. Her belly now stuck out more noticeably and bumped into his hips. His next impression was that she did not appear to be in distress.

He pulled away from the embrace and looked her over. Perhaps she was putting on a cheerful act and really was upset about the day's events. After all, this was the woman who was proud of her new independent ways and probably wouldn't want to admit she had felt defenseless and vulnerable.

But she walked back to the cookstove and flipped something over. "Guess what? I'm making potato pancakes and using my own potatoes that I grew myself!" She smiled again. "Want one?"

"Sure." He took a seat across from Magpie—who was essentially ignoring him—still feeling confused. He couldn't seem to form the words, he had so many questions he wanted to ask Etta. He knew he should start with inquiring about the cowboys today and her sobbing, but he couldn't help wanting to ask first: What about *the dance* and his horrible attempt at *kissing* her? Was it all forgotten? Were they just going to act now as if it hadn't happened?

Etta turned around once again from the stove and smiled warmly. So okay, apparently so. And if so, then his plan for them to be just pals had suddenly become a lot easier. He could do this. He really could.

He could distance himself enough from this woman so his feelings would no longer get hurt.

He decided to wait for everyone else to arrive before he started grilling Etta about the day's events. He knew they all wanted to know the specific details as much as he did. He looked over at Magpie, "So what you makin' this time? A shirt for me?"

Magpie looked up and snorted. "No. You have clothes." She went back to sewing.

Etta butted in. "Magpie's making another shirt for Tinker. He's been filling out."

He looked over at Etta. "So have you."

"You think so?" She brushed down her skirt with her free hand. "The baby's been kicking more." She then turned back around to the stove quickly. Collan knew why. That slip had just been a reminder to them both of the night of the dance. He blew out a breath. Sometime they were going to have to talk about it. But not today. And not in front of everyone else.

Etta placed her concoction on a plate and put it in front of Collan. She waited while he took a bite of the pancake and then asked, "So what do you think?"

He looked up at her. "It's good."

"I know! And I got more still coming in. This was just the first crop of potatoes I picked."

Tinker walked in unobtrusively and took a seat next to Magpie. She scooted over a bit to give herself more room to continue sewing. Etta didn't bother to ask but placed a pancake in front of Tinker.

He looked up at her and gave her a good stare. She smiled and said, "Potato pancakes with potatoes from my own garden. Eat up, Tinker."

Collan wanted to say to Tinker: Yep, you heard her correctly. She's excited about her potatoes. Forget about the fact that she was potentially mauled by five scoundrels today. We're talking about her potatoes. Isn't that nice?

At that moment, Abner and the Farrar brothers all walked in the open door, taking seats at the table.

Clint looked over worriedly. "Hi, Miss Henrietta. You feeling better?"

She smiled. "I got potato pancakes. Want some?"

Clint frowned, not fully comprehending the situation.

"It'll just be a moment to make some more." Etta turned back to the stove.

Ike placed the basket in front of himself and started pulling out dishes and unwrapping napkins. "Finally. Hank wouldn't let me eat until we got back here."

Etta turned back around and looked over at Hank. "Why ever not?"

Hank shrugged. "I thought we should get back."

"Well, never mind. You all can have potato pancakes with what's in the basket."

They watched her fuss over her stove—all except Magpie who kept on sewing—and remained quiet until she had taken a seat with them and was eating one of her pancakes herself.

Abner was done waiting for the conversation to start. "I'm sorry to hear what happened to you today."

Etta frowned. "I can see why everyone is so mad at Whyte. He certainly is an arrogant one."

Collan leaned back and crossed his arms. "Etta, why don't you tell everyone exactly what happened today."

Etta swallowed. "Well, first Whyte and his five cowboys all rode into my yard and surrounded me."

Collan frowned. "Did they threaten you?"

"Not in so many words. But that Mister Whyte told me he had business to discuss."

She took another bite and Collan motioned with his hand for her to continue. "And then what?"

"Well, actually I got angry. I didn't like the way they were looking at me and if you must know, I was wearing my oldest, most faded dress—it's just so comfortable—but that's still no excuse for the staring that went on." She shook her head disapprovingly.

Collan frowned. He could just imagine the lascivious looks she had gotten. But the question was whether the men had acted on it in any way. "So what did you do? Did you try to defend yourself?"

Etta sat straighter. "I served them tea on the porch."

There was a collective: *"What?!"*

"Well, somebody had to teach those men some manners and the proper way to behave with new acquaintances." She chuckled. "You should have seen them holding up their pinkies to drink out of the cups. I had pulled my fine porcelain set out of the trunk just to make it more difficult." She giggled. "It was so funny, actually." Magpie smiled but kept sewing.

"Did Whyte find it amusing?" Collan already knew the answer but asked anyways.

Etta shook her head. "Not particularly. He basically insisted we talk business. So I finally let him because I could see that his men had all finished their pieces of pie by then."

Ike interrupted. "You got any more pie, Miss Henrietta?" He looked at the empty plate that was all that remained from the one she had placed in the basket. "I didn't get near nothing from this one."

Etta got up and went to her cupboard. She returned with a jar full of cookies and sat back down. "Just these."

Ike took one out and around a mouthful asked, "Then what happened? How come you were bawling out in the yard?"

She waved her hand dismissively. "Oh, Whyte just said that this was not my property, and I informed him in no uncertain terms that yes, it was." She turned to Abner. "What happened when you talked to him? Didn't you go over there to have a word?"

Abner straightened. "Yes, I did. Let's just say that it turned into a wordy row."

Etta nodded and Collan looked at her, narrowing his eyes. She was acting nonchalant either because she had managed the situation just fine or she was holding back something.

Ike frowned. "But I don't get it. Why were you crying?"

Etta drew in a breath and said in a high-pitched tone, "Well, the whole state of affairs just finally got to me and I couldn't hold it in anymore." She sniffled once.

Collan nodded sagely and said, "Oh, I bet." as Clint blew out a sorry breath and slumped.

Collan raised both brows and gave her a suspicious look which she caught. He knew Etta and he knew every inflection of her voice. That weeping had been just an act. She briefly frowned at him, then turned away and said, "But everything is perfectly in control and I'm sure this will all turn out as it should."

Collan persisted, "So is your place going to be surveyed?"

Etta nodded. "That's what he said."

"And where is your title?" he asked.

Etta ignored the question and asked, cheerfully, "Does anybody else want a cookie?"

They all shook their heads.

As Collan said again, "Your title?" Etta jumped up and said, "Look what Magpie's making for Tinker. Oh, and Tinker, I meant to tell you that your playing was just lovely at the dance. I didn't know you were musical."

Collan saw her blushing after inadvertently blurting out another reference to that embarrassing evening, but nobody seemed to noticed.

Tinker nodded. "Thank you, Henrietta. I haven't touched a fiddle for a while. Didn't know if I could, but I suddenly had a hankering."

The table then turned to look at the shirt Magpie was holding up. But something was up with Etta. She was discreetly trying to get Collan's attention by craning her neck towards the door. She wanted to talk to him outside.

He couldn't resist and asked, "Is something wrong with your neck, Etta?"

She frowned, "No, why would you ask, Collie?"

203

He chuckled. "No reason. Want to show me where your potatoes are growing?"

"Yes! Let's go outside." She hurried towards the door but turned back around to say, "You all can just relax and enjoy yourselves. This will only take a moment."

Collan followed her out the door and they headed towards her garden plot. Once there he turned to her and said, "Okay, so you played one of your pranks with the tea party, Etta. But where's your title?"

She clasped her hands together. "Well, see, I'm not sure."

"*What*?"

"The family who owned this place were supposed to mail it to me, but they haven't yet."

Collan held his head in his hands. "Oh, my God." The purchase of her cabin had taken place before he had arrived. He had assumed everything had proceeded as it should.

She wrung her hands. "See, I bought it when Alex was away doing his lawyering so I couldn't get his advice. But I asked when he returned and Alex said that I probably had done okay but to let him know if anything went wrong. I just forgot about the title with everything else that's been happening."

"What did you do on the day of the sale?"

"Well, the family signed over their copy of the title in front of me so I know they did that. But then the husband said that I had to register it in Denver, and I told him that I didn't know when I was going to Denver, and he said that they were going there next before they moved to Wyoming, and I asked whether he would mind registering it for me, and he said he would and then he would mail the title back to me, but I realize I never got it."

"And you don't actually know if this property is registered in your name."

She blew out a breath. "No. But I wrote a letter to the family today, asking for the title." She pulled an envelope out of her pocket. "I'll try mailing it with tomorrow's stage."

He looked at the address: To the Postmaster, Wyoming Territory. He looked up. "You don't know where they actually live."

She shook her head. "No."

"So I guess you're going to Denver to find out what happened."

"Well, first I want to see if they write me back. I think I should give it a few weeks. Then I'll go to Denver if they don't."

He blew out a breath. "Or I can go to Denver for you."

"Would you?" She looked relieved.

"Yes, but . . ." He hesitated. He hadn't planned on getting involved with the next topic just yet, but plodded on, knowing it was the correct thing to do. "I think you should go yourself. And . . . and have your baby there—where you can get help if anything should go wrong."

Her eyes filled with tears. "I know. I've been worrying about that. But Collan . . . I'm so afraid. I could lose the baby just on the bumpy stage ride there."

Collan looked at her and felt hopeless. He wondered whether the initial warm greeting had been because she had honestly been happy to see him or whether she was just more interested in him helping with the title. He felt a jab of that familiar hurt feeling again. He tamped it down because . . . did it matter? There was going to be no distance between them. He could not view her as just his pal. She always drew him in.

Chapter Twenty-two

Henrietta sat on her front porch, petting Ring and Sally, trying to remain calm. She had waited several weeks, but no title had arrived in the mail. Luckily at least, she had also seen no sign of a surveyor.

But she also fretted about what to do with her baby. The weather was decidedly colder, and they had recently even had a couple brief snow storms though the dusting had melted quickly. But if she was going to leave the area and have her baby with adequate help, she had to do it now.

Everyone seemed to be worried about her and she had had frequent visitors the last few weeks. Abner and Tinker both had swung by a couple times, inquiring after her, though Tinker had spent most of his time talking to Magpie and even going on a ride with her along the river.

Clara had brought her a baby outfit that she had sewn, and Sal had given her a small quilt that she had made, but neither Clara nor Sal would tell Henrietta what she should do. Finally, yesterday afternoon the Farrar brothers had stopped by with a cradle they had constructed in the evenings and the situation had suddenly seemed even more real. Henrietta had burst into tears, saying how she was so moved by their kindness, but the truth was also that now she felt in an uproar, trying to decide what to do.

She continued stroking Ring and Sally, pondering. The one person she had not seen for weeks was Collan, though Abner and Tinker had passed on salutations from him. She had thought that they had gotten over any awkwardness between them when he had visited the day of her famous encounter with the cowboys. But in thinking back now she realized that she had been the one acting as if things were completely the same between them while he had not been exactly his usual easy going self around her.

She blew out a long breath. She wasn't going to fret about Collan. There were just so many things she could get upset about at one time, and she tried reassuring herself now as she had the last few weeks that eventually relations between Collan and her would return to how they had always been. How could they not? They had known each other for too long to let a drunken attempt at kissing her come between them.

She briefly glanced up at her ridge now and saw Collan's familiar silhouette. She felt an immediate jolt of excitement and jumped out her chair as Ring and Sally started wagging their tails. She smiled warmly and waved and waited for him to enter her yard. She could see as he approached that he also was smiling—though kind of a held-back version—and she warmed inside.

She descended her steps as he dismounted in her yard. "Hi, Collan. Nice to see you." She wanted to give him a hug—that was so strange that she kept having that urge lately when seeing him—but refrained, somehow sensing that it wasn't the thing to do between them just now and perhaps never again.

He turned to look at her as he slipped the bridle off his horse and placed a rope collar around his horse's neck. As he led his horse over to the stable, he said. "You're getting big, Etta. You look ready to pop."

She smiled some more. She couldn't hold in her happiness at seeing him. Somehow, she felt everything was going to be okay now that he was here. "Want something to eat? I got stew cooking."

"You bet. I'll be inside in a minute. Let me just hitch my horse."

She turned and strolled to her cabin, holding her hands behind her back. She couldn't seem to shake this feeling of exhilaration at seeing him. She shook her head. Carrying this baby sure did funny things to her emotions. She entered her cabin, walked over to her cook stove and began stirring the pot.

A few moments later, he entered her home and closed the door. He looked around. "Where's Magpie?"

"Hunting with Ike. She said she'd be back later today."

Collan sat at the table and she placed a bowl of stew in front of him, then served herself. She felt a little strange being with him alone. Perhaps because it so seldom had occurred before. She took a bite of her stew. She couldn't seem to calm down and swallowed with difficulty. She looked over at him. He was playing with the meat in his bowl. Were they back to being completely awkward with each other? She started to feel disappointed when he finally spoke up. "Etta, we have to talk."

She nodded, wondering which topic he found important—the baby, their relationship, or the title.

209

"I want you to go to Denver to have the baby. Will you do that for me? I'm too worried that something will go wrong if you have it here." He frowned, waiting for her to argue.

But she looked at him and nodded. Her decision was suddenly made. And she wasn't quite sure why his asking her to go made all the difference, but it did. "Yes, I'll go. I guess I should leave this week."

He nodded. "There's a stage you can take tomorrow to Denver. I passed by and chatted with Clara before I came here. Clara thinks it's probably the last one for the season."

"A stage. Yes, I see." And abruptly one of her main concerns about leaving returned full force. She blinked back tears and pushed her bowl away, her hunger gone.

Collan frowned again. "It's not that bad. Perhaps you can return in the spring—"

She interrupted. "Of course, I'll come back. It's not that. It's just . . ."

"What?"

She looked at him earnestly and whispered, "Do you know how much this baby means to me? I think I'll about pass away from grief if I lose it."

He shook his head. "Don't say that, Etta. You have your whole life ahead of you."

She raised her hands. "But I'll have nothing . . . nothing to remind me so much of Charles. Do you know how much we wanted children and they never came? This baby would have meant so much to Charles. I don't want to lose it." Tears ran down her face now.

Collan tried to give her the reassurance he couldn't give. "You won't lose the baby . . ."

"I hope not. But I can't forget how bumpy the ride here was and I'm *terrified* if I step on that stage that all the juggling will cause something to go wrong."

He shook his head exasperated. "Well, you can't walk there."

She nodded. "I know. I was thinking that perhaps I could ride there on my horse and then when I get to an uneven part I could get off and walk for a bit and then get back on to ride when the trail is smoother again."

He blew out a long breath. "You want to ride there."

She looked at him. "Yes."

He shut his eyes briefly then opened them again. "Well, I'm not letting you go by yourself."

She hoped she wasn't looking too pleadingly at him, but she really wanted him to come to the next conclusion.

He looked at her hesitantly. "And I suppose by your look that you would like me to go with you."

"Would you?" She hadn't thought it all the way through before, or perhaps she had and never thought it would come to pass, but suddenly now it was very important that Collan come with her. She wanted his support. She knew she could trust him. She did not want to go without him. "Please?"

He started chuckling disparagingly and placed his head in his hands. "No matter what I do, I can't . . ."

She looked at him and bit back a smile, knowing he was going with her. "You can't what?"

"Escape you." He raised his head.

"Escape me? Why would you want to do that? Haven't I always been your sole source of entertainment?" She wiped her tears with her sleeves and grinned widely. She was so happy.

Collan scowled. "You do know that if I go and something happens, I know squat shit about how to have a baby."

She waved her hand dismissively. "I'm sure the baby's not due for weeks still."

Magpie heard her as she opened the door. She smirked. "Baby come soon."

Ike followed her in. "How soon, Miss Magpie?"

They all looked at her expectantly. Magpie would not answer so Henrietta said, "Collan has agreed to ride with me to Denver to have the baby. Isn't that wonderful?"

"I come with you." Magpie said.

That made Henrietta even happier, but then she realized the implications. "But who will watch over my homestead and the livestock while we're gone?"

Ike lifted the lid over the pot of stew. "Can I have some? Smells great. I thought I was going to be eating more trout today. Anyways, Clint, Hank and I can watch over your place. We'll take turns."

"Oh, thank you. I'll make sure there's plenty of cooked food the first few days." Henrietta kept smiling.

Ike sat down at the table. "Then I'll take the first shift. Did you make any pie, Miss Henrietta?"

She stood up. "Yep. Let me get you some stew first." She turned to Collan who was staring into space, thinking about something. "What about your homestead,

212

Collan? Do you think Tinker will mind being there by himself?"

He came out of his reverie. "Huh? Oh, no. Tinker will be fine. I just hope I can say the same for myself."

She laughed. "You've turned into such a worrier, Collan. I'm sure things will be just perfect now that we've made our plan. I'm suddenly very hungry again. How about you, Collan?"

He stood. "No, thanks. I've had enough for today."

Three days later, Collan, Etta and Magpie started out towards Denver on what appeared to be an unseasonably warm day. Etta was cheerful at first and couldn't keep from chattering away. Collan grunted replies when necessary, but he wasn't sure exactly how he felt to be part of this baby parade.

Part of him felt grateful that as soon as he got her to Denver, she would no longer be his responsibility for at least a while, but another part didn't want to say goodbye to her and wondered whether she would actually ever return to Estes Park. That thought made him sad despite all he had tried to do over the last couple of months to get over his romantic feelings for her. And though he could admit he liked the idea of being a small part of such a momentous occasion in her life, he felt let down that the baby would not be his. In fact, he couldn't see how this baby fathered by another man was not going to put another barrier between them and yet he kicked himself that he wasn't happy about this easy solution to his feelings for her. So Collan rode in a jumble of emotions.

Etta finally tired of talking after a couple of hours and complained briefly that her back was giving her some problems despite the fact that they had travelled by way of the easy toll road. They took a break for her but resumed riding after fifteen minutes. Collan was soon later trying to estimate how far from home they were when Etta announced the path had become too rough. She dismounted and walked while Collan took the reins to her horse. Her gait had turned into a distinct waddle and did not make for easy passage over the rocks. Multiple times he dismounted himself to help her over some hindrance. The going progressed extremely slowly. He hoped they could gain back some time when they eventually reached the plains. They stopped to eat by the Saint Vrain River.

Etta now said that her back was really bothering her. Magpie frowned, but Collan figured it made sense since she was carrying such a load around with her. They progressed further but did not make much distance. Collan now realized that they would be camping for the night at a location much farther from Denver than he had supposed. He wondered whether the trip to Denver would take an extra couple more days than he had originally figured. But Etta trudged on and Collan yearned to do the walking for her. He hated seeing her struggle so, but she put on a brave face and smiled at him often.

Eventually the shadows from the trees grew long and Etta said she had to stop for another break. She was gripping her back with both hands now so Collan helped her gingerly to the ground. He stood over her and said, "Etta, we should stop for the day now. There's just so much you can do." He looked around at the grassy area beside the river. "This place seems as good as any."

Etta shook her head. "Oh, no. Just give me a moment. I'll be fine in a minute and we can go on."

Magpie snorted, dismounted and began gathering sticks for a fire. She obviously thought they were done for now so Collan looked for rocks to put around the flames.

Etta started shaking her head and trying to stand. "No, really. Don't stop because of me." She suddenly lowered herself quickly back to the ground. "Oh, no."

Collan and Magpie looked over worriedly. He asked, "What is it, Etta?" but somehow he already knew.

His thoughts were confirmed when Etta answered, "My water broke! The baby's coming."

Chapter Twenty-three

Collan looked over at Etta horrified and asked stupidly, "Are you sure?"

Etta nodded. "I guess I was a little late in leaving Estes Park."

"You think?!" He exclaimed loudly and sarcastically. He couldn't control himself. This was a disaster. "I thought women knew about these things. You figured the baby wasn't due until the new year. That's over a month away! My God, now what are we supposed to do?" He looked around frantically. "Have the baby out here?! Your brother is going to kill me. I was supposed to look out for you."

Etta shifted her dress and looked at her wet hand from the soaked cloth. She seemed amazingly serene. "You know, I was wondering if that fluttering I sensed the month before I felt that big kick the night of the dance was the baby moving around, but I just was too scared to hope so. Well, now I know."

Collan huffed. "You felt *fluttering* a month before and didn't bother to mention it?"

She looked up. "Yes, fluttering. I didn't think you would find it interesting." She stared at him a moment and started chuckling. "You know, Collie, I think this could go down as the biggest prank I ever played on you."

"How can you make a joke out of this?!"

She puckered her brow. "Well, because there's nothing we can do about it now. We're just going to have to make the best of it."

Collan's mouth dropped as he shook his head. He was in way over his head. He wanted to rail at her some more, but she suddenly gripped her back again and said, "Ow, it really hurts now."

That snapped him out of his rant and he knelt down beside her quickly and raised his hands hopelessly. "What can I do?" He was so scared for her.

Magpie answered, "Get me more logs for the fire, Collan. Keep walking, Talks to Hawk. Baby comes faster."

Collan and Etta obeyed without question. And as Collan gathered sticks and tinder, he felt a slight relief that Magpie was taking charge. She gave the impression that she knew what she was doing. Thank God.

An hour later, the fire was blazing and Magpie had made a bed for Etta out of dried grass and a blanket. Etta gratefully lay down after changing into her nightdress and a coat, declaring she didn't think she could walk anymore. But Collan could do nothing but pace. Etta was moaning at regular intervals now. Magpie bathed her forehead and muttered soothing words, adjusting another blanket over her.

An eternity seemed to pass in a similar fashion except Etta was no longer joking, and she shook as if with chills despite the intense heat from the nearby fire. Collan was beside himself with worry. He was grateful when Magpie gave him chores such as giving Etta some water, and then hooch mixed with water, and then building up the fire again and boiling some water, and then even washing the soiled cloths and drying them by the fire. Anything to take his mind off of what was happening. He did not know at all if things were progressing as they should. She had said her life would end if she lost the baby. He now felt his life would be meaningless if he lost her.

Hours later a faint light shone through the trees and a new day was beginning. They had all been up all night except for a slight lull in the action when they all took a quick doze. But now Collan looked over at Etta with growing concern. Her locks curled damply around her face and she was intensely grimacing, though too fatigued to utter a word. Her eyes were closed as if she wanted to try to sleep through the ordeal. She seemed to be fading away. He glanced over at Magpie and he sensed she had similar thoughts. She motioned with her hand for Collan to follow her and they walked toward the stream.

"What are we going to do, Magpie?"

"Talks with Hawk is tiring." She stopped and gazed at Collan fiercely. "You give her your—" She raised her hand in a fist.

"But how?"

Magpie explained in broken English, but Collan got what she wanted him to do. He walked back over to Etta and took her hand. "Etta?"

"Huh?" She opened her eyes. "Oh, Collie it hurts all the time now. I can't get a break."

He smoothed his hand over her head. "But you have to try longer to bring this baby into the world."

Tears came to her eyes. "I know, but I'm just so tired, Collie. What if . . . what if I can't do it?"

"You will, Etta, honey. We're going to help you."

Magpie was moving Etta's legs open to have a look. She nodded at Collan.

Collan crouched down kneeling, leaning his back against a nearby tree trunk. He reached over and picked Etta up in his arms and positioned her so she was essentially sitting in his lap.

She muttered, "What are you doing, Collie? I want to lie down."

"No, you don't. You want to lean back against me." He wrapped his arms around her and took both her hands in his. "I'll keep you squatting. Magpie says the baby might have an easier time coming out."

She started panting. "A really bad one's coming on."

"Push, Etta. Push." Collan held her tightly as Magpie leaned on Etta's belly with all her might. They repeated the same for several more intervals.

Etta was panting vigorously. "I don't know if I can take more of this."

"Yes, you can. I love you, Etta, and you're going to do this for the baby and me."

"I love you, too, Collie." She then yelled, "Oooh! Something's happening! I have to push. I have to push. I feel it."

Collan straightened out his legs, keeping Etta against him, and Magpie positioned herself between Etta's legs.

Magpie shouted, "Push, now. Push."

Etta strained with all her might, then broke off panting again.

Magpie looked at her smiling. "I have the head. When I say push, you push like Indian woman."

Etta nodded.

"Push!"

Etta screamed and gave it all she got.

Magpie scooped out a moving, slimy baby with a long curly cord attached and grinned.

Collan's mouth dropped. Etta started weeping.

Magpie held the baby by its legs and spanked. A loud cry pierced the air. Collan and Etta looked at each other and started laughing.

Magpie swung the baby into her arms. She glanced over. "A boy."

Etta looked up again. "Did you hear, Collie?" She smiled. "I have a *boy*."

Tears came to Collan's eyes. "I heard, Etta. And a strong one at that." He squeezed her hand.

Magpie was back to business. "Take the baby, Collan."

"You want *me* to hold the baby?"

Magpie smirked and rolled her eyes as she handed the baby over to him. "Talks with Hawk have more to do."

Collan nodded. Oh, yeah. The stuff that comes out last. He tried to gently place the infant in his arms but then gripped firmly. He did not want the slippery boy to fall.

Magpie then directed Etta. "Be brave like *Indian* woman. No scream, Talks with Hawk."

The next few moments went by smoothly and quickly. Magpie tied string to the cord and cut the cord with a hot knife she had placed on a rock by the fire.

Magpie took the boy from Collan and bathed the baby with the warm water he had placed in a pot. She told Etta to lift her gown. Etta unabashedly raised her hem above her breast. He knew he should look away but was mesmerized by the scene. If Etta wasn't going to protest the new intimacy, neither was he. She positioned the baby and after a little coaxing with her nipple, the baby began to suckle.

"What are you going to name him, Etta?" He asked softly.

She glanced up at him. "Oh, that's easy. Charles *Collan* Herman Schodde."

He smiled. "I think I like the sound of that."

"I thought you might." She smiled back.

Hours later, Henrietta yawned and lifted her head to look around the campsite. Charlie lay next to her sleeping. Across a softly glowing fire, Collan and Magpie both snoozed side by side on bedrolls. She could tell by the shadows that evening was rapidly approaching. She felt overwhelmingly fatigued but exhilarated. She peeked underneath her blanket. She felt as sticky dirty as she looked. She also was famished.

Gently, she picked Charlie up with his blanket and placed him between Collan and Magpie. She gazed at him lovingly for a moment—such a sweet miracle.

She turned towards the stream. She knew it would feel icy cold but headed in its direction anyways. At the edge, she tested the water with her toe and quickly withdrew it. Then with a great gulp of air, she took a few steps forward, knelt and immersed herself, gown and all, in the swift current. She gasped at the feel of the frigid water and ran to the shore.

She hurried back over to the campfire, grabbed her blanket, and began drying herself with it. She looked over and caught Collan's eye.

"What the hell are you doing, Etta?" He sat up and started chuckling.

"Shsssh. You'll wake Charlie," she whispered and then smiled.

Collan stared at her a moment. A look about him she had never noticed before crossed his face. She could swear it was a look of desire.

She glanced at herself and saw that her wet gown clung revealingly to her body—her plump breasts and big belly, down to her now chubby legs. She swung the blanket quickly around to cover herself. She puckered her brows. She had a vague recollection of Collan telling her that he loved her. She shook her head inwardly. What nonsense. If he had said the words, he surely hadn't meant it. *Had he?*

Charlie started sniveling softly. Magpie awoke and smiled. Genuinely smiled. She picked Charlie up in her arms and cooed to him softly in Cheyenne.

She looked over at Henrietta and frowned slightly, obviously puzzled.

Henrietta walked over to her saddle bags where she had a change of clothes. "Just let me get out of this wet gown and I'll take him, Magpie."

Magpie scarcely paid attention and went back to talking to Charlie in Cheyenne. Henrietta walked behind a pine tree and stole glances as she put on a dry dress.

When she reemerged, Collan was standing and stretching.

"Is anybody else starving?" she asked just as Charlie began wailing.

Collan turned. "Looks like he is."

Henrietta took Charlie from Magpie and sat on a fallen log. She started unbuttoning her dress and then looked over at Collan and stopped. He was still watching her intently. Suddenly, what she had done naturally in front of him only hours before seemed too intimate now.

He blinked and seemed to come to his senses. He turned quickly away, but before he did, Henrietta could have sworn this time that there was a look of sincere disappointment or even hurt that flitted across his face. He said brusquely, "I'm gathering more logs for the fire."

She said to his retreating back. "Okay, then perhaps we can make some food."

He grunted back a reply she could not make out.

After they ate, Henrietta slept, then fed Charlie, then slept some more until the time seemed to pass in a blur of resting and awakening for Charlie. Nothing else drew her attention for hours until she awoke at first light to find Collan saddling the horses.

She suddenly felt a little let down, the brief idle of yesterday, coming to an end. Of course, it was time to move on, and yet she wanted . . . what? She puckered her brows, thinking.

She wanted the warm glow she was feeling to go on a little longer. She wanted the special intimacy of the situation to continue. She wanted to feel especially close to Collan again—wait, *what?*

She shook her head, exasperated. Becoming a mother was making her sentimental or something, that's all there was to it. Her mixed up emotions were causing her yearnings for her husband at such a momentous occasion to be skewed and transferred to the next available man present—who just happened to be Collan. Surely, that was all there was to it. My God. She would never do something as foolish and risky as becoming especially close to Collan . . . to actually letting herself possibly fall in love again. If something untoward should then happen to him, she would not be able to bear it. No, not again. She stood and shook out the dress she had slept in.

"Ah, you're awake." Collan turned to her smiling.

She smiled back. "Yes, ready to return to my home."

He frowned. "What did you say?"

"I'm ready to—"

He held up his hand. "I heard what you said. Surely, you don't mean it."

She puckered her brows. "Why ever not?"

He blinked a moment. "I thought you were still going on to Denver. Perhaps see about your title when you felt better and then—I don't know—stay with Clarissa."

"Clarissa? I can write to her. And Denver and that title thing can just wait. You almost sound as if you want to get rid of me." She crossed her arms.

"Of course not." But then a guilty blush appeared on his face.

Her eyes widened. She was flabbergasted. How could they have such completely different reactions to the incredible events of the last day? She suddenly felt angry and hurt and wanted to lash out at him, but then Charlie started wailing.

She hurried over to pick him up and turned her back on Collan as she unbuttoned her dress, lifting her breast to Charlie. She grabbed a nearby cloth to cover herself even more while Charlie suckled.

Collan continued saddling the horses, not saying a word so she remained quiet also. Magpie appeared from the surrounding trees just as Charlie finished and passed out in her arms.

Magpie smiled. "Give him to me."

She tied him in the beautiful beaded cradle board she had made, and he continued sleeping soundly despite the confining quarters. She lifted him and the board and showed Henrietta how she could hang him from the cloth hook on the back of the board that then attached to her saddle while she rode.

Henrietta blew out a breath. The whole contraption looked too dangerous to her. What if the set up broke loose? What if the horse started galloping and fell suddenly? She shook her head. "Magpie, no. Couldn't I carry him in a blanket tied around my neck as I ride?"

Magpie shook her head. "This is better."

Collan now spoke up. "You plan on holding him while you're riding, Etta? Lordy, that's a recipe for disaster. You can scarcely ride by yourself, let alone with an infant around you."

225

She turned on him and huffed. "Oh, thanks a lot, Collie, for all your support. I suppose you have a better idea."

He looked away a moment and then turned back to her with a resigned look on his face. "And you're determined to return to Estes Park."

She nodded once. "Estes Park is my home."

"Then I suppose you should ride in front of me on my horse while holding Charlie."

She suddenly felt like smiling. "Oh, yes. That's a good idea." She turned to Magpie. "Perhaps when he's a little older, I will feel better about him riding in the board as you said."

"Yes, baby brave Cheyenne." She turned and walked towards her horse.

Charlie a Cheyenne? Whatever did she mean?

Hours later, Henrietta couldn't help snuggling into Collan's shoulder. She just wanted to take a little nap on the ride home.

Chapter Twenty-four

Spring
1876

Henrietta sat at the table, darning a pair of socks, occasionally glancing at Magpie who was humming while she sewed a pair of moccasins for Netse—little Eagle. Henrietta had preferred to call her child Charlie but had given in to popular opinion. She supposed with his watchful eyes and the few fair sprouts on his head that he did appear a bit like an eagle. Ike had thought so when he first heard Magpie use the name and had anglicized to the extreme the Cheyenne pronunciation of Netse to Neddie and then finally Teddie. Charlie had responded with smiles—or gas—and fists waving excitedly when the men had all started chanting Teddie, Teddie. So Henrietta had surrendered to the merriment and begun calling him Teddie Charlie, then just Teddie. That was months ago and the pet name had stuck. So now she had a baby that seemed to not only comprehend Netse or Teddie as himself but was learning a whole slew of other Cheyenne words.

That was because Magpie was a changed woman—she chatted as much as a Magpie. She cooed and sang songs and smiled at the baby constantly. Magpie had declared shortly after Teddie made his

227

entrance into the world that she "wanted to live now." The day she had divulged that secret Henrietta had been surprised—she hadn't known that Magpie had felt so low before Teddie had come into her life. So Henrietta and Magpie had resided the last few wintry months in their blissful little cocoon, isolated, with few sporadic callers. They had lavished attention on Teddie while sharing in the chores.

Oh, the men had all made a point of stopping by during the year end festivities for brief visits, but on the whole, she and Magpie had been on their own due to the rough weather—some of the worst they had ever seen with lots of snow and drifts so high they often covered her front door until she shoveled her way through.

Henrietta stopped darning and looked over. "Magpie?"

"Hmmm?"

"Thank you."

She looked up. "For what?"

"For being my friend. For helping me. For loving Teddie as if he were your own. I think I always felt a special connection with you because we were both women, trying to make our own way alone in the world, but . . . I have come to really treasure our bond." She looked at her warmly.

Magpie got up and stood by Henrietta a moment. She stroked her hand once over Henrietta's head. "I like you too."

They smiled at each other and went back to their work.

Yesterday the weather had warmed and Tinker had appeared. Magpie and Tinker had taken Teddie out for a ride with them, Teddie strapped contentedly in his cradle board. Henrietta had watched from her window, initially to see how Teddie was doing, and then out of curiosity for Magpie and Tinker had stopped a bit of the way down the river, dismounted, put a sleeping Teddie on the ground next to them and then had lain together in the grass and shrubs. Henrietta had watched a moment longer just making out their entwined outline. Once she realized precisely what was taking place though, she had turned away. She had been a bit surprised but also pleased for Magpie—even if they were sinning since they weren't married. Henrietta faulted no one for seeking happiness wherever they could find it. One never knew what the next day could bring.

It was almost a year now since Charles had passed—with Teddie looking more like him every day. Her sorrow was less raw, but she still burst into tears on occasion at a remembrance. How unfair that Charles could not experience the wonder of his son growing up.

She thought about Collan now and frowned slightly. The few times he had visited her the last few months he had been different—perhaps even distant. He hadn't wanted to hold Teddie for longer than a brief moment. He had scarcely joked with her. A shadow seemed to have fallen on him. Perhaps he was concerned about making it in the cattle business or just plain exhausted—calving season had begun. But Collan just wasn't the type to let any enterprise he was involved in keep him down for long. She did not believe he was still embarrassed about trying to kiss her at the dance last year. The incident, undoubtedly due to drink, seemed like ancient history after all that had happened. So what exactly was the matter then?

She tied off a yarn and shook her head slightly to stop her musings about Collan. She really didn't want to think about him and go over every nuance of their relationship. After all she was fine with the new status of their friendship. Truly she was. And yet . . . seeing Magpie and Tinker yesterday made her realize that she missed being intimately close with someone—which . . . whoa. Halt. Stop.

Where had *that* thought come from? She wasn't planning on being with anyone. Ever again. Even the thought made her feel guiltily uncomfortable as if she was betraying the memory of her husband. And yet, would Charles, now in heaven, think so? She wasn't sure. Probably because of his line of work and all the sudden tragedies he had been involved in, Charles had always expressed the thought that life should be lived and never wasted. She just would have liked if he could give a sign—anything—letting her know how he felt about things—about Teddie, about her life now, about how she should proceed in the future.

She reached in the basket for the next sock with a hole. But if she wasn't going to be intimate with anyone, couldn't she at least have an especially close friendship with someone? Particularly since someone she had known for years lived just nearby. Was that too much to ask? Apparently so.

Teddie started crying in his cradle in her bedroom and Henrietta looked over at Magpie and stood. "I'll get him. He's due for a feeding." She walked into her bedroom and lifted him up.

She lay down on her bed and positioned Teddie next to her, offering him her breast. He suckled for a brief moment then pushed her breast away irritably. She picked him up and carried him over to the trunk that held the clean rags used for his drawers. She changed him on her bed. He kept crying. She offered him her breast again. He turned his head away. She walked with him over to Magpie. "He's really fussing."

Magpie nodded. "Netse wants food. He tired of milk."

Henrietta shrugged. "Perhaps so."

Magpie took Teddie as he continued to sob. Henrietta mushed down with a fork some of the remaining stew in the pot on the stove. She offered a tiny spoonful to Teddie. He turned his head away and wailed pitifully.

Magpie felt his head and then shook her own. "Netse good." She reached a finger into his mouth and felt around. "No problem."

"I wonder what's the matter."

Henrietta and Magpie were still wondering well over an hour later. They had tried *everything* and yet Teddie still cried.

Henrietta was just considering riding to a friend for some advice when she heard a knocking and saw the door opening. Collan stood there, adjusting his eyes to the sudden dimness while Ring and Sally wagged their tails eagerly around him. He looked around the cabin. "What's all the racket about? I could hear Teddie from a mile away. I came because I should talk to you about your title, but I didn't realize I would be interrupting what sounds like some sort of terrible torture. What's wrong with him?"

"We don't know." Henrietta shook her head sadly. "He just won't stop."

Collan walked over and took Teddie from Magpie's lap. "Hey, little one. What's going on?" He took Teddie out of the house and stepped down into the yard. He rocked him back and forth some.

Henrietta and Magpie stared in amazement, mouths open, as Teddie finally quieted.

Collan started chuckling. "Oh, heck. He was just tired of you old hens. He wants to be around a man for a while." He raised Teddie in the air and gazed up at him, grinning. "Isn't that so, Teddie?"

Teddie drooled and smiled down at Collan.

Collan walked back over to the porch to give Teddie back to the women, but Teddie whimpered and held on to him tightly. He shrugged. "You either got a way with babies or you don't, Etta." He smiled smugly. "I obviously do."

Henrietta bit back a chuckle. She was pleased to see Collan acting the most like himself as she had seen for a long time. "Well, come in and have some stew."

He looked at Teddie. "What do you think? Should we torment ourselves with their womanly company for a while or not?" He tickled Teddie's belly.

Teddie smiled and giggled.

Collan stepped into the cabin and handed Teddie over to Henrietta as he took off his coat. "Teddie says yes. But only for a bit because the weather looks as if it might be turning again."

Henrietta glanced at the low clouds approaching. "Collan, you can at least stay for a meal."

He sat at the table and motioned for her to give him back Teddie. Magpie resumed sewing the moccasins as Henrietta walked over to the cook stove.

He chuckled. "I bet you don't know there's a wager going concerning your son, Etta."

She turned around, puckering her brows slightly. "My son?"

"Yep. You can get in on it if you want. So can you, Magpie. But it will cost you both a penny." He smiled.

"What is it?" Henrietta smiled back.

"The folks are betting whether the first words out of Teddie are going to be Cheyenne or English." He grinned at Henrietta. "I bet English. I know how much you can talk, Etta. He's bound to pick up some of that chatter."

Henrietta chuckled. "I do not talk that much. Do I, Magpie?"

Magpie smiled. "Netse speak Cheyenne first."

Teddie started patting Collan's face happily and Collan pretended he was going to bite his hand. Her son giggled gleefully.

Henrietta went back to heating up and stirring the stew. When she next turned around again she saw to her amazement Collan lying on the floor, raising Teddie up with his arms playfully, while the dogs ran around Collan excitedly. "You like that, Teddie? Watch this."

He stood and then threw Teddie up into the air a foot before catching him as he fell back down.

Henrietta was alarmed. "Collan, you can't be so rough—" But her protest was drowned out by the dogs barking, Collan chuckling and Teddie screaming with delight.

"Etta, for God's sake, how much have you been coddling this boy? No wonder he was crying. He was bored out of his wits." Collan threw him in the air again. Teddie squealed happily.

"Collie, you can't just—"

But Collan had again sprawled back down on the floor and as the dogs slurped his face, Teddie tried climbing all over him. "You want to try walking, Teddie? Let's try walking."

"He hasn't even started crawling yet—"

Collan held him standing on his belly as Teddie wiggled his feet, smiling.

"That's it. Now let's fly like a hawk." He swooshed Teddie through the air above him. "Weee, weee. We're flying away from the boring women. Weee. We're heading to the saloon for some poker."

"Collan!"

He stopped and looked over. "What?"

"The stews ready." Henrietta bit back a smile as she placed a bowl on the table.

Collan stood. "Thank God, Teddie, huh? Now we're going to have some real man food. None of that sissy milk for us."

Henrietta shook her head. "No, Collan. We already tried giving him some real food. He didn't want any."

Collan broke off a piece of potato and spooned some into Teddie's mouth. "He didn't?" Teddie eagerly gummed some and swallowed as the rest dribbled out of his mouth. Collan took a bite of the stew himself and then pulled a tiny nibble of the meat from his mouth. "How about this, Teddie?"

Teddie swallowed and smiled. He then passed gas and turned red in the face, straining.

Collan's eyes widened. "Whoa. Whoa. Not while we're eating. Oh my God." He handed him quickly over to Henrietta. "The stink!"

Henrietta took Teddie and looked at Magpie. "Perhaps that's why he was crying, he was blocked up."

Magpie looked over. "Huh?"

"He couldn't poop." Collan interpreted. "But I still contend you all bored him to pieces." He took another bite of stew.

Henrietta headed for the bedroom with Teddie. She said over her shoulder, "I don't think so, Collie. I'll have you know, we both play and sing all sorts of games with him like patty cake and this little tea pot and—"

Collan guffawed. "Girls games, Etta. Teddie wants to ride and rope a bronco."

"That's ridiculous." She placed Teddie on her bed and pulled off his dirty rag, then washed him with the damp rag she kept in a bucket and put on a new rag. Then she picked up Teddie and carried him and the soiled rag out the front door and around to the back of her cabin where she shook what she could off the rag. She looked up and noticed the dark, low clouds were almost upon them. Then she went back into the cabin and placed the soiled rag in another bucket she kept behind a chair in her bedroom that was filled with water to soak off the stains before she washed a group of them in the river. She walked out of her bedroom again finally and announced, "You don't know babies, Collan. They like to be cuddled and talked to *gently.*" She raised her voice to the pitch that always got Teddie's attention. "Isn't that so, Teddie?"

Teddie smiled sweetly.

Collan reached out his arms. "Give him back to me, Etta. Let me feed him some more stew."

She handed him over. "Yes, he probably does want something solid now also." Henrietta scooped some more stew into Collan's bowl. She watched Collan feed Teddie some gravy and meat slowly. She always had recognized that Collan would be playful with any future children he had, but she stared mesmerized now at the considerate attention he was now showing Teddie.

The scene was almost too sweet and something her husband should have been doing, and yet . . . it somehow didn't seem out of place or wrong. She realized she was feeling emotions she was not used to with Collan and it made her slightly uncomfortable so she got up to gaze out her window.

"Oh, my God! Look at that!"

Collan stood with Teddie and walked over. Magpie joined them. In the sudden quiet of the room they all noticed that the wind was now howling. Outside snow was coming down in slanting thick sheets.

"It looks like a blizzard!" Henrietta quickly walked over to the front door and placed her arms wide in a barring gesture. "You can't leave. I won't let you go in this weather. I had heard that the snow storms were worse in the spring, but I didn't believe it. Did you? This is *incredible.*"

Collan rolled his eyes. "For heaven's sake, Etta. Of course, I'm not riding in this storm. I'm no fool." He sat back down with Teddie at the table and took a spoonful of stew for himself.

She lowered her arms and walked back over to take a seat. "Just what were you doing out today? I haven't seen you for ages."

He frowned slightly. "Been busy, Etta."

"Practically *all* winter?"

"Why?" He half-smiled. "Did you miss me?"

Henrietta drew in a breath. "Well, as a matter of fact, I did notice your absence. I mean, we have been friends for a long, long time and it would be nice if you would occasionally—"

"Friends." He glanced at Magpie, who was now sewing in her bedroom, then said in a lowered voice, "Perhaps we're not. Perhaps—"

Henrietta stood. "How can you say that?!" She suddenly felt hurt. "We're not even *friends*?"

Teddie then burst into tears at her outburst.

Well, he wasn't the only one who was upset. Henrietta motioned peevishly with her hands for Collan to hand Teddie over. "Oh, he's probably tired now. Just give him to me."

But Collan patted Teddie's head and smoothed his hand down his back and as Teddie quieted, he snuggled, sucking his thumb, into Collan's shoulder. Collan then stood and said softly, "I'll put him to bed."

Henrietta turned away, feeling letdown by Collan now. "I'll clean up the dishes." As she scrubbed, she heard Teddie fussing again as Collan tried lowering him to his cradle. Then she heard nothing except for her

237

bedroom door closing and the wind still whistling loudly.

She looked out the window once she had finished straightening the room and saw that darkness had descended. She opened her front door a crack. A gust of snow and wind overwhelmed her and she slammed the door close. At least an inch appeared to be on the ground already. She turned back around. Now Magpie's door was closed also.

She stomped over to her bedroom door. She couldn't believe that Collan hadn't come out to discuss their friendship some more. Didn't it bother him that they were at odds? She opened her door brusquely and stopped short at the sight that greeted her.

Collan lay on her bed with his arm protectively around Teddie, both fast asleep. Her insides melted again at the image before her.

She tiptoed quietly and grabbed the extra quilt off the chair in the corner. She was just lowering it over them when Collan raised his head sleepily and said, "What are you doing, Etta?"

She startled and frowned slightly. "Covering you both. You must be cold."

Collan groggily stood and picked up Teddie. He then pulled back the covers and sheet on the bed one handed and slipped into the bed again with Teddie, facing away from her, pulling back the covers over them both.

She watched, mouth open. After a moment, he glanced back over his shoulder at her. "Just get into bed, Etta. I don't want to sleep on the floor and neither do you." He yawned. "For heaven's sake, I'm not going to ravage you." He turned away from her again and snuggled deeper into the covers. Teddie kept on sleeping.

She stood motionless for a moment, then shook her head. The whole situation was at once incredulous and yet made sense at the same time. She grabbed her nightdress off the hook and changed in the adjoining room before extinguishing the lantern. She fumbled her way back over to the bed.

She refused to sleep next to Collie. It just wasn't proper and besides she was still upset with him. She climbed over him—with him grunting as she elbowed him in the face—and slipped into the bed on the other side of Teddie. At least Teddie would serve as a barrier between them. She tossed and turned for several minutes, certain she would never fall asleep, but the soft snoring of both Collan and Teddie lulled her eventually into oblivion.

Chapter Twenty-five

The next morning, she awoke to lightness in her cabin. She looked over to her bed companions. Teddie had curled sometime during the night out from the covers and was asleep almost like a puppy on the edge of her pillow, crammed up against the headrest of her cast iron bedframe.

She remembered sometime during the night Teddie crying to be fed and drowsily lifting her nightdress for him to suckle, noticing that Collan at the time was dozing, turned away from them both. But she and Teddie must have fallen back asleep during the process because as she now looked down she realized that her dress was still raised up over her breast and Collan's large hand—oh, Lord—was covering it. She looked at him alarmed. He was still asleep, but she could swear he wore a contented smug expression on his face. The air was cold in her bedroom and his warm hand felt good so she didn't immediately move. Yes, that was why she was permitting it.

But then he mumbled something in his sleep— he sounded like he was joking—and she hurriedly moved his hand aside. He awoke with a start and she quickly lowered her nightdress back over her breast. He smiled sleepily and said, "Well, hello, Etta. Fancy meeting you here this morning."

She raised herself on her elbows and smirked. "What does that mean? This is my bed."

"And so it is." He chuckled. "And I'm in it."

"That's only because you demanded I sleep with you."

He smiled. "Did I?"

"Yes!"

He shook his head, thoughtfully. "I don't think so. I think you've turned into a loose woman."

"Oh, for heaven's sake." She grabbed at her pillow, dislodging Teddie, and used it to whack Collan firmly.

Collan chuckled and Teddie then raised his head and giggled. Collan grabbed the pillow and handed it over to her. "Do it again. Teddie thinks it's funny."

"I'm getting up and starting coffee." She elbowed her way over Collan, purposely grinding her arms in at his belly this time.

"Ooomph." He slapped her rear playfully as she slipped to the floor. "Keep it up, Etta. I like feisty harlots." He turned back to pick up Teddie and placed him sitting on his chest.

She stared at him flabbergasted a moment, pulling her nightdress firmly over her rear. "I can't believe you just did that."

"Believe it, Etta. Just believe it."

She headed towards her cook stove, then changed her mind. She grabbed her coat hanging by the front door and sat on the bench at the table, pulling on her boots and tying them. "I want to go see about my animals first."

"In your nightgown?"

241

She slipped her arms through her coat sleeves and then waved dismissively. "I'll change when I get back."

She opened the front door and stared. The sky was blue and the wind was gone, but her whole yard was blanketed with about a foot and a half of snow. "Oh, my gosh."

"Hey, you're letting in the cold air."

She turned back around. "Collie, get up. You have to see this." She faced the outside again and Collan joined her at the door, holding Teddie.

"We got some snow," he uttered.

"*Some* snow. We got tons."

Magpie now stood at the door and took Teddie. "Snow gone fast. It spring."

"I'm heading out." Henrietta cautiously stepped off her porch with Ring and Sally following. The snow came higher than her boots. "Oh, this is going to be cold." She heard the door close behind her. She took several more steps, practically wading through the soft flakes. She then heard a swishing behind her and felt a handful of the freezing stuff fall down the back of her collar. She gasped and turned. "Collie Wallace, I'm going to get you."

He laughed and ran a few feet away. She grabbed a handful of the snow and threw it at him. She grazed the sleeve of his coat. He hurried and scooped up some more, forcibly shoving it down her coat again.

She screamed and ran after him laughing. "You are such a *schweinehund*, Collie." She threw another handful and missed him entirely.

He turned and taunted her some more, walking backwards. "I see your aim hasn't improved one bit, Etta." He grabbed a handful and threw it at her, hitting her elbow.

"Oh! I hate you." She threw another handful and got his leg.

"No, you don't. You love me, Etta. You told me so yourself." He got her on her chest.

"When?!" She hustled to get closer to him and missed again.

"When you had Teddie and after I told you I loved you."

She stopped suddenly, mouth open, remembering.

He got her in the face. "Ooops, sorry, Etta. Didn't mean to do *that!*"

She glared at him and wiped the snow away. "Well, I really hate you now, Collie. And besides, how do you know we weren't just saying those things at the spur of a special moment?" She reached down for more snow. "*You* said you don't even want to be friends anymore. Just *yesterday*." She ran towards him and slipped, landing on her rump.

He walked over, chuckling, and looked down. "That's correct. I want to be lovers. I'm officially courting you now, Etta Schodde, so just watch out."

She lay back and swung her arms and legs in the snow to make an angel. "This is incredible. Just when did you come to this ridiculous decision?"

"This time?" He paused, looking skyward a moment. "Sometime last night."

"So that's why you came over?"

"Oh, no. Before I got here yesterday I was sure I didn't want to be near you more than necessary. No, I had convinced myself that I was purely coming over to ask if you wanted me to see about your title since I'm going to Denver for business soon. I mean I thought I should at least help with that—"

"What? How long are you staying in Denver?"

He reached down and scooped her up in his arms and started walking towards the stable. "A few days. Why? You going to miss me?"

"I'm not sure." She frowned. "Perhaps." She paused in thought a moment, then huffed. "You scarcely came to visit this winter and now you say you couldn't abide my presence and before yesterday you wouldn't even hold Teddie for a second and you were distant and I really don't think it's been long enough for me to be courting any one and perhaps it's just too risky to ever truly—"

He placed her on her feet in front of the stable. "Shhhsh. Now Etta, I know this is going to mess with your mind, but just give it a chance, will you?"

She opened her mouth to speak, but he stopped her again, holding up his hand. "Don't say a word. Just think about it." He turned her to face the door of the stable. He opened it and waited for her to proceed before him. "Now let's hurry. It's freezing outside and I'm hungry. I want some breakfast."

She walked into the stable, muttering, "If this is your idea of romance, Collie, you got a lot to learn."

"I heard that, Etta." He chuckled. "You can teach me, then."

She turned back around to face him. "First off, you don't court women in their nightdress on their way to giving grain and possibly mucking out stalls. That's for starters."

"You think?" He chuckled. "I'm surprised."

A while later as they sat at the table, eating pancakes with Magpie and Teddie, Collan discreetly, but slowly, winked at her. She felt immediately flustered and knocked over the bottle of syrup. But they no longer had any further opportunity to discuss their new relationship because as soon as she had cleaned up the mess, there was a knock on her door and her friends entered with disturbing news.

Collan was grateful for his friends being worried enough about him to go looking for him, but he had been hoping to spend some more time alone with Etta. But it was not to be for at least the present. He tried to concentrate on what Abner was saying, but his mind kept wandering to last night when Etta had climbed into the bed. That was when he had discerned, whether she realized it or not, that she was ready for a relationship with him.

Etta and he had been raised to be "good kids" by their parents. Collan had strayed, though not terribly, but Etta certainly had not. And for her to climb into bed with him, unmarried, even if it did make sense, was outrageously scandalous for her set of morals. And then when he had awoken and realized that he hadn't just been dreaming about squeezing her breast, he had felt triumphant.

But Abner was speaking. "So after Tinker informed me at first light that Collan hadn't returned last night, we decided to split up in huge half circles. I rode over to the Fergusons and then over to the Evans and then looped back here while Tinker set out for the MacGregors and then you Farrars before heading here."

Etta asked, "So how are the Evans and Fergusons and MacGregors?"

Abner shrugged. "Oh, they're all fine. Aren't they, Tinker?"

Tinker nodded.

Ike spoke up. "Are there any more pancakes, Miss Henrietta?"

Etta stood. "Let me just make another batch. How were you able to ride through all this snow?"

"Slowly." Tinker said around a mouthful.

Abner shrugged again. "We didn't have any choice. We didn't know what had befallen Collan."

"I appreciate your concern." Collan nodded.

"You would have done the same for us." Abner rejoined. "But finding you isn't the biggest news from this morning. Guess who else I ran into." He didn't wait for a response. "That devil Whyte."

"What did the shithead have to say?" Hank suddenly glanced at the women. "Sorry for the language, Miss Henrietta. Sorry, Miss Magpie."

Ike chuckled loudly until Clint kicked him underneath the table.

"Ow!" Ike exclaimed.

"Could I please have some more pancakes, also, Miss Henrietta?" Clint asked politely.

Etta turned around from the stove and smiled. "Certainly." She puckered her brow slightly. "You're looking a little thinner."

Ike started chuckling again. "That's cuz we've scarcely been around here visiting this winter. Hank can't cook for shit—you know that."

Clint kicked him again underneath the table.

"Ow!" He glared at Clint, then smiled and said, "But we'll be coming more as soon as the weather warms up again, Miss Henrietta."

Etta smiled. "Oh, we'll like that. Won't we, Magpie?"

Magpie raised one corner of her mouth in a smile. "I teach you to hunt again."

Ike waved his hand. "Oh, you go on, Miss Magpie."

Teddie perked up in Magpie's arms and patted her head. He murmured baby talk. "Waawaw."

"He speakin' Cheyenne or something, Miss Magpie?" Ike grinned.

Magpie smiled back. "No, but Netse happy now."

"Can we please hear what Whyte said?" Hank frowned. "Go on, Abner."

Abner swallowed, then continued. "Well, it seems he's been plotting these last few months. He's got a new plan for the Dunraven holdings." He looked around, confirming he had all their attention. "He's going to fence in entirely all of their property."

Collan threw his cloth napkin onto the table. "Son of a bitch."

Ike frowned. "What do you mean, Abner? But then . . . but then how are we all supposed to get back to our properties if we leave them for a while to go hunting and then want to return by Dunraven land?"

"You aren't. That's the point." Hank muttered.

"Can he do that, Hank?" Ike leaned back his head, astounded.

Hank shrugged. "Don't know." He looked at Abner and Collan, inquiringly.

Abner answered, "I'm not sure, either. I'm going to talk to Alex once the snow melts. I think we all should have a community meeting with Alex as soon as we can and get his lawyerly advice."

Everyone nodded.

"Pancakes ready." Etta placed a couple on the plates Clint and Ike held out. "Some more will be done in a minute."

"But he said something else when he heard I was heading over here next to see about Collan."

Etta looked at Collan and rolled her eyes. "I bet he saw about my title sometime the last few months."

Collan nodded. "What did he say, Abner?"

Abner shook his head. "No, he didn't say anything about your title, Henrietta." He turned to Magpie. "He threatened you."

"Hmmmph." She snorted.

"Threatened how, Abner?" Tinker frowned.

"Did you know that Custer was sent on an expedition through Dakota Territory?" Abner asked.

Tinker nodded. "Yeah, I read something about it in the papers. Custer discovered goldflecked rocks in the Black Hills. Good luck getting at it. That area is sacred to all sorts of Indian tribes."

"We make treaty." Magpie frowned. "Black Hills for Indians."

Tinker nodded. "That's correct. The last treaty gave that location to the Indians."

"But what a treasure, Tinker. Do you really think they can keep the miners out?" Collan asked.

"But how was Magpie threatened?" Tinker inquired again.

Abner explained. "Well, it seems the government is expecting trouble and apparently there have already been skirmishes so this winter the government commanded all Cheyenne and Sioux living outside the reservations to report in."

"Last *winter*?" Etta exclaimed. "But how could they when the weather is still cold even during this spring? Do they expect the families with children and old people to just trounce through the snow as easy as pie?"

Magpie shook her head. "They stupid."

Abner continued. "Whyte asked me if you were Cheyenne or Sioux, Magpie, and whether you still lived with Henrietta. I lied and told him I didn't know. But I think he's going to cause you trouble, Magpie."

"Let him try. Just let him try." Tinker muttered grimly.

"Oh, my gosh. What are we going to do?" Etta asked worriedly. "They can't mean Magpie. She's not a hostile warrior. Why is Whyte doing this? What has Magpie ever done to him?"

"Nothing, Etta. But he figures Magpie and you are close and he's trying to actually harass you." Collan explained.

"Well, he's being successful." She looked at Magpie earnestly. "Don't you worry, Magpie. I'll give him what he wants if he'll leave you alone."

"Oh, you shouldn't give in so easily, Etta." Collan blew out a breath. "But I don't know what there is to do."

"Nothing." Tinker shrugged. "Magpie's doesn't have to go anywhere."

"But if the government says," Etta continued wailing, "then—"

Tinker interrupted her. "Magpie and I are married. They can't take my wife even if she is Indian."

Tinker looked over at Magpie then. Magpie said nothing but raised Teddie up before her, smiling and speaking Cheyenne to him. Teddie gave a drooly grin back.

"What?" Etta dropped her spatula on the floor. "But you can't—" Then Etta raised her hand to her mouth to shut herself up.

Collan frowned. Yes, of course, it was surprising that they were married—and just when in the hell had they done that—but he knew his Etta and there was damn sure a lot more going on here than just the marital revelation. But what? He had no idea.

He thought some more. Tinker was probably lying. That was it. They undoubtedly weren't married at all. He was just protecting Magpie. Collan then looked over at Magpie. She was still happily cooing at Teddie. Then again, didn't those Indians have simple ceremonies? Perhaps she was married if she had just said her Indian vows to Tinker. However, Etta had said, "but you can't" before she had quieted.

250

Why couldn't they? Surely, Etta wouldn't have a problem because they both weren't Indian. Collan knew she didn't harbor that kind of prejudice in her. He looked at Etta. She was still mulling something over in her mind. She still hadn't congratulated the couple.

He would however. He got up from the table and walked over to where Tinker was sitting. He gave him a clap on the back. "Great news. I'm happy for you, Tinker. You, too, Magpie."

Magpie looked over and smiled at Collan.

Ike then stood, agitatedly. "Wait a minute, Miss Magpie. What does this mean? Aren't you going hunting with us no more?"

Magpie looked over at him. "I hunt."

"Okay." Ike sat down, but then another question quickly occurred to him. "So are you moving in with Tinker now?"

Tinker raised both brows at Magpie, obviously also waiting for her answer.

Magpie shook her head. "No, I live with Netse." She then shook her head teasingly into Teddie's belly. He giggled and Magpie spoke some more Cheyenne to him.

Collan sat back down at the table and looked over at Etta. She was slowly lowering herself to her chair at the end of the table, her pancakes forgotten. She muttered, "This has got to be the craziest day ever . . ."

Collan chuckled. "Isn't it?" He gave her a knowing look and her eyes widened.

Chapter Twenty-six

After Collan departed her cabin, Henrietta spent a day or so fretting about whether she should let Collan harbor any intentions to court her. She had fancifully asked her husband in heaven for a sign from him about what she should do with her future and Collan had appeared at her door. Could something so mystical possibly have some meaning? But what if her husband would have approved of her moving on with her life, how did *she* really feel about it? The truth was, she couldn't help feeling afraid still of becoming so romantically attached to another person and then possibly losing that person—it would kill her. Perhaps that made her a weak person, but that was the way of it, at least for now.

But her disquiet was all for naught because whether Collan wanted to romance her or not, he was simply too busy to do so. Calving season was still going on. Collan could not afford to lose any cow as she struggled to bring her calf into the world. Collan might be land rich, but he was becoming increasingly cash poor, trying to make a go at ranching.

Henrietta at least had some pennies coming in from her baked goods for the tourists were beginning to trickle in again. Magpie was also selling beaded trinkets and wares she had made. Henrietta had asked Magpie as soon as the men departed whether she was actually married. Magpie had nodded.

Henrietta had tried to reason with her. "But Magpie, have you told Tinker that perhaps you are already wedded? We don't actually know where your husband is."

Magpie had shrugged. "He gone. I don't want him. I'm not married to him."

"But were your vows at a fort? Was there a man of God present?"

"A black robe? Yes."

"Oh, no. Then you're still *married.*"

Magpie had shaken her head. "No. I tell him when he comes again I don't want him."

"Oh, Lord. Do you think he's coming back?"

"He comes to mountains in spring . . . if he still alive."

Henrietta had shuddered at the thought. She had then worried whether she should discuss the marital situation with Tinker but had decided it was none of her business what actually went on between them both.

Collan had swung by a few days later on his way to Denver for a quick meal. Despite his teasing smile, he had looked fatigued. He had divulged that Abner, the Fergusons and he were considering building their own sawmill. He was going to look into the price of equipment. He would also see about her title. She had given him money to buy beads, cloth and spices for her. A week later he had returned on his way back from Denver, hauling a cart, partially filled with her purchases. He had only wanted to stay at her place for a bit which she couldn't help finding disappointing. He still had to talk to Abner and the Fergusons about the sawmill and he was worried how his homestead had faired while he was gone. But Collan had revealed the good news that the title to her property was filed in her name. At least that was one less worry.

The following week more tourists arrived and the weather was warm enough for her to set up her tea service on the front porch. She got the Farrar brothers to build her another small table and benches and made a tablecloth for the setting—Collan had bought her particularly pretty fabric—and the travelers told her how charming they found her homestead.

A surprising visitor then came knocking on her door one day. Herr Big Blade had shyly asked if she could make him some strudel. She had agreed and he had returned a couple days later to pick it up. Apparently, Herr Big Blade had then spread the word to his fellow cowboys that she held no grudge—indeed, they paid quite well for her baked goods—and she started having a regular business like a bakery instead of the haphazard visits from just tourists. She contemplated investing in a bigger cook stove with oven.

Teddie then surprised her next. He started crawling. Before this he had been satisfied to ride along in his cradle board while Magpie and she had done their chores. No longer. He wanted to explore on his own. And though he hadn't voiced an official Cheyenne or English word yet, he had no trouble spouting his opinion in his own way. What was delightful at first to Magpie and her became a real concern.

Teddie tried eating dirt, he picked up dung, and one day he headed towards the river before she caught him. So the Farrar brothers built her a playpen—Ike called it a cage—that saddened Henrietta a little, but which she realized was a necessity. At least now that Teddie was less delicate, the men—especially Ike—played with him more and also found him more entertaining.

Collan and Tinker came by again when everyone was sitting down for supper. They took a seat at the table and Henrietta served them some biscuits, elk roast and gravy. They both still looked exhausted and thinner.

"Isn't calving season done yet?" she asked.

Collan nodded. "Mostly, but we've been taking turns at night watching for the bears, coyotes, and wolves—at least until they get a little older."

"Oh. Sounds like you could use some more help."

"You bet. You volunteering, Etta?" He smiled and raised both brows at her.

"Of course not, but perhaps I should pack you some food to take home with you."

"That would be great. We've gotten plum tired of our own cooking, haven't we, Tinker?"

Tinker nodded.

"That was one of the reasons we came over here—so we could get a decent meal." He then turned to Magpie. "Let me hold Teddie for a bit."

Magpie handed him across the table. Collan positioned Teddie in his lap and gave him a piece of biscuit. Teddie spit it out and struggled to get down until he was underneath the table.

Ike chuckled. "Oh, watch out now. He's in a frisky mood."

Henrietta looked underneath the table and tried reaching for him. "Teddie, come here. You have to learn your manners."

Teddie crawled further away from her and patted the pants legs of Clint and Hank before pulling on Collan. Collan scooped him up again. "What are you doing, Teddie?" He tickled his belly and Teddie giggled gleefully. "Giving your mama a difficult time?"

Teddie smiled into Collan's face. "Papa."

Ike stood up. "Did you hear that? Did you hear that? Teddie said his first words!"

Henrietta puckered her brows. "He doesn't even know what Papa means."

But Clint was equally excited. "Sure he does. You point to your husband's picture and say Papa, Miss Henrietta. I've heard you."

Hank smiled. "He spoke English first. How much is in the pot for the bet?"

"Oh, for heaven's sake." Henrietta put down her cloth napkin. "I don't think this really counts. Do you, Magpie?"

She crossed her arms. "Netse Cheyenne baby. Netse speak Cheyenne first."

Tinker put his arm around her shoulders, consolingly. "Oh, come on, Magpie. He hasn't spoken any Cheyenne yet. You know that."

Magpie sulked.

Henrietta straightened. "Well, if he did say Papa, he probably just thinks it means 'a man.'" She looked over at Collan.

Collan was grinning and pointing to himself as he spoke to Teddie. "Yes, Teddie. You can call me Papa.

I'm Papa." He looked over at Henrietta and chuckled loudly. "Guess *he's* made his decision of whom you should marry next."

Ike gaped. "You getting *hitched*, Miss Henrietta? To Collan? I thought you both half hated each other after what you did as sprogs."

Henrietta felt herself turning red. "This is ridiculous. We're not even—"

Collan interrupted loudly. "I want to announce to everybody that I'm officially courting Etta now."

"You *are*?!" Ike was still flabbergasted.

Clint kicked him. "You're such a stupid oaf. Everybody can see they love each other."

Henrietta felt even hotter. "Now, Clint, nobody has said anything like that—"

Hank cut in. "We should start a new wager—"

"Hank, don't you do any such thing!" She turned to Collan for help, but he was now on the floor, pretending to chase Teddie while crawling.

"Collan!"

He stopped and looked up. "What?"

She took a deep breath and raised her hands in appeal. She decided it was best just to change the subject. "Don't you want to finish your meal and tell us the other reasons you came for a visit?"

He smiled at her, laughingly. "Oh, sure, Etta." He stood and handed Teddie back to Magpie who immediately started whispering Cheyenne words to him. Teddie smiled at her.

Collan sat at the table and took a bite before announcing, "Abner says everyone should meet at the MacGregors' in exactly one week to discuss the planned fencing of Dunraven holdings—or I should say the planned blockage to the fencing of Dunraven." He turned to Henrietta. "Abner also said it's going to be a pot luck."

Henrietta nodded. "Oh, sure. I can make some food to bring. What time are we supposed to be at the MacGregors'?"

"Around five."

"Oh, but it could be dark when the meeting ends."

Collan nodded. "Yep. I'll pick you up and bring you there and back, Etta."

Ike snorted.

Henrietta tried ignoring the outburst. "Yes, I suppose that is the sensible thing to do."

Ike then bit back a chuckle.

She pressed on. "Do you think we should bring Teddie?"

Collan shook his head. "He's too little. Tinker says he'll stay with Magpie and watch them both while we're at the meeting."

Ike dropped off the end of the bench, guffawing loudly. "And they think I'm stupid."

Henrietta turned red again.

Chapter Twenty-seven

Collan swung by Henrietta's place the following week as promised. She had been dreading and yet feeling excited about seeing him again. She felt butterflies in her belly as he rode into her yard. She wasn't sure what to expect between them now.

She had Buzzie already saddled and was finishing packing some bread, a pie, and an elk roast when Collan stopped in front of her. She tightened the cinch, trying to pretend calm. She glanced up and saw Tinker ride his horse immediately over to the cabin. He waved at her, before dismounting and throwing his reins loosely over the rail. Tinker entered the cabin and closed the door.

She looked at Collan again. He was eying her horse dubiously. "You really think you should ride Buzzie? We shouldn't be late."

Henrietta straightened. "Now, Collan. You saw how well I rode on the way to having Teddie."

Collan shrugged. "Yeah, he does do better when following." He smiled then. "But don't you want to ride in front of me. We can snuggle."

She quickly tried mounting. "Certainly not. I'm sure everybody's already heard that you're trying to court me." Buzzie took a step and Henrietta faltered in getting into the saddle. "Just when do you think you're going to start this romancing? Tonight? Oh, nooo. Not in front of everybody."

Collan dismounted and held the bridle so Buzzie would stay still. "Now, Etta. I can see that you've been letting your mind go all in circles over us. So let's just get it over with."

"Get what over with—"

"This." With his free hand he pulled the back of her head quickly forward, giving her a smooch on the lips.

She pushed on his chest firmly with both hands. "Oh, my God. Stop that! They could be watching from the cabin!"

Collan chuckled. "I'm sure they've seen it before. In fact, I think Magpie and Tinker are going at it themselves now. You saw how quickly Tinker got into that cabin."

Her mouth dropped open. "In front of *Teddie*?"

"Oh, hell, Etta. He's probably in his cradle, playing with his feet, not even paying attention."

"Give me a hoist. I'm not listening to this anymore." She put her foot in the stirrup.

"Sure thing, Etta." Collan squeezed her rear as he pushed her into the saddle.

She glared down at him. "You're incorrigible. Let's get going so we're not late."

Collan chuckled as he mounted himself. "You know, I think I'm really going to like this courting, Etta. It'll be like when we were younger, only naughtier."

She narrowed her eyes. "It better not be, Collie. You have a lot to learn about what independent women like and will allow." She clicked and squeezed Buzzie with her legs. "Come on, Buzzie. Let's get going."

Buzzie took one step and then stood motionless. Collan shook his head. "Give me your reins, Etta. I'll lead him for a bit."

She huffed. "Oh, very well. But only until he realizes that I'm the boss."

"Sure, Etta. I'll hand the reins back as soon as we arrive."

"Have I told you how much I hate you yet today?

Collan laughed. "I love you too, Etta."

Henrietta looked around as she took a seat between Clara and Sal. Everyone had shown from the community except, of course, the enemy.

The men were all loitering by the front, joking and slapping each other on the backs.

Sal motioned with her head. "Look at them. Acting as if they aren't worried. As if they don't all realize that this place is the best thing that ever happened to them." She shook her head.

Henrietta asked, "Are things still going fine, Sal?"

She nodded. "Better than ever. The tourists just keep arriving. We've never had so much money coming in. We're not giving up without a fight."

Henrietta turned around to Clara. "I see you're building more cabins."

Clara nodded. "Yep, to house the tourists who don't want to camp. I've been sending them your way for baked goods. Have they been coming?"

Henrietta nodded. "I think I might want a bigger oven."

"That's wonderful."

"Whatever happened with your mother's dispute over her land?"

"She's offered to swap his parcel with property by Fall River. I think he might take her up on it."

Sal leaned over. "Well, if the fella is smart, he'll build a tourist resort over there."

Henrietta turned back to Sal. "What about your dispute with Whyte?"

"We've offered Whyte to trade our daughter's claim for land we want. I think he's going to take it. Then we can build more accommodations, also, for the tourists. But if he fences everything in . . ." Sal shook her head.

"Alex has a plan." Clara blew out a breath. "I hope it works."

At that moment, Alex asked for everyone's attention. He stood at the front with his neatly trimmed beard and mustache, wearing a business suit. He presented himself as a capable and reliable person that everyone wanted to take charge. Abner took a chair next to him, and though in casual clothing, and short compared to Alex, he appeared determined and rugged, one who everyone could relate to and wanted on their side. The remaining men scattered in the audience. Collan took a seat behind Henrietta.

Alex put his hands on his hips and began. "I'm sure you're all aware that Whyte has proposed fencing in all of the property that Dunraven owns without any provision mentioned for the folks to pass through the land to get to their own property."

There was a low murmuring from the crowd.

"Well, while that kind of thing might be perfectly acceptable in England, I can assure you with certainty that such practice is not tolerated in America."

The crowd cheered and Alex motioned with his hand for everyone to quiet again.

"What I propose is that we settlers petition the Larimer County Commissioners to lay out three public roads through our area so that all can reach their property. Such an action is protected by law in America, and I do not foresee any problem obtaining permission."

The crowd roared.

"I have put by the food table a drawing showing where I feel the three roads should run. I want your opinion for whether you also agree. Talk to either Abner or myself. At the end of the evening if I feel I have a consensus, I will contact the county and handle all pertinent documents. Abner plans to notify Whyte of our actions and will keep you informed."

Hunter Ferguson spoke up. "Is it true that Dunraven is planning to build a hotel?"

Abner nodded. "So I've heard."

Sal leaned over to Henrietta and whispered, "The son of a gun tries to take over the cattle ranching, and now he wants to drive us out of the tourist business."

Hunter then asked, "Where is he planning on locating it?"

Abner shook his head. "Not decided yet as far as I know."

Sal smirked. "Just watch. He'll put it plum down next to ours."

Henrietta puckered her brow. "But surely if everyone keeps their rates reasonable and provides good service, there'll be enough business for all."

"Let's hope."

No further questions were asked and everyone slowly wandered over towards the drawing and the food.

Henrietta let the group look at the map first before she studied it herself. She saw that one of the planned roads would follow the river by her and pass near her homestead. She was pleased about that. She saw that no road extended to where Abner and Collan lived. The area was still too isolated from the rest of the settlement.

Collan appeared at her side. "So what do you think?"

"This is good for my bakery business. Are you disappointed?"

"Nah. I didn't expect any road to come by me. In fact, I'm kind of happy that I'll still have the area to myself and just a few others."

"Did you get enough to eat?"

"Yes, and you?"

She nodded.

He yawned. "I'm kinda tired. I'm ready to leave if you are."

"Let me just say goodbye to my friends and I'll meet you by the horses."

She joined Collan a few minutes later and mounted Buzzie, slapping at Collan's hand to get away when he offered to help. Collan chuckled.

Buzzie cooperated when she urged him to move forward. She looked over at Collan proudly.

Collan smirked. "Yes, it's amazing how amenable a horse can be when he knows he's heading home."

Henrietta decided to ignore that comment and they rode quietly side by side for several minutes. There was a half moon rising and a few scattered clouds slowly drifting by, giving an enchanting appearance to the landscape around them. They heard some coyotes yipping in the distance and then an owl screech, then peacefulness. They rode further.

A sudden streak of light raced across the dark sky. "Did you see that, Collie?"

"Now you have to tell me what you yearn for, Etta."

She closed her eyes and halted. "If I could get my truest desire, it would be . . ."

Collan drew rein. "What?"

"That I never have to lose anyone else that I love ever again." She looked over at Collan, suddenly blinking back tears. She bit her lip and sniffled. "Oh . . . oh . . . I didn't mean to . . . suddenly become so sad." She looked away.

Collan reached over and scooped her gently into his saddle in front of him, positioning her sideways. She didn't want to resist. She cuddled into his shoulder, the side of her face resting into his chest.

He leaned over, trying to look into her eyes. "It's okay, Etta. You're not going to lose anyone any time soon. I promise."

She looked up at him, then wiped her tears with her sleeve. "I don't know why this happens to me with you. I go days—no *weeks*—without crying lately and then I see you and you say something simple like 'tell me what you want' and I go to pieces again."

"That's because you can, Etta. Because you trust me with your feelings. Heck, we've always had some sort of connection, even when we were fighting kids. I guess it's fate for us to always be close."

She puckered her brow. "Then why do you forever give me a difficult time?"

He chuckled softly. "Ah, now that's because it's fun."

She shoved him playfully. He grabbed at her horse's reins and kicked his into moving.

"Wait. What are you doing?"

"Taking you home."

"I can ride myself."

"Yes, yes, Etta. You can ride. You've proved yourself to be an expert horsewoman—"

"About time you noticed."

"But see I wanted to get home sometime this century and at the pace you were setting I didn't know if that was possible."

"You are so full of—"

"Now, now Etta. Watch your language—"

"What's that?" She sat straighter and sniffed. "Is that smoke?" She smelled the air again.

"Yeah."

"But that's too much to just be somebody's campfire or chimney."

"I know." Collan urged his horse to go faster.

BOOM!

She looked around, frantically. "That was gunfire."

"I know." Collan frowned and urged his horse to go faster. They came to the ridge overlooking her homestead. They looked down and to their horror, red flames and smoke were rising from the back end of her cabin.

"Teddie!" Henrietta screamed. "I got to get to Teddie!" She clutched at Collan's shirt front.

"Hold on, Etta. Let's get down there as quick as we can." Collan dropped her horse's reins and traversed the ridge to her homestead, descending at a rapid pace.

BOOM!

"What's going on, Collie?!"

"We'll find out in a minute, Etta." Collan looked angry but determined. He urged his mount to make risky jumps over fallen debris and rocks as they raced faster, Henrietta clutching Collan to stay on.

As they got closer, Henrietta could hear Teddie wailing, but she couldn't make out where he was. His crying was muffled at times by a horse whinnying and Beauty mooing. She heard Beauty kicking her stall. She saw Magpie running from the milking shed with a bucket. She dipped it into the horse's trough and ran into the cabin. She came out of the cabin with the bucket a moment later and ran toward the river. She returned, hurrying back into the cabin.

Collan finally reached the yard and Etta hustled down. She looked around frantically as Ring and Sally jumped on her excitedly. "Teddie! Teddie!" She could hear Teddie sobbing loudly but couldn't see where he was. She turned and turned around again, searching.

"He's over here, Etta." Collan ran into the chicken coop and emerged a moment later, holding a sobbing Teddie, chicken feathers falling off his head.

Henrietta hastened over and took him from Collan.

BOOM! BOOM!

"Get your head down, Etta, and run to the stable, behind the door." Henrietta obeyed Collan with Ring and Sally following her, but she kept watching through a crack, holding Teddie. Magpie retrieved more water. Collan ran into the cabin and she could see him grabbing a quilt and batting at flames.

A moment later, Tinker emerged from the pines behind her cabin and hurried limping into her home, carrying her husband's old rifle. He snatched another blanket and worked at extinguishing the fire while Collan joined Magpie running back and forth to the river with buckets.

Henrietta heard no more gunfire and the smoke finally lessened that had been billowing from the rear of her home. Collan, Magpie, and Tinker eventually emerged out of her front door and all sat down wearily on her porch steps. Henrietta walked tentatively out of the stable, cradling Teddie, and Collan motioned her over.

"Oh, my Lord. What happened?" Henrietta asked dazedly, sitting down next to Collan.

Before anyone could answer, the Farrar brothers came thundering into her yard, jumping off their horses. Henrietta saw that Ike was holding Buzzie by the reins.

The Farrars all looked around, gaping, but Ike was the first to speak. "Have you all gone crazy?!"

Chapter Twenty-eight

Henrietta had just finished mopping the floors, Magpie had just laid Teddie in his cradle, sucking his thumb, and Collan and the men had just completed nailing some boards over the gaping hole in the rear of the bedroom Magpie had claimed, when they all heard a loud crack. Magpie watched in muted horror as the corner of her bedroom roof suddenly sagged and dropped a foot.

They all were a bit too jaded at this point to show much reaction, but Hank walked over and kicked and pushed at the damaged structure. He then turned back around and said, "I think it will probably hold for tonight."

Henrietta nodded and said dolefully, "Oookaaay. Does anybody want some coffee?"

Everyone nodded, took their seats at the table and watched silently as she prepared a pot. It had been decided to finish the work required before stopping for any lengthy explanation from Magpie and Tinker for what had occurred this evening.

As she poured the cups and then took a seat herself, Collan turned to Tinker and said, "So tell me exactly what happened, moment to moment."

Tinker nodded once. "Well, like I already said, Magpie and I were just starting to eat some supper when we smelled smoke. So we saw that it was coming from her bedroom—"

"Did you leave a candle burning there? Did a lantern tip over?" Hank asked.

"Oh, no. Definitely not. In fact, I told Magpie that the fire seemed to be coming from outside because the logs were just smoking, but there were no flames inside her bedroom. At least not yet."

"Then what?"

"So I walked outside and headed toward the rear of the cabin. Sure enough there was a pile of logs burning fiercely by the back corner. Some had even been shoved underneath and were catching fire. But while I was looking at that, the smoke got worse in the cabin so Magpie picked Teddie up and was heading toward his playpen in the yard when we both heard gunfire. Magpie swore a bullet went just by her so she ran instead to take cover with Teddie behind those rocks by the chicken coop. I scurried into the house and grabbed that old rifle that Henrietta has—I hadn't brought my own gun over here tonight—and crept into that timber where the gunfire seemed to have come from."

"Whoa. Hold on. Who the hell would want to take aim at Magpie?" Collan asked amazed.

Magpie crossed her arms and stared straight ahead, saying nothing. Henrietta blew out a long breath ready to answer when Tinker continued. "That's what I was wondering, but then I caught glimpse of some fella dodging through the trees. So I followed as best I could and tried getting him with that darned old rifle but missed. He kept moving, until he took cover behind some rocks and then tried to get me. I fired back but missed again. By then I could see the flames rising over the trees and hurried back to help save the cabin. By then

271

Magpie had stashed Teddie in the chicken coop and was running buckets back and forth."

Collan shook his head. "This makes no sense. Who would want to do harm to this homestead? To these women? *Any* woman?"

Henrietta sat straighter. "Well, as a matter of fact . . ."

Collan's eyes widened. "Are you kidding me, Etta? You have an answer for this and you're just telling us now about it?!"

She raised her hands. "Now I can explain. And Collie stop getting angry. You always do that when you don't have to."

"Explain what?! That you both have been in harm's way and didn't say anything before now, knowing that Herm wanted me to protect you." He stood and frowned. "And knowing how much you mean to me. This is unbelievable."

Tinker turned to Magpie. "What the hell, Magpie." He uttered some Cheyenne words to her, but she turned her head away.

Ike stood then. "Hey, what about us? We're your friends and nearest neighbors. How come you didn't tell us?"

Clint nodded and glared at Henrietta.

Hank shook his head, disgustedly. "Now, everybody, *sit* down. Let's hear what she has to say."

"Thank you, Hank." Henrietta said.

Collan and Ike sat down. Clint crossed his arms and began to look hurt.

Henrietta started. "See, one day I was looking out my window and across the river I saw that Magpie was getting in a fight with a man—who turned out to be her husband—and I went outside to help her. Now I hadn't met Magpie before this, but her husband was obviously mean. So anyways, he tried to hit me in the head with a rock, but before he could Magpie got him in the leg with a gun." She turned to Magpie. "That was his leg, wasn't it? I can't quite remember."

Magpie nodded.

"So anyways, he collapsed because actually he was so drunk, also, but then he got up and threatened us saying he was going to get us. And then he rode off." Henrietta paused, thinking. "Oh, and then Magpie decided she was going to live with me."

"And you didn't tell anyone this *because* . . .?" Collan asked incredulously.

Henrietta shook her head. "Well, obviously, we couldn't."

"Why not?"

"Pay attention here, Collie. For heaven's sake. Magpie is an Indian and Indians can't attack one of our race. She could get into big trouble. You men are so prejudicial about these things." She rolled her eyes at him. "Except . . ."

"Except what? Oh, and by the way, Etta, you failed to mention that he looked like me and you in your story."

"Well, anyways, there might be a slight problem."

"Oh, *God*! Now what?"

"That horrible Mister Whyte might have seen the whole thing. He was on the ridge when I looked up at one point. I can't tell. He didn't say anything when he came here for tea, but he seemed to recognize Magpie. I'm not really certain."

"So Mister Whyte might also be involved."

Henrietta shrugged. "I'm not sure. But if he says something I'm just going to tell him that *I* assaulted her husband, not Magpie, after he attacked me—if only I was a better liar."

Tinker started speaking angrily to Magpie in Cheyenne. Magpie narrowed her eyes at him. Henrietta could only imagine what was being said, so she tried to intervene. "Now, Tinker, you have to see that we weren't even sure if her husband was still alive or would ever return, but if he did Magpie had told me that she was going to tell him that she wasn't married to him anymore. So the only issue would be whether something has to be told to the church that married them initially." She tried to smile pleasantly and reassuringly.

Tinker continued scowling.

Collan shook his head. "This is *unbelievable,* Etta."

She hung her head. "Yeah. I guess so." After a moment she looked up and asked, "Do you think one of you all could teach me how to use a gun properly? Oh, and Hank, just how long do you think it will take to fix that room?"

Collan interrupted before Hank could answer. "Why, Etta? Do you have plans on living here still?"

She straightened, puckering her brows. "Ah—"

Collan stood and pointed at her. "Oh, no. That's out. Don't even consider it, Etta. Until this husband is caught, you're staying away from here where he can't find you easily."

"But, perhaps he's run away for good now."

"Yeah, and perhaps not."

She stood now also. "But what do you expect Magpie and me to do, Collie?" She stamped her foot. "Oh, no. I am *not* living with my sister."

He paused a moment, frowning at her determinedly, before answering, "You're moving in with me."

"What? We can't do *that*! How would it *look*?" She started to pace towards the door, before turning back around. "And how would we explain it? We can't tell anybody what happened. Magpie could get into trouble." She then narrowed her eyes at all the men. "And none of you better squeal about this to anyone or you're going to get it from me."

Clint widened his eyes. "We won't, Miss Henrietta."

Ike stood and smiled. "I got an idea. Why don't you move in with us, Miss Henrietta? You could still do all the cookin' and Magpie can hunt—"

Collan glared at him. "Shut up, Ike."

Clint kicked him. "You better sit down. You're getting Collan angry."

He sat back down grumbling.

Collan placed his hands on his hips. "Why do you have to explain anything to anybody? You simply say, 'My cabin got damaged in a fire and I've moved until it can be fixed properly.'"

She looked at him incredulously. "Into your cabin? *With you?* I'll be labeled a loose woman."

He looked at her a moment. "Then marry me."

She raised her hands into the air, helplessly. "We haven't even courted properly yet."

He shook his head. "Etta, we've been courting each other since we've been little kids whether you realized it or not."

"Not!" She started pacing again. "You've lost your noodles, Collie. And I'm not marrying a man who proposes only because I got some scoundrel after Magpie and me." She looked at him earnestly. "Marriage should be taken seriously and sweetly and mean something special and—"

Hank raised his hand for attention. "I got an idea."

Collan and Henrietta both looked at him irritably. "What?"

"Why don't Magpie and you move into Collan's cabin where Tinker and he can keep a watch out for you both and why don't we all build another small cabin for Collan? Working together we could complete it in a few days. Just say this cabin requires repairs because your roof collapsed. Nobody will think twice." Hank shrugged. "Simple."

Henrietta opened her mouth to protest, then said, "That actually sounds fine."

Chapter Twenty-nine

Etta had been living with Collan for three weeks in Willow Park—or as Abner and Collan liked to refer to it as, "moraine park" since there was a downpour nearly every afternoon this summer. At first she had fretted that everyone would find out the whole truth and possibly think poorly of her, then she had worried that nobody would discover anything and not realize how they could even visit with her. But before they had locked her cabin door, she had nailed a paper on it stating where she could be found for her baked goods. They had also hauled her precious cook stove over to Collan's so before long Etta was prospering just as before. Only Collan got to see her more—which he liked.

Tinker was still annoyed with Magpie and it was uncertain whether they would ever make up. He still lived alone in the cabin he had built for himself the year before. Collan now resided in a small hut adjacent to it and across the pasture Teddie and the women reigned in his former home.

He scarcely recognized the place any more. Etta had added all her girly touches, such as bouquets of flowers and table cloths. The porch was now her tea shop. And his roof was no longer made of peat. Abner, the Fergusons and he had established their saw mill on Steep Mountain. His roof and the sod roof of the Fergusons were now replaced with shake shingles.

Collan was proud to show Etta all he had accomplished—she had never visited his place before this move—yet he sought more. He yearned to buy her pretty presents. He wanted to prove he was capable of raising a family. He coveted being a successful rancher. He hoped to pay loyal Tinker who was still working for just board and room. And he aspired to be prosperous enough so that he could enjoy more leisure time with Etta. Currently he was so busy with his cattle and the saw mill that he saw Etta only for a quick meal at best— and that he often had to skip also—which was better than when they had lived on separate properties but still not enough.

But Teddie deserved his attention also. He was playful and seemed pleased to see Collan whenever he arrived. Collan thought he should show Teddie the type of devotion a man could provide—he dreamed of going fishing and hunting with Teddie one day. Collan no longer thought of Teddie as Etta's husband's child—hell he had helped bring the tot into the world.

Yet he realized that it was going to be a struggle for many years before he actually was established and had the luxury to do all he desired. He had some savings still from the sale of his family's general store, but he didn't want to go through it all quickly and lose any sense of security.

So far, there had been no hide or sign of that scalawag of a husband, and Collan wondered how long it would be before Etta insisted she move back to her property. He wanted to keep her with him as long as possible. The Farrars were fixing her cabin but still stopping by for occasional meals. He wanted to tell the brothers to slow down in their work but refrained, not wanting to appear too forlorn for Etta's company.

Therefore, considering all these churned emotions, when a letter arrived with a surprising message, he greeted the news with mixed feelings. They were all sitting outside on the porch—Collan, Etta, Magpie, Teddie and Tinker—enjoying an outdoor supper when the Farrars arrived.

Ike was full of excitement as they all dismounted. "You probably haven't heard the big news yet."

Clint nodded. "We got the mail and the latest newspapers before we swung by here."

Hank handed a bundle of meat to Etta.

She got up from the table and took the package. "Thanks, Hank. I made some bread and meat pies for you to take with you before you leave. Let me just put this package in cold storage and then I'll serve you some of our supper. Have a seat." As she headed to the locked root cellar that Collan had dug next to his cabin, she said, "Ike, wait until I get back to the table before you spill the beans."

Clint, however, gave Collan and Tinker each one of the newspapers, ignoring her request. Collan quickly read the headline and his eyes widened. This *was* huge news. He looked over to see Tinker's reaction but saw him merely smirking, as he handed the paper to Magpie who, though she could not read, could gather from the illustrations what had happened.

Etta returned from the cellar and scooped some stew into bowls and placed them in front of the brothers.

She sat back down. "Okay, Ike. Tell me what has occurred."

Ike raised his hands in the air for affect. "You won't believe it, but Custer and his men were slaughtered fighting Indians in Montana Territory."

Etta gasped. "You're kidding?"

Ike shook his head. "Nope. Over a couple hundred men lost their lives. The Indians were having some kind of big powwow when Custer attacked, but I guess they were overrun by the savages. That Crazy Horse and Sitting Bull were thought to be there also."

Magpie adjusted Teddie's sleeping position in her arms and smiled. "I'm happy. I think Cheyenne Dog Soldiers got him. Custer very bad man."

Collan shook his head. "No, Magpie. He was a great American hero. Brave and honorable—"

"Bullshit, Collan." Tinker exclaimed.

"What did you say?" Ike asked astounded.

"If you call attacking innocent Indian children, old folks and defenseless women—brave—and then treating your own subordinates cruelly and shamefully—honorable—then I got some swamp land for you to buy."

Ike looked puzzled. "But I thought . . ."

Tears came to Tinker's eyes. "You don't know the horrific atrocities I and others were forced to partake in, the stories I heard and know to be true. . . ."

Etta hurriedly stood and walked over to give Tinker a hug from behind. He patted her arms silently, then continued. "How that animal Custer was ever allowed to take command again, I'll never be able to comprehend. Glory hungry and reckless, that's all he was. My God, he was court-martialed! Why was he ever

280

reinstated?" Tinker wiped his eyes with his sleeve and Etta sat back down. "Oh, of course. This is about that golden bootie in the Dakotas. The Indians were resisting giving up their land, and I bet the commanders in charge just knew that Custer would be overly aggressive and violent—that's actually what they probably wanted without having to take the responsibility themselves—so they let Custer loose. Little did they realize what they were up against with those Indians."

Etta shook her head. "Well, I feel sorry for those men fighting with him and also, for their poor wives."

Tinker nodded. "Honest enough. But I'll tell you that his brothers were probably there, also, and they were scarcely a sight better than him. And his wife was either a fool for sticking with him or just as grasping for prestige as he and either way I can't respect her."

"Why do men fight in battles at all? Why can't they sit down and just talk? Look at all the people on both sides of this war who are forced to suffer." Etta looked so upset. Collan reached out and squeezed her hand.

"Well, I reckon there's going to be some big trouble for those Indians who won this battle. It ain't over yet." Hank commented.

"That's for sure." Collan nodded.

"The Indians go—" Magpie motioned wide with her fingers.

"I agree." Tinker said. "They'll scatter."

"Do you think you know any of them, Magpie?" Etta asked.

She nodded. "Yes. I have cousins. They are brave warriors."

281

"When was the last time you saw any of them?" Etta wondered.

"Many moons."

Tinker chuckled ruefully. "I wouldn't be surprised if one of them showed up here. News travels amongst those folks. Magpie ran across that old one called Lone Wolf last year while she was hunting with you Farrars."

"She did?" Ike asked incredulously. "You didn't tell us, Magpie."

Magpie shrugged.

"He got his name because he ventures alone, but he spreads the news to his kind." Tinker added, "Her tribe probably realizes now that Magpie lives here and associates with you Farrars."

Ike scrunched his expression. "I'm not sure if I like that. What if they go after us?"

Magpie chuckled and then shook her head. "No, you are my friends."

Hank blew out a breath. "Well, thank God for that." Hank then turned to Clint. "What about the letters?"

Clint stood. "Oh, I forgot." He walked over to his saddlebag and withdrew a couple envelopes. He walked back to the table. "These came for you, Collan and Miss Henrietta. I thought I would save you a trip fetching them."

Etta smiled warmly as she took hers. "Thank you, Clint. You're always so sweet."

Clint turned red as Ike snorted.

Ike then asked, "Well, aren't you going to read it, Miss Henrietta?"

Clint whacked his brother. "It's her private bees wax, you oaf."

Collan watched as Etta hesitated at first. Letters were precious on the frontier—something to be cherished. But she obviously didn't want to disappoint those naturally curious so she opened her envelope. Collan glanced down at his and was puzzled by the return address so he quickly broke the seal on his own.

There was a moment of silence as they both read. Etta broke the quiet first. "Oh, my Lord." Her eyes widened.

Ike asked, "What is it? What is it?"

She looked over. "My sister Clarissa is coming for a visit."

"Oh, is that all?" Ike scoffed.

Etta stood. "She's bringing the whole family." She turned to Collan. "What am I going to *say*? About *everything*?"

Collan chuckled. "Nothing."

"*What* do you mean nothing? I haven't told her a thing about being here." She frowned. "You didn't blab again, did you, Collie?"

He shook his head.

"Well, at least I don't have to explain about some events. But still, we're practically living together. OUT OF WEDLOCK."

"Now I told you how you could correct that."

"Oh, would you shut up?! I have to think." Etta started to pace. "Clarissa is not stupid. And she snoops. First thing tomorrow, you have to move *all* of your stuff out of this cabin, Collie."

He ignored Etta's rant and went back to reading his letter. He got to the end and looked up. "Jesus Christ."

Etta nodded vigorously. "Yes, this is serious, but don't use the Lord's name in vain, Collie."

"Oh, I'm not talking about your bossy sister, Etta."

She stopped in her tracks. "What is it, then?"

"Remember you met my uncle once?"

"Your father's brother? Yes. I thought he passed."

"He did. This is about my mother's brother. The one that visited from Philadelphia."

"Yes, I kind of recollect him. We were both little then."

Collan nodded. "Well, he passed."

Etta sat and reached for his hand. "Oh, I'm sorry, Collie."

"Thank you, Etta. But I scarcely knew him. He was like a stranger." He shook his head, amazed. "Seems he named me to inherit. None of his own family remained. A lawyer wants me to travel to Philadelphia to decide how to finish his estate."

Etta stood again. "Oh, yes, Collie. You should leave. *Immediately.* Before my sister arrives." She shrugged, smiling. "That way I can tell her this is my place. I'm sure I can act my way through that one."

Collan frowned. "There's a lot to consider before I go."

"Like what?"

"Well, how about Magpie's husband? Forget about him, Etta?"

She waved her hand dismissively. "Oh, he's gone. Long gone."

"I'm not so certain."

Tinker spoke. "I can watch out for them, Collan. I can handle the cattle also."

Hank added. "We can hang around here more and help Tinker."

Collan nodded. "Thanks, Hank. Thanks, Tinker."

Collan wanted to ask, but aren't you going to miss me, Etta? We are just starting our relationship and I could be gone for a few weeks. He realized, though, that he would only sound desperate. He hesitated a moment longer, pondering, then said, "I guess I'm going to Philadelphia."

Etta smiled widely. "I'll help you pack."

Chapter Thirty

Henrietta held Teddie as she waved goodbye to Collan. He kicked his horse into a trot, and she watched until he disappeared over a ridge. Despite initially encouraging him to leave, now that the time had come for him to actually depart, she felt saddened. She realized she would miss him—a lot.

He must have sensed her feelings because she had given Collan such a long hug goodbye—not wanting to let go. He had assured her that he would return as soon as he could. He planned on taking the train from Denver back East. They both figured the trip would take about a week. He hoped to stay no longer than a week there and then spend another week returning to Denver. So with luck, he would be back with them by three weeks.

She walked slowly into the quiet cabin. She placed Teddie in the playpen, hoping she could get through baking some bread and a strudel before he demanded some more attention. She gave him the tiny horse George had carved for her—Teddie loved holding it, and Henrietta regretted not asking George to make some other animal forms before he had departed. She also tossed into the pen the cloth doggy stuffed animal she had sewn for him. Teddie pointed to the dining table and said, "*Nahqui.*" Hanging over the edge was the toy bear Magpie had sewn for him made out of soft fur and

Henrietta handed him that also. Henrietta was now learning some Cheyenne herself because half the time Teddie called the toy bear the Cheyenne word for it.

Henrietta then started mixing the ingredients for strudel dough and kneading it. She broke off a couple pieces of raw dough for Ring and Sally who were lounging at her feet—they loved it that way—before letting the dough rest for an hour. Next she shaped the bread dough into loaves—she had made it a couple hours before and it had already risen. She placed the bread into the oven to bake just as Teddie started giggling. He threw his doggy stuffed animal out of the pen.

Henrietta shook her head. Oh, no. He was already getting bored. Daily he was becoming more active and curious about the world around him. Yesterday he had even tried standing before plopping down quickly—she was glad that Collan had had the opportunity to witness that event before leaving.

She wished again that Collan was here now. Her son always enjoyed the rougher play Collan favored and slept well afterwards. Ah, well, Teddie was just going to have to make do with mainly her for the next few weeks.

Magpie was currently riding the range with Tinker, looking in on the cattle. They were spending more time together again and Henrietta knew it was not just because Tinker could use the help. Magpie seemed particularly happy at present and Henrietta was glad for her.

Henrietta started preparing the filling for the strudel. Making strudel was always more time consuming than any other baked goods and had only been made in her family for special occasions, but she persevered because the strudel these days was one of her best sellers—more so than the pies.

Bash. Thump. Whack. She looked over. Teddie was on his back, kicking the side of his playpen. Darn. She didn't want to stop now because the strudel dough would soon be ready to finish preparing.

She blew out a breath. She didn't like to give Teddie her cookware because it meant more washing for her, but she realized she didn't have a choice. He looked ready to wail. She gathered up a baking dish, a pan, a pot, and her largest spoon.

"Here, Teddie. Pound on these." She placed the collected items in his pen.

Teddie gleefully used the spoon to bang on the pot and Henrietta starting rolling out her strudel dough. She had to make the dough paper thin and brush it with butter so the crust would be delicate and flaky. But after what seemed like only a short while later, Teddie began howling in protest. Oh, no. She absolutely could not take a break at this point.

Henrietta then did what she always considered her absolutely last, all-else-has-failed, effort—the thing she knew she should not do and had only discovered by chance one day that it worked. She looked down at Sally and said, "You're such a good dog. Would you like some cookies?"

Henrietta then took her cookie jar out of the cupboard and placed it in the pen. She looked inside and saw there were about nine remaining. She picked up Sally and put her in the playpen with Teddie. She could never do this with Ring—he didn't tolerate the indignity—but since he was wagging his tail, also, realizing what was going on, she gave him a cookie.

She looked at Teddie who had quieted. "Now give Sally a cookie, Teddie."

She gave Teddie a cookie and he grinned. As he held it to Sally she snatched it from his hand with her mouth and gulped it down. Teddie giggled happily and repeated the process as best he could—which was essentially letting the pooch eat from the jar. Henrietta returned to her baking, placing her filling on the dough, then rolling it into a loaf shape. She was just placing her strudel in the oven and removing her bread when she glanced over and saw that Teddie had curled up asleep next to a snoozing Sally.

Henrietta smiled. She so wished Collan could see the sweet scene. She decided to bake cookies with the time just gifted to her. An hour later, the bread, cookies and strudel finished, and the baking dishes washed, she looked over at the playpen again. Sally was wagging her tail again and Teddie was grabbing hold of the side of the pen, trying to stand.

Henrietta lifted Sally out and then reached for Teddie. "What are you doing, Teddie? Do you want to try walking?"

She placed Teddie on his feet in front of one of the benches. She helped him grab hold of the edge of the bench and he unsteadily remained standing. She knelt down a few feet from him. "Come to me, Teddie. Come to me."

Teddie let go of one hand and fell down.

"Oh, no, let's try it again."

She placed him before the bench again. He let go of a hand, but this time he remained standing.

She smiled encouragingly. "That's it. Come to me." She held out her arms.

With shaky concentration, he took a step and fell into her arms. She held him to her for a moment. "You did it, Teddie! You did it!"

She tickled his belly and then stood, holding him. "I'm so proud of you."

Henrietta was amazed and then she remembered her husband Charles telling her once that he had matured quickly and started walking at nine months of age also. She stepped outside the cabin with Teddie and looked up at the sky. "I hope you saw your son just now, Charles."

She then gazed at Teddie and said, happily, "We have to show Papa Collan when he returns, don't we, Teddie?"

Teddie searched around the yard. "Papa."

"No, Papa went away. He'll be back though. He promised us."

As Henrietta walked back into the cabin with Teddie, she admitted to herself for the first time ever, the full extent of her feelings. She was obviously, without any doubt, deeply in love with Collan. The thought was exciting and exhilarating and momentous and everything wonderful that life could offer . . . and yet still a bit scary when she thought how vulnerable that made her. So now what was she going to do about it?

"I think you should consider courting him, Henrietta. He's handsome and successful and would make a wonderful father for your son." Her sister Clarissa sat down on the porch chair and took a sip of her tea.

Henrietta shook her head. "I'm not interested."

Clarissa rolled her eyes. "You said that last year, but surely you must be getting over your husband by now." She took a peek at the noise coming through the cabin door. "Eddie, put that down. Wally! Stop teasing your sister."

Ellie burst into tears. Clarissa held out her arms. "Come here, Ellie. Come to Mama."

Ellie toddled onto the porch and sat in Clarissa's lap.

Henrietta's brother-in-law, Edward, appeared at the door. "I found the fishing equipment in the corner of your bedroom, Henrietta. Thanks for letting us borrow it. I'll take the boys now. Wally, get away from those cookies."

Clarissa and Henrietta watched in silence as Edward stepped off the porch and headed toward the river, his boys eagerly scampering behind him.

Clarissa puckered her brows slightly. "Since when have you taken up the hobby of fishing, Henrietta?" She shuddered. "You couldn't get me to do that."

Henrietta didn't bother to respond.

"But then I wouldn't have moved to this uncivilized settlement either. I told Edward so on the way here—not in this lifetime I said." She looked around at the scenery. "The landscape is beautiful, though. I'll give you that. The mountains, the pretty pasture, the river flowing through it." She took another sip of tea, then continued. "Did you know you wrote such detailed directions to your cabin, we didn't have to ask a soul how to find you?"

Henrietta had been counting on that. Clarissa and her family had come in their own wagon, following the stage, and had been instructed when and where to veer off, thus avoiding Henrietta's neighbors who might have said something she didn't want her sister to hear.

"So let's talk about Ernest again. How about if you come visit me next and I'll introduce you both."

Henrietta inwardly groaned. She was only on the first day of this vacation visit of Clarissa's and she wanted to gag her. "No, Clarissa. I'm not attracted to the prospect in the least."

Clarissa pursed her lips. "Oh, my Lord. I just had a thought. Are you attached to some fella *here*?" She answered her own question. "No, you couldn't possibly find this rugged type appealing."

"Why not? We both grew up on a farm, remember."

"Well, that perhaps is so. However, there was refinement in our home. Our parents weren't country bumpkins no matter if Daddy tilled the soil."

"And there's refinement here if you know where to look for it. Not everyone is some uneducated buffoon."

Clarissa pointed. "Oh, look. I think that must be your son Teddie coming over here now with your servant. What did you say her name was? Magpie? That sure is a funny name."

Teddie had been fussing before Clarissa had arrived and Magpie had taken Teddie outdoors to entertain him. He was resting in her arms now as she

292

carried him toward the cabin. Henrietta watched a moment, then answered her sister. "Magpie is not my servant. We're friends."

"Oh." Clarissa stared in silence, gazing closer. "But she's . . . an Indian." Her eyes widened then. "You made acquaintance with a squaw."

Henrietta smiled. "Yes, in fact she's one of my best friends now. I don't know what I would do without her."

Clarissa shook her head, astounded. "But aren't you afraid? She's an Indian."

"You already pointed that out. And no, I'm not scared. I also know she would give her own life to protect Teddie. She adores him."

"He's wearing moccasins!"

"He also speaks some Cheyenne words."

"Good Lord."

"Clarissa, just behave. We were lucky enough to be raised without prejudice by our parents. Don't act ignorant now."

"You're correct." Clarissa nodded. "You're absolutely correct."

As Magpie approached nearer, Clarissa stood and placed Ellie on her feet. She walked up to Magpie. "Can I hold him? I'm his Aunt Clarissa."

Magpie nodded and placed Teddie in her arms.

Clarissa smiled sweetly. "Hi, Teddie. I'm your aunt. Aren't you such a handsome boy. You look just like your father." She turned around, holding Teddie, with tears in her eyes. "Oh, Henrietta. He's lovely. Just lovely." She motioned with a hand. "Come here, Ellie. Meet your cousin Teddie."

And Henrietta remembered again why she loved her sister so dearly. Perhaps she would be able to make it through the next three days.

Magpie decided to reside in Collan's small cabin across the pasture while Clarissa visited. But Teddie saw a lot of his relatives. Henrietta could see he enjoyed especially playing with his cousins who were indulgent considering Teddie's infant age. Ellie tried carrying him once as if he was her own baby. Henrietta thought how nice it would be to have another child and give Teddie a sibling.

Clarissa asked about Collan casually in passing, knowing he was out of town. Henrietta divulged nothing of their changed relationship. She didn't want one question to lead to another just yet. Tinker and the Farrars all stopped by briefly to say hello to her sister. All were wearing their work clothes and looked like a cross between cowboys and old mountain trappers. She had caught Clarissa staring initially, mouth agape, but her sister warmed as the Farrars spoke kindly and politely and even teased her while Tinker struck up a conversation with her husband.

The tourists kept arriving and Clarissa was suddenly in her element. She helped serve pie and tea and chatted amiably, especially with the obviously wealthier customers. Her husband and the boys loved the fishing and hiking and all slept soundly each night.

By the time the hour had arrived for her sister to leave, Clarissa and Henrietta both felt disappointed the visit was at an end and they hugged each other tightly.

Clarissa broke the embrace first. "You have to write more, Henrietta. And visit us."

Henrietta nodded. "I will."

Clarissa looked around once more at the view. "You know, Henrietta. I can now see the appeal. This place is . . . enchanting."

"It is. Come again. Will you?"

"Perhaps even next year." Clarissa shrugged and smiled. "I might even bring a fella for you to meet." She then chuckled impishly and stepped into the wagon. Henrietta just shook her head.

No sooner had Clarissa and her family departed, then Henrietta received another set of visitors, one of them being the most annoying who had ever come a-calling.

Chapter Thirty-one

Lord Dunraven was arrogant and condescending, though Henrietta could see he was not much older than she. He was also fascinating to listen to in a curious sort of way. So, Henrietta sat down at the table across from him and served him tea with her best set. Lord Dunraven had just finished telling the story of his encounter with a mountain lion in these parts. She was not sure if she believed him. But the other guest present obviously did.

Albert Bierstadt shook his head. "I never tire of hearing that tale—to think you conquered the beast by yourself. Amazing."

It certainly was, Henrietta thought wryly. She had heard through gossip that the Lord was a world traveler and had once worked as a journalist in a war zone. With that kind of impressive personal history, why did he feel he had to tell a story of self-aggrandizement? But then his pursuit of an immense cattle ranch, his own personal game preserve, and dominance over Estes Park was more of the same, now, wasn't it?

She decided to give the other guest some attention and turned, asking, "Would you like some more strudel, Mister Bierstadt?"

"*Ja, bitte, Frau Schodde.*" He smiled. "*Es schmeckt.*"

"*Dankeschoen*, I'm glad you like it." Henrietta smiled warmly back. She had taken an immediate liking to the artist of German heritage accompanying the lord. She placed another piece on his plate. "What brings you to Estes Park, Mister Bierstadt?"

"I paint landscapes and you cannot get better scenery than here in these mountains." He looked around and stood. "With your permission, I would like to walk around your property first before I eat some more."

"Absolutely."

He bowed and clicked his heels very German like before descending the porch steps and strolling towards the nearby pasture. His parents had immigrated to America from Germany when he was a youth, but the artist had returned to the homeland to study.

The Lord commented, "Albert is part of the Rocky Mountain School of Landscape Painting. I plan to commission several works from him."

Of course, you do Lord Bragalot Henrietta thought. She looked more closely at his fine attire. She was glad she was at least wearing the new dress she had made for herself. But since she was stuck with just him for the moment she made another effort to be polite. "Perhaps you'll use the paintings to adorn the hotel I hear you plan on building."

The Lord nodded. "Indeed. My hotel will strive to have only the best. Luxury accommodations surrounded by the most spectacular scenery. The place should be a far sight better than what is available now. And Albert with his superb eye for detail has agreed to help me pick out the location."

"Well, you do realize that this area here is already claimed."

"Yes, however, Mister Whyte informed me that the moraine just south of here is mine. He also suggested that since you were developing a reputation for your pastries and this quaint tea shop we might consider stopping by." He paused a moment and then with an inquisitive frown said, "I heard you moved from your original cabin to here after a fire occurred in somewhat questionable circumstances."

"Who told you that?"

"Mister Whyte."

"And questionable circumstances? How so?" The Lord was irritating Henrietta without even trying. And why did the description of her tea shop as *quaint* sound so demeaning coming from him?

"Mister Whyte said that it appeared to him as if the fire might have begun on the outside corner first—as if someone purposely set it."

She had had enough. "So Mister Whyte was poking around *my* property? What business is it of his to do so?"

Lord Bragalot smiled confidently. "You must have become aware that everything that occurs in these parts is our business. Especially concerning property in dispute. But I'm sure you didn't set the fire out of spite because you realized you were going to have to forfeit the cabin."

"Certainly not!" she sputtered. "The title is in my name—"

"But a survey confirming the boundaries of the property has not been completed as yet or so I've heard."

"I'm sure there will be no discrepancy."

He smiled smugly. "Of course not. But I have informed Mister Whyte that he should resume all avenues of attaining property including completing surveys."

Oooh, she really did not like this man. She had wondered if the reason she had not heard from Whyte for months concerning her property was because he was ashamed of harassing a widow or perhaps he had thought his fencing the whole area scheme would be enough. Whatever the reason, Lord Bragalot obviously wanted Whyte to aggressively obtain property once again.

Pleasant Mister Bierstadt returned to the porch at that moment, smiling at Henrietta, and resumed eating. Henrietta summoned to memory all the German she had once known. She knew it was rude to speak a foreign language when someone in the party did not grasp it.

So that's exactly why she spoke the lengthiest conversation in German she had had in years. She only wished Collan could have been there. She imagined he would have instantly recognized her devilish motive and then laughed his head off.

Collan burst out laughing, gleefully happy, then caught himself. After all, his uncle had sadly passed away and this stuffy lawyer was explaining his inheritance in the most solemn tone of voice. But to think he was going to receive this much money and then more when his uncle's home was sold was just unbelievably great.

Oh, Collan wouldn't be rich, as if he were one of these new industrial tycoons—not even close—but he would be comfortable and have a buffer against disaster.

He bit back a smile and tried to concentrate on what the lawyer was droning on about now. But he suddenly had a memory of his mother saying that her brother could be miserly at times. Well, thank you, Uncle, for that, because Collan knew of plenty of ways the money could be spent.

He attempted a somber, sorrowful expression— the lawyer was explaining now how Collan was the only living relative remaining because of the misfortune of these relations who he scarcely remembered even meeting—but a chuckle again burst forth. The lawyer frowned and Collan again shut his mouth. Oh, come on. His uncle's wife had passed when she had leaned too far out an upstairs window, gossiping with a neighbor. Who would even think to make something like that up? He couldn't wait to tell Etta.

But the lawyer was now requesting that Collan stay in town until all the required paperwork could be completed by him and then Collan could sign the documents since he now knew Collan's decisions about the estate. He surmised that would take another three days.

Collan could live with that. He definitely could. He would still be back with Etta within the three weeks he had expected.

The next day since he had time to spare he decided to visit the "Centennial International Exhibition of 1876" that was taking place that summer in the city. The first official World's Fair in the United States was a huge exposition which had been organized to commemorate the hundredth-year founding of the country.

Multiple nations were participating with pavilions displaying their successes and wares. Some women's group even had their own structure and a *gal* showed how she could master a mechanical machine. Collan continued wandering from building to building, but the one containing the multitude of devices all working at once was particularly impressive *and noisy*. Machines were sewing, newspapers and wallpaper were being printed, logs were being sawed, but towering higher than a house above all others was the Corliss Steam Engine, powering the *thirteen* acres of machinery in the building by *five* miles of connecting shafting. And there sat only one attendant calmly reading a newspaper next to the engine giving power to the *hundreds* of machines—it boggled the mind.

Collan also saw clever new inventions on display. An electric light bulb, spinning machines and a typewriter drew large admiring crowds, but something called a telephone scarcely got anyone's attention—though Collan found it intriguing, what were they supposed to do with *that*?

Lines were long for drinks in the sweltering heat—the officials had initially tried to ban beer but had ended up caving in to the crowd—and as Collan waited, he thought how much he would have enjoyed bringing Etta and Teddie to this event. He could imagine how Teddie would have been in awe of the new sights, and Etta probably would have gotten a kick out of the dishwasher. Of course, he would have had to avoid the hawkers and scantily dressed strumpets dancing on stages in abundance just outside the fairgrounds but still there would have been plenty to see.

The next day he decided what items he would like to keep in his uncle's house. He experienced odd emotions initially since he felt as if he was intruding in a stranger's private environ, but then he recognized a portrait of his mother when she had been just a girl and was more at peace. His uncle was an educated man who had become a whiskey distiller. Collan packed nearly every book he found in his uncle's library—these were precious on the frontier. He wrapped expensive bedclothes, drapes, linen, and rugs in bundles. He boxed his uncle's tools and took away all the pictures. Then he pondered what to do about a piano, a sofa and some other nice furnishings. He finally arranged for shipping in crates back West by train.

He spent the remainder of the day and the following morning buying presents for those back home. He bought tons of beads and a colorful shawl for Magpie, toys for Teddie, and almost purchased a cheap fiddle for Tinker. But then the music shop owner had shown Collan an expensively made, but used fiddle, and Collan instantly realized that Tinker would value that one more. He also bought a pistol with a carved handle for Tinker and a rifle for himself.

Etta, however, was the most difficult to choose for. He wanted her presents to be extra special and have some meaning. He bought her expensive fabric, a necklace, and perfume, but was still not satisfied. Then he came across an item that he just had to buy for her, despite the damn thing being massively heavy and as unwieldy as hell. Swearing some more, he trudged back to the train station to arrange further shipping. God, what he did for this woman.

That afternoon he returned to the lawyer's office and finished what was necessary for the time being. The lawyer would handle the sale of his uncle's home and remaining possessions and deposit the money in Collan's bank account.

Before returning West, Collan thought about visiting the home where he had grown up, but some memories he still found too sad, especially concerning his brother who had not returned from the war. He pondered his life the last few years while he packed his baggage and admitted he had latched on to Etta with a kind of emotional desperation after the loss of his brother. But he hadn't voiced anything of the sort to Etta. She could not have grasped that his feelings for her had taken such a shift at the time. And he had ended up crushed when she had married her husband. He hadn't been at peace after that, roaming restlessly through life, including making the initial sudden decision to move to Estes Park. Her brother had been accurate when he had warned Collan that he couldn't run away from his inner thoughts. They came with you where you went.

But Collan didn't feel as if he was running restlessly from anything anymore—denying what he truly felt inside. He was running *to* something. Eagerly. He had a life full of hope and promise in Estes Park and he could not wait to get back. He boarded the train the next day. He was ready to go home.

The vote was counted and Colorado became the next state to join the union. Clara decided to hold a celebration and all were invited. Henrietta rode over to

303

her place in a wagon with Magpie, Teddie, and Tinker on a warm late afternoon with no clouds in the sky.

Nearly all in the community turned out for the festivities. Tables were set up for the food the women brought which was then eaten picnic style with blankets on the ground. Clara had arranged an area for dancing and a small band was playing.

Everyone was in a jovial mood and Henrietta yearned for Collan to be there also. However, he had not returned yet from his trip back East, though he was due any day now as long as nothing untoward had occurred.

Henrietta spread her blanket next to the one Clara and Sal were sharing. Magpie took Teddie in her arms and pretended to dance with him in front of the band. One musician recognized Tinker and handed over another fiddle to him. Tinker smiled and began playing.

Sal commented, "Well, now that we are a state, I say it's time the women were allowed to vote. Why should the Wyoming gals be the only ones with that privilege?"

Clara shook her head, disgustedly. "Men."

"One of my tourist guests told me how the vote went in Wyoming." Sal added, smirking.

"What do you mean?" Henrietta asked.

"Apparently one political party didn't really think much of allowing the women to vote even though it would draw more females into moving to their territory but just said they were in favor to *embarrass* the opposing party who they were sure were not for the notion and would upset the womenfolk with their views. But before those stupid men realized what was happening the idea passed. And you can bet those gals are not giving up that privilege." Sal smiled and then motioned with her head. "See that fella talking with my daughter?"

Clara and Henrietta followed her gaze.

Sal chuckled. "He's turning into a real regular guest. I wouldn't be surprised if they become hitched before the end of the year. So how is the tourist business progressing, Clara?"

"Steady, however, not everything has been going our way. We're having trouble with the toll road."

Sal nodded. "Oh, I think I heard something about that. Weren't your toll gates torn down?"

"More than once. Parts of the road have become in disrepair due to rock slides and washouts. People are complaining we're being neglectful, but there are just so many hours in the day."

"You can say that," Sal huffed. "Those whiners should try building a road themselves."

Magpie walked over and handed Teddie to Henrietta. "I dance with Abner."

"Sure thing, Magpie." Henrietta placed Teddie in her lap. He promptly squirmed out of it when he saw Hank walking by.

Teddie squealed and Hank stopped to pick him up. "Want to go look at the horses, Teddie?"

Teddie grinned.

Henrietta nodded. "Thanks, Hank."

"No problem." He smiled.

"Hank sure is one nice fella." Clara mused as they gazed at them walking toward the stable.

"You bet." Sal said. "And handsome enough, too." They all giggled. "He'd be married already, I'm sure, if there were more women out West to choose from."

Sal then turned and said, "However, on the other hand, look at that drunk tourist stumbling along over there. My mother used to have a saying—for a gal out in the frontier, considering the overwhelming number of men, the odds are good she'll find someone. Unfortunately, the *goods* are often *odd*."

Henrietta grinned, then watched Magpie dancing a moment. "Abner said his parents are moving in with him soon."

Clara smiled. "Oh, that's nice. You'll have more near neighbors."

Ike ran up to them then. "Did you all hear the latest news?"

Sal chuckled. "Yes, we've been gossiping."

"Huh?" Ike frowned.

"Never mind." Sal motioned with her hand to continue. "What do you have to tell us?"

Ike widened his eyes. "WildBill Hickok took a bullet to the back of his head while he was playing poker."

Henrietta gasped. "How did that happen?"

Ike shrugged. "Nobody has found out yet for sure."

"By some crazy person I suppose." Sal shook her head. "Now that's a sorry story. Can't say I'm surprised though. That's what seems to happen to rough men in tough country."

Ike frowned. "That's all you're going to say? I was expecting you to get more excited than *that*."

"Sorry to disappoint you, Ike." Clara tried to explain. "But we've just been talking about how men do stupid things."

"Aw, heck."

They chuckled as Ike stomped off.

"I guess some people called me foolish also when I bought my cabin." Henrietta mulled over.

Sal patted her hand. "Not me. I was proud of you."

"Thanks, but I scarcely realized what I was getting myself into."

"Yet you've done so well, Henrietta." Clara inserted.

Henrietta blew out a breath. "But with everybody's help."

"And what's wrong with that?" Sal asked.

"Nothing. I mean I'm so grateful. It's just . . ."

"What?" Sal frowned.

"Well, I still can't say I've ever been truly independent. I make my own decisions now, but I haven't proven myself yet. Not really."

"Well, I think you have. I mean as much as any of us has." Sal insisted.

Henrietta shrugged noncommittedly. "Perhaps."

"And perhaps the more important question is why being independent is so important to you." Clara gazed at her searchingly.

Henrietta looked back at Clara, unsure how to answer her. "I guess I just want to know that I have it in me to be so."

Sal snorted. "Believe me, you do."

Just then Henrietta heard a wailing and saw Hank approaching, carrying a crying Teddie back to her. "He's angry I wouldn't let him sit on the big stallion's back."

"You're kidding? He actually wanted to do that?"

Sal chuckled. "Oh, Teddie's going to be a handful when he grows up, Henrietta. Just watch my words."

She shook her head. "Good Lord."

A couple hours later, as they all returned home Magpie and Tinker said they wanted to look in on the cattle again and Henrietta didn't bother to question why since it sounded like an excuse to her for them to spend more time alone.

They watched her carry a now sleeping Teddie into the cabin, and Henrietta waved goodbye from the doorway. As she placed Teddie in his crib, Ring and Sally curled up next to him on the floor. There was some light still remaining on this long summer evening and Henrietta decided to sit outside for a while. It had become chillier so Henrietta grabbed her coat before leaving the cabin, closing the door on the pooches and her son and sitting down on the chair with the best view at the end of the porch.

As she gazed at the surrounding mountains, including magnificent Longs Peak, she felt content—her thoughts about not having attained a sense of true independence temporarily forgotten again in her peaceful surroundings. Life was treating her better now than just a year ago. She had enjoyed relaxing that afternoon with people she now considered her good friends.

And Collan was due home soon.

A waft of air suddenly blew the branches of a few nearby pines. But Collan had situated his cabin close to a rocky outcropping, acting as a break from the gusts. Henrietta liked that the wind was settled at his cabin. Her home by the river had felt every breeze.

Henrietta heard her horse neigh loudly by the stables and gazed across the pasture to determine why. She stood up out of her chair and took a step forward not seeing anything untoward when a rough hand clamped firmly over her mouth. Just as suddenly a beefy arm grabbed her by the waist from behind. She was struck with terror and frantically struggled to get free but was held tightly. She tried to scream but was unable. She twisted and writhed but was only held more forcefully.

She felt herself being hauled off the end of the porch. The chair she had been sitting in fell over as she tried to kick her attacker. Ring and Sally started fiercely barking inside the cabin. Teddie began wailing.

She was dragged across the yard to behind the stables and forced to lie on her front, a knee to her back holding her to the ground. She managed a short scream before a dirty rag was shoved into her mouth and then a cloth swung around her head to gag her. Her hands were tied behind her back and then her feet knotted together.

She continued to struggle to break loose but suddenly felt herself being lifted and roughly thrown sideways over the front of a saddle. With a heave, she managed to fall off but tumbled awkwardly to the ground.

Then a boot held her in place. "You stupid bitch."

She turned her head to get a good look at the man for the first time. It was scarcely necessary. Even though it had been a year, she fully recognized the voice.

She was then whacked in the head by the end of a pistol with such ferocity that she saw nothing more.

Chapter Thirty-two

Henrietta awoke with a pounding in her head. She opened her eyes and scrutinized her surroundings. She was lying on her front over dirt and sparse grass, still gagged and tied. She saw through the faint light coming from the start of a new day, the outlines of trees and a large rocky outcropping nearby—a scene so familiar and yet not. For all she knew, she could be anywhere in the vast range of mountains.

She then heard loud snoring off to her side. She wriggled until she could get a better view. The husband who Magpie hated was sprawled on his back, holding a bottle of whiskey in one hand and a gun loosely in the other. She was looking at her worst nightmare come to life.

But an even more frightening thought then came to fore. She wondered if Magpie had returned to the cabin to find her son or had she decided to spend the night with Tinker instead. Henrietta imagined all the horrible events that could occur to Teddie before he was discovered—what if he had managed to climb out of his crib and then opened the door and then had got lost trying to find her. He was walking now. Lord, anything was possible. He would never be able to defend himself against the beasts that roamed about. He didn't know how to swim. What if he got to the nearby river?

Henrietta struggled desperately to break loose from her ties, but she was restrained too tightly. She started blinking back tears of frustration but then caught herself. She had to stay calm and think. She looked again over at her attacker. If she could get his gun . . . but of course she was still tied. She had to somehow convince him to loosen the ropes and then she could try escaping. She started squirming closer to him so she could kick him awake. When she was practically on top of him she lifted her legs and let them fall heavily on his torso.

He jerked awake with a yelp, frowning deeply at her. He roughly shoved her legs off of himself and groggily announced, "So you finally came to, you stupid bitch."

He then stood, placing his gun in its holster. He stumbled a few feet away to crudely relieve himself in front of her. She was suddenly filled with rage instead of terror and tried to speak around the rag in her mouth. To her surprise, he then returned to where she was lying on the ground and removed her gag and the tie around her arms.

He sneered. "Go ahead and scream now all you want. Nobody's going to hear you out here."

She moved her stiff arms, placing herself in a sitting position. "Where are we and what do you want from me?"

He ignored her, picking up the whiskey bottle and taking a swig before placing it in a saddle bag.

He crouched down in front of her and studied her in silence. Henrietta stared back. He wasn't as old as she had first thought—perhaps in his thirties—but he certainly was filthy, haggard, stinking, weary and worn.

Henrietta wondered what Magpie had ever seen in the likes of a man such as he. But then he smiled briefly and sadly and though it was unsettling, there was a ghost of what the man might have been like before.

He then admitted, "I don't know what I want from you. I apparently did when I was on my latest drinking spree, but I don't now."

"Then let me go."

He shook his head. "No."

"Why not?"

He smirked. "And hang for kidnapping? Besides I might find some use for you. If not, I can try selling you into slavery down south." He eyed her. "Though you are a bit old."

She gasped. "You wouldn't."

"Try me." He stood and walked back to his saddlebag, taking another nip. "I can do anything while drinking."

"Then *stop*."

"I can't." He held the bottle up as if in a mocking toast. "I've tried, but I can't."

"But Magpie says it's killing you."

He smiled again sadly. "I know."

Henrietta shook her head taken aback. There was obviously no reasoning with a man who viewed himself so hopelessly—who could also be dangerously violent when drunk. She was going to have to escape. She looked around at her surroundings, feeling fraught again.

He read her mind. "Don't think of running. We've already travelled far into the frontier. You'll

313

either get lost and starve or be eaten by some animal. Your only chance is to stay with me."

She blinked back tears again, knowing there was some truth to what he said. But surely, they would eventually run into somebody who could help or perhaps he would stop for supplies at a settlement. Then she could try to escape. For now, she just had to stay alive.

He walked back over to his saddle, lying on the ground, and removed a coiled long rope. She noticed then that his horse was still sleeping hobbled nearby. He then proceeded to make a noose out of the cord.

"But just to make sure you don't get any foolish ideas." He placed the looped rope over her head and twisted the other end around his wrist. "We better go with this for a while."

She was back to feeling angry.

He tossed a blanket at her then. "Get some more rest. We'll be travelling far as soon as I finish packing up again."

Henrietta didn't think she could possibly fall asleep, but when she opened her eyes next—the knock on her head must have caused her drowsiness—it was now full morning and the pounding in her head was gratefully lessened. Her captor had his back turned to her and was tightening the cinch on his saddled horse.

She watched him a moment silently but found she could not give up the hope of reasoning with him again. From their brief conversation already, she knew he was not completely ignorant—just a pathetic drunk. Perhaps if she tried being friendlier, she could make some progress.

"I'm Henrietta. I don't know your name."

He turned around, appearing a bit startled at first. He hesitated before answering, then said, "Alec."

"Well, Alec, would you please untie my feet and take the rope off my head. Nature is calling for me."

"Huh? Oooh." He then shook his head. "I can untie the feet, but the rope remains."

"But I want some privacy." She turned red.

He shrugged. "Too bad." He cut the ties on her feet with a knife he had hanging from his belt and motioned her towards nearby shrubbery.

She felt like a dog on a leash but walked as far as she could before squatting. He at least had the courtesy to turn around. She hurried through her business as fast as she could, wiping with some leaves. An incongruent remembrance of changing Teddie's dirty cloths suddenly came to mind and helped stifle the degradation she was feeling. Whatever happened to her such as humiliating situations such as this one, really didn't matter, she tried convincing herself. She just had to stay alive she told herself once again and get back to her son.

And Collan . . . oh, Collan.

She did not want either of them to know the hurt of losing a loved one.

She brushed down her skirt and decided to continue with her plan at being amiable. She walked back to Alec with a pleasant smile. "All done. Should I make us breakfast before we leave?"

He looked at her confounded, obviously puzzled by her cheerful mood. "No. We'll eat jerky along the way. Get on the horse."

"What's his name?"

315

"Who?"

"The horse."

Alec frowned. "I haven't named him."

"Now that's a shame." She stroked the mount's mane a moment. "I think we should call him . . . Intrepid."

"Intrepid."

"Yes, you know like—"

"Fearless. I know what it means. I'm not stupid. Just get on the horse, Henrietta. Enough of your games."

She mounted, trying her best to pull her dress over her ankles.

Alec watched her a moment silently before seating himself behind her. He then curled his end of the leash around his waist. She noticed that his hands shook. She realized he was probably getting the shakes from not drinking. So he was going to try to stay sober while he fled with her. Yes, unfortunately, he was not stupid and this was going to be a long, long day.

Blessed nightfall came what seemed like an eternity later and they finally stopped for the evening. She practically crumbled on the ground when dismounting, her legs were so weary. Henrietta tried to guess how far they had travelled, but with all the twists and turns it was nearly impossible to know. They had mostly followed animal paths that Alec seemed to recognize with familiarity—she remembered that he had once been a trapper.

Despite her best efforts, conversation had been lacking during the day as Alec became increasingly irritable without his drink.

316

Alec now looked up at the sky. "You can make us dinner tonight. The clouds will mask the fire." Alec had managed to kill a rabbit during one of their rests by merely throwing a rock at it.

They had stopped by a creek and Alec and Henrietta first headed over there for a drink and to wash their faces. He studied her a moment and then took the rope from around her head. "If you're foolish enough to run now, you'll be a goner. Remember that."

She nodded. "I will."

"Gather logs for the fire while I unsaddle and put my horse to graze."

An hour later, they nibbled on roasted rabbit with beans.

Henrietta finally asked what she had been wondering all day. "Why did you take me instead of Magpie."

Alec chuckled mirthlessly as he took a drink from his bottle of whiskey. "Magpie is trouble. She wasn't always, but she is now." He shrugged. "Besides your looks please me better."

Henrietta swallowed uneasily. There had been a gleam in his eyes that had become increasingly uncomfortable throughout the day. She now felt that her plan to be friendly was backfiring on her.

She stood quickly. "I'll go wash our plates by the creek."

He watched her every move while he downed some more. She returned and took a blanket. The evening was warm and she longed to remove her heavy coat but didn't dare. With a calmness she did not feel, she lay on the ground and wrapped the blanket around her. She looked over at Alec. "Well, goodnight. See you in the morning." She turned away from him then, hoping he would leave her alone.

And he did while he drank for the next hour. But she was sweltering with the blanket and her coat on so as discreetly as she could she undid the buttons to her coat and lifted the blanket some so she could feel the breeze. Finally, too tired to stay awake any longer watching out for him, she fell into a fitful doze.

But she awoke with a jolt from the pressure of him straddling her as he roughly clasped her hands over her head. She just had to stay alive she told herself once again and get back to her loved ones, including her dear son, who for all she knew was now cold and hungry and pitifully crying for her.

Chapter Thirty-three

Henrietta struggled to get out from underneath him. "Alec stop. Please stop."

He ignored her pleas and Henrietta realized with terror that he was too strong for her to resist, despite her turning and twisting frantically. He pushed away the sides of her coat and with a yank, ripped off the buttons to the front of her dress. He then harshly grasped one of her breasts while he opened the front of his pants.

Now falling full-length on top of her, he clutched her hands again with one of his. He was so heavy she couldn't breathe. She really could not get in any air.

So she quit fighting him and lay passively. He was going to smother her otherwise. Despite his drunken haze, he sensed the change in her and lifted slightly to look down at her. She gulped in a precious breath of air.

"You won't fight me?"

She shook her head tearfully. He raised the bottom edge of her dress to her waist and lowered her drawers. Oh, God. It was really going to happen.

She closed her eyes and tensed, waiting for the final violation.

But . . . it didn't come. And when he still hadn't entered her a moment later, she looked down and realized with disgust that he was actually fondling himself, his—oh, my God—*his limp thing.*

Seeing her expression of horror, he shouted at her angrily, "You touch me."

She wanted to throw up but obeyed tentatively.

"More." He whispered as he breathed rapidly, but it soon became obvious that he was incapable of performing the deed.

A minute later, he rolled off of her and covered his face with his arm. He then mumbled, "I can't even do it *with you.*" He turned his head, glaringly. "So what good are you?"

She didn't respond, unable to express all the churning emotions pitching through her—helplessness, humiliation, hurt, rage, shame, and even a weird fleeting sense of triumph for him being thwarted, though she was still his captive. As she pulled her dress back down and buttoned her coat, she then inanely wondered if he drank because he was incapable or was he incapable because he drank. She almost chuckled drearily because . . . what did it matter? He was crazy. He was violently unstable.

She gathered her strength and got up to a sitting position. She then pointed to his bedroll forcefully. "Go to sleep and leave me be."

With relief, she watched him rise and stagger over to his blanket, collapsing on the ground.

She took a deep breath and let it out slowly. She had survived. She was still alive.

The next morning, he was sober once more and she vainly tried to reason with him again. "Take me home, Alec."

He shook his head. "No."

"Why not?" She looked at him earnestly. "You can go your way and I'll go mine. Nothing seriously

320

harmful has occurred yet. I won't take you to court. It would be too . . . embarrassing for us both."

"I find I still want you by my side." He busied himself, straightening the saddle on his horse.

"Why?" She raised her hands helplessly. "I can't do anything for you."

"Can't you see?" He seemed so despairing as he looked at her. "I don't want to die alone."

It was such an unexpected plea for humanity and so startling that he was showing some emotion other than his usual contempt that she actually felt sorry for him. For this pathetic creature of a man . . . however, one who was capable of such atrocious acts when drunk.

She inwardly shook her head. Perhaps she was the one who was now turning crazy. But she tried to use this temporary truce to her advantage and suggested, "You could come home with me and stay there." She knew it sounded ridiculous the moment she suggested it.

So did Alec and he suddenly became angry again. "Just mount up, Henrietta. We got another long ride ahead."

Alec was quiet the remaining part of the morning and Henrietta had no desire to talk. As she rode in the saddle in front of him, her mind wandered again to escaping. It would be so easy now. He was giving her as much freedom as she wanted. But the thought of trying to make it back home by herself through this unknown territory was just so daunting. Alec was correct. She would most likely get hopelessly lost. Even when they occasionally ascended above the tree line all she could see surrounding her were unfamiliar mountains upon mountains. And if she didn't get lost? Well, then there were the bears and coyotes and mountain lions and wolves and god-knows-what-else to contend with. No, she was safer sticking with Alec for the time being.

She eyed his gun and knife out of the corner of her eye. But perhaps she could grab a weapon and force Alec to return to her cabin. He would certainly know the way. But would he actually take her home? He knew he would hang once there so why should he obey her command even with a gun pointed at him?

Alec began to shake more vigorously from lack of drink by the afternoon. Henrietta knew enough about withdrawal from what Charles had told her that if Alec was forced to quit abruptly it could kill him. She wondered if he had enough whiskey to sustain him until he could resupply. So now she had another worry. She had to keep Alec alive until they got to a place safer for her to escape from him.

She wondered whether Alec realized the danger he was in. Probably so. He wasn't just keeping sober to flee more easily. He knew he had to ration his supply of drink. Didn't he? She had to find out.

"Alec, you're shaking a lot. Perhaps you should take a small nip."

"Yeah, I think I will." He reached into his saddle bag and took a swallow from his bottle.

She turned around and glanced at him. "Did you know that you could perish if you stopped drinking abruptly?"

"Does it matter?"

Huh? What was going on in his mind *now*? "Yes, it does."

"Well, time will tell." He took another swig. She turned facing forward again.

"Don't fuss with me, Henrietta. You'll see that my drinking will scarcely be of concern to you in the future."

He was talking in some kind of riddle.

"Henrietta?"

"Yes?" She kept facing forward. She could tell by his tone of voice that his whole mood was changed. She intuitively realized that he had made some kind of decision or had resigned himself to something and he was at peace with whatever that was. Somehow the thought frightened her instead of calming her—he was so volatile.

"I want you to know that I wasn't always such a disgraceful, vile shell of a man."

"Alec—"

"No. Let me finish. I was raised by respectable parents and received an education. I enjoyed life and came West for the adventure. I fell in love with Magpie and she was good to me. I . . ." He trailed off.

Henrietta turned around again. "But, Alec. It doesn't have to be this way. You can quit drinking, but slowly, and—"

"No. I can't." He shook his head.

Their conversation stood still a moment. She faced forward. Her mind raced. How could she get through to this man? And what was actually going on with him?

Alec began speaking again. Oddly cheerfully. He started telling her a story about the first time he met Magpie. But she couldn't concentrate on what he was

323

saying. She repeated to herself what he had said about how his drinking would not be a concern for her in the future. Why?

Oh, Lord. It hit her then. Because she wasn't going to be alive in the future. He was going to kill her. Of course. She was of no use to him. If he rid himself of her, he could go on with his life. Who could possibly prove that he had abducted her? And did he hope to get back together with Magpie? Was that why he was talking about her now? In his warped mind, was he trying to explain and justify to himself why he was going to do away with his captive?

She felt cold with fear. She had to do something. But, what?

She could try slaying Alec first. She could grab the knife and . . . she dismissed the idea as quickly as she thought it. Besides being unlikely that she could overpower him, the concept was so out of character for her that it was laughable. And what if she was wrong and just imagining that he wanted to rid himself of her? She would be horribly guilty of an unforgivable sin and here all alone in the rough country, attempting to find her way back home.

She blew out a deep breath. She had to remain calm. She really didn't know what his intentions were if any. But then it occurred to her that even if he was thinking the worse, she could attempt *her* best weapon against him. She could reason and talk him out of it. So she returned to her original plan—she was going to make a friend out of Alec. And he had just finished his story about meeting Magpie.

"So, Alec, did you ever own a dog?"

324

Chapter Thirty-four

Collan rode into Willow Park with as much anticipation and excitement as he had ever felt in his life. He could not wait to see Etta again. Her hug goodbye when he had departed had been prolonged and sincere. He just knew that they had a real future together now. As he ascended a rise and got his first glimpse of his cabin, he hurried along, his presents stuffed in his saddle bags flying up and down. He hadn't brought with him everything that he had bought. The larger items were still being shipped by train to Denver. He would pick them up with a wagon from the station once they arrived. But he had a token present for everyone now as a surprise.

He saw the cabin door open and eagerly expected to see his first sight of Etta. But he could make out even at this distance that it wasn't Etta, but Magpie standing in the doorway with Teddie in her arms, waiting to greet him. He squelched his disappointment. He would see his Etta soon no matter where she was now. Once in the yard, he drew rein and dismounted quickly.

He practically jumped onto the porch and took Teddie from Magpie, grinning widely. "Hey there, little man. You've grown. Where's your mama?"

Teddie patted his head happily as Collan turned to get an answer from Magpie. But he quickly realized that Magpie wasn't talking but swallowing as she tried to hold back tears. Collan's whole insides clenched. Something was wrong. Terribly wrong.

Oh, God. Not his Etta.

He suddenly had no strength in his arms and he slowly lowered Teddie to the porch. Magpie picked Teddie up and carried him into the cabin. Collan silently followed and sat at the table with them.

Magpie took Collan's hand in hers and said tremulously, "She's gone. We don't know where. We're trying to find her."

He frowned. He couldn't register her words. "What do you mean she's gone?"

He then heard the sound of horses approaching and looked through the doorway to see the Farrar brothers and Tinker dismounting. He went out to the porch again. "What in the hell is going on?" he practically roared.

As he waited for someone, anyone, to give him an explanation, he saw that all the horses had been ridden long and the men were wearing grim, weary expressions. He felt his legs give out and he plopped down suddenly onto a porch step.

Tinker spoke first. "Collan, I'm so sorry. You trusted me to watch out for the women, but I failed. The last time I saw Henrietta was three nights ago when I escorted her back from a celebration and watched her and Teddie enter the cabin. Uh . . . Magpie and I then went off on our own for a while and when we returned a few hours later and opened the cabin door, we found Teddie crying in his crib, the dogs barking and Henrietta gone. That porch chair on the end was turned over so I surmise there was some kind of struggle, and I worry that Magpie's first husband has abducted Henrietta."

"Why Etta?" Collan frowned. "Wouldn't you think if the bastard was going to take anyone it would be Magpie instead?"

Tinker nodded. "All along I thought Magpie was in the most danger. Not Henrietta. It's my fault. All my fault."

Collan shook his head. "Don't think it, Tinker. All of us became slack after so long without any trouble. I should never have departed for back East. I should have stayed." He straightened. "So what has been done to try to find her?"

"Well, that very night I rode out with the dogs and a lantern to see if I could track her. Best I could tell he dragged her behind the stables and rode southwest from there. But after a few hours, I realized I could use help so I returned and rode over to the Farrars. Luckily, they were home. We've been trying to find her the last couple days, riding out on different paths and back."

Collan looked around. "Just where are the dogs?"

"They come and go now. Scarcely stay put. I think they're actually trying to find her themselves."

Hank tiredly sat down next to Collan on the porch step. "Abner is watching the cattle and keeping an eye on the place. Unfortunately, the Ferguson men are on a trip to Denver—not that a Ferguson would know these mountains any better than us. Abner rode over to tell Alex yesterday. Alex departed immediately to try to get the sheriff of Fort Collins to help, but he isn't hopeful about getting any assistance soon—this probably isn't even his area. We really don't know who to find to help search other than other men in the settlement."

Ike added, "We rode back this time to try to gather a posse."

Collan stood. "That'll take too much time. I want to ride out again now. I got a map inside the cabin. I want you to show me where you've already been and we'll go from there."

Clint shook his head sadly. "Whoever took Miss Henrietta wouldn't do her any harm." He looked over at Collan. "I mean he just couldn't. Who would hurt a woman? Nobody is that crazy."

Ike then burst out with, "Clint, you fool. What if an Injun grabbed her?" He turned to Tinker. "You even said one of those Cheyenne or Sioux who are supposed to be on a reservation now might wander down here."

Magpie shook her head, angrily. "No. Indians know Talks with Hawk my friend. Indians do not hurt her." Teddie started crying in her arms and she walked back into the cabin.

Hank turned to his brothers. "If you don't have anything helpful to say, shut the hell up."

A day later, Collan rode back into his yard, exhausted and frustrated. After only a few hours of riding he had realized the futility of the situation but had persisted longer out of fear for what was happening to Etta. He wouldn't entertain the notion that she was possibly already permanently gone. The thought was too wretched.

But the range of mountains from which she could have disappeared were vast. None of them were experienced trackers—damn it all, he had only being a merchant, a miner and a cattle rancher to his credentials. Any trail was surely cold—or at least too hidden for their combined talents.

They were going to have to find some help and that would take time. He hoped with all his being that Etta could hold out that long.

Chapter Thirty-five

The rest of the day Henrietta persisted in her plan to try to forge a sort of peace with Alec so she could eventually convince him to take her home. At first, she was amazed that Alec and she could chat together civilly at all, let alone for hours. Of course, part of the reason was that he was remaining his version of sober, only imbibing when the shakes started again. But suddenly their ability to converse—and for her to find him even witty at times—made sense to her. Why else would someone as independent and strong-willed as Magpie have stayed with a man such as Alec for so many years if he had been a complete brute. Magpie obviously could get along by herself if she had to and would have departed from him way sooner than she had if she had wanted to.

She found herself thinking that Alec wasn't all bad—just cruelly damaged by drink. He wasn't a happy drunk but a violent one. Perhaps he truly was salvageable, his personality not yet fully consumed by drink.

Yet she couldn't get over her persistent unease at this change in mood. She was sure something must have caused it. Some momentous decision and the uncertainty of what that was continued to be unsettling.

That evening they made camp on top of a high steep ridge with views for miles of the surrounding undulating mountains. Before their meal, she noticed Alec taking off his belt—with the gun and knife attached—and placing it next to his saddle on the ground instead of wearing it while they ate, and she became more hopeful that she had made some progress and could eventually convince him to return her home. She might even be able to get him to stop drinking and save himself. So when she wrapped herself into her blanket by the fire, she felt more relaxed and fell into an exhausted sleep.

But Henrietta awoke what seemed like minutes later yet could have been hours since the moon was now out. She realized Alec was calling to her.

"Henrietta, wake up. *Henrietta*, I want to talk to you."

She sat up, still somewhat befuddled with sleep. Alec was standing at the edge of the cliff yet she realized that there was no sight he could possibly see in the dark. "What do you want, Alec?"

He staggered a few feet and she recognized with dread that he had been drinking heavily again.

"I want you to forgive me."

She hesitated. Just which of his atrocious acts was she supposed to absolve—all of them? She didn't know if she could do that.

He pleaded further. "Please, Henrietta. Say you forgive me. It might save me from going to hell."

He swayed and looked briefly over the edge of the ridge and Henrietta realized in a flash what was going on. He planned on jumping off the cliff. He was never going to kill *her*. He had made the decision some time during the day to kill *himself*. And oddly enough that had given him some calming resolution. Good Lord. Did all people who took their lives become peacefully resigned before they accomplished the deed?

She hurriedly stood and held out her hands in supplication. "I forgive you, Alec. Please come away from that cliff—you could fall. I don't want any harm to come to you." She took a step towards him, but he teetered on the edge some more. She screamed and he thankfully walked toward her a stride.

He took a deep breath. "Listen to me now. Keep going northeast until you start recognizing some mountains—"

She shook her head. "Alec, no. Don't do this."

"You should have enough food for a couple of weeks. If you can't find water . . . uh, give Intrepid his lead. He will find it for you. And . . . build a fire each evening to keep away the animals and have the gun ready—"

"Alec. Don't leave me. We can work this out. I can help you get better—"

"If it gets cloudy, stop until you can get your direction again." He swallowed. "And tell Magpie I'm sorry. She deserved better."

He took another staggering step backwards. "Goodbye, Henrietta. I think I could have loved you, too."

He turned away from her, gazing over the ridge again.

"Alec, nooo." She charged towards him.

As soon as she reached him, he suddenly crumpled on the ground, chuckling mirthlessly. "God, I can't even do this properly. I'm such a weak coward."

He lay on his back a moment, peering up at her with blurred eyes. "You're the problem, Henrietta. You know that, don't you? You made me realize what I can't have anymore. What my life used to be like . . . that I can't live like this anymore . . ."

He then slowly arose and the drink again took its usual hold on him. He glared and swayed before her. "Yes, *you're* the problem!"

Henrietta stood motionless, terrified and not sure how to handle this latest irrational drunken foray.

He dropped his head, took a deep breath and when he looked back at her, she could see he was filled with crazy rage again. "What good are you anyway? All you can do is *talk*. At least Magpie can . . . hunt . . . and feed me." He took a few unsteady steps in the direction of his horse. "I'm getting Magpie."

She followed him. "Yes, Alec. Let's get Magpie. That would be good to go back—"

He turned around. "Shut up, you troublesome bitch! *I'm* getting Magpie. Not *you*. You're the *problem*, remember?" He frowned at her. "And you'll tell everyone what I did!"

She shook her head. "No, I won't. We're friends now, aren't we, Alec?"

"Shut up! I can't think with you jabbering at me all the time." He stared at her a moment, scowling, then uttered, "I have to get rid of you. It's the only way." After announcing such a disastrous decision, he suddenly grabbed her arms and started pulling her toward the cliff edge.

"Alec, nooo. What are you doing?" She struggled to break loose from him. "Think, Alec. Think.

This isn't the way." She tried digging in her heels frantically.

But he ignored her and as they got relentlessly closer to the edge, she was filled with a devastating hopelessness, knowing that drink had made him unreasonably violent again with a strength that was overpowering.

They reached the ridge and he suddenly let go of her arms, looking just ready to push her over.

"Nooo, Alec," she screamed. And a startled expression came over his eyes, stopping him for a brief moment.

Was he finally coming to his senses or . . .?

The ground abruptly gave way beneath both their feet. She found herself slipping and tumbling over the edge with Alec. She bounced and skidded on her rump several feet on loose dirt and pebbles, then she twisted herself and grasped at the ground, trying to find some traction. She slid some more over the rapidly descending rocky landscape. Her hand finally found a thick root stump sticking out and she grabbed hold with a strength she did not know she possessed.

Her slide came to a halt.

She took several deep breaths to steady herself as she heard Alec in his drunken state helplessly yelling and tumbling further down. Finally, there was a disgusting grunt and thud as if he had hit some rocks.

Henrietta slowly let go of the stump. By cautiously crawling and digging in with her feet, she made it back to the top of the ridge.

She lay on her front and peered over the rim. She saw nothing in the dark.

"Alec," she yelled.

"Alec!"

Still he gave no response and she heard no groaning or moaning. She briefly thought about trying to climb down and see if she could help him. But the thought was ridiculously dangerous and she dismissed it. Even if she could make her way to where he was at, Alec was still undoubtedly hopelessly drunk. She would have to wait until the morning to see if he was still alive.

She walked unsteadily back to the fire that was still glowing and added a couple more logs, before collapsing on the ground. She looked over to where Intrepid was standing. He was flicking his ears and stamping a foot. After a moment, she strode over to the agitated horse and stroked his mane.

She then heard a coyote howling. Then another. Oh, God. Were they surrounding Alec already? She ran to where Alec had placed the saddle and found his gun belt and knife still in front of it.

She quickly swung the belt around her waist. She took out the gun and pulled the trigger to try to scare the coyotes away. The yipping stopped momentarily.

She then searched through his saddlebags. Yes, there were more dried beans, flour, sugar and jerky. She also found another bottle of whiskey. She even discovered to her surprise a clean pair of pants and a new looking shirt. So, he hadn't lost all sense of dignity.

But her thoughts quickly returned to the excited coyote howling which had returned louder and more persistent—as if they weren't at all scared of the gun.

She shook her head. There was no way, if he was still alive, that he was going to survive the night.

She fired the gun once more to no effect. The howling continued. She wanted to cover her ears to the horrible noise, but she knew that would be foolish. She had to stay alert. She walked back to the fire, dragging the saddlebags with her. She positioned herself with a rock against her back and cautiously looked around the campsite. It was going to be a long night.

Hours later, the sky finally started lightening in the east. The yipping of the coyotes had ended hours ago, but Henrietta had remained awake, too scared to possibly fall back asleep. She also wasn't hungry in the least. She just wanted to try to make it home.

But first she had to see to Alec. She walked toward the edge of the ridge and crawled again the last few feet. She looked down. All she could see were rocks and a few scattered trees. Where was Alec? She searched some more and saw his hat. She studied the surrounding ground. She couldn't find him anywhere. She turned around and sat up, holding her head. The coyotes had probably dragged him off. There was nothing she could do. She only hoped he had not been alive to experience it.

But the realization that she was completely alone now hit her full force. Up until this moment, she had held a faint hope that she would find Alec and at least have some guidance from him on her way home. She started chuckling grimly. She had wanted her independence and to prove herself. Well, now she was going to get it and then some.

She wasn't going to give up, though. She had Teddie and Collan and her family and friends to live for. Perhaps they were still looking for her. But she knew not to count on that. None of them really had the experience to find her. The Farrars hunted, but she didn't think in the country Alec had taken her. The trails had seemed old and overgrown—as if they had not been used for years for finding game.

She looked up at the sky. If only her good friend Rocky Mountain Jim was still around. He would have certainly known how best to locate her.

She got up and walked over to Intrepid. First things first. She was finally going to have to learn how to handle a horse, so help her God.

Chapter Thirty-six

Though Collan and the others all had the urge to just keep moving—whether going off alone to search for Etta or finding men to help them, Magpie had insisted on feeding them a meal and then that they all lay down for a quick nap before continuing. Everyone had disagreed until she pointed out that the horses required rest if nothing else.

So Collan found himself waking a couple hours later from a fitful sleep as he heard a rapping on the cabin door. He got up and opened the bedroom door. Clint, Ike, and Hank all sat up in their bedrolls. Tinker was holding Teddie at the table. Collan wondered if he had slept at all. The man was consumed with guilt.

They all watched as Magpie greeted a stranger at the entrance to his cabin. But instead of telling him that no, there weren't any baked goods for sale, she opened the door wider to let the gentleman in. He took off his hat. He was dressed in a dapper fashion but in outdoorsy clothes. He looked as if he had bought his outfit from some fine hunting store back East.

Collan frowned. He was in no mood for a chat. "Magpie, what's going on?"

She turned around. "He says he wants to speak with Talks with Hawk. He is a friend of Rocky Mountain Jim. She always tells me stories about that man."

"What?"

The man stepped forward and held out his hand. "How do you do? I'm Hugo Jaska. Is Henrietta Schodde perhaps at home? I was told I could find her here."

He shook his hand. "Collan Wallace." The news had apparently not spread that far and wide yet that Etta was missing. "What concern do you have with her?"

"I've been travelling on business for my sporting goods store but didn't want to return back home until I thanked the woman who helped a good friend of mine when he could use it the most. We were trappers many years ago and traipsed all over these parts together. I have very fond memories of our time together. Rocky Mountain Jim was like a brother to me."

Ike stood. "Miss Henrietta is missing. We think she's been kidnapped."

Hugo eyes widened. "Kidnapped?"

Collan explained. "A few days past. We've been searching for her but returned for help. Who told you that you could still find Henrietta here?"

"A woman by the name of Evans."

Collan nodded. That made sense that she would not know the news about Etta. Nobody talked to an Evans unless they had to, ever since the family started associating with the English Company.

"You say you were a trapper?" Hank asked while folding up his blanket and Hugo nodded.

"How are your tracking skills?" Tinker handed Teddie over to Magpie, suddenly looking a bit hopeful.

"Fair to middling. It's been a while. But I remember these parts like the back of my hand. Where have you looked for her so far?"

Clint reached into his saddlebag and hurriedly spread out a map on the table. They all studied it intensely. They showed Hugo the areas they had searched.

"Do you have any idea who might have taken her?"

Collan answered. "Yeah, a fellow who also once trapped in these parts with Magpie here."

Hugo nodded sagely. "Then he probably knows the old routes."

Collan added, "But Magpie's directions to where they once went involve finding things like a large rock with a hole in it. The map is meaningless to her."

Hugo turned around and addressed Magpie. "The large rock with a hole in it by a river?"

She nodded.

"Did you ever go by an extremely steep ridge where you could see for miles?"

She looked puzzled. Tinker tried translating.

Magpie then answered excitedly. "Yes, yes."

Hugo raised his brows. "There's a trail you haven't searched yet."

"Where?" Tinker asked desperately.

Hugo put his hat back on. "If you'll allow me, I'll be happy to lead the way."

Henrietta had Intrepid saddled and ready to leave. She grabbed his reins and mounted him, settling herself in the seat. She reached down to pull her dress over her ankles as far as possible and then had a thought. She really did not want to ride wearing a dress, especially when there were a perfectly good pair of pants and a shirt in one of the saddlebags.

She dismounted and changed into the clothes, adjusting the pants cuffs and sleeves and then pulling the belt with the gun and knife tightly around her waist. She then had another idea. As cautiously as she could she descended the cliff and retrieved the hat Alec had lost in his fall—it really had not dropped that far from the ridgetop—and with a string she found in a bag tied it around her head. If she did come upon some strangers, she hoped she would not look like a helpless woman—at least from a distance.

She mounted Intrepid again. He turned his head and seemed to look at her warily. She had always been told that if a horse sensed you were afraid, then the horse became scared also, wondering what the danger was. Henrietta blew out a long breath and tried to calm herself.

She smiled and then said, "Intrepid, this is it. We're going home. Don't you want to see Magpie again? Don't worry. Everything's going to be just fine."

Intrepid snorted loudly. Henrietta found that encouraging. She reined Intrepid around pointing east and nudged him with her legs to get going. He took one step and then lowered his head to munch on some grass. Oh, no. Not again.

Henrietta pursed her lips. She had been told a million times that she had to take command of a horse. She had to believe and show that she was the boss.

She pulled Intrepid's head up with the reins and said firmly, "Intrepid, get going. I'm in no mood for this kind of nonsense." She gave him a kick and Intrepid trotted off.

Henrietta slowed him to a walk and then guided him into a circle, then backwards, then trotting, then a walk, then a short gallop and finally a walk again. He never stopped to graze. Henrietta couldn't help grinning widely. She was so proud—if only Collan could see her now. But enough expert horsemanship, she thought. She had a ways to travel.

Henrietta kept to a northeast path as Alec had instructed as best she could—but the animal trails twisted and turn and she did not think she should always follow them. Occasionally she had to backtrack after she found herself on precipitous rocky ledges or the terrain became too rough. By the afternoon she was feeling her lack of sleep and clouds had rolled in. She stopped to rest and dozed for a few hours, holding the loaded gun in one hand with her back against a tree trunk. When she awoke, the clouds had broken up again and she was able to follow a direction again.

She rode as late into the evening as she dared. She still did not recognize her surroundings at all and tried not to feel dejected. That quickly became easy because her overriding emotion suddenly became sheer fear as she heard a low growl while she was unsaddling Intrepid. A bear was in the vicinity and it surely smelled her food.

Henrietta rapidly gathered some logs and tinder. Despite shaky hands, she managed to light a fire. She dragged the saddlebags closer to the flames and sat down next to them. She didn't know if she was capable of defending her food supply so she shoved a piece of jerky into her mouth—better to eat now while she still had something.

She grabbed the gun as she heard more growling. Intrepid then neighed loudly and stamped his foot. Henrietta stood. "You get away from here," she shouted.

But as she turned around frantically to peer into the surrounding shadows, it wasn't a bear that appeared but—oh, Lord—a mountain lion. Henrietta had never seen one before except in pictures, they were usually so elusive, but she recognized the animal by its coloration and long tail. Intrepid nickered loudly and attempted rearing despite being hobbled. The mountain lion growled again and Henrietta pulled out the knife with her free hand, waving it high.

Even at this close distance, she knew her aim with the gun was unreliable and she certainly didn't think she could win a knife fight. She figured she had no choice. Keeping her eyes on the creature, she dropped the gun and knelt. She fished around quickly in a saddlebag and found some jerky. She flung it as far as she could over the mountain lion's head. The lion turned and ran toward the meat and then seemed to retreat through the trees—Henrietta heard no more snarling.

"Well, I'm definitely not staying here for the night" She said aloud.

She saddled Intrepid and packed her belongings. Once mounted, Henrietta rode what she thought was northeast, picking her way around fallen trees and rocks. Luckily the moon could now give her some faint light. But she really didn't want to possibly stray too far out of the proper direction so after another couple hours, she stopped again. She remained awake the rest of the night and was on her way at first light the following morning.

Just a few hours before, Collan had been hopeful that Hugo might be able to lead them to Etta. But they found no sign whatsoever of anyone having passed through the trail they were currently following. Hugo seemed undaunted, but Collan could see the weary disappointment on the faces of his friends. Had they been foolish to start out again without more men to widen the search? At least this time they had brought more supplies so if they found something encouraging they could easily stay on the path for a few more days.

Several hours later, the light was fading when Collan squinted to get a better look at a distinctive formation in the distance. "Hugo, is that the rock you were talking about?"

Hugo followed Collan's gaze. "Why, yes, it is. The trail follows just by it."

The men trotted to get closer and then dismounted to look around. Once again, there was nothing to indicate Etta had passed this way. Hugo suggested making camp for the night. If it got any darker, they could miss something important.

They talked little the remaining evening—all realizing that they could be fully wasting their time again, riding in the wrong direction.

The next day was more of the same and the men debated turning around. But in late afternoon Hugo stopped his horse and looked up at the sky, frowning.

"What is it, Hugo?" Collan blew out a breath. He was ready to give up.

"I have a sudden recollection of . . ." He reined his horse more westerly. "You men keep following this path. There's another one not too far from here I want to have a look at."

"I'll go with." Collan looked at his friends. "We'll catch up with you further on."

Three hours later, Collan was hopeful again as Hugo and he charged into the camp his friends had made. "We found signs of a recent fire and trampled grass. We'll follow that trail in the morning."

Henrietta spent another day not recognizing her surroundings. She felt horribly lost and started counting out how many more strips of jerky she had remaining. She tried to console herself that at least the animals seemed to be leaving her alone and she was becoming quite the expert horsewoman now. But when she stared into her fire that evening she couldn't hold back her tears.

The next morning Henrietta came to the conclusion that she better try hunting for some food. Lord knew how long she would remain lost. She watched a rabbit scurry across her path and dismounted Intrepid. If there was one rabbit, there were probably a dozen in this area. She gathered small rocks and took up a position behind an outcropping. She had seen how easily Alec had obtained one with an accurate throw. An hour later she was ready to give up and move on. No rabbits had appeared.

Suddenly she caught some movement in the grass. She couldn't quite make out what it was but hurled a rock at it. She heard a squeal and ran forward. A dazed raccoon was lolling on its back, still alive.

"Oh!" Henrietta grabbed her knife. "Oh! You poor thing!" She felt so sorry for it, but she stabbed it in the neck.

"Oh, *Lord*!" Now the precious thing was writhing. She saw a large rock nearby and ran to it. She heaved it at the raccoon's head. The raccoon finally lay still.

Henrietta sat down next to it. She was so disgusted with herself. *Why* hadn't she thrown the large rock at its head before making it suffer with her ineffective knife slash? Next time she would know better. She vowed she would never make another animal endure so grievously.

She gutted it and then hung it from the saddle with the noose Alec had made. She continued on her lost way.

Late in the afternoon Henrietta gazed at a mountain and tried not to get too excited. She didn't want to fool herself, but it did really look as if there was a beaver head next to the tip.

"Oh, my God. That's Longs Peak."

Longs Peak was the highest in this range of mountains, but because nearby ones came close in height she wasn't always sure of its identity unless she also saw Longs Peaks most distinguishable feature. Part of its rocky side looked as if a beaver was climbing it. Depending on one's location, the whole beaver from head to tail could be seen or just a portion. Henrietta was now thinking that she was viewing part of its head. And if that was so, then . . .

"I'm going to find my way home. Intrepid, we just have to discover the area where the beaver looks the same as at the cabin and then wander around some. Yippee! We did it!"

Intrepid turned his head around and gave her one of his looks Henrietta now found so familiar. She stroked his mane. "Let's get going."

A few hours later, Henrietta was about to make camp when she caught a whiff of smoke. But then it was gone and as she looked around, she saw no fire. She rode a bit more and got another trace of the same. She was now on a ridge and gazed down into a valley with a narrow creek meandering through it. Along the river edge, she finally caught sight of a large blaze. She doubted just one person would have built such a huge fire.

She wanted to shout with excitement, but then realized it could be anybody down there—perhaps even outlaws. But she was going to find out now even though it would soon be dark. She rode slowly towards the camp, straining to hear voices that she might recognize. As she got closer, night came but she thought she heard Collan talking—or was her mind playing tricks because she yearned so for him?

No. That was him! She was sure of it. She charged into the camp, reining in a circle and a quick stop. She jumped off Intrepid and grinned widely, glancing around. "Hi, everybody! I'm back!"

All her friends were here with one stranger—all standing, mouths agape.

"It's me. Henrietta. Don't you recognize me?" She looked down at her outfit. "I guess I am a bit dirty."

She reached for the rope on her saddle and held it up. "Anybody hungry? I caught a raccoon."

Collan started chuckling as tears came to his eyes. "What *the hell* happened to you, Etta? I'm so happy to see you I could eat *you* up." He ran to her and swung her and the raccoon around in a hug.

Henrietta started laughing and broke from the embrace as he put her down.

She handed the raccoon to Collan and then walked slowly over to Clint, who was quietly weeping. She put her arms around him and patted his back. "I guess I gave you a scare." Clint nodded.

"You sure did, Miss Henrietta." Ike said. "I thought you were a goner for certains. Now give me a hug."

After Ike, she looked at Tinker, who had collapsed in a crouch on the ground, appearing overcome. He shook his head. "Thank God you're safe. I'm so sorry I didn't protect you better. It was Magpie's husband who took you, wasn't it?"

She nodded. "But it wasn't your fault. After the celebration, I decided to sit outside on the porch and he grabbed me from there. Please tell me that Teddie is fine."

Tinker nodded. "He misses you, though. As does Magpie."

"I'll be so glad to see them."

Hank walked over and embraced her next. She smiled up at him. "Can you believe I caught a raccoon?"

He chuckled and pointed to himself. "*I'll* cook it over the fire for *you* this time."

Ike stomped his boot. "Awww, heck. Hank will burn the coon for sure, Miss Henrietta."

His brothers said at the same time, "Shut up Ike."

Henrietta approached the stranger next. She held out her hand. "I don't believe we've met. I'm Henrietta Schodde."

He shook her hand. "Hugo Jaska. I wanted to thank you for seeing to my good friend Mountain Jim but found out about your current troubles when I arrived. I stuck around to see if I could help."

She smiled. "I know you. I mean I know all about you. So you're Mountain Jim's Hugo Jaska."

He nodded.

She looked up at the sky and yelled, "Thank you, Mountain Jim. I knew I could count on you." She then grinned at everyone.

Ike raised his brows. "Oh, Lordy. Do you think she's gone plumb loco?" Ike eyed her up and down. "And look how you're dressed, Miss Henrietta."

Collan frowned. "Well, I'm sure there's a story behind that. But first I want to know just where this son of bitch is now."

Henrietta shook her head. "Gone."

"What do you mean gone, Etta."

"He . . . he's gone. Please don't make me talk about the details now, Collie. I'm too happy for such unpleasantries."

Chapter Thirty-seven

The next morning Etta was still acting too cheerful as far as Collan was concerned. She had to be covering up a lot of emotional turmoil. After eating that critter of hers, everyone had fallen fast asleep—everyone except Etta and Hugo, who had chatted throughout most of the evening. Collan knew that because their *laughter* had occasionally woken him up. He had tried to stay awake, but once he had put his head in Etta's lap as a playful gesture, he had found that just the reassurance of being able to touch her again had lulled him quickly into slumber.

He also didn't like that she still wouldn't talk about any of the details. She would have to eventually, he knew, but he didn't press her when she refused again on the ride home. At least with her new riding skills, they made good time, trotting instead of walking a good portion of the way back.

Soon they entered the yard in front of the cabin—everyone except Hugo, who had said his goodbyes an hour before.

Magpie, Teddie and the dogs burst out of the door to greet them. Teddie toddled over to Etta.

Etta jumped off her horse and picked him up, squeezing him tightly, while the dogs tumbled around her, but the sweet reunion was abruptly ended as they all heard riders approaching.

Collan recognized the lead man and inwardly groaned. This was the last thing anybody should have to deal with after what they had all gone through.

Theodore Whyte stopped in front of Etta and his rough cowboys formed a line in back of him. The gesture made Collan, the Farrar brothers and Tinker fashion a row behind Etta. The battle was about to begin. But then Collan looked more closely and he could see that the lackeys refused to meet Etta's or anyone's, for that matter, eyes. Aha. Whatever Theodore Whyte had planned they were embarrassed by it and obviously wanted no part of it.

She looked up to Whyte since no one had dismounted but her. Collan didn't like that since it put her at a disadvantage. At least she had changed out of her peculiar outfit this morning and was wearing a dress. But the hem was dirty and soiled and she was wearing her coat despite the warmth of the day. She also looked exhausted. Anyone with any kind of noodle in their noggin would realize that something untoward had happened to her and leave her be. Whyte obviously didn't have a clue or preferred to ignore it.

Etta being Etta addressed him politely. "What brings you our way, Mr. Whyte? Would you like a refreshment?" She looked to Magpie for help. Magpie took Teddie back.

Whyte shook his head. "Not this time, Mrs. Schodde. I'll state my business. Our surveyor has informed us that while your land is not on the property of Lord Dunraven, your cabin is."

Oh, my God. How many more blows could Etta take before she crumbled, Collan wondered. Etta said nothing for a moment but then straightened her back and said, "Well, Mister Whyte, I will have to see what *my* surveyor thinks first. But supposing that is correct . . . hold on a moment." She turned around and looked at Collan. "Will you sell your cabin to me?"

"What?"

"You heard me. Will you sell it or not?"

"Etta, for heaven's sake. I don't think that will be necessary—"

"Collie, just answer the question." He could see she had begun to shake. She had finally hit her last straw. Now was no time to argue with her so he said, "Of course. Whatever you want, Etta."

She turned back around. "You can inform the Lord that he can purchase my remaining land if he desires. But tell him that it will not go cheaply. I have had absolutely enough of these antics from Dunraven. He is an arrogant, conceited, selfish creature that should just stay in England though England probably can't tolerate the man either. Now if you will excuse me, I have had a hectic last few days." She stormed into the cabin and slammed the door.

Magpie smiled while everyone else, including Teddie, gaped.

Hours later, Collan tried to talk to Etta. She still wasn't herself. After first playing with Teddie for a while, she had wanted to take a bath. She had stayed in the tub so long scrubbing herself that Collan had made Magpie go into her bedroom to see that she was okay. Collan had then suggested that she take a nap. She had refused. And now she wouldn't stop moving, insisting that she serve dinner to Collan and Magpie—she had reheated some stew—even though they were perfectly capable of getting some themselves. Teddie was already dozing in the crib Magpie had placed in her bedroom and the Farrar brothers had long departed for their home. Even Tinker had just wanted some sleep in his own cabin.

But perhaps worst of all, she was back to being cheerful again. Collan couldn't stand it anymore. "Etta, sit down. I don't want any more stew."

"So tell me about your trip, Collie. We haven't discussed it at all." She sat down across from him and tried keeping her head steady. But Collan could see she was on her very last legs and her head was tipping back as if begging for some sleep.

"That's it." Collan got up and walked around the table. He placed his arms underneath her legs and lifted her up.

As he headed toward her bedroom she protested, "What are you doing?"

"You're going to rest." He placed her on the bed.

"No. I don't want to. I haven't even changed into a nightdress."

He covered her with a quilt. "Etta, indulge me for once and just try to go to sleep."

He waited for her to argue some more as he placed the blanket around her, but when he glanced at her face once more he saw that she had already passed out. He muttered, "Thank God," then quietly closed the door.

He sat down across from Magpie. "She hasn't cried once. It's as if she wants to deny what happened to her."

Magpie nodded. "She be well when she cry. She rest now."

"I don't feel comfortable leaving her for the night. I think I'm going to sleep here instead of that other cabin I built."

Magpie stood. "Yes. You sleep here in my bed. Teddie and I go with the dogs to Tinker. I want to bring him dinner and stay with him."

Collan glanced out the window. There was still some light. "Do you want me to take you there?"

Magpie chuckled and shook her head. "Teddie and I will be fine."

But after everything that had happened, Collan stood on the porch and watched her walk with Teddie all the way across the pasture until she reached Tinker's cabin.

Etta slept quietly for hours, but in the middle of the night, Collan awoke to Etta moaning.

"Nooo.

"No.

"Nooooo. Don't do that."

Then she screamed. Collan was in her room in a flash. He had kept a lantern lit on the kitchen table and had remained fully clothed, having expected just something like this to occur. He could now see that she was sitting up in bed, panting.

He sat on the bed and embraced her. "Etta, honey. You're safe. I'm here."

She clutched at his shirt desperately as she looked into his face. "Oh, Collan. It was really horrible." Then, *finally*, she burst into tears.

Collan lay down next to her and he placed her head on his shoulder as he wrapped an arm around her. "Tell me what happened, Etta."

She curled into him and he started to stroke her head, but she winced.

"He hit me there and knocked me out when he first grabbed me. I was struggling so to get away from him."

"I'll kill him, Etta. I swear to God."

"You can't. He's already passed on. He fell over a cliff."

"Oh, Lord. And you had to witness that?"

She nodded.

"Start from the beginning. I want to hear everything."

As Etta flooded him with details he wondered at the courage and resiliency she had shown. He was so proud of her. But after a while he sensed she was leaving something out.

"Etta," he whispered. "Did he lay with you?"

She started crying again and Collan swallowed. "Tell me. What happened?"

Through broken tears she said, "He tried to, but he . . . couldn't. That thing stayed limp."

Collan burst out in a chuckle. He couldn't help himself. "That *thing* stayed limp. Very descriptive, Etta. You should be an author."

And to his surprise, she started laughing through her tears. "Stop it, Collie. I'm being serious."

"I know. I'm sorry. I take it he ripped your dress?"

She nodded.

"That's terrible. Truly. But, well, I must say, though, that at least the incident encouraged you to change into that attractive attire you were wearing when you arrived. I really liked the look—those baggy pants, a shirt practically hanging down to your feet and the belt complete with gun holster and knife. Oh, and let's not forget that oversized hat tied with a string. Now that was priceless."

She punched him in the arm playfully but snorted back a chuckle.

So Collan kept going, just knowing that he was handling the situation as he should. This was what they did. They teased each other. They always had and this tragedy was not going to be any different. He knew she would get better faster if they could joke about it. "And just what the hell did you do to that raccoon, Etta? It looked as if a train had hit it."

"I hate you, Collie."

"Now, Etta. We've been over that. You actually love me."

"Well, I don't now."

She looked up at him. "Aren't you even proud that I managed to kill it? I was very clever. I threw a rock at it."

He kissed the top of her head. "Yes—I'm immensely proud of you. You did extremely well for yourself."

She sat up, smiling. "And what do you think about my new riding skills?"

"Excellent, Etta. Did you bludgeon the horse also to get it to obey?"

She laughed and Collan smiled, he loved her so.

"Actually, I took command—just as everybody has always told me to do. I told Intrepid what's what. But, Collie, Intrepid gives me these looks. I've never had a horse give me such looks."

"What looks?"

"I suppose he's trying to talk to me. He finds me odd, I think."

"You don't say—how surprising."

She whacked him playfully in the arm again and then settled down next to him again with her head on his shoulder. She was still so tired he knew. "Now tell me about your trip, Collie."

"You should rest."

"Please. Give me something else to dream about." She yawned.

"Okay. The short version is that I have inherited enough money that I now have a buffer against disaster. I can live more comfortably."

"Really?"

"Yes. Now go to sleep."

"I don't want to have another nightmare. Tell me something more to think about."

"How about this?" He leaned over her and kissed her gently on the lips. "I love you, Etta, more than life and I plan to marry you—"

"But—"

He placed his finger on her lips. "Let me finish. Now I know you've been through a lot and should have some time to get back to yourself. But I'm going to court you proper and make you love me as much as I love you."

"Collie."

"Yes?"

"I came to a conclusion while you were away."

"What?" He suddenly wasn't sure if he wanted to hear what she had to say.

"I really love you, too."

He grinned. "Now isn't that exactly what I've been saying all along?"

She smiled back and then yawned again. "Will you stay with me here until I fall asleep?"

"As long as you like, Etta." Within minutes she was fast asleep again.

When Collan next awoke the room was light. Etta was still passed out next to him in a deep sleep. She had started moaning once more during the night but had calmed as soon as she realized Collan was next to her. Collan now quietly got out of bed and closed the door on her soft snoring.

He made some coffee and sat on a chair out on the porch. He was feeling lazy and tired himself and didn't want to put in a full day's work yet. Collan then saw in the distance that Magpie was walking with Teddie hand in hand in the pasture, apparently picking flowers. When she noticed Collan she waved high above her head. Collan pointed to his cabin and tried to sign that Etta was sleeping by putting his hands together against his tilting head. She seemed to grasped what he was motioning and then she pointed to herself and then his cabin and shook her head. Collan nodded. Etta and he were going to be alone at least for the day.

He went back into the cabin and started making breakfast. When nearly finished, Etta appeared in her bedroom doorway.

She looked around perplexed. "You're cooking bacon and eggs? What time is it?"

"Late morning. Have a seat, Etta. Let me serve you. You want some stale biscuits and jam I found, also?"

She nodded as she walked towards the table and sat down. "Where is everyone?"

"Magpie and Teddie are over by Tinker's place, picking flowers."

She shook her head. "I didn't hear a peep out of them all last evening or this morning."

"They slept at Tinker's."

"What? You mean you and I were here last night alone unchaperoned?!"

Collan chuckled. "You're really such a prude, Etta." He put the food on the table and took a seat across from her.

She started eating as if ravenous. "No, I'm not, Collie," she said around a swallow. "But I have a reputation to maintain. Are there any more biscuits?"

He got up and put a couple more on her plate.

She bit into one even though it was obviously dry and tough. "And speaking of that, how much do you want for your cabin?"

Collan frowned. "I'm not going to *sell* you my cabin. You can stay here for free as always."

"Absolutely not." She put down her fork. "I won't be some kept woman. Now that everybody's going to find out that I lost my own cabin—and it's not just being repaired—I must have a place of my own."

Collan rolled his eyes.

"So how much, Collie?"

"A dollar. You can have the cabin for a dollar. Take it or leave it. I'm not negotiating anymore." He crossed his arms.

Etta huffed. "You're impossible." She then stomped into her bedroom. A moment later she handed him the money. "There." She sat back down and resumed gnawing on her biscuit.

Collan smiled. "I love you, Etta."

"Stop saying that—you know I'm frustrated with you presently."

He raised a brow, suggestively. "Yeah, I'm frustrated with you, too."

Her eyes widened and she stopped chewing midbite, grasping his implication. She then pretended not to catch on and stood. "Well, I better get going. Lots to do."

Collan shook his head. "No, Etta. You're getting more rest. You look like hell."

"Oh, thanks loads, Collie."

"Etta, you're the prettiest filly I know, but you look as if you could sleep for a week."

"Is this what you call *courting*?"

"Oh, I've got some surprises up my sleeve."

She sat back down, interested. "Like what?"

"If you'll take another nap, I'll give you one of them when you wake."

"You got me a present?" She smiled.

He nodded. "Uh, huh. From back East."

"Well, I guess I am still a little tired."

Collan peeked in on her fifteen minutes later and she was passed out again.

Chapter Thirty-eight

Henrietta awoke to the smell of cooking again. She looked around her bedroom and could see by the light that it must already be late afternoon.

She changed into another dress and opened her bedroom doorway. Collan was at the stove again with his back turned to her. On the table rested not one wrapped present but several. She smiled. "Hello, Collan. What are you making?"

He turned around and eyed her up and down. "You look better, Etta. Potatoes and elk steaks."

She walked over to him. "Here, let me do that. Where is everyone?"

"Still gone." He grabbed her by the waist and gave her a quick kiss on the lips, surprising her, and then he grinned. She smiled back. Despite the fact that she had known Collan nearly her whole life, she had never realized that he was such an affectionate person. She loved that but still felt inexplicably shy with him.

"Open your presents. I can handle the meal. I want to know if you like them."

She picked up the first box and unwrapped it. "Perfume?" She put some on. "Oh, it's wonderful. I love perfume."

"I remember. Once you poured your mother's whole bottle on yourself." Collan chuckled. "You stank for a week, Etta."

"Well, I was only about five, Collie. I didn't know any better."

"Uh, huh. Open the next one."

Henrietta reached for a slim box. Inside she found a golden chain with a small jewel locket hanging from it. "Oh, Collie. You shouldn't have. This is so pretty." She put it on and went to look in the mirror.

"It reminded me of you—it's delicate."

She turned away from the mirror and stared at him.

"What?" He frowned slightly.

"That's the sweetest thing you've ever said to me."

"Well, I guess I do have my moments. Unwrap the last present. I really didn't know what I was doing with that one, but I gave it my best try."

She ripped open the paper and found folds upon folds of luxurious fabric. The patterns were beautiful.

"Oh, Collie. You couldn't have picked better. How did you know what to choose?"

"By the price tag, Etta. What do you think—that I hang out in fabric stores all the time? Oh, okay, and I also thought one of those would go with the color of your eyes."

"I never knew you could be so romantic."

"Etta, you're embarrassing me now." He turned back to the stove.

She laughed and put her arms around his waist from behind. He turned back around and smiled. She raised her arms to around his neck, smiled back, and kissed him on the lips. She had meant it to be a quick buss, but he then embraced her tightly—as she heard the spatula dropping on the floor—and caressing her back up and down, deepened the kiss. Her first reaction was to break away—she wasn't ready for this. She had only kissed her husband like this and . . . and . . . oh! Collan kissed her differently than her husband. She had always loved her husband's kisses, but . . . but . . . she really liked this, too. She put her hands in Collan's soft hair and tilted her head. He moved his mouth down to her neck. Oooh. That felt really good. God, it had been a while since she had relished something like this.

"Mama! Papa!?"

They jumped apart and Collan started chuckling as he turned back to the stove. "You explain this one, Etta."

"Teddie! How nice. We're making dinner."

Teddie frowned, obviously puzzled, but was then distracted as the dogs bounced in next, followed by Magpie and Tinker.

Magpie gave a knowing look that Henrietta ignored. "Have you all eaten yet?"

She nodded and sat at the table beside Tinker. While Collan and Henrietta ate, the rest opened presents. Teddie took to the toy train, studying with fascination as he turned the wheels. He also liked the spinning top. But he especially enjoyed throwing the big ball for Sally. Sally claimed it eventually by carrying it over to her bed in the corner.

Magpie's eyes lit up when she received the shawl. Next she opened the box with all the beads.

"Oh, Magpie. That will be very useful when I explain to you what Hugo told me," Henrietta said excitedly.

"What?" She was wrapping the shawl around herself and smiling.

"He wants to buy from you every moccasin you can make—especially the baby sizes—for his store back East, and the price he will pay is three times what you receive usually."

"Three times?" Tinker grinned. "You'll be making a lot more money, Magpie."

"So will you, Tinker. I can finally pay you a wage." Collan said around a mouthful. "Do you like the pistol?"

"Very much. It's well made. I'll try it out tomorrow." Tinker then looked at Magpie. "Do you want to tell them or me?"

"I tell them. I'm having a baby." Magpie smiled.

There was stunned silence a second and then Henrietta jumped up from the table and hugged Magpie. "I'm so happy for you and Teddie will have a playmate. I thought you looked especially content lately." She straightened and clasped her hands. "Oh, this is such wonderful news."

"Congratulations, Magpie," Collan said. "When are you all getting officially hitched?"

"We are married. We said our vows to each other." Tinker said.

Collan smiled. "Fair enough."

Henrietta hoped they would get married with all the proper ceremony someday but knew that as a common law couple what they were doing was very accepted out West, especially since there often was no preacher to be found. It was not unusual for some couples to wait years before they got married—often at

365

the time of their first child's baptism—or never at all. Of course, their community now had a preacher, but none of them or their friends had much to do with him. He lived up Longs Peak and they scarcely saw him.

Collan looked at Henrietta and winked. "I guess if Magpie's now living with Tinker, I can move into her bedroom."

"What?" Henrietta was amazed he had even suggested it. "No, you most certainly cannot. They might be married, but we aren't. That will be Teddie's bedroom now and that's that."

"Prude."

"Oh, be quiet, Collan."

He chuckled, but then he looked at her seriously. "Etta, I don't think you should be alone at night—at least not for a while."

"But I'm already feeling so much better and the danger's past."

"Collan," Tinker got his attention. "Magpie doesn't necessarily want to spend every night in my small cabin. It's very common for Indian brides to have their own tepee, especially if the husband marries more than one."

Collan looked at Henrietta. "Well, if she's not here, then I'm sleeping on the porch, Etta."

"You're being ridiculous."

He shrugged.

"There's more news." Tinker suddenly looked uncomfortable.

"Oh, now what?"

"One of Magpie's cousins came for a visit. He's resting at my cabin now."

Collan put his head in his hands. "God Almighty. I would really like to know what it's like to have a boring life." He looked around at everybody. "Wouldn't that be nice? Everything always uneventful. Nothing making the waves. Sit on your ass all day and pick your nose—"

"Collan! Let Tinker talk." Henrietta turned to Tinker, smiling pleasantly. "Go on. Tell us about him."

"Well, he's a youngish fella—I'd say late teens and he doesn't want to go to a reservation. He's heard what they're like. He's good with horses and I think I could teach him how to run cattle."

"Oh, how nice. I'm sure Collan could use the help."

"Etta, how do you know I won't end up in jail for harboring a Cheyenne?"

"Nonsense, Collie. We can just say we didn't know we were doing anything wrong."

Collan blew out a long breath. "Tinker, he can stay only if he follows these rules. Etta and Magpie get him dressing like you and me. He cuts his braids or wears a hat to cover them up. I don't want him looking Cheyenne—at least from a distance—if he can help it. And he learns English as fast as he possibly can. And no tepee."

Henrietta smiled, suddenly excited. "I can help with *all* of that."

"Etta, he's not one of your strays. Try not to embarrass the boy."

"Oh, poo, Collie." She turned to Magpie. "What's his name?"

"It means mountain lion."

"Hmmm. Mountain lion's a little long. Why don't we call him Leo?"

Magpie nodded. "I think he is a good boy."

Henrietta smiled. "Oh, I'm sure he is."

Collan stood. "Well, I think I've had enough for one day. Now am I sleeping on the porch or in my cabin tonight?"

"Collie, I really think Magpie should spend the night at Tinker's. Leo might be frightened otherwise. I mean he's just arrived after all."

"Etta, Leo has probably been a warrior in more battles than we can count. I doubt he's scared." Collan then turned to Tinker. "Oh, and no war paint."

The next morning, Henrietta shooed Collan off her porch at first light—she also informed him that she considered his dozing there only a smidge more respectable than sleeping inside. He just laughed.

But she had slept without any nightmares and felt even stronger today than she had yesterday. And yesterday she had been a lot better just talking to Collan. She then found Magpie and told her what nice things Alec had said about her. Henrietta stated that in the end she blamed everything on his drinking and not on the person so she forgave him. Then she divulged to Magpie the full details of what happened to Alec. Looking back now, Henrietta informed her she wasn't completely sure whether he had come to his senses just before the ground had given way beneath them. Magpie had nodded sadly and then departed without any comment. Henrietta let her be, realizing that this had to be traumatic for her also—she had probably once loved the man. Magpie would come to talk to her again when she was ready.

Henrietta then kept busy baking throughout the morning and just when she planned on sitting down for a bit of sewing, Clara and Sal rode into the yard and dismounted.

She went out to the porch and waved. "Oh, I'm so happy to see you."

Sal eyed her up and down. "The Farrars told us you were doing fine, but we wanted to see for ourselves."

"Well, I'm feeling even better than when the Farrars saw me last."

Clara smiled. "That's good. We brought over a couple meals. We didn't know what you felt up to."

"Thank you so much." She took the basket from Clara and peeked in. "Oh, a stew and a roast. How nice. Would you like some now?"

Sal shook her head. "I smell just-baked bread. I'll take a slice of that." She plopped down on a porch chair.

"Me, too, Henrietta." Clara took the seat next to Sal.

Henrietta returned a few minutes later with tea also.

They all ate in silence a few moments, then Sal took her hand. "Henrietta darling, you know you can discuss anything with me, anytime you want."

Henrietta swallowed. Her friends were sure the worst had happened. She had to explain. "He was too much of a drunk to do me any harm."

"Really?"

Henrietta nodded. "Honest, Sal."

"Well, at least that. But surely you must have been scared."

"Of course." She smiled wryly. "But at least I got my taste of true independence finding my way home."

"Oh, Henrietta. We love you." Clara reached over and gave her a hug. "You *are* doing fine. We were so worried."

"I know it will take some time before I'm really my old self, but I'm getting there. Please don't fret about me. And please inform everyone else, so I don't have to repeat the story."

Sal nodded. "We will. I heard you think he's gone for good."

"He is. He passed away, but out of respect for Magpie—he was her husband—I don't want to give the details."

"Sure, honey. You only tell us what you want."

Clara waved her hand. "Look, Abner is coming."

A few minutes later, he joined them on the porch. "I'm so glad everything turned out fine, Henrietta. You sure gave us a scare."

"Thanks, Abner. Would you like some bread and tea?"

"Don't mind if I do." He took a seat. "So I heard you bought this cabin from Collan."

Henrietta smiled. "Yes, it's all mine." She was quick to add, "Collan lives now in that cabin across the pasture."

Abner shook his head. "It's a shame that Dunraven caused you such grief." He turned to Clara. "I heard Alex wants to hold a community meeting at your place about Dunraven next week. Will there be a dance afterwards, also?"

Clara looked at Henrietta. "I told Alex this morning I wasn't sure whether we should cancel the whole event—if it was too much for you."

"Oh, no. I think the sooner I get back to enjoying living, the better."

Sal patted her hand. "That's my gal."

They then all turned, hearing riders approaching.

Sal murmured, "What do *they* want?"

Abner and Henrietta stood as Herr Big Blade and couple of the other men who worked for Whyte and who had stopped by on their own in the past for baked goods, rode into the yard.

They all took off their hats but stayed mounted.

Herr Big Blade did the talking. "Miss Henrietta, we wanted to tell you that we was sorry for what Whyte did to you the other day. Word just trickled in to us what happened to you this last week. We want you to know that if ever you require help in the future, to come to us."

"How kind of you." She smiled warmly—she was actually quite pleased—and the men seemed to relax.

"And Miss Henrietta?"

"Yes?"

He held out a small basket. "We brought you some dried cherries. My maw used to put them in her strudel. I thought you might like them."

She stepped off the porch and took the offering. "How sweet of you all."

They smiled shyly.

"Come by again, day after tomorrow. I'll have some strudel made by then."

He put on his hat and smiled. "Thank you kindly, Miss Henrietta."

As they reined around and rode off, Sal muttered, "Well did you ever."

Chapter Thirty-nine

Collan rode into his yard with a wagon load full of rocks. It had only been a few days since Leo had arrived, but the kid was already making himself useful—he freed up Collan to pursue other activities other than his usual ranching chores.

Leo could ride as if he was one with the horse—Collan had never seen anyone better and it was a beautiful sight. He performed tricks such as hanging off his mount at full gallop, snatching at grass. Collan had no doubt that if he bought another horse, the kid could train the mount to become a cutting horse—efficiently removing a calf from its mother for branding—something Collan could use. Hell, Collan could even see possibly trying to raise horses now as a sideline.

Tinker had already taught Leo how to rope cattle and he worked at it so diligently and got so quickly proficient that Tinker also had to tell him to stop harassing the livestock with his practicing.

Oh, and of course, Etta and Magpie were already fussing over him—altering some of Collan's old clothes to fit him. Leo, though, refused to cut his braids but wore them tucked into his shirt. And on further thought, Collan really didn't want to force the kid to lose his entire culture. He only wanted him to blend in better to protect him—and also Collan—from getting into any kind of unnecessary trouble.

Etta had decided to try teaching Leo English during and after the usual midday meal break. To everyone's surprise, Magpie joined in for the lessons. Yesterday Etta had started teaching letters and numbers and showed Magpie exactly how much more money she would make sending her wares to Hugo. Magpie had smiled proudly. That nobody had thought to help Magpie with her education and fledgling business before Hugo and Leo had arrived now appeared shameful to Collan. But, hell, with everything that always seemed to be occurring, he guessed they could be forgiven.

As Collan jumped off the wagon now, he chuckled to himself. His Etta was such a natural tutor— just figured, considering how much an annoying pet she had been when they had received their education as youngsters. He grabbed the hammer, the small posts he had made at the sawmill and the string from the wagon and began pacing next to Etta's cabin.

Just as he finished pounding in the last stake and tying the string to it, Etta rode into the yard. Abner had informed him yesterday that his parents had arrived and Etta had wanted to give his mother a special greeting by bringing over some baked goods.

She dismounted and walked over to Collan, "Oh, she's so nice, Collie. We had such a pleasant chat. I can see why Abner turned out so wonderful."

Collan chuckled. "Well, now. I'm certain he'd just love hearing how he's such a good mommy's boy. I'll be sure to tell him."

She stomped her foot. "Don't you dare, Collie. That's not what I meant and you know it."

"Uh, huh."

She looked around at his work. "What are you doing?"

"Plotting my next home."

"What? You didn't tell me you were building another cabin."

He shrugged.

She frowned then. "And why here? This place is only one more smidge proper than you sleeping on my porch. It won't look respectable us living next door to each other."

"Prude."

"You have to move the site."

"No, Etta. This location has the best views on my property and is sheltered from the wind. I'm building my home here."

She rolled her eyes. "If the community doesn't start calling me a hussy, it'll be a miracle."

Collan chuckled.

She looked around at what he had done. "This place is going to be big."

"Yep. But I'll try to finish just a portion immediately so I have a roof over my head."

"Well, you'd have a roof already if you'd just stay in your cabin at night across the pasture."

"Can't. Gave the place to Leo."

"Then bunk with Leo."

"I'm a man of means now. The place isn't good enough for me any longer."

She looked him over. "Is that so? Sounds pretty uppity to me."

Collan chuckled.

She went back to surveying the plot and stepped to a section of it. "I suppose you'll want your kitchen here."

"No, I was thinking over here." He walked to the opposite corner.

"Oh, but I'm sure you'd like your kitchen window to face east. That way it's cheery first thing in the morning."

"What else are you sure I'd want?"

She pursed her lips. "Let's see." She walked a few feet over. "Here you'd want your parlor to get the afternoon light." She yanked on one of his stakes and pulled it out. "But you'd want the angle of the room to be slightly different so it's not full west." She looked up at him. "Too glaring, of course."

"Of course."

"Since there's the sawmill now—you'd want a framed clapboard house with shingles?"

He nodded.

"Oh, how lovely." She tapped her lips. "But since your home will be so large, you'd probably want a front parlor for visitors—you know, a fancy room—and a back morning room for relaxing—but then that room should face eastward also. No, westward. Let's just call it the back parlor." She heaved out more stakes.

Collan blew out a breath. "What else are you sure I'd want, Etta?"

She started motioning with her hands, trying to visualize something. "Actually, you'd want the whole house to be turned just so." More stakes were jerked out. "The front entrance, front parlor, front dining room with the spectacular view . . . no wait, it would be so much easier if the dining room were closer to the kitchen."

She grabbed a stick and started drawing a plot in the dirt with it. An hour later she was describing the westward facing small *sewing room she was sure he would want* upstairs. She did concede then that he would want a small library for himself on the first floor below it so the whole house he would want several feet wider or he would want to make an addition later.

She looked up at him smiling then, obviously pleased with herself. She walked over to the wagon next. "These rocks are for the simple foundation I suppose."

"You're sure I'd want them?"

"Well, moving the root cellar below the house would be nice—you'd want that, certainly."

He groaned. "But not necessarily?"

"No. You'd want to start with a kitchen big enough for your table, a parlor, and a set of stairs on the first floor with a couple bedrooms over that upstairs. The remainder of the house you'd want to build as time allows and as in the plan we just made—I mean you showed me you wanted."

Collan chuckled and shook his head.

"This is fun. I'll help you pound in the stakes again, Collie."

"Good. Because I plan on sleeping in at least a roughed in kitchen area within the next week."

Etta smirked. "Well, as to that, Collie—just keep quiet about it—"

"I know. It's only a smidge more respectable than your porch—"

377

"—and I'm going to pretend I didn't just hear that and you're sleeping in your cabin *across the pasture.*"

"Prude."

An evening later, Henrietta looked around the huge dining hall that Alex had built among the trees. It was so big that the meeting was going to be held in it shortly and then a dance following. A babysitter had been hired for all the toddlers present—her son was so excited at all the playmates—so Henrietta felt free to enjoy herself.

Sal leaned in to talk quietly to Clara and her. "Guess what I heard about the Evans woman?"

Clara and Henrietta raised their brows.

"She's grumbling that the first official post office was put at your ranch and you're the postmistress, Clara, instead of her."

Clara blew out a breath. "Well, that figures it's a point of contention. The Evans and I should say Dunraven lose tourist business by not having the post office at their spread."

Sal smirked. "Or perhaps she doesn't like not having something important to do."

Alex called for everyone's attention then and they took their seats. Alex began, "As you remember Whyte, acting on behalf of Lord Dunraven and the English Company, has threatened to fence in totally the land they own, closing off trails and keeping settlers from reaching their property. Whyte has now realized that access is legally protected in America and has agreed to open thoroughfares over their land if gates are placed where the road enters and leaves their property and everyone tries to keep the gates closed."

Abner then stood. "This sounds reasonable to me. The gates could help keep the cattle secure and also might discourage tourists' horses from wandering where we don't want them."

Alex nodded. "I agree with Abner, but we should take a vote."

Overwhelmingly the crowd agreed.

Alex continued. "Next I want to say that although sportsmen have only been visiting our area in droves for essentially a couple years, you fishermen in the crowd would probably agree with me that the trout population has decreased significantly. I'm now building dams along Black Canyon Creek for a trout hatchery but possibly more should be done. Perhaps we should consider petitioning the new government for some sort of regulation."

There was grumbling in the crowd at that.

Alex shrugged. "Think about it is all I'm asking for now. Finally, I want to inform you of the details that I learned about the new hotel Dunraven is having built as it looks as if there will be plenty of opportunities for work if you so desire." He pulled a note from his pocket. "Let's see. The hotel will be three stories high and forty by one hundred feet long, costing approximately fifteen thousand dollars."

The crowd was stunned silent at the astounding figures.

"It will be constructed of bricks, rocks and timber with 'quote unquote' finely appointed furnishings and rooms for billiards, cards or just lounging. The location will be along Fish Creek south of their current ranch and in addition to a well-maintained lawn, it will have tennis courts, a nine-hole golf course and its own blacksmith, butcher shop and dairy. They also plan on forming an artificial lake large enough for small boats by damming Fish Creek."

The gathering exploded at that.

He then yelled to be heard. "Meeting adjourned. The dancing and refreshments should begin shortly."

Sal looked over. "Oh. My. God. How can we all compete? He'll ruin us."

Clara shook her head. "Don't be so sure."

Sal continued, "And I thought we were being so grand by naming our place The Ferguson Highlands. Better change that to Ferguson Gone Broke. We just finished attaching a dining hall and a larger kitchen to the main building. I was so proud that we had sixty paying guests this summer not only from Colorado, but the eastern states and even foreigners—"

Clara interrupted. "But Sal, imagine how much he's going to demand to stay there. Most people will want our more affordable rates."

Sal frowned. "How much are you charging?"

"Well, now that we have that series of log cabins on the north side of Black Canyon Creek we expect seven dollars a week for meals, room and washing. Stabling a horse is fifty cents a day without the feed."

Sal pursed her lips. "Hmmm. We're charging eight to fourteen dollars a week, depending on whether the guest is in the main building or one of the five three-room cottages or five tent houses we have."

Clara nodded. "That's reasonable."

"I suppose so. We've certainly made money."

Henrietta finally spoke up. "Well, I can't imagine anyone wanting to stay at a place *he* owns when they could enjoy either one of your companies."

"Oh, heck, Henrietta." Sal harrumphed. "My guests aren't asking about me. They all want my husband to be their fishing guide. Let's go get something to eat. I'm hungry."

Collan found Henrietta just as she had finished eating a piece of pie. "Dance with me, Etta? Please?"

Henrietta nodded. Her husband Charles had passed away over a year ago—certainly no one expected her not to dance in public. Charles had been a wonderful singer, but Collan could dance. She had guiltily enjoyed the few times she had danced last fall. She wanted to sashay and spin now without any regret. She knew her husband would not want her mourning any longer.

Collan took her out onto the floor and she sang along while dancing—Well, the camptown ladies sing a song, doo dah, doo dah—and Collan laughed as she stepped and turned. But he did not remain her partner for long—it seemed as if every male acquaintance of hers eventually asked to cut in. When a waltz finally began, Collan appeared again. But they didn't stay on the dance floor. He edged them toward the fringes and out the door.

"What are you doing?"

"Do you honestly think I'm going to keep you in there so I can be flung away again. This is my dance, Etta. We can hear the music out here."

"But what about appearances—"

"Etta, please just dance."

A moment later she was no longer protesting. Collan held her closely and firmly the way she enjoyed and she became caught up in the wonderful sensation of being led and twirled to the music. She didn't pay attention as Collan steered them further into the trees until she realized she could only faintly hear the melody. She stopped short.

"Now what are you doing, Collie?" She asked innocently enough, though she already suspected.

He smiled. "Courting you as promised."

"Oh, does that mean you'll get me another piece of pie"

"No, I can think of something better to do."

"How about some punch?"

"Only if it was adequately laden—it's not loaded for some reason tonight."

She chuckled as she shook her head. "That is not what you're supposed to say to a gal you're courting."

"Surprising. How about that you look lovely tonight."

She smiled. "You honestly think so? I wasn't sure if I should wear this dress."

"I mean you're not as attractive as I suspect you would be if it was entirely off, but it will do."

She gasped. "If my parents had known what a scandalous mind you have, they never would have let you even come around the house."

"Now, Etta. I didn't always want to see you naked—just the last fifteen years or so." He grinned.

She bit back a smile. "You are absolutely the worst, Collie."

He started laughing, sheepishly, obviously regretting what he had just said. "I know. Truly, Etta, I know. And I meant to tell you all these pretty things that I figure you would like to hear, but . . ."

She looked at him puzzled. "But what?"

He guffawed. "It's always just been too much fun to try to get a rile out of you."

"Well, I'm going back to the dance."

He quieted immediately and took her hand. "Etta, no. I love you so much. I really do." He put his hand gently behind her head. "Please give me a kiss."

She looked around to make sure nobody could see them. "Well, just one." But the problem was, that not only was Collan a good dancer, he was such a good kisser—Who knew? Certainly not her with their kind of history—and she quickly melted in his arms. So much so that she turned into a disheveled mess.

She finally broke free and tried straightening her clothing. "How do I look?"

"Like that tart you were afraid of being called." He began chuckling.

She started walking back. Collan followed. "Now Collie, try to control yourself. Remember you're supposed to be telling me pretty things since I'm letting you court me."

"Oh, sure. I almost forgot again. What do you say we do that again in a couple minutes, but how about if you take off all your clothes now that you're officially a—"

"—Don't say it—"

"—wanton woman."

She stopped and turned. "You really can't help yourself, can you?"

He shook his head. "No, I guess not. Isn't it fun?"

"No." Henrietta answered as she turned, but she bit back a smile.

About three weeks later, Collan was sleeping soundly in the kitchen of his new house when he was awoken by the sound of Etta screaming next door and then the dogs barking and Teddie crying. He quickly threw on a pair of pants over his longjohns and ran next door. Etta, with tears in her eyes, opened the door to his pounding, holding a still weeping Teddie.

Collan took Teddie from her and he quieted. "Hello, big fella. Nothing to be afraid of. Your mama and I just want to talk for a while. You go back to bed now. I'm sure you're sleepy."

Teddie didn't protest as Collan placed him back down in his crib, and as Collan stroked his head, he fell back to sleep.

Through the full moonlight coming through the window he found Etta, sitting at the table, sniffling. "Back to bed for you, also." He picked her up in his arms and lay down next to her on the bed. She curled into him and rested her head on his shoulder.

"Oh, Collan. Do you think I'll ever be completely better? I had another nightmare."

"Etta, I'm so proud of how strong you are. I'm sure to friends like the Farrar brothers you appear as always to them. But, honey, I think you and I made a mistake. You have to talk to me more about what happened. Keeping your thoughts inside are just coming out in your nightmares. What were you dreaming about tonight?"

"I have this fear of leaving Teddie all alone to fend for himself. This time I couldn't find my way back and then I fell off a mountain top."

"Well, Etta, if that happened, I would just make sure I caught you before you landed because my life would be over without you. But, Etta, I promise you that I will always watch over Teddie. I love him like a son."

"Thank you, Collan."

"Etta?"

"Yeah?"

"Let me sleep in Teddie's room at night."

"But—"

"Etta, listen. Nobody has to find out—it will be our secret. I worry that your nightmares might start affecting Teddie if something occurs like this evening again. I want to be closer so that if I hear you getting upset, talking in your sleep, I can get to you faster to comfort you."

"Teddie was so scared hearing me."

"So you'll let me?"

She nodded.

"I also think we should go on a little vacation together. Get you away from the same surroundings for a while—give your mind something fun to think about. I hear Manitou Springs is nice. We could ride to Denver, then take the train there and see the fall colors. We'd only be gone from Estes Park for a few days. What do you say?"

"Well, it sounds nice, but . . . who would be our chaperone? I mean—"

"Teddie."

"Teddie?"

"Yes, Teddie." Collan chuckled. "Take it or leave it, my little prude. I'm not negotiating anymore."

"Fine." Etta sat up and smiled. "How soon can we leave?"

Collan sat on the front veranda of the Cliff House in Manitou Springs with Etta and Teddie, drinking a fancy refreshment. The place was an elegant inn and stagecoach stop that they were residing at for a day. In fact, a lot of establishments in Manitou Springs were swanky and he could see Etta was enjoying herself immensely. She was wearing a dress she had made out of the expensive fabric he had given her and she looked lovely. He had put on his best suit. They had already viewed nearby Pikes Peak. But Collan had enjoyed the Garden of the Gods better. The tourist location had gotten its name because Indian legend claimed that Gods came out of the sky and landed there. Collan didn't know if he believed anything about this Indian tale, but he did like its massive rocks in peculiar and unusual formations.

Teddie climbed out of Etta's lap and into Collan's, playing with the toy stagecoach they had bought him. Etta smiled warmly at them both.

"Marry me, Etta. I love you so very much. Please become my wife." He had planned on asking her in some elaborate way in the near future, but somehow that instant seemed the best time.

She gasped and then smiled. "Oh, Collan. Yes. Absolutely yes. I love you so much, too."

He leaned over his chair and gave her a soft kiss on the lips.

"When do you think you first really fell in love with me, Collie?"

"Breckenridge when your husband stole you away."

"We mined in Breckenridge years ago." She looked at him in surprise and wonder. "That long ago?"

"Yep. But I would say I didn't admit my true feelings to myself then. I just knew that I felt restless and unhappy without you. If I had, I probably would have punched your husband when he first talked to you."

Etta chuckled.

"So when do you want to get married, Etta? We could find a preacher here."

"No. I would like a big wedding with all our friends and my family present."

"But winter will be coming on soon. Your brother and sister won't want to travel in possible snow."

"So next spring. Would that be fine?"

"Etta, considering how long I've been desiring you, I can certainly wait a few more months."

The next day they took the train back to Denver. Collan had another surprise for her. They met the Farrar brothers in the hotel lobby he had arranged to meet them at. He had hired them to help haul his uncle's belongings back home. Etta knew nothing about what was going on.

"I didn't realize you all were coming here. How nice to meet up with you." Etta smiled.

Ike winked. "She still doesn't know, does she?"

Collan shook his head.

Etta puckered her brows. "Know what?"

Ike winked again. "You'll see."

They headed over to the storage area of the train station and Collan broke into the lid of a large crate. He climbed atop a smaller box and peered inside. "Looks all here."

"What is?" Etta asked excitedly.

Clint took Teddie from her as Collan stepped down and pointed to the crate. She climbed onto the box and gazed inside the crate. "Oh, my gosh. Oh, my gosh. It's the most beautiful stove I have ever seen."

She turned back to glance at Collan. "And I think there is an oven on *either* side of the middle griddle instead of just one."

"I was assured back East it's the latest stove available."

She went back to gawking. "Oh! Oh! It's so wonderful. I can't wait to try it."

"Let me see, Miss Henrietta." Ike complained. "You're hogging the view."

"Ike." Hank frowned.

"No, I'll get down. Have a look."

The brothers all took their turns, then Hank asked Collan, "Are these other crates going as well."

Collan nodded.

Clint exclaimed, "Oh, that's a lot of stuff. What all you have in them?"

"Let's see. If I remember—books, a dining table, a fiddle, linens, pictures, a sofa—oh, and one contains a piano."

Etta bent over, laughing.

The next few months flew by for Henrietta. She kept busy arranging the new house and planning her nuptials. A few happenings stood out, though.

Magpie became her own businesswoman, so to speak, handling almost all aspects of making and shipping her goods. Henrietta was so pleased for her but also nagged her to take it easy since she was carrying a baby. Magpie would only chuckle and then go about her own way.

The first official wedding took place in Estes Park in December when Anna Ferguson, the daughter of a proud Sal, married the Longmont merchant Richard Hubbell, officiated by Reverend Coffman of Longmont and witnessed by Abner and John Buchanan, one of their neighbors.

Henrietta told Sal that Anna looked lovely. "I suppose Richard Hubbell wanted his own preacher for the ceremony."

She raised a brow. "Yes, you could say that."

"I can tell there's something more as to why Preacher Lamb did not perform the ceremony, considering he just lives up Longs Peak."

"Preacher Lamb is not a Ferguson kind of person. Oh, he's industrious like us. He's raising cattle and putting up tourists—even guiding them further up Longs Peak for five dollars a trip. But do you know I heard he's put in a toll road to his spread? But guess when he's charging them? Not at the bottom, but surprising them at the top when they have to pay to get back down."

Henrietta chuckled. "I see. I better ask your Reverend if he'll come to my wedding, also."

The next occurrence of significance was that the Farrar brothers finally came to an agreement with Whyte and traded their homestead cabin for forty acres along Fall River. Whyte was shrewd. Although at first look, one would think he might have gotten the short end, considering how much land he had obtained, but actually where the Farrar brothers' cabin stood was now becoming the crossroads of their settlement and would appear to be the most valuable land in the future. Realizing her proximity, Henrietta sold her original property to the English Company for a very good price.

In March, Clara informed Henrietta that the Evans woman had stomped over to her place with a commission as the new postmistress, demanding the key. Clara had handed it over unhappily. The town feud with the English Company simmered.

Finally on May third, Collan and Henrietta tied the knot. Clara had offered to host the wedding, since they had built the large dining hall. Family and friends gathered. Henrietta wore a light pink dress she had made from the fabric Collan had bought. She carried a bouquet of spring flowers. Tinker began playing with the fiddle Collan had given him that had been packed in the crates from back East.

The music was their cue. Henrietta looked down the aisle to where she should begin walking. Collan handsomely stood at the front, smiling at her. Next to him were her brother Herman and sister Clarissa, who would serve as witnesses. Herman had already promised to return again later that summer for a visit. Henrietta did not think she could be having a happier day.

She took a few steps with Teddie, holding his hand, smiling to either side of the seated crowd.

She suddenly halted and said excitedly, "George Bode. I didn't know you could make my wedding."

Tinker stopped playing.

George turned red. "*Ja, naturlich,* Henrietta. Clara wanted me to surprise you."

"How lovely." She smiled cheerfully. "I can really ride horses now. You should see me."

He turned even redder, glancing around uncomfortably.

She whispered loudly, "I'll show you after the wedding." And she meant to start walking again, but then she saw her three strudel cowboys seated next to him. They were wearing clean pants and new shirts and had obviously tried to spiff themselves up. She was pleased. "You look *so nice,* gentlemen." They smiled shyly.

"Henrietta! Everyone is waiting." She turned to see her sister Clarissa, frowning at the front.

But then Collan started chuckling, quietly at first, but rapidly turning into loud roars of laughter. Her sister was now staring at him, horrified.

Henrietta quickly motioned for the music to begin again. Collan and she managed to make it through the rest of the ceremony uneventfully.

At the reception, Collan walked over with a cup of punch for her. She took a sip. "Oooh. This is strong."

"What do you expect, Etta, when you invite cowboys to your wedding?"

"Well, it was about time they mingled socially."

"Uh, huh. Give me a kiss." He bussed her on the lips and she smiled.

Sal walked up, wearing a long apron over her party dress. "Got some news for you all. Magpie whispered to me during your vows that her water broke."

Henrietta gasped. Collan chuckled. "Figures, Etta, we can't even have routine nuptials."

"Where is she?"

"I got her over at the cabin George claimed. I told George he can spend the night at our spread."

"I want to see her."

"But just for a moment, Henrietta. You should enjoy your wedding. She's doing fine and has already progressed quickly. I wonder if this is her first baby, but I didn't ask."

Fifteen minutes later, Henrietta was beside Collan again, after having been shooed out of the cabin by Sal. He handed her another cup of punch.

"Thanks." She did not pay attention to how rapidly she drank it down. "I'm so worried, Collie."

"Imagine how Tinker feels. Let's get the musicians to play a waltz. I want to dance with you."

Once on the floor, others joined in. But in the middle of the next melody, Henrietta heard the distinctive cry of a new baby. So did everyone else. Collan grabbed Henrietta's hand and they hurried over to the front of the cabin, followed by the remaining guests. The door opened and Tinker appeared on the porch. "I have a son." He smiled widely and the crowd cheered loudly.

The celebration really began then. Hours later, by the stable, Collan helped Henrietta onto the seat of the specially decorated buggy. Big bows, cans and old shoes dangled behind it. Teddie would spend the remaining night there and Collan and Henrietta would have their new home to themselves.

"Waaait! I almost forgot." Henrietta stepped quickly down and strode over to a saddled Liebchen. She mounted astride, pulling down her dress, and smiled at George who was standing to the side of the crowd. "Watch this!"

Collan stood in the buggy. "Etta, for heaven's sake, remember how strong the punch was."

"Oh, Collie, I'm fine."

She performed a trotting circle around George and then backed the horse up, then circled him again the opposite way before stopping in front of him. "What do you think?"

"*Wunderbar*, Henrietta."

"Thanks, George." Henrietta grinned proudly.

Collan shook his head, smiling.

She jumped off the horse. "I'm coming, Collie." Henrietta ran to the buggy and scurried into the seat.

They gave each other a kiss and banged, bashed, and thumped their way home.

Three months later, Henrietta stepped out of their house to have a word with Collan, who had just ridden into the yard.

"Well, hello, Etta. Fancy meeting you here." Collan smiled and dismounted, giving her a quick smooch on the lips. "What's for supper?"

"I was in the mood for elk *sauerkraut* pie so I made one. Hope you like it." She grinned.

"Etta, it sounds atrocious. . . ." He stared at her. "I think you're trying to tell me something."

Henrietta nodded.

"When?" Collan looked ecstatic.

"Let's see, nine months is the start of next year."

He swung her around before saying, "It sure took a while to get you, but I would do it again if I had to."

"I love you, too, Collie."

Epilogue

That summer the English Hotel, as it was referred to by the community, opened with a grand ball. The attendees included the visiting mucky-muck along with certain town guests. But relations were not easily ameliorated. By the fall, settlers had made a criminal indictment against Evans and Whyte over the misappropriation of thirty head of cattle. The Evans family departed the community within a few years to become lodge owners in a nearby town. Whyte stayed in Estes Park for decades more, raising a family, eventually managing to ingratiate himself into the settlement.

Within a couple years of the hotel being built, Dunraven was bored with Estes Park and suffering from staffing issues and the like to run the hotel properly. He wrote from the hotel to another Lord in 1879 that he would not be sorry if he never came back to Estes Park—where the garden boy was the cook and he had only Charlie to wait on him. He apparently made at least one trip back years later, scandalizing the community by bringing his mistress with him. But Dunraven finally sold his holdings after supposedly having difficulty paying his taxes and the English hotel burned down in 1911.

Abner Sprague persisted as a leading member of the community. His mother started serving dinner to tourists, but when some requested to stay, he built a hotel which was described as having scrupulous neatness in every board and corner. His mother also operated a small general store which sold items such as canned goods, cigars, and fishing tackle. Ice cream could be bought for fifteen cents. By 1880, the settlement had grown so large that the back of the store served as an additional post office. Abner also began acting as a guide to locations such as Middle and North Park. In the 1880's, he prospected in Lulu City, a local mining camp and worked as a surveyor. He eventually married and survived to his nineties. Sprague Lake in Rocky Mountain National Park honors him.

Ferguson Highlands thrived yet did not become the largest resort in the area—that distinction went to the Elkhorn Lodge which was formed by the gentleman who had originally squabbled over land with the mother of Clara MacGregor. The Ferguson Highlands did endure as the place to go for fish guiding services.

Alex and Clara continued to raise an amazing family. Unfortunately, in 1896, Alex died from a lightning strike while prospecting on a mountain near the ranch, leaving Clara to raise three sons on her own. However, a few years after the passing of her husband, she died at the young age of forty-eight. The oldest son of Alex and Clara carried on, eventually accumulating three thousand acres of land and also fathering one child who inherited, a daughter Muriel. She never married but became a lawyer and rancher, and upon her passing in 1970 donated the family holdings as a ranch working museum that can be visited by tourists to this day.

There is a public record from 1879 of a Mister George Bode marrying Miss Sylvia Brubaker in an adjoining county.

But most wonderfully of all, Collan and Henrietta had a baby girl named Caroline and lived—teasing each other happily—for many years to come.

Readers,

The history of the West is fascinating to me. The Black Hills of South Dakota, which was mentioned in the story, in particular intrigues me. I am aware that Mount Rushmore is not viewed with pleasure by Native Americans who consider it an intrusion in land they consider sacred. The Crazy Horse Monument is still not completed and being sculpted in a nearby location. Late in the last century the United States Supreme Court decided just compensation, including interest, should be given to the Sioux Nation for the Black Hills. The Sioux refused to take the millions, or should I say now, the billion—they had never agreed to sell the land in the first place and accepting payment would legally terminate any Sioux demands for the return of the area. The money remains, accumulating interest. I think Magpie would have taken pleasure in that.

Although snippets of the Farrar brothers and their kindly acts repeatedly appeared in histories of Estes Park describing the 1870's, frustratingly I could never find what actually happened to them over the decades.

But Teddie and family, including Magpie—who you probably have already guessed are completely fictional—will be in the next sequel, taking place about thirty years later in Estes Park shortly before the formation of Rocky Mountain National Park.

All the best,
Kari

P.S. I sincerely hope you enjoy reading my books as much as I take pleasure in researching and writing them. But spending any time marketing my novels instead of actually creating them is loathsome, as I am sure most can imagine.

Please help me out by leaving a review on Amazon or Amazon UK of *Settling the Wind*—just a couple lines of your thoughts will do. I thank you truly in advance. Look forward to hearing from you.

Visit my author webpage at kariaugust.wordpress.com

Want more Kari August novels?

Reaching Rocky Mountain Jim

Set amidst a rugged, stunning frontier just beginning to realize its potential, the novel recounts the true compelling romance between Jim Nugent and Isabella Bird, a rough trapper and a strong-willed Englishwoman in the Colorado Territory of 1873.

Consider also reading about the romping adventures of a medieval king:

The Arrival of Richard III

"Entertaining, original, exceptionally well written . . . impressive storytelling talents." Midwest Book Review.

Or

Richard III and Clarence

Amusing and quirky, fans of merriment are sure to be delighted.

All available on Amazon.